THE
RUSSIAN BRIDE

THE
RUSSIAN BRIDE

ED KOVACS

Minotaur Books

New York

For Virginia Rose; I can't repay the countless acts of kindness and
love, but I'll do my best to pass them on.

THE RUSSIAN BRIDE. Copyright © 2015 by Ed Kovacs. All rights reserved.
Printed in the United States of America. For information,
address St. Martin's Press, 175 Fifth Avenue, New York, N.Y. 10010.

www.minotaurbooks.com

Designed by Omar Chapa

The Library of Congress Cataloging-in-Publication Data is available upon request.

ISBN 978-1-250-04700-7 (hardcover)
ISBN 978-1-4668-4737-8 (e-book)

Minotaur Books may be purchased for educational, business, or promotional use.
For information on bulk purchases, please contact the Macmillan Corporate and
Premium Sales Department at 1-800-221-7945, extension 5442, or write to
specialmarkets@macmillan.com.

First Edition: April 2015

10 9 8 7 6 5 4 3 2 1

ACKNOWLEDGMENTS

Sincere thanks to Christopher Graham and Richard Curtis. Michael Homler, Hector DeJean, Kate Davis, a terrific art department, and all the rest of the good folks at SMP have my deep appreciation for their hard work and efforts on behalf of my books.

Pilots and aviation raconteurs Carl Scholl and Tony Ritzman provided aviation expertise that fit the bill perfectly. I owe them many thanks for their ongoing generosity and support.

Special thanks to a former U.S. Army defense attaché, who wishes to remain unnamed, for providing background information and insight into the world of military attachés. Col. John B. Alexander, U.S. Army (Ret.), generously shared his knowledge of electromagnetic pulse and directed energy weapons, and pointed me in the proper directions for further research. I'm proud to be able to call John and his lovely, catalyst-of-a-wife Victoria, my dear friends.

Warren Sessler, a Korean War–decorated hero from the brutal siege of Outpost Harry, helped out with my research in Las Vegas. Warren is just a great guy; he and his beautiful wife, Captain Xiao Sessler, U.S. Army, are true American Profiles in Courage.

The Phoenix Group, as always, deserves special mention for all of the unsung assistance they afford me behind the scenes.

I'm fortunate and grateful to have such a terrific, loving family.

I not only offer my heartfelt thanks to my wife, children, and other family members for taking such good care of me and being so supportive, but I must also ask their forgiveness for my long absences.

Very specific and hugely significant thanks go to David Reeves of Bedlam Group in Las Vegas. Serendipity brought our families together, and how grateful I am for that. David is a brilliant, generous soul who was instrumental in contributing astute technical advice, and other input. Thankfully, he's also a devious genius who enjoys a good Scotch, a fine cigar, and a hot cup of well-brewed coffee; please, David, accept my most humble thanks.

AUTHOR'S NOTE

Thanks in advance to my readers for understanding that while most of the locations in this book are real and worth a visit, others are purely fictional.

The mask-wearing militants who have appeared in eastern Ukraine and taken over government buildings represent the latest face of Russia's tradition of *maskirovka* (mas-kir-OAF-ka). It's a word literally translated as *disguise,* but Russia has long used it in a broader sense, meaning any military tactic that incorporates camouflage, concealment, deception, disinformation—or any combination thereof.

—*Time*, May 23, 2014

Denial and Deception: (Russian: *Maskirovka,* Маскировка) is a term which describes a particular type of information operation employed by a government agency, often an intelligence service. This sort of operation both blocks an adversary's access to accurate information regarding one's actions or intentions and, simultaneously, convinces said adversary of the accuracy of false information regarding those actions and intentions.

—Wikipedia

The Russians have been successful at using sophisticated deceptions for over 600 years.

—"Todd," a former U.S. Air Force Intelligence Agency officer

CHAPTER 1

The big sky hung low. Charcoal-hued cumulus clouds crowded the airspace above Interstate 80 east of Evanston, Wyoming, like they were moving in for a takedown. The weather made Irene Shanks's ankles hurt even more than the walking did.

"Rain coming soon," said Irene, without even glancing up. At seventy-eight years old, she didn't need a barometer; the swelling in her joints told her everything she needed to know about the weather forecast. She loosely held the L-rods favored by most dowsers as she hobbled her grid pattern over the hard soil.

"Will we have to stop?" asked Lily Bain, the pretty, blue-eyed blond woman who had shown up unannounced two days earlier on the doorstep of Irene's Tucson home with a lucrative proposition to come to the Salt Lake City area for a quick dowsing job.

"No, this shouldn't take long at all. Locating buried cables is child's play for me. Howard, my deceased husband, taught me how to find buried cables over forty years ago."

Lily and her partner Dennis had flown Irene first-class to Salt Lake City, put her in a nice hotel to rest, and then set out early this morning for the drive east on the interstate into Wyoming. Irene wasn't sure exactly where they were now, but back in Tucson she had map-dowsed the couple's Wyoming property using a pendulum. She had marked an area on a large-scale map they had provided her of a two-acre-sized plot where she felt the buried cable would most likely be found. And since the homemade map contained no reference that identified the actual location, Irene wondered if they were really treasure hunters trying to disguise their true intent.

They had all arrived from Salt Lake City in a rented four-wheel-drive GMC Yukon about thirty minutes earlier. Irene had set to work quickly and found the area that corresponded with the points she had marked on the map. She was now carefully walking a grid pattern on the desolate, gently sloping land, letting a moisture-laden prestorm breeze rich with ozone blow wayward strands of silver hair into her eyes.

Irene looked up. The foreground roller-coaster horizon didn't reveal much perspective; she knew they were close to I-80 and civilization—at least truck-stop civilization—but the view only suggested that they stood in the middle of nowhere. Something nagged at her as she slowly covered more ground; it wasn't the approaching storm bothering her, but she couldn't put her finger on it.

"Can I ask what you two are going to do out here in the boondocks that you're worried about the location of this cable?" asked Irene.

"We haven't decided that exactly," said Dennis, smiling. At thirty-four years old he stood six feet three, and even with a long-sleeved shirt covering his torso, one could see that he clearly was no stranger to the weight room. The bulk contrasted with a babyish face and pale skin featuring perennially rosy cheeks. His golden hair was combed back and made darker by using some kind of cream or gel. "But since the county has misplaced the maps showing where the cable is located, we want to know where *not* to dig or build something."

"I mean, you'll have to construct some kind of real road just to drive in here and . . ."

"It's amazing that you dowsed a water well for the Tucson water utility," said Lily, gently changing the subject. Only in her mid-twenties, Lily was slender, her ghost-white skin freckled out from the nose, and her smile was completely sweet. Irene thought of it as a "cutie-pie smile." Lily had explained away her slight accent as the result of spending her high school years in Prague, where her business-man father had been working. Lily's limp, straight hair was not cut fashionably, making Dennis appear to be the vain one of the young couple.

"But I got a call from the Tucson water company telling me I was wrong," protested Irene.

Dennis and Lily suddenly looked aghast. "Wrong?"

A smile came to Irene's lips, since she knew she had them going. "The water utility executive told me they drilled on the spot I had marked, and that they found water at exactly one hundred forty-three feet deep, just like I told them. But he said they were getting two hundred and two gallons a minute from the well, not two hundred and one, like I had said." *Nothing wrong with a little bragging from a seventy-eight-year-old,* thought Irene.

Dennis visibly relaxed and, smiling again, flicked his cigarette. "Sounds like your late husband, Howard, taught you well."

Suddenly, Irene's L-rods, made from pot metal similar to coat hangers, pointed sharply to the ground. "Found it. Could you mark it, sweetheart?" Irene asked Lily.

Irene reached into a nylon pouch slung across her chest, re-trieved a small pink plastic surveyor's flag on a metal rod, and gave it to Lily, who inserted it into the ground under Irene's L-rods. Irene concentrated her efforts on this area now, and soon a line of pink sur-veyor's flags bifurcated part of the property.

"That's good enough," called out Dennis as he crossed toward the Yukon. "You have earned your money, Irene. We can easily deter-mine the path of the cable now. Come here before the rain starts."

"I thought you wanted to know how deep it's buried."

"Oh, yes, of course! Sorry."

Irene handed her L-rods to Lily and then removed from her pouch a quartz crystal on a silver chain. She stood over one of the pink flags and held out the pendulum in her right hand. "Right for yes, left for no, thank you," whispered Irene, with her eyes closed. Then in a normal voice she said, "Is the cable buried between one and ten feet deep?"

Lily watched with obvious interest as the crystal quickly spun left. The young woman squinted, looking more closely, as if trying to catch Irene manipulating the movement of the stone.

"Is the cable buried between ten and twenty feet deep?"

This time the crystal spun to the right. "I'm going to go with a hunch," Irene said to Lily as she grasped the crystal to make it still again. "Is the cable buried at fifteen feet deep?"

The pendulum spun wildly to the right. "Fifteen feet deep it is, then. Seems awfully deep for a cable," said Irene, shaking her head as she put the pendulum away.

"Let's go. The rain is almost here," said Lily.

As Lily gently took Irene's arm and helped her walk the twenty yards to the SUV, Dennis opened the rear doors, retrieved a large black plastic tarp, and spread it onto the ground next to the rear of the Yukon.

"Can you stand on the tarp and use your dowsing rods to see if there's something there?" asked Lily.

"What am I looking for?"

"Just tell me if you get any sense of something. This will only take a moment, and then we are finished."

Irene thought the request a bit odd, but the size of the tarp was so small, it would indeed only take a moment. She held out the L-rods and slowly stepped onto the black tarp.

"I know dowsers who can locate crashed airplane sites, dowsers who find gold, silver . . . and buried treasure."

"We just wanted you to find the cable, I promise you that," assured Dennis.

She had no real reason to doubt him. But after taking a few short steps, she stopped. "I almost feel like Howard is trying to warn me about—"

Irene turned to face Lily and saw the sweet young lady holding a handgun that was pointed right at her. There was a black tube attached to the end of the gun barrel, and Irene heard several very soft sounds come from the gun before her world went black as the tarp.

The seventy-eight-year-old fell perfectly onto the center of the plastic sheet. Her swollen ankles would never bother her again.

"Did you hear what she said? She said her dead husband was trying to warn her, and that was exactly when I pulled my weapon."

"Just a coincidence," said Dennis, sizing up the fresh corpse, the easy smile gone from his face. "How deep did she say the cable was?"

"Fifteen feet."

"That sounds right. This old babushka must weigh a hundred kilos," he said disdainfully.

And with that, Dennis rolled her up into the tarp, and he and Lily grunted as they lifted Irene's body into the back of the Yukon.

Dennis closed the doors and then barked commands in Russian into a two-way radio. Lily crossed over to the pink surveyor's flags and replaced them all with small chunks of broken concrete painted to match the brown earth.

In less than a minute, a Ford F-350 pickup towing a backhoe on a trailer and carrying three men appeared over a slight rise and drove up to the Yukon.

"Get the camouflage netting up first," yelled Dennis, speaking in his native tongue of Russian to the workers. "Dig down to exactly fourteen feet. We work in between passes of the spy satellites."

CHAPTER 2

The Bennings family home sat on a hillock just off narrow and wind-ing Carbon Canyon Road in Chino Hills, California. Chino Hills was once a rustic ranch community in the southwest corner of San Ber-nardino County that went somewhat upscale with the influx of mon-eyed Chinese American and Chinese immigrant householders, and it's part of the smog-choked Los Angeles megalopolis that consumes a good chunk of Southern California. When the traffic gods are smil-ing, the drive to downtown L.A. only takes forty minutes.

Thirty-one-year-old Staci Bennings sat in her late father's airy home office on a pleasant spring morning, but her view out the win-dows was of a muddy brownish gray pall clinging to the horizon like a judgment that couldn't be expunged. To be sure, there was blue sky, but Staci would have to crane her neck at least 45 degrees to see it. She appeared to be lost in thought, staring out the windows.

The home office was decorated with all kinds of aviation memo-rabilia: models of commercial jets painted in the old TWA paint scheme occupied bookcase shelves; an airline captain's hat sat next to a U.S. Air Force officer's hat; and the control wheel from a 747 rested on the desk next to the PC where Staci sat. She shifted her gaze to the computer monitor, clicked on a different Web page, and twisted her troubled countenance into an angry scowl. Tall, slender, and very capable, Staci was the kind of person who usually wore a smile, not a frown; the sour look on her high-cheekboned, elegant face was like a clanging alarm, and her mood was not due to the dirty air tainting the skyline.

"From the look on your face, this is not good," said Staci's mother, Gina, weakly. "I don't understand what's going on."

Staci clicked on yet another Web page, then locked her gaze on her mother. "It's called identity theft, Mom. Some thief has hacked your life; the bank accounts are drained, your credit cards are maxed, new credit lines have been opened . . . I mean, wow, this is not good. I was just thinking about what I need to do first."

In frustration, Staci blew air from her mouth upward, causing some of the bangs of her shoulder-length brown hair highlighted with blond to flutter.

"New credit lines? Oh, my lord . . ." Gina Bennings put a hand on her chest and swayed slightly.

"Mom, sit down," said Staci, springing to her feet and crossing quickly to Gina. She eased her into a chair. "It's a mess right now, but I can take care of it. Don't worry, the banks, the credit card companies will make good on the money. I promise."

Gina Bennings had been an Italian fashion model thirty-eight years ago when she married her late husband, Tommy, an American citizen and commercial airline pilot. She gave up her catwalk career in Milan to be a wife and mother, giving birth to and raising three children in Southern California. But when her husband and youngest son died in a plane crash four years ago, she snapped. She had a nervous breakdown from which she never fully recovered. She also physically let herself go to seed, and she looked older than her age of sixty. Gina couldn't even take good care of herself anymore, so Staci had been living with her and attending to her needs while at the same time stepping in to help run the family aviation business.

"We should call Kit."

"He's overseas, Mom. I'll tell him the next time he calls."

"Where is he stationed now?"

"I've told you a hundred times: he's doing one of those things he can't talk about."

"Kit can help. We need a man in the house. Why doesn't he move home, anyway?"

"Don't worry, I can take care of this," said Staci, running her hand through her mom's unkempt gray hair and then giving her a gentle kiss on top of the head.

"Staci, someone has stolen all of our money. Please call Kit."

Staci checked her chronograph: 8:00 A.M. Pacific Time meant it was 7:00 P.M. in Moscow. The timing was probably okay. Kit would be calling in a few hours, anyway, as he did every day without fail since the plane crash that left him as the sole "man of the house." She knew she was only to call him if there was an emergency, using the encrypted satellite phone, or sat phone, he had given her. As she thought about it, she figured this qualified, even if her brother was involved in some kind of black ops. Having spent several years in the army herself, including a stint in Iraq, she knew better than to ever ask her brother what he really did.

Staci could take care of the damage control well enough with all of the financial institutions; it would be a time-consuming mess, but she'd do it and do it well. She took no offense at her mom's insistence on notifying her big brother. A day never went by that Gina didn't ask Kit to please move back home and live with her and Staci. An extremely close-knit family had been torn apart the day her dad and younger brother died in that crash. Selfishly, a part of Staci would like Kit to come home, too, and help ease the burden of being Gina's sole caregiver.

Yes, the view from the window was murky; sometimes you needed help to remember to look up and find the blue sky.

"You're right, Mom. I'll call Kit."

Staci knew that Kit had friends at the NSA, National Security Agency, and those freaky geeks could do virtually anything in the digital world they wanted to. Congressional oversight? Court orders? Search warrants? The politicians wanted people to believe that all of the snooping was legal and about terrorism, but oversight was a gray area at best, and Washington power politics was a constant exercise in abuse of power. The more spying that was allowed in the name of "keeping Americans safe," the more risk every citizen ran of becoming a target in the crosshairs of a government agency or employee or politician with an agenda; it happened frequently, regardless of what the politicians or the press led the public to believe.

But the flip side of the coin for Staci was that Kit's cyber-warrior pals would indeed abuse the system to find the jerk who did this, and then make them pay. So she crossed to the desk and dialed a number into the sat phone.

Just back from a long workday, Major Kit Bennings stood at the foot of his bed and, with no wasted movement, changed out of the civilian clothes—slacks, dress shirt, and tie—that he usually wore while on duty as an assistant defense attaché at the U.S. embassy in Moscow. He could faintly hear his roommates arguing over a game of cards in the main room of their shared apartment off Voykova Street in the Golovinsky District.

His three roomies were army personnel posted to the embassy. Careful scheduling assured that at least one of them was always present in the ground-floor corner apartment, thus preventing agents of the Russian intelligence agencies from ever gaining surreptitious access and bugging the place, as they did at most American government workers' living quarters in Moscow. Bennings turned up the volume on his digital music player, and the chords of "Boom Boom" by legendary bluesman John Lee Hooker filled his room and masked the indistinct chatter of his roomies.

Bennings's quarters were a safe room within a safe house; from the exterior, no one could see the bricked-up windows and floors and walls lined with lead. Or the trapdoor leading to a secret tunnel down below.

Kit sat heavily at a small vanity. Recent stress and fatigue lines and dark circles had become fixtures under his thirty-five-year-old brown eyes, indicating a need for more sleep and relaxation. In a preventative effort to fight off the enervating migraines that sometimes plagued him, he used reflexology on himself and dug his right thumb hard into a pressure point on his hand. He winced from the sharp pain but then pressed harder. Then he released and pressed again. Sixty seconds of sharp pain from pressure-point stimulation was far superior to three days of debilitating agony from a migraine. Army doctors had prescribed Imitrex, Zolmitriptan nasal spray, and other medications, but they didn't help, and instead, infused him with crippling fatigue. So Bennings had come to rely on acupuncture and acupressure to fight off the debilitating migraines.

"Massage" finished, he ran a hand through short-cropped, brown hair as coarse as steel wool and scratched his head vigorously, as if trying to wake up his brain. Tall without being too tall, fit without drawing attention to the fact, Kit had a narrow face, slightly crooked nose, and strong chin highlighting a visage that could blend in easily in Latin America, the Middle East, the West, Russia, or most any-where, excluding Africa or Asia. And he had often done just that in the years he had spent conducting dangerous operations for a secret army unit originally designated ISA—Intelligence Support Activity. This secret detachment of fearless, highly-trained soldiers went out and gathered intelligence in harm's way before the boys from Delta or DEV GRU—SEAL Team Six—went in to do their dirty business, although ISA had their share of "shooters," too.

Sometimes, as during the raid to kill Bin Laden, ISA operatives worked hand-in-hand with Six or Delta or DIA, Defense Intelligence Agency agents or officers from the CIA's SAD, Special Activities Division. The ISA folks made for some of the spookiest spooks, and while ISA wasn't even their official name anymore, it didn't matter: they were referred to by those in the know, usually in whispers, as simply, the Activity.

Kit Bennings felt tremendous pride in having achieved so much success as a member of the Activity. But tonight he was tired, and that could be seen in his most striking feature, his eyes. Even though brown is the most common color of all, his eyes simply . . . simmered. Not with rage but with intensity and luminosity. He could accuse, judge, and sentence a suspect in one brief glance. They cut like a diamond saw. Were they eagle eyes? Hawk eyes? They were the eyes of a predator, for sure, and when he directed them with intent upon a person, it was like having the red dot of a weapon's laser pointing at your vitals.

Since his eyes could be a giveaway, a red flag to the opposition, he had to remember to smile to soften his gaze; or he had to look away to stay unnoticed by others, since his hard countenance was so physically intimidating. He could imply a malevolence in his stare that made men, even hard men, think twice about trying something.

In the past, friendly acquaintances who didn't know the true nature of his work had felt reassured by simply being in Bennings's presence, within the aura of his confident physicality, not knowing he was usually involved in something that could get himself and everyone around him killed.

After delivering a final scratch to his scalp, he slid open a drawer in the vanity and silently calculated: within a month, this Moscow duty would be over. The sacrifice on his part to pull off the counter-intelligence operation could stop, and he seriously looked forward to that day. He wanted to get back to L.A. to see his mom and sister. He was worried about them; he was always worried about them since the demise of his dad and brother.

He let out an audible sigh, as if signaling some kind of transition, an acquiescence to the next phase of the evening's activities, and then with delicate precision that belied his large hands and powerful forearms, he popped in green contact lenses, applied eyeliner, and tugged on a shaggy, dirty-blond wig. Then he crossed to an antique armoire and found the rest of tonight's costume. He squeezed into tight black jeans and pulled on a slim-fit Maroon 5 T-shirt. Completing the transformation into some kind of quasi-goth hipster, he draped a red shoulder bag over his shoulder and lifted the trapdoor, ready to climb down to a dim netherworld, when his encrypted sat phone rang softly.

He checked the caller ID and then quickly answered. "Staci, is everything okay?" Bennings immediately felt a little self-conscious, standing there in front of a full-length mirror looking very nonmilitary;

it was like his sister wasn't calling on a phone from thousands of miles away but had just walked in on him while he was pretending to be Iggy Pop.

After apologizing for the call, she quickly filled him in about the identity theft. "I'm so sorry to interrupt anything, but Mom insisted, and I..."

"I'm glad you called, that's why I gave you the phone. Listen, I'm busy right now, but you remember my friend Jen Huffman, right?"

"Yes. How is she?"

"Ask her that yourself when she calls you. Tell her everything, give her whatever she needs. Trust her like she's one of the family, because that's what she is."

"Sounds great."

"She's a magician with this kind of stuff. We'll make everything right, I promise."

Staci exhaled audibly. "I have to say that's a big relief."

"Give the phone to Mom, and I'll say hi to her real quick."

"She's fallen asleep in the chair."

Kit bit his lip. "At eight o'clock in the morning?"

"I'll tell her you said you love her."

"I do love her. And I love you too, Staci. And say hello to that fiancé of yours."

"His name is Blanchard. When are you going to start using it?"

"Maybe when he's my brother-in-law. But what kind of first name is Blanchard?" asked Kit, smiling.

"What kind of first name is Kitman?"

"I shortened it to Kit, remember? But if you shorten Blanchard, you get Blanch. 'Hey everybody, meet Blanch. Great guy with a woman's name from a Tennessee Williams play!' Got to go, Sis," said Kit with a smile to his voice.

"Stay safe, big Brother."

The tunnel ran between Bennings's five-story walk-up concrete-block apartment building to an identical building next door. Identical, in fact, to thousands of other apartment buildings in Moscow. At two feet deep by three feet wide, the crude underground passageway had taken engineers six months to secretly build, the same six months that Bennings had to spend in the Pentagon's Defense Attaché System training program.

Bennings manually pulled himself along the tunnel while lying on a flat cart that rolled on small sections of plastic rail. The four- or five-times-a-week ritual was an exercise in blind faith and total surrender. He hated it. Undercover operators don't generally remain successful due to blind faith and total surrender.

He climbed up through the trapdoor into a ground-floor apartment of his neighboring building, a unit decorated in goth musician chic and that faced away from his real apartment. Hidden timers controlled the lights, TV, and water usage, to give the appearance to any utility snoops that someone actually lived there. But to be extra careful, Bennings grabbed his Fender Stratocaster, the same electric guitar he had played as a so-so lead guitarist in a high school blues band called Chord on Blue. He plugged into a small Marshall amp, sank into the secondhand sofa, turned up the volume, and started playing a bad rendition of Stevie Ray Vaughan's "Cold Shot."

Thirty seconds into the song, the old lady who lived next door began pounding on the wall. He turned the volume down and finished up the tune. Practicing his blues guitar licks for only three minutes wasn't improving his shoddy musicianship, but it helped establish with certainty that a human being lived in the apartment, and in Moscow, this was no small thing. Bennings also simply loved to play, and even three minutes a day, even a frustrating three minutes of wrong notes and missed chords, helped to lighten his mood.

He switched off the amp. After checking concealed security cameras that showed the hallway outside the apartment door to be empty, he slid on a pair of very dark sunglasses, adopted a slack posture, and with a bouncy walking gait unlike his own, disappeared into the night.

CHAPTER 3

Bennings rode the Metro to Chistye Prudy station. The only way to be certain he wasn't being followed required time and patience. He spent over an hour using elaborate countersurveillance moves to ensure there were no shadows on his tail. All the walking gave him ample opportunity to call Jen Huffman in the States and ask her to help out his sister with the identify-theft issue. Jen had spent several years with the NSA monkeys at Fort Meade before transferring to USSOCOM, the United States Special Operations Command. She was a bona fide cyber-wizard.

Bennings changed into sweats and switched wigs in a grungy public squat toilet next to a KFC. He turned his shoulder bag inside out, and the red bag became black. He stashed his rock-and-roll clothes in the bag, and then stepped out into the cool Moscow spring evening. He grabbed a couple of greasy piroshki to go from a kiosk on Marosejka.

After another ride on the Metro and some judicious walking, he found himself pretending to peruse a menu inside the TGI Friday's restaurant on Tverskaya in the city center. Right away he spotted Julie Rufo, his target for the night, and her dinner date.

Bennings strolled back outside and crossed the street. He pretended to window-shop while finishing off a piroshki, as the perpetually insane chaos called Russian traffic played its never-ending street dramas, such as five cars trying to simultaneously occupy the space of one. Conducting foot surveillance with only one person and not an entire team was outlandish but had so far worked fairly well here in Moscow.

Bennings felt tired but good. He enjoyed operating on the edge, with a lot of risk involved. And while he preferred functioning as an intelligence collector and not a counterintelligence spy-catcher going after his own people, he was well suited to accomplish the task. His day job as a defense attaché was a necessary charade, for it gave him access to many of the most sensitive areas of the U.S. embassy. But working undercover with a lot riding on the outcome was what got his blood pumping. His "night job" of uncovering moles in the American embassy was the real reason he'd been sent to Moscow.

His Russian cell phone vibrated with an incoming text. Bennings checked it and then moved to the curb. He never took the same route twice when going to meet Sinclair, and they never met at the same place. If he ever led a tail to Herb Sinclair, arguably the most successful American spy who ever operated in Moscow, it would most likely cost the man his life. Which is why the U.S. government spent the money to construct the secret tunnel connecting Bennings's apartment to a sterile one.

Herb Sinclair was a CIA Special Activities Division "illegal," a deep-cover American spy operating without official cover. As a defense attaché, Bennings held diplomatic immunity; Sinclair had no such thing.

Looking without appearing to look, Bennings held out his arm at 45 degrees to the ground, the Russian gesture for those trying to hail a taxi or hitch a ride, and a panel van pulled over. He quickly got in and closed the door.

"She's having dinner in the TGI Friday's across the street with one of the embassy marines," said Bennings in perfect Moscow-accented Russian as Sinclair pulled into traffic. They always spoke Russian as part of good operational security.

"Isn't that the restaurant chain that got busted back in the States for watering down the hard liquor?"

"That's why I distill my own sake back home. Cold sake is the bomb."

"Distilling sake sounds too much like real work. Just give me a Dos Equis, ice cold, with a lime, thank you very much," said Sinclair, winking. Herb Sinclair had thick hair becoming more salty than peppery, and he constantly pushed up the heavy black-framed glasses on his nose as he drove. He'd put on weight since he was posted to Moscow, but if you tapped his belly, it was like hitting a side of beef.

Herb was a legendary spook because of his now-long-term deep-cover penetration in Moscow. The Russians were adept at planting dozens of sleeper agents in America, while the CIA, mostly due to the nature of Soviet/Russian society, had few such operatives. Sinclair had originally gone undercover in Moscow for a single op, having assumed the identity of a Russian carpenter. But his superiors saw the value of keeping him in place and ordered him to become a "stay-behind" agent, something of a sleeper who was only activated for very sensitive operations. So for the last five years, Sinclair ran a small but thriving Moscow remodeling business as his cover.

Part of his success was due to the fact he was off the books. He had zero contact with the CIA's Moscow station, and few in the agency knew he in fact existed. He preferred to work alone as a "singleton," and had actually refused to take part in some operations because he felt it risked his exposure.

But Sinclair would work with partners on ops run by the SAD, the Special Activities Division, if he had previous experience with at least one team member he could trust.

Kit Bennings, though twenty years younger, had saved Sinclair's bacon on an op in Iran once when they were both with the Activity, and that's the only reason they were working together now.

Sinclair's primary forte was as a close-in "knob-turner," and he was one of the best COMINT—communications intelligence—geek maestros ever to walk the planet. If the NSA was gathering up the personal digital data of all Americans in the States, then Herb Sinclair was being even more invasive into the private affairs of all Americans working for the U.S. embassy in Moscow. The justification was simple: an American spy ring in the Moscow embassy had been passing sensitive information over to the Russians during the last eighteen months. Bennings and Sinclair had secretly uncovered two of the moles; one more was believed to remain.

So Sinclair operated as the COMINT element of the two-man team, with Bennings handling HUMINT—human intelligence.

Bennings's and Sinclair's spy-catching detail had been crafted by Secretary of State Margarite Padilla, with presidential backing. Kit Bennings had been pulled from the Activity and seconded to the Diplomatic Security Counterintelligence Directorate while simultaneously being transferred into the Defense Attaché System training program in preparation for the Moscow mission the two men were now conducting.

"So you tailed Rufo from the embassy?" asked Sinclair.

"No, just some good hard intelligence collecting called scuttlebutt. The embassy gossip mill is in high gear twenty-four/seven, and I'm plugged in."

"I'm surprised she's going out with a marine."

"The dinner date is just for show. For both of them. She'll ditch the marine after dessert without sleeping with him," said Bennings.

"Why do you say that?"

"She's eating with Shaw."

"Oh. One of the doughnut punchers. They must have made the date in person at the embassy, because I didn't pick it up on any of her comms."

"Which is why you knob-turners need HUMINT guys and gossipmongers like me," said Bennings.

"So which gay marine is she with?"

"I just told you, it's Shaw."

"Oh, right, the bean queen," said Sinclair. "He likes Hispanic guys."

Embassy marines don't have big secrets to spill, but you still wouldn't want them giving up what they know. While in-the-closet gays are theoretically more susceptible to blackmail, Sinclair and

Bennings had already ruled out any of the marines, including the gay ones, as being the remaining mole.

Special operators are very pragmatic individuals; both Bennings and Sinclair had worked with plenty of gays and had no issues in that regard whatsoever. Just as with the color of people's skin or their religion or gender, the only thing that mattered was were they good at their jobs and could you count on them in the clutch?

"One of the things I miss most living here in Moscow is Mexican food and Mexican ladies."

"So I guess that makes you the bean king," said Bennings.

"The bean king in exile. My kingdom for a good taco."

"It makes sense Rufo ditches the marine, whether he's gay or not," said Bennings. "She seems to be in love with the Russian guy, Sergei Lopatin."

"Well, she's peeling his banana every chance she gets."

"Lopatin is handsome and smooth. Rufo practically swoons when they're together."

"He's a little too handsome, too smooth. Something's not right, and you know it," said Sinclair.

"Be nice if it was a real romance."

"Has your brain turned to sap? We'll be getting her on tape passing information to Lopatin any time now."

"I like to give people the benefit of the doubt, but . . . you're probably right," said Bennings.

"Anyway, you know that I read her e-mail and cell-phone texts. He's coming to her place at ten. We don't need to waste time tailing her. Let's just take up position outside her apartment building."

Sinclair accelerated but drove carefully, unlike most of the other vehicles on the road.

"She's in a sexual relationship with a Russian national and hasn't reported it," said Sinclair. "Thanks to Putin's expansionist exploits in Crimea and Ukraine and all the other places, the imbeciles in Washington have finally figured out that the Russians are not our good buddies. 'Reset relations' my ass."

Bennings nodded. "So Rufo's in a little trouble already." Kit polished off the last piroshki from his sixty-ruble dinner. "Intensive sur-veillance for another week should tell us if she's the third mole. One way or another, I just want to wrap this operation up and get back home." Bennings shrugged.

"You've been here a few months and you can't wait to go back. I've been here five friggin' years."

Bennings looked intently at his partner. "You telling me they won't pull you out?"

"Bingo. Some suits back at Langley are making their careers based on the work I do here. They know I want out, but I don't even ask about it anymore."

Bennings knew that the Activity—an army unit—would never do that to one of their people. But the CIA was a much different ani-mal. He wanted to ask Sinclair more about the situation, but it wasn't his business, and his partner changed the subject back to Rufo and made further convincing arguments as to why he thought she was the third mole.

Be sweet if we could catch her in the act tonight, thought Bennings.

CHAPTER 4

Twenty minutes later, Bennings and Sinclair sat parked on the side-walk half a block down from Julie Rufo's ten-story concrete apart-ment building painted beige. Rufo was an E-5 who worked in the communications room at the embassy. She wasn't anything special to look at, but a lot of guys wouldn't kick her out of bed, either. It was a toss-up as to whether she might have been targeted by Sergei Lopa-tin in a classic honey-trap intelligence operation. Sensitive informa-tion that came through the communications room had been passed on to the Russians, but that information may have been leaked by one of the two moles whom Bennings and Sinclair had already iden-tified, or by someone else.

Both exposed moles, a senior diplomat and a mid-level consular official, had been quietly picked up and taken back to Washington.

They had resigned their positions, and no arrests had been forth-coming. In spite of hard evidence of damning leaks—espionage against the United States—the current presidential administration, already reeling from scandals, was keeping a lid on the whole affair.

"I hear your girlfriend, the SECSTATE, is coming to town," teased Sinclair.

"Padilla? Yeah, I have to attend the ball in her honor at the am-bassador's residence. As I think about it, what rotten luck for her to handpick me, pluck me out of the Activity and force me into six months' worth of attaché training. Just to establish my cover! I mean, half a year to establish a cover," said Bennings, shaking his head.

"A good cover is a wonderful thing."

"Yes, except all defense attachés are assumed to be *spies.* So my cover in Russia is 'American spy.' I still have a hard time wrapping my mind around that."

"Everyone at the embassy thinks you're spying on the Russians, not *them.* We're ferreting out American traitors, my friend, on the deep down-low. What we're doing here is historic. I mean, for Secretary of State Padilla to not even trust her own counterintelligence people in Diplomatic Security but to go to the president to authorize using us instead . . . that tells you just how sensitive and important this whole business is. Do you know that the SAD doesn't know about this op?"

"What?" asked Kit, shocked.

"We're both working under a secret presidential 'Finding.' The DCI had this shoved down his throat by your friend Padilla, is what I heard."

Kit whistled softly. "Padilla has a set of brass ones. It's no secret she hates the director of Central Intelligence."

"Screw them all," said Sinclair bitterly.

"I don't do what I do for the pricks in D.C., that's for sure. And I don't like working counterintelligence ops, but it felt damn good to catch those traitors," said Bennings. "So I guess the six months of attaché training was well spent."

"Becoming an attaché helped smooth out some of your rough edges, Bennings. Now you get to go to fancy balls, wear your prissy uniform, and suck up to a lot of creeps like the ambassador."

Bennings broke into a big smile. "You damn well know I didn't want to become a defense attaché."

"You're an *assistant* attaché, junior."

"You're jealous because we attachés are always having to throw cocktail parties for the idiots we're spying on and we get to flirt with their hot dates."

"You serve watered-down drinks, right?" asked Sinclair.

"Russian champagne. Which can also be used as paint remover."

Bennings yawned, then rubbed his eyes, as if trying to shake off fatigue. Sinclair stole a look at his partner, and his voice softened. "How's your mom doing?"

"Well . . . not too good," said Bennings.

"But your sister lives with her, right? Taking care of her."

"Yeah. They kind of take care of each other."

"I know you're pulling double duty—the embassy all day and then out with me for half the night. But if Rufo is the third little birdie singing to the Russians—and I think she is—I won't be going home, but at least you will."

At exactly ten on the dot, Bennings and Sinclair watched Sergei Lopatin, a handsome, confident dark-haired man in his late twenties, as he entered Rufo's apartment building. The men used laptops and earbuds to watch and listen in via the bugs and cameras Sinclair had already planted. Video showed Rufo and Lopatin go through their usual routine in her apartment: the couple drank a bottle of red wine while listening to soft Russian pop as he quizzed her on the boring details of her life since they last met.

Rufo's eyes sparkled, her smiles beamed cherubic, a glow of happiness engulfed her; even on the laptop screen she looked like a person in love. As for Lopatin, Bennings couldn't help suspecting it was just an act, as Herb Sinclair had been suggesting.

Twenty minutes of drink and chat later, the heavy petting began, and then five minutes later they made the short trek into her bedroom.

This part of the evening didn't interest Bennings—his job was to follow Lopatin when he left the apartment—but he kept an earbud in one ear as he thought about his mother and sister and wished he was with them to help. His mom was no slouch with computers, but that had been before her nervous breakdown. She either got sloppy and gave up her personal information in a phishing scam or maybe a Web site she trusted had been hacked and her data had been stolen. Either way, she had been aggressively targeted, and he felt a strong need to set things right.

At 2:17 A.M. Bennings stood in shadows watching as Sergei Lopatin emerged from Julie Rufo's apartment building. Tailing the Russian on foot, without assistance, was not ideal, but Bennings had performed similar tasks dozens of times all over the world.

But there would be no footwork tonight; a shiny black Mercedes with tinted windows squealed around the corner and stopped just as Lopatin reached the curb. The Russian hopped in and was gone in moments. Sinclair was not to attempt to follow.

Bennings started walking toward the nearest Metro station. Fourteen minutes and three blocks later, Sinclair stopped his van next to him, and Bennings piled in.

Neither man looked happy.

"That car had 'mob' written all over it," said Bennings.

"Maybe, but my money is on our friends in the FSB, the *Federal'naya Sluzhba Bezopasnosti,* or one of the other intelligence services. Sloppy for them to pick him up right in front of her place."

"How is she passing him the information? What have we missed?" asked Bennings, frustration evident in his voice.

"I hate to tell you, but you're going to have to tail her to and from work. Maybe he slipped her a cell phone or a netbook we don't know about. Maybe she's using a dead drop along her route to the embassy."

"Just what I need . . . less sleep." Bennings templed his fingers together, thinking. "Okay, but I can't start this morning. I have a breakfast meeting with Viktor Popov."

"The ex-KGB warhorse?" KGB stood for *Komitet Gosudarstvennoy Bezopasnosti*, or Committee for State Security, the former main intelligence agency of the old Soviet Union. Kit nodded. "I see him once a week. Makes me look like a real defense attaché, collecting information about the Russian's nonlethal weapons program. I'm supposedly here in Moscow to get secrets from Russians, remember?"

"Be careful with Popov. People trying to get something from that old spy bastard usually get dead."

Dennis Kedrov, the big blond Russian chief henchman of Viktor Popov's American operations, stood under camouflage netting as the sound of heavy equipment rumbled around him. All vehicles and equipment at the site were shrouded with similar camouflage, as was the heavy equipment currently doing the digging.

Smoke from a Turkish cigarette clenched between his teeth curled up into his eyes. He squinted, ignoring the smoke, and settled into a putting stance while holding a collapsible travel putter. He took two short practice strokes, then putted a yellow golf ball right into a Styrofoam coffee cup lying on its side in the dirt four feet away.

He took a final puff, then flicked the cigarette aside, smiling. He sat on a folding hunter's chair, poured a small shot of vodka from a silver flask, and knocked it back. An ice chest served as a desk for his laptops. He was uplinked directly to satellites and stayed in secure communications with Popov and other members of the specialized teams assembled for the current operation—a complex, brilliant scheme and a stellar example of Russian *maskirovka*: the use of deception and deceit, a technique employed by the Russians ever since they defeated the Golden Horde of Genghis Khan 120 miles south of present-day Moscow. Although originally used in terms of military operations, it was a concept long-embraced and used by Russians in everyday affairs.

Dennis knew that the current deceptions were so clever that with a little luck, the Americans would never learn what actually happened. Eventually, they might come to suspect the truth, but it would be far too late by then. The chances were excellent that Dennis and his fellow *vor v zakone*, "thieves-in-law," were about to pull off the biggest scam in the history of the planet.

Dennis glanced at his laptop screens, then sharply craned his neck at the sound of the backhoe going silent. He checked his watch, then yelled, "What now?"

A rail-thin Russian worker walked up to him holding a tape measure. "We're at fourteen feet."

CHAPTER 5

The Moscow Marriott Grand was one of the better hotels in the city center. Security was tight; goons in black suits packing heat lurked everywhere, and one had to walk through a metal detector to enter from the street. An efficient staff provided good service, and the generous breakfast buffet in the lobby was top-notch and usually packed with foreign businessmen in town on a never-ending pursuit of rubles, regardless of which country Vladimir Putin was destabilizing at the moment.

"Are you sure you wish to place your knight there?" asked Viktor Popov with a sly smile.

Kit Bennings was dangling his white knight over position e8. The chess set was a small travel size that barely fit on the table crowded with a coffee urn, plates of cheese, pastries, yogurt, fruits, and piles of ham, bacon, and sausage. Viktor enjoyed large breakfasts; Kit had stopped after half a croissant.

"Not trying to psych me out, are you?" said Kit, smiling. He placed his knight in the e8 square.

They sat at a table as far from the buffet as possible, giving them a bit of privacy from the other guests, since most of the hungry diners liked to sit close to the goodies.

"In this instance, no. Just trying to prolong the game a bit. But, alas . . ." Viktor moved his knight. "Checkmate."

"Damn . . . I didn't see that coming."

"It would seem there have been a few things you and your government haven't seen coming lately," said Popov, smirking.

Kit glanced at the general. The old man never missed a chance to dig in the needle.

"You're not too sharp this morning, Major. And you look terrible. A pretty Russian girl keep you awake last night?"

"I prefer American women, General."

"Perhaps you will change your mind about that."

Viktor Popov was a very tall, large man, who at sixty-seven was still physically intimidating and in incredibly good shape. A deep bass voice enhanced the command presence he conveyed, keying even strangers to the fact that he was an authority figure. One moment Popov could be absolutely charming, the next he would snap orders with a tone that suggested dire circumstances if the instructions weren't carried out immediately.

His longish gray hair was combed back and meticulously held in place with hair gel, suggesting he paid attention to his looks. His gray eyes moved slowly, always lingering, as if they didn't want to miss a detail, however insignificant. Big hands betrayed enlarged knuckles, suggesting Popov had been no stranger to fisticuffs in the past. A bone-colored raw-silk Burberry blazer that must have cost a hundred thousand rubles looked as good on Popov as it would have on a young male catwalk model; the general was a bit of a dandy.

"Smart," "slick," and "deadly" were three words Kit Bennings had written in a report after his first meeting with former KGB general Viktor Popov.

Viktor poured them shots from a carafe of vodka—not an uncommon sight at Russian breakfast tables. "Hair of the dog," he said, holding up his small crystal vodka glass. "To beautiful Russian girls."

Kit didn't want the drink, but social protocol called for it. "To beautiful women everywhere."

They clinked glasses and drank. Bennings had been meeting Popov regularly every week. As an attaché, he was expected to solicit relationships with knowledgeable foreign nationals, including military and intelligence types. A kind of camaraderie without trust had developed, at least for Kit, and he sometimes would not even bother to pump Viktor for any information. Since they were both avid pilots of fixed-wing and rotary aircraft, they often argued over performance specs between Russian and American craft. But today Bennings didn't feel like talking airplanes.

"Speaking of beautiful Russian ladies," said Viktor, "and at the risk of offending you, I have a favor to ask . . . for you to consider."

Bennings quickly went more alert. *A favor?*

"It goes without saying that I'm not recording this conversation, you're not," said Viktor as he placed a sophisticated bug detector on the table and ran a check, "and it seems the esteemed intelligence agencies of Mother Russia aren't recording, either."

Now he had Kit's full attention, and Bennings didn't mask his wariness.

"My niece Yulana," Viktor said, handing Kit a photo. "She's twenty-eight, beautiful, divorced, and wants to move to the United States. I'm not talking about visiting as a tourist. She wants to live there. So I want to help her do that. Legally. I've given you much valuable information these last few months and asked for nothing in return. But I was hoping you could be of help in this matter."

"There are people at the embassy I can pass this on to. . . ."

"No, no, you misunderstand me. The U.S. State Department and myself are no longer on such good terms. My name can't be connected to this."

Kit handed the photo back to Viktor. "I'm sure you know that I'm not in any position to order or even politely ask the consular folks to grant your niece a visa. But I can keep your name out of it, forward the paperwork, and request that she gets a fair hearing."

"I was thinking of a different approach." Viktor's eyes locked onto Kit's; they were like two predators sizing each other up.

"I truly appreciate the tidbits you've given to me, General Popov, but you haven't shared any earth-shattering information since we've been meeting," said Kit firmly. "Give me something juicy and I can make the visa happen."

"I don't have anything 'juicy' for you Americans right now."

At this point, Bennings wished he *were* recording the conversation. He knew what a sly fox Viktor Popov was, since he had studied his background closely.

Viktor Popov had met many foreign "businessmen" at the Marriott Grand for meals and drinks since the collapse of the Soviet Union. Like many former high-ranking KGB officers, Popov had scrambled to position himself to cash in on the chaos of the early 1990s, as mob wars raged across Moscow and criminals penetrated literally every division, agency, and department of the Russian government.

Incredibly, the huge arsenals of the Russian military were simply plundered. With the help of his scientist wife, who worked and lived in Samara—a large industrial city on the Volga River with major defense plants—Popov had looted an entire warehouse full of electromagnetic pulse and directed energy weapons and sold them on the black market. He brokered the sale of an entire squadron of Mi-28 helicopters based in Kyrgyzstan, to Kenya. Trucks, munitions, secrets, technicians—he sold, rented, and bartered what he could to capitalize himself for bigger things and to grow and groom a legion of loyal minions, all operating under a criminal code, the principal tenets of the Russian mobs, the *vor v zakone*—"thieves-in-law."

The newly installed Russian reformers in the 1990s had been wrong: it wasn't a revolution for the people, it was a revolution for the Mafia. And Viktor Popov, like so many others, had intended to cash in on it.

Bigger things did come to Popov that decade, but so did trouble, as the ruthless Russian mob ranks in Moscow and elsewhere grew fat with brutal, greedy men bailing from the intelligence services and military. Massacres of rival gangs and even their families became common. To survive, Popov attached himself to an emerging oligarch. But that wasn't enough; he needed more friends, powerful friends, and so in the late 1990s he sold some secrets to the Americans. Popov held many secrets; he had them to spare, actually, since he'd been the KGB general in charge of the Eighth Chief Directorate. He personally supervised the unit that had been responsible for successful penetration operations against foreign cryptographic outfits and personnel, like America's NSA and Britain's equivalent, GCHQ Government Communications Headquarters.

In return for Popov's help in those unsettled times for Russia, the grateful D.C. intelligence wonks opened the doors to America—"The Big Store," the Russian mobsters call it—and Viktor Popov walked through with his legions of thugs and cyber-crooks to settle in Los Angeles. He quickly made allegiances with the other larger, more-powerful Russian mob outfits. Seeing the need to specialize, Popov avoided the usual drug, gambling, prostitution, and fuel scams and insurance fraud common to the other Russian crime groups in the United States, and early on he concentrated on what he knew best: cyber-crimes and cyber-spying. He grew wealthy, but his personal wealth ran only into the tens of millions, not the billions, making him a minor player at best in *très* expensive Moscow, a town that had more billionaires per capita than any city on earth. Popov now spent half of his time in the Russian capital, currying favors with the rich and powerful—crime lords—and trying to weasel his way back into Vladimir Putin's favor now that the quest to re-establish the old Soviet Union was out in the open.

He was tolerated by the police state of Putin, mainly because of the valuable information he provided gratis to the Kremlin. Information, in fact, had long been Popov's stock-in-trade. There was less downside to obtaining and then selling sensitive data than there was to monetary theft. Steal money or material, and people come after you. Steal information, a more ephemeral commodity, and institutions and states don't like it one bit, but they tend to write it off to the cost of doing business in a digital age.

So Popov's people, experienced "black hat" hackers, vacuumed up facts, figures, statistics, gossip, plans, blueprints, proposals, secrets, strategies, and data of any value. Popov sifted through all of the stolen information and then brokered it, acting essentially as a free-lance spy, a "paper merchant" or a "paper mill," selling intelligence to the secret services of Iran, China, India, Brazil, France, Germany, Russia, the United States, and any other country with hard currency.

But now, here he was sitting across the table from Bennings with some kind of a proposition that he didn't want taken to the embassy. Kit recalled Herb Sinclair's earlier warning about Popov: "People trying to get something from that old spy bastard usually get dead."

"I'll give you a hundred thousand dollars to marry Yulana. When you return to the States, take her with you. You won't have to live together or anything like that. Your government doesn't check on such things."

Bennings stared at Popov for a long time with unforgiving intensity. "We shouldn't be having this conversation."

"Humor me. We are speaking in private."

Bennings shook his head. "You're not joking?"

"No, I don't joke when it comes to business. Wait just a moment, please."

Popov suddenly stood up and crossed to a young Asian couple having breakfast with their daughter, who looked to be about two years old. Kit had seen him do it time and time again, whenever a toddler was present. Popov would always approach the parents and tell them what a cute child they had, inquire as to the age, and then gently touch the child's fingers. He'd make small talk and then politely leave. The first few times, Kit was suspicious that the parents were agents of some sort and that Popov was passing or receiving information, so he always watched very closely. Finally Kit came to realize that the general liked kids. But since spies are not trusting types, Bennings never took his eyes off of Popov.

Viktor Popov absolutely loved the pure humanness of toddlers. The selfishness, the kindness, the overt manipulation of the parents and others, the emotional and physical needs and wants laid bare without malicious artifice. Oh, sure, toddlers could be arch-schemers, but without intent to hurt anyone.

It was the intent that made the difference. Every action in Viktor's life, as far back as he could remember, had been a product of artifice, underscored with vile intent. Indeed, he'd become a grand master of ruthless *maskirovka*—deception. His endless machinations hurt people all the time, often in the form of collateral damage: his children, wife, lovers, family, friends, peers. But so what? Life was hard and unforgiving, and the bumps along the road, sometimes big bumps, could and should make one stronger for having survived them.

And then there were his plots designed to absolutely hurt others, "hurt" actually being too tame a word. People would be targeted to be financially ruined, their careers destroyed, their lives taken—necessary outcomes for his deceptions to succeed. This was part and parcel of the way he did business. Viktor held little but contempt for the weak, the losers, the victims.

As he stood towering over the Asian couple and their toddler in the lobby restaurant of the Marriott Grand, the child muttered baby talk and grasped Viktor's index finger. The purity of the very young made him melancholy for something he'd lost. Doting on toddlers was no artifice for Viktor, but a form of worship, a ritual of remembrance that was possibly the most genuine action Viktor Popov was capable of performing.

"Please have a safe trip home, and take good care of your little girl," said Viktor, smiling and with a slight bow.

As he crossed back toward his table, he shifted his thoughts back to the proposal he'd made to Bennings, and he knew he'd never have another pleasant conversation with the man. It was a pity, because he liked talking about flying with the American spy. But business trumped everything else.

"Visiting from Japan," said Popov as he sat back down. "An adorable little girl. Twenty-one months old."

"How old are your grandkids now?" asked Kit, making an obvious effort to direct the conversation to other topics.

"They are all spoiled, troublemaking high school brats," said Popov without warmth. "My wife and I had four children, but only my two sons survived past the age of three."

"Your twin daughters were murdered." The words had been uttered gently, but Bennings's gaze bore into Popov's, as if looking for his reaction.

Viktor realized that this was the first time Bennings had ever brought up an event from his past, especially such a sensitive one. "Yes." For a brief moment, Popov's eyes clouded over. He pulled a gold locket from his pocket and opened it, revealing two black-and-white photos of his girls. "By mobsters. I've tracked down and personally killed every man responsible, except one." He turned to Kit. "The murders of my daughters is not common knowledge," he said, without emotion.

"I'm a spy, remember?"

Viktor waved off the remark as if it were meaningless. "If you say so. Anyway, you don't have children, Major. But I can assure you that they are so precious the first few years of their lives. They are such a gift. When they're older, they become assholes like everybody else."

"I'm truly sorry for the loss of your daughters."

"Thank you. So you see I am something of a father to Yulana," said Viktor, swiftly shifting the conversation back to business.

"Children are precious, and so is the sanctity of marriage," said Kit.

"Sorry to inform you, but marriage, even in the best of circumstances, is a business deal. I know you are aware that in the past, more than a few of the embassy marines have gotten thirty or forty thousand dollars for a fake marriage to get a U.S. visa for a Russian woman."

"I've heard rumors to that effect. And I'm sure those marines came under suspicion."

"But nothing was done to them. They remained in the service." Before Kit could interrupt, Viktor went on: "Chinese regularly pay fifty thousand dollars to be smuggled into the U.S. *illegally*. With no legal status once they get there."

"Illegal immigrants to the USA don't have much to fear these days, do they?"

"That's beside the point. You have a much higher status than a marine, Major Bennings. One hundred thousand dollars to you is a fair price."

Kit looked at Viktor evenly. Popov could tell the man was trying to rein in his temper. "I'm sorry you think so little of me to even consider I might be for sale or for rent, for a hundred thousand or for one hundred million. Please go find a marine for fifty thousand, is my advice. Now you'll have to excuse me."

"She's my niece. Even though it's a fake marriage, I want it to be with a good man, a person with integrity. With you. I'll make it two hundred thousand. Cash. Untraceable bills."

"You think I have integrity? That's why you're trying to bribe me? You said you wanted her there legally, but she and I would be committing fraud. We could both go to federal prison." The irritation in Bennings's tone had ratcheted up a notch or two.

"If I offered one million dollars—I could have it delivered to you within the hour—would you consider it?"

"I would consider that you were trying to co-opt me, and that it had nothing to do with marrying your niece," said Bennings.

"And your answer would be the same?"

"Of course."

"In my experience, Major, everyone has their price. But just to clarify, I'm not offering one million, I'm offering two hundred thousand, which is a lot of money for a U.S. soldier, and only because Yulana is my family."

Bennings stood. Popov watched him carefully; he'd gotten under the major's skin, and Bennings seemed to work hard to muster up a pleasant countenance. "General Popov, thank you for all of your valuable time that you have so generously given me in the past. Goodbye, sir." Bennings didn't reach to shake Popov's hand but turned and walked away.

Popov had been 95 percent certain that he wouldn't take the bribe. But since he liked Bennings, he wanted to give him the opportunity to accept the money and therefore avoid a much darker outcome, a hurt that would be foisted upon Kit and his family as a result of the current deceptions that should make Viktor Popov the wealthiest man in Moscow.

Everyone does have a buying or selling price, but sometimes the payment isn't rendered with money. You will be the one paying a dear price, not me, my American friend, thought Popov, reaching for his cell phone as he watched Bennings leave the restaurant.

CHAPTER 6

As Bennings sat at his desk in the Embassy of the United States, Moscow, Russia, he considered what to include in his report on the meeting with Viktor Popov. Yes, his cover was an assistant defense attaché, but that meant he was a real defense attaché and had to perform as such. No one in the DAO, the Defense Attaché Office, or in the entire worldwide program, not even General Alexander, commander of the Moscow attaché office, knew Bennings was really in town working undercover to catch American traitors.

If he wrote up the report indicating Popov's attempt at a bribe—a significant one at that—it could unleash a series of events that would pull in the embassy CIA spooks and go all the way to the ambassador. They might even want him to accept the bribe and use him as some kind of bait in an attempted sting against Popov. Since that kind of attention was unwelcome, Bennings opted to write an incomplete report, omitting any mention of the marriage-for-money offer, and he silently cursed Popov as he wrote it.

After finishing the report, he considered the pros and cons of bugging the embassy communications room so he and Sinclair could spy on Julie Rufo. Planting a surveillance device in such a sensitive area would be terribly problematic and probably counterproductive, so Bennings abandoned the idea. He planned to follow Rufo when she took her lunch, but then he was ordered by General Alexander to go to Sheremetyevo Airport. Not only was Secretary of State Margarite Padilla arriving in Moscow today, but one of the Joint Chiefs of Staff, a four-star army general, was traveling with her. Which meant that as a mere assistant defense attaché from the army, Kit Bennings had to go and carry the luggage for the four-star. Ah, the glamour of being an attaché posted to a major foreign capital.

Bennings made it back to the embassy by five and was able to follow the suspected mole, Julie Rufo, from the embassy all the way to her apartment block. He saw absolutely nothing out of the ordinary, and that irritated the hell out of him. By the time he got back to his own apartment, he was exhausted and failed to make his usual call home to Chino Hills before dropping off to sleep in his clothing.

Gina Bennings finished her third cup of strong Italian coffee in her flower-adorned hilltop kitchen, but she still felt tired. Either the medications she took made her tired or the depression the meds were supposed to treat made her tired—she wasn't sure which. She had good days—enough time had elapsed since the accident to ensure that—but the bad ones outnumbered the good. This was a bad day.

She'd led something of a charmed life from the moment she'd met Tommy Bennings in Milan almost forty years ago. But for the last four years, since the deaths of her husband and youngest son, Michael, her charmed life had become a dark place.

Yes, she was grateful for her children Staci and Kit, but no parent should have to bury a child. It wasn't fair. And now, with the development that someone had stolen her life savings and sent her deep into debt, well, she prayed daily to God that he take her to join Tommy and Michael.

The phone ringing startled her out of her self-pitying interior monologue.

"Hello."

"Hi, this is Paula Duvan from Town and Country Bank. Is this Mrs. Gina Bennings?"

"Yes."

"You're aware of the problems we're having with your account?"

The female voice sounded vaguely European to Gina, but she couldn't place it. Her bank had become so multicultural over the years, she sometimes wondered if there were any American-born employees left. Of course, Gina Bennings wasn't American-born, either.

"Yes, but my daughter, Staci, is taking care of all those things."

"Can I speak to Staci then, please?"

"She's at work. Can you call her at—"

"Mrs. Bennings, since it's your account, is there any way you could come in to the bank this morning? I don't think it's necessary to bother your daughter at work. It's a mere formality. We need your signature on some documents."

"Just a signature?"

"Yes. We're trying to get all of your money put back into your accounts, so if you could come in right now, that would help a lot."

"Right now?"

"Yes, can you do that?"

"All right, I don't see why not."

"How soon can we expect you?"

Gina checked her watch. "Thirty minutes."

"She's backing out of the driveway now," said the Russian speaker, acting as lookout on the street opposite the Bennings residence.

"All units copy. We are a go," said the cute blonde with the cutie-pie smile: Lily Bain, who had gone by the name of Paula Duvan a few minutes earlier on the phone with Gina.

Lily sat in the front passenger seat of a Lincoln Navigator holding a two-way radio. Dimi, one of Viktor Popov's thugs, worked on a big wad of chewing gum as he sat behind the wheel. Both the Navigator and a Ford panel van stood parked on the shoulder of Carbon Canyon Road, just down from Gina Bennings's home.

"Unit two copies."

"Three, copy."

"Four copies, moving in behind her."

This would be a snatch using four vehicles. Lily, whose real name was Ludmilla Babanin, had executed many such kidnappings, and had in fact executed many *people*. In cold blood. A hardened street prostitute at age fourteen, she'd been recruited at age seventeen by the SVR, *Sluzhba Vneshney Razvedki,* the foreign intelligence service of the Russian Federation, and excelled in all aspects of training. At age twenty-four she went to work in America for Viktor Popov. Life had been mostly good ever since.

"Unit four to unit one: she's turned onto Carbon Canyon. I'm behind her and now dropping back."

"Copy," said Lily.

Unit four was a pickup truck with amber lights mounted on the roof, and metallic signs stating: EMERGENCY VEHICLE. The truck slowed, allowing Gina to disappear down the hill, then turned on its flashing lights, slowing all other downhill traffic.

An identical pickup, unit three, had already done the same thing to uphill traffic. As Gina Bennings entered a series of sharp S turns, there was no one else on the road . . .

. . . except for a black Navigator and a white panel van now blocking Carbon Canyon Road. Lily and some thugs stood next to the vehicles.

Lily Bain had carefully calculated that in the middle of this S curve not visible from any houses, Gina would have plenty of time to stop. Her goons would then grab the old lady, toss her into the panel van, and one of them would drive Gina's car to a rendezvous point. It would be over in less than thirty seconds.

But when Gina rounded the sharp curve, Lily got a sinking feeling in the pit of her stomach. She could see the panic on Gina's face as her car lurched forward—*accelerated*—and swerved to miss the roadblock, then hurtled into a heavily wooded arroyo just off the shoulder. The noise of the crash could have been worse. Gina's car missed hitting trees and nose-dived into hard earth about twenty feet below the road.

"Chert poberi!" shouted Lily. *Damn it all to hell!* She then reined in her anger and calmly spoke into her radio: "Three and four, hold the traffic, hold the traffic." She waved frantically at Dimi. "Park the vehicles on the shoulder, there!"

As Lily and the thugs raced into the arroyo, Dimi and the other driver parked the Navigator and panel van at the point where Gina's car had left the roadway, blocking the site from view.

Lily Bain slid down the slope and was the first to reach the driver's compartment, where she put on thin white cotton gloves. "The air bags didn't deploy. And this car is almost new."

"This is America. She can sue," joked one of the thugs.

"Shut up," she snapped.

Gina Bennings, still wearing her seat belt, looked dead to Lily. Her nose was smashed into her head, blood oozed from numerous gashes, and her awkwardly angled neck didn't look right. But Lily checked her pulse in two places. She eased her cell-phone screen under what was left of Gina's nostrils and checked for condensation.

"She's dead," said Lily, pulling off her gloves and stuffing them into a back pocket of her jeans. "Quick, let's go."

In seconds the Russians were back in their vehicles and pulled onto Carbon Canyon Road. "Units three and four, release traffic." Lily lit a cigarette. "All she had to do was step on the brake."

"We should have grabbed her at the house," said the driver, Dimi, who then blew a bubble with his chewing gum.

"That's why you're just the driver. That house has more alarms and CCTV cameras than a bank. We still have plan B."

Lily reached behind her to get the white gloves from her back pocket, but there was only one glove, not two.

Ohooiet'! Holy f*ck! A flash of panic swept over her freckled face. Did she lose a glove at the accident scene? She felt sick in the pit of her stomach, but then quickly balled up the glove into her hand and stuffed it into her front pocket.

Dimi glanced over at her, but she ignored him. Even if the police found the glove, how could they possibly connect it to her? Lily relaxed and thought about plan B.

.   .   .

Gina Bennings groggily opened her eyes. She was only half there, maybe not even that much. She silently recited the prayer she'd been saying for the last four years, asking to be taken to join her deceased husband and son.

Then she closed her eyes, and God answered her prayers.

CHAPTER 7

Kit awoke at 4:00 A.M. to make sure he'd be in place at Julie Rufo's apartment building by 7:00. He didn't use the tunnel and so he picked up his usual tail when he left his apartment. As a defense attaché / assumed spy in an adversary nation, the Russians followed him everywhere. It was only when he used the tunnel in disguise at night that he could leave and enter his residence unnoticed.

Since he'd never had occasion to ditch his tail before, their guard was down, and he easily lost them at a Metro station. Still, he spent a solid hour of countersurveillance to make sure he wasn't followed to Rufo's.

Kit easily followed her to the Presnensky District, but he dropped back as they neared the embassy complex at Bolshoy Deviatinsky Pereulok No. 8. His shadows were waiting for him, and he didn't want them to connect him to Rufo. Once again, she had done nothing out of the ordinary during her commute.

As soon as Bennings walked into the embassy's defense attaché office, he could feel something was wrong. Everyone gave him strange looks. Everyone. Strange look, quick nod, then look away.

"Major Bennings." It was Jan, a young secretary. "General Alexander wants to see you immediately."

Damn! Does he know about Popov's bribe attempt? How could he? It wasn't in the report, but . . .

"This way please, Major." Kit tensed his stomach muscles and followed Jan right into the general's office. The secretary quietly closed the door as she left.

"Please sit down," said General Alexander, a white-haired man in his late fifties. He wore a shirt and tie, just like all the male attachés in the office. Kit couldn't read his face as he sat across the big wooden desk from his commander. He'd only worked for the general for a few months and hadn't yet established any kind of personal connection; their dealings had been brief and very formal.

"I'm guessing you haven't checked your e-mail this morning."

"No, sir, I was going to do that first thing after I arrived."

"And you have some kind of satellite phone?"

The question surprised Kit. *How does the general know I have a sat phone? Oh, hell, there's trouble coming for sure.* Kit felt for the device in his pocket. "Yes, sir." He pulled it out. "Would you like to see it?" Kit quickly checked the phone. "Sorry, General, looks like the battery is dead. I was so tired last night I went to sleep without charging it. But, sir, my regular cell phone with a Russian SIM card is right here." He produced the cell phone, which he seldom used. "It's working. Your office has this number and—"

"Settle down, you're not in any trouble. Your sister back in the States has been trying to call your sat phone. She finally called the Red Cross, and they called us. So I guess I'm the one who has to tell you: your mother was killed in a car accident. She apparently couldn't negotiate a sharp curve and ended up in an embankment. I'm very sorry. Tell me what I can do for you. We can get you on the first thing smoking out of Moscow. You can leave today if you want."

Kit sat in stunned silence holding on tightly to the arms of the chair. He hadn't called home last night. He'd forgotten. One day his mom's bank accounts were raided, the next day she was dead. What in the hell? And worse, he wasn't even there to have helped. His head was spinning.

He simply couldn't believe it. He had exactly one family member left in the world, his sister, Staci.

"Major Bennings?"

"Yes, sir." It came out automatically, in almost a whisper. Kit realized his eyes had moistened. He squeezed the armrests as hard as he could, then bit down on his tongue till it almost bled. He worked hard to consciously swallow the emotion and keep it from rising to his head.

General Alexander stood and poured a glass of water from a pitcher on a side table. He handed it to Kit.

"Thank you, General." Kit drank deeply from the water as his intellect overrode the emotion, as he'd been trained to do. His mind raced. "Sir, I have a few things to wrap up. I'd like to fly back to Los Angeles tomorrow afternoon, if that can be arranged."

"Consider it done."

He saluted and managed to walk out without shedding a tear.

The general provided a private office with a phone, and Kit immediately called Staci at home in Chino Hills. She cried for most of an hour, but he held the space of the emotional anchor point, the solid rock of reason to her wailing sorrow. Her fiancé, Blanchard, was a globe-trotting financial adviser currently closing a big deal in Tokyo; he couldn't get back to Chino Hills for at least a week without blowing his multimillion-dollar deal. But Rick and Maria Carrillo were with Staci. Rick had flown with Kit's father, Tommy, during the Vietnam War; he had flown with Tommy as an airline copilot, and he had been a founding partner in the aviation company Tommy had started. Rick and Maria had been best friends to Tommy and Gina for decades and were like an uncle and aunt to Kit and Staci. *At least Rick and Maria are there.*

Bennings then sent a coded, encrypted message to Herb Sinclair saying he was leaving Moscow due to a personal emergency. Sinclair had the communications of so many embassy employees wired, there was a good chance he already knew about the accident. Either way, it was instructive how when "life" intrudes upon your world—in this case life being death—so much that had been terribly important suddenly becomes meaningless. Like the search for the third mole.

CHAPTER 8

"This isn't plan B, this is plan XYZ," groused Dimi, the Russian driver, as he popped a chunk of pink bubble gum into his mouth. This time, Dimi sat behind the wheel of a silver Ford Crown Victoria. He began loading tranquilizer darts into a special pistol as lights twinkled in the darkness from homes on the nearby hills.

"And what difference does it make to you?" quizzed Lily Bain. There was no cutie-pie smile, just a quick, sharp look flashed like a shiv at Dimi. She sat in the front seat and returned her gaze to a tablet computer as a video feed suddenly appeared showing the driveway leading up to the Bennings house in Chino Hills. A blueprint of the home lay on the seat between them.

The Crown Vic sat parked next to the white panel van on a deserted turnout. Ten more thugs sat crammed into the van.

"Why not wait until the old couple leaves?" asked Dimi.

"Because Viktor wanted it done fifteen minutes ago. Would you like me to call him for you and express your concerns?"

Dimi looked at Lily. He wasn't intimidated by her and certainly wasn't squeamish about killing, he just liked to kill smart. He disagreed with almost every tactical decision Lily Bain made, but he had to tread lightly, since she occasionally slept with the boss and had Popov's confidence. For now.

Suddenly, a disembodied voice crackled over the two-way radios. "Phone line is cut, alarms and CCTV are hacked and down. All cell-phone signals are jammed within a quarter mile."

"Okay, let's go," said Lily into her radio.

The van moved out first, with lights out, and arrived at the target within one minute. The armed ten-man team crept up the Bennings's driveway, where a Mercedes and an Audi sat parked, and assumed their prearranged positions around the house. The hilly nature of the subdivision ensured that no neighbors lived too close or had a direct line of sight, especially at night, to the front of the house.

Dimi pulled the Crown Vic into the driveway. With its antennae, the Ford sedan looked like an unmarked police car. Lily wore a pantsuit, Dimi a sport jacket as they crossed to the front door and rang the bell. Dimi remembered to spit out the gum, and then he smoothed down his jacket.

Ricardo "Rick" Carrillo, an athletic man of sixty-two with gray hair and a mustache to match, moved to the front door as the bell gently chimed. When he reached for the doorknob, he noticed the alarm system was down. Rick stopped short of opening the door and instead turned in Staci's direction. "Staci, did you turn off the alarm?"

Staci looked up from her chair in the living room. "No."

Rick punched in the code to turn on the alarm, but nothing happened. "It's not working."

"It was working this morning," said Staci.

"Are you expecting someone?"

"Maybe it's flowers. From Kit or Blanchard, or—"

"Flowers at this hour?"

Rick was already plenty upset, but he was also a cautious man. He knew very well that Gina Bennings had driven through the S turns on Carbon Canyon Road hundreds, no, *thousands* of times. He was having a hard time accepting his old friend's death.

Rick looked out the front door peephole and saw a man and woman standing there. To Rick they looked young, both well under thirty.

"Staci, check the CCTV cameras," he said, just loudly enough for her to hear. She quickly got up and crossed to her late father's office.

There was nothing flimsy about the Bennings home; it was solid construction, and the thick, hardwood front door provided a substantial buffer between occupants and the occasional traveling salesman. Hence there was an intercom, and Rick engaged it.

"Can I help you?"

"San Bernardino County Sheriff's detectives," said Lily, using the intercom as she and Dimi held up fake, but authentic-looking police IDs and badges.

"Homicide?"

"Yes, we're here about Mrs. Bennings," said Lily.

"Does Captain Clark, the homicide commander, know you're here?" asked Rick, who quickly squinted through the peephole to see their response.

Dimi stared back blankly; Lily's eyes rolled up for a split second before she answered.

"Sir, our investigation uncovered some troubling information. You're welcome to accompany us to the station, or we can talk here," said Lily.

"So Clark approved this visit at this late hour?"

"Sir, I'm now in charge of the investigation. We're here to ask questions, not answer them."

"Hold on, I'm not dressed," said Rick into the intercom. He then quickly moved away from the door as Staci emerged from the office.

"The cameras aren't working, either," said Staci.

"If they're cops, I'm Kermit the Frog!"

"What?!"

"Imposters, pretending to be police." Rick pulled out his cell phone. "No signal!"

"What's going on?" asked Staci, alarmed.

"Are the guns still kept in your dad's old office?"

Dimi couldn't help but smirk. He might just be the driver, but he was ten times smarter than Lily. Her plan B was already unraveling. She should have only cut landline and cell-phone service and kept the alarms and cameras working until the front door was opened. Dimi was a former *Spetsnaz*, Russian Special Forces, operator and knew exactly what should be done.

"They're suspicious. They won't open the door," whispered Dimi.

"Yes they will."

"You didn't answer his questions about this Captain Clark person."

"He's getting dressed, then—"

"He's finding out the phones don't work and he's getting a gun, is what he's probably doing," said Dimi, no longer whispering. "If he starts shooting, the whole neighborhood will hear." He spoke into his radio, "Remember, do not shoot the girl. Go, go, go!"

Before Lily could react to her authority being usurped, Dimi unholstered a sound-suppressed KRISS Super V, a compact .45 caliber subgun, from a special shoulder rig, and then emptied the magazine into the door-lock mechanism. The gun was quiet, the sound of wood splintering and rounds hitting metal door hardware less so, but the nearest neighbor was a hundred yards away. One kick from Dimi, and the big door gave way. He charged into the house with Lily following.

Staci held a 9mm Beretta 92F, the same type of sidearm she had carried in Iraq, and scrambled toward the kitchen, shouting, "Maria!"

Rick's short, silver-haired, slender wife, Maria, appeared in the kitchen doorway and was then immediately riddled with suppressed rounds from behind. Her face a mask of confused shock, she dropped to the floor a bloody mess. A black form appeared in the doorway behind Maria, and Staci put three rounds into the man, the booming reports of her weapon echoing throughout the house like a cannon.

She heard more people moving in the kitchen, but then gunfire erupted from behind her.

Rick stood in the office doorway, firing a shotgun. The man and woman—the fake cops—dove to the ground and scrambled behind furniture.

Someone will hear this; help will come, thought Staci as her world went into slow motion. Two more men charged through the front door. She sighted her weapon and started firing, not stopping until the slide locked back, the magazine empty. Both men went down hard, with blood leaking all over the parquet floor.

The blond woman stood and fired several times, hitting Rick Carrillo. He fell back onto the white office door, then slid to the floor, blood streaking the wood.

Staci heard a pop, and a piercing sting burrowed into her chest. The man in the sport jacket had fired it, but she turned to the blonde; since she was out of ammunition, Staci threw the Beretta at her head. The blonde charged her, and Staci, who had studied Brazilian jiujitsu for years, feinted, then delivered a spinning back kick to the face of the blonde, knocking her down.

As more men crowded into the room, Staci turned to face the man who'd shot her. But her legs wobbled, her vision blurred, and she fell . . . right into the arms of Dimi, the driver.

CHAPTER 9

They got him just outside Barrikadnaya Metro station near the embassy. Two college-age females distracted him, pretending to be lost, when a third lady hit him with a blackjack.

Kit Bennings woke up chained to a solid wooden chair in some kind of cold warehouse. Waves of pain shot through his head, seemingly timed to the constant dripping of water from a leaking pipe onto a dirty cement floor.

As he struggled to focus, he saw it wasn't a warehouse at all, but a meat locker. Slabs of beef hung from hooks that slid on overhead rails. And it was not just cold, it was very cold. Bennings fought not to shiver, since six big strong irritated men stood around watching him. One of them moved off into another room.

"Can you write your names down for me?" asked Kit in Russian, grinning, as he studied their faces. "Because I'm going to kill every last one of you."

"Don't be so cocky," said Viktor Popov, stepping into the meat locker. "Or they'll turn you into *shashlik*."

He hadn't started putting it all together until he left the embassy. Popov's people had hacked his mom's bank accounts to create financial panic within the family. But when Popov had made the generous money-for-marriage approach, Kit had rebuffed him. So then they killed Gina as a message that he'd better reconsider. He understood that all of this had nothing to do with his secret counterintelligence work with Sinclair, because the intelligence agencies would never kill a family member of an opponent. But the Russian mob had no such gentlemanly compunctions. They often killed family members of their adversaries—that's exactly what had happened long ago to Popov's twin daughters. But what was it that the former KGB general, now a Mafia don, really wanted from him? Just to marry his niece Yulana? No way; there was something else.

"They won't do a damn thing to me," said Bennings with contempt. "You didn't go to the trouble of killing my mother just to bring me here and do the same."

"No one killed your mother. That was an accident," said Popov, checking his smartphone.

"It won't be an accident when I shove that phone down your throat."

"Your sentiments are duly noted. Regretfully, the abduction went bad. Your mother accelerated instead of braked, and crashed her car," said Popov, matter-of-factly.

Bennings digested the possibility he was telling the truth. "Even if that's true, that doesn't erase your responsibility. She's dead because of the actions of your people, who were following your orders."

"She is of no use to me dead!" snapped Popov. "I've no leverage over you if she's a corpse."

Oh, crap. I didn't warn Staci. Staci! Bennings's mind raced. He had to protect Staci, had to agree to any demands or offers until he could secure her safety. But he couldn't appear to be too anxious to cooperate.

"I'm starting to get the picture that you want me to marry your niece, and you'll go to a lot of trouble to make it happen. Where is she?"

"You'll be meeting her soon enough." Popov gestured, and one of the men opened a laptop on a huge slab of butcher's block and booted it up.

Kit wasn't sure what the laptop was for; he simply had to steer away from his sister whatever was coming.

"You've kidnapped an American diplomat. I doubt the Kremlin would approve. In fact, they might kill you for this."

"You're correct in that regard. But I don't think you'll be filing a complaint or mentioning our new arrangement to anyone."

Damn. Popov is so sure of himself. His people must already have grabbed Staci in California. "Let's cut to the chase. Give me your niece's passport, and I can get the visa done on the spot. She can fly out with me tomorrow." Bennings spoke with the tone of a man who had some leverage in the deal and not someone who was chained to a chair, surrounded by amoral killers.

"Before, you said you could not get her a visa unless I gave you something juicy."

"I lied. And I'm going to need lots of cash to cover the losses from my mother's bank accounts. It was obviously your people who wiped out most of my family's assets."

Popov grinned slightly. The thug who had previously left returned with a chair, and Popov sat down, showing no sign of discomfort from the cold air. "So, now that your mother has died, you are for sale?"

If Kit hadn't been restrained, he would have killed Popov with his bare hands on the spot. Instead, he ignored the remark and spoke without emotion. "Like you said at breakfast yesterday, everyone has their price."

"Yes, and *you* said that even one hundred million was not enough to engage your services."

"Don't be ridiculous. Who wouldn't sell out for a hundred million?" asked Kit. He was very smoothly trying to suggest the very opposite of the truth: that he was ready and willing to deal. "You said your offer to me of two hundred thousand for the fake marriage was a fair price, but I don't agree. I could lose my military pension for marrying your niece, and that's worth a lot more than a lousy two hundred grand. And since relations between our two countries are in the toilet after what your government has done in Crimea and elsewhere, do you think I'd be allowed to keep my security clearance if I married a Russian?"

Popov shrugged, as if the conversation had started to bore him.

"You mentioned the figure of one million American dollars delivered in cash. Make it two million and you have a deal," said Bennings, salting a little desperation into the tone of his voice.

"This line of conversation leads me to ask you something. Perhaps one-tenth of one percent of Americans understand what perestroika was. Do you?"

Popov was a master of manipulation, including of conversations. Kit badly wanted to maintain some control of the dialogue, believing that his sister's safety hung in the balance.

"We should be talking money now, not political history," said Kit.

"Trust me, we are talking money. So what was perestroika?"

Since refusing to answer would only anger the general, Kit played along. "It was the program under your President Gorbachev that led to the collapse of the Soviet Union. It was a restructuring of the whole system."

"And do you know why the *nomenklatura*—the government and economic and military elites of the Communist Party—went along with it?"

"Sure I do. They saw the opportunity to steal *everything*, not just the chunks they were already getting, but everything."

"Yes!" exclaimed Popov. "The entire government morphed into one big criminal outfit. It was complete and utter corruption of the state. The KGB ran out of people to control the stolen wealth. There was so much, they had to turn to the mob for help. Money—perestroika was all about vast sums of money, money, money." Popov let out a long exhale.

"And you didn't get much, did you? What was it, twenty million, maybe thirty? So many of your peers, people not as smart as you, became just filthy rich, didn't they? That must be galling."

"I'm still young enough to put billions to good use. Some of us just have to wait longer in life for our true destiny to unfold. But life is so . . . tricky. That's why people have insurance. To make sure they will be kept whole."

"Insurance is a scam, a legal scam," said Bennings.

"That, my friend, is cynical. Insurance can be very effective. When one of my mob associates accepts protection money from say, a restaurant, you can be certain that no other bad guys will disturb that place. It's a certainty. And since I believe that money, money, money does not really work as a motivational tool with you, Major Bennings, I need some insurance."

Uh-oh. Kit had a bad feeling about where this was going. "I'm happy to take your money, but now I'm wondering if you can afford to pay me two million. No offense."

"No offense taken. Don't worry, I'll give you some money, but you see, like you, I am a spy, too. And just as you knew my twin daughters were murdered, I know something about you. I've known from the beginning that just giving you money is not enough. I need some certainty that you will do exactly as I ask and won't make trouble for me."

Damn, he's talking about Staci; we've come all the way back to Staci.

The man at the laptop looked up at Popov. "It just came in."

Popov gestured, and the thug took the laptop over to Bennings and held it in front of him.

"Play the home movie for him."

The thug clicked on PLAY.

Bennings steeled himself and looked at the screen with dread. Shaky camcorder footage showed the aftermath of the gun battle in Chino Hills. Kit sucked in air audibly as he watched footage showing the bullet-riddled bodies of Maria Carrillo and her husband, Rick. Then the screen went black, and new footage showed Staci being held by a man. Her face was bruised and she looked drugged. The man nudged her and she looked into the camera.

"Kit, they killed Mom and Rick and Maria. But don't you dare do a damn thing for them!"

A blond woman then entered the shot, grabbed Staci's wrist, and wrenched it; the sound of bones breaking rang distinct. Staci screamed in utter pain. As the man held her fast, the blonde delivered a crunching kick to Staci's knee and then threw her to the floor, where she screamed and writhed in agony.

The thug turned off the video.

Bennings silently seethed with rage inside his shackled body. Popov was a dead man walking. He didn't know how, when, or where, but he would kill the Russian bastard. But he had to be smart; he had to protect Staci; he had to make sure they didn't hurt her again; he had to set her free. He decided then and there he would do whatever it took, regardless of the consequences to himself. Starting right now, Kit Bennings held no doubt that the course of his life had just been irrevocably altered.

His mother was dead and his sister kidnapped all because he was sent to Moscow on a mission he didn't particularly want to be part of. The whole scenario made him unbelievably angry. And anger, not money, worked much better as a motivational tool for Bennings.

Popov nodded to a thug, who then stepped forward and administered a shot into Bennings's arm with a syringe.

"A sedative that will wear off in an hour," said Popov.

Bennings almost immediately felt deeply relaxed—too relaxed to move. The thug then cut loose the restraints, and two men lifted him to his feet.

"I'm told your sister is your last living relative. Call me at exactly ten o'clock tonight—not before, not after—and let me know if you want to keep her that way."

CHAPTER 10

"I can have six men at your mom's house in ninety minutes," said Buzz Van Wyke emphatically. A slender man of medium height in his fifties, Van Wyke stood on a café patio talking into his cell phone on a breezy morning, just after 9:00 A.M. in California, with the blue Pacific Ocean just behind him.

"Buzz, I appreciate your willingness to help, but don't BS me," said Bennings over his encrypted sat phone in his safe room at his apartment. It was just after 8:00 P.M. in Moscow, and he was putting on his army mess dress uniform that was worn at more-formal social occasions. He washed down four aspirin with hot matcha Japanese green tea with a high caffeine content to shake off the grogginess from the sedative and tend to the throbbing pain from getting slugged with a blackjack. Bennings needed to be sharp, considering what he hoped to do at the ambassador's ball in honor of Secretary of State Padilla.

"I'm in San Diego," said Buzz. "Angel Perez came here with me— he's inside finishing breakfast. We're visiting my son, Randy, who, if you'll remember, is on SEAL Team Three down here in Coronado. So it'll be me, Angel, Randy, and some of his SEAL buddies."

"I wouldn't want your son and his friends to get into trouble for helping me."

"Too late. I've told them some of the unsung things you've done in service to your country, and I happened to mention some of the times we've been in the soup together. Do you think I could keep them away if I wanted to?" asked Buzz.

"Well . . . please tell them I'm grateful," said Kit humbly.

"We can make Chino Hills in an hour and a half, no problem. And we won't go light," said Buzz, meaning they would be heavily armed.

Buzz Van Wyke was retired from a distinguished thirty-year career with various federal law enforcement and intelligence agencies. But he still worked as a part-time CIA contractor, mainly as a pilot. A smart, levelheaded strategist, Buzz was often sought by Kit for his unofficial counsel on covert operations. A widower and father of three grown children, Buzz wore one of his trademark cardigan sweaters as he chewed on the stem of a pipe, looking more like a soft-spoken professor than a cagey field agent.

"Okay, sounds good," said Kit. "I called one of my mom's neighbors, who told me sheriff's deputies are all over the place. The cops know I'm flying in tomorrow, but I haven't spoken with them yet. Find out what you can at the crime scene."

"Will do. I can get us a safe house, too, if that's okay. The CIA has a few in L.A., and I can access one."

"Unofficially?" asked Bennings.

"Very unofficially."

"Do it."

"Kit . . . how are you?" asked Buzz with fatherly concern in his voice.

"I'm focused, Buzz. I'm focused. See you tomorrow at LAX."

Chino Hills contracts with the San Bernardino County Sheriff's Department to provide law-enforcement services to its more than seventy-five thousand residents. Homicide Detail Detective Bobby Chan stood in the foyer of the Bennings house and shook his head as he surveyed the maelstrom of activity. Dumb like a fox, he stuffed an entire Snickers bar into his mouth, stuffed the wrapper in his pocket, and wiped his hands on his dark slacks held up with black suspenders.

There was a time when Asians and Asian Americans were generally of smaller physical stature than other races. Those days are long gone, as forty-one-year-old Bobby Chan stood testament to. He measured in at a hulking six feet three inches and was a combination of muscle and flab, weighing in at 285 pounds. He loved watching stand-up comics on TV and was always joking around, mostly as his way of processing the horrible results of violence he witnessed on a daily basis.

"I haven't seen this much blood since my ex caught me cheating with that Eskimo hooker," said Chan, trying to get a laugh from some crime scene techs.

"Yeah, but you don't bleed red, Bobby. You bleed yellow from all the cheap beer you swill," teased a female crime scene techie.

Chan turned around and saw Sheriff Jim McCain enter the house with an aide. Bobby figured the sheriff would be showing up about now, and he had a spiel ready for his boss.

"So, Bobby, what do you have here?" asked McCain, who sipped from a cup of gas station take-out coffee. The fifty-one-year-old sheriff wore a sharp business suit, colored his hair dark brown, and looked more like a lawyer than a cop.

"This ain't the kind of crime we see in Chino Hills, that's for sure, Sheriff. Hell, the last real investigation we ran here, and it's been a few years, was that rancher who got pinned by his horses up against a gate and was crushed to death."

"Skip the history and give me the current events."

"Well, aside from the two victims here—Mr. and Mrs. Carrillo—bloodstains and trails going all the way down the driveway indicate three or four other victims were removed from the scene. Based on the amount of blood, I'd bet at least two, maybe three of them have assumed room temperature by now."

"What?! You're saying maybe five homicides here?"

Chan nodded. "Staci Bennings, age thirty-one, is missing. That's her Audi out front. The Benz belongs to the dead couple here. Forensics will tell us if Staci's blood is here in the house. If so, chances are she's worm food, because she didn't get taken to any area hospitals.

But there was a gun battle here, and I'm guessing the other two or three missing bodies are bad guys."

"Christ almighty, was this some kind of drug beef?"

"No indication of that right now, Sheriff. Bennings and the Carrillos co-own an aviation company out at Chino Airport. Were they up to no good? Give me some time and I'll tell you."

"Any neighbors see anything?"

"No, but the neighbors are in agreement they heard maybe fifteen shots. Fifteen to twenty maximum. But we've found sixty-seven shell casings and counting. Different calibers. That tells me suppressed weapons. The phone line was cut, the alarm systems are off-line. The attackers shot open the front door. This was one hell of a whack job. A big-time professional hit with enough shooters to make sure the bad guys would win. The perps came in through doors and windows all around the house."

"So, Bobby, if this Staci Bennings's blood isn't present in the house . . . hell, even if it is, we might have a kidnapping here."

"I'll give those knob jobs at the FBI a heads-up. Oh, Staci Bennings has a brother named Kit who's active-duty military overseas. He called a neighbor and said he's flying in to LAX tomorrow. I already called DHS and got his flight number," said Chan, referring to a scrap of paper that contained the flight information provided by the Department of Homeland Security.

The sheriff moved in close to Chan and spoke softly. "I don't have to remind you that I'm up for reelection, and a whole lot of rich campaign contributors live here in Chino Hills."

"I'd like a new big-screen TV, so I'm happy to know you've authorized unlimited overtime," said Chan.

"I'm not just talking about OT. I'm signing off for you to bust the budget on this one. Do whatever it takes, and do it yesterday. Send some people to meet Mr. Bennings at LAX and bring him in for questioning."

"I might just go myself."

"Take Ron Franklin with you. Partner up with him on this case. I want to know what the hell was going on in this house."

.   .   .

Six heavily armed men in two vehicles reconnoitering a busy crime scene on a quiet residential street were the ingredients for a recipe Buzz Van Wyke didn't care for. So, having arrived in Chino Hills before noon, he sent his son and the other three navy SEALs to the safe house in El Monte, about thirty minutes away. The SEALs were loaning the use of weapons, ammo, radios and communications gear, optics, audio and video surveillance equipment, and other exotic goodies you can't find at Walmart.

So only Van Wyke and Angel Perez, an army master sergeant currently assigned to the Activity and a longtime friend of Kit Bennings, went to the house in Chino Hills. While Perez waited in the car, ironically enough at the same turnout the killers had used, Van Wyke simply jogged up in running shorts, sweating like a pig, and showed fake credentials, identifying himself as a retired police officer, to a deputy standing at the driveway leading to the Bennings house.

Buzz also pretended to be a local homeowner and soon enough got the deputy talking. Within ten minutes he had most of the same details the sheriff had been given by Homicide Detective Bobby Chan. And what he heard, he didn't like at all.

CHAPTER 11

For the last eighty years, Spaso House, on 10 Spasopeskovskaya Square, has housed American ambassadors in Moscow. An opulent neoclassical mansion, the residence is ideal for entertaining. Over the decades the historic building has hosted countless meetings, balls, receptions, parties, dinners, concerts, and ceremonies. Bennings had attended two cocktail parties there during the past few months, and so he knew the symmetrical floor plan well.

His first stop was the Chandelier Room, where the gigantic crystal chandelier cast a warm topaz glow from wall to white wall. A pianist tinkled a strain of bossa nova—the secretary of state's favorite music. The light, lilting melody of Antônio Carlos Jobim's "Waters of March" rang as counterpoint to Bennings's heavy, overburdened mind-set. He made a beeline over the lush Oriental carpet centering the room and steered right toward the bar.

"The Macallan. Three fingers."

The bartender smiled and poured the hefty drink into an Old-Fashioned glass. Bennings took a healthy taste. He was a light drinker, but tonight just might be an exception. Especially considering what he needed to do in the next thirty-four minutes, since it was already 9:26 P.M. and Staci's life depended upon him making a ten o'clock call to Viktor Popov.

Bennings reconnoitered the Music Room, making quick greetings with many acquaintances, mostly diplomats from the American and other embassies. He excused himself and made his way toward the library, stopping for a moment to toss back the rest of his Scotch. As he turned to look for a passing waiter, an arm grabbed him.

Instinctively, Bennings grabbed the hand and was about to maneuver it into an arm-bar hold, when he stopped himself; the hand belonged to General Alexander.

"Whoa, cowboy."

"General, so sorry."

Bennings quickly released Alexander and looked embarrassed.

"I'm not sure a reception for the secretary of state at the ambassador's residence is the right place for you to put on a martial arts demonstration."

"You startled me, sir. I reacted on instinct. Very sorry."

"I wasn't expecting to see you here, Major."

Bennings didn't say anything, just kept the general's gaze.

"You don't look too good."

"Well, I thought I looked okay, sir." Bennings was actually immaculately turned out: starched white shirt and black bow tie, waist-length dark blue mess jacket, black cummerbund, high-rise blue trousers with a yellow stripe running up the outside of each leg, red suspenders matching the jacket's red lapels, high-gloss patent-leather shoes, and all the appropriate gold trim and miniaturized medals and Combat Service Identification Badges, such as the 75th Ranger Regiment, and the U.S. Special Operations Command.

"You know what I'm talking about. Hell, son, you're wound up tighter than a drum."

"I'm fine, General. Really. And sir, the SECSTATE and I . . . I've known her for several years. I used to brief her when she was the national security adviser and I was a DIA investigator. She's been something of a mentor to me, since I didn't understand much about Washington politics."

"Is that right?"

"I just wanted to say hello to her, sir. I won't stay long."

"Well, I think she might be upstairs in a meeting with the ambassador."

Bennings scowled slightly, then checked his watch: 9:37.

"I can give her your regards."

"That won't be necessary, sir. I'll do it myself, and then go home."

Kit fixed the general with a firm stare, in effect suggesting that he wasn't going to budge. The general would have to order him to leave, and under the circumstances there wasn't much chance of that happening. But you never know. He mentally prepared his counter-arguments should Alexander demand he leave.

"Very well," said Alexander, a little reluctantly.

The general moved off, and Kit strode over to the front stairway covered in lush burgundy-colored carpet. Beginning under a graceful arch, the foot of the stairs curved slightly, and then the body of the stairway straightened out to a gentle incline.

But there was no sign of the secretary of state. He checked his watch again and toyed with the notion of just walking up and looking for her. That would cause a huge stink, but he no longer cared about such things.

He caught the attention of a passing waiter and put his empty glass on the man's tray.

"Have you seen the secretary of state?"

"Sir, she's right now dancing in the ballroom."

"Thanks."

Bennings walked as fast as he could without drawing too much attention to himself. The Ballroom Annex was crowded with the real crème de la crème of Moscow's diplomatic elite and high society. The designer ball gowns were custom-fitted and not off the rack from Saks; the hundred-thousand-dollar strands of diamonds weren't on loan from Harry Winston; the men wore watches that cost more than Kit made in a year.

Speaking of watches, as he entered the ballroom, Kit checked his TAG Heuer chronograph: 9:44.

The Palladian windows, plush velvet draperies, and parquet floors of the grand room were almost enough to upstage the preening, lordly attendees. Almost.

Bennings spotted Margarite Padilla looking very elegant in a gold Valentino gown. Unfortunately, she was dancing with the American ambassador, Harry Thorn, and he seemed to be having the time of his life butchering a simple two-step to some generic fifties tune.

There was simply no time to be polite, so Bennings crossed directly to the couple in the middle of the dance floor and decisively interrupted.

"Madam Secretary, excuse me. Mister Ambassador, I'm very sorry to interrupt, but may I cut in, sir?"

Thorn couldn't quite believe the intrusion and flashed angry. "Just who do you think you are, Major?"

Bennings saw from the corner of his eye that security agents were already heading his way. Then he locked his eyes, lasered them, onto Padilla. When she saw the look on Kit's face, she gently patted the ambassador on the back.

"Harry, please indulge a middle-age lady," said Padilla as more of an order than a request. With dyed-black hair up in a rather traditional chignon, Padilla wasn't slim but carried the extra weight she'd put on as she had aged with refined dignity. A sly D.C. insider and the widow of a distinguished senator, Padilla had parlayed brains, loyalty, contacts, favors, and lucky timing into a very successful political career. Some even touted her as future presidential material. "Major Bennings here and I are old friends. And you might not have heard, but his mother passed away suddenly yesterday. I'd very much like to dance with him right now. But you shall have the next one."

Ambassador Thorn swallowed his pride, shot Kit a dirty look, then plastered a phony smile on his face as he turned away and waved off the security pukes. Bennings had been schooled in all kinds of formal dancing as part of his attaché training, so he took the lead and crisply danced Padilla across the floor.

"Did you have to cut in like that?"

"I'm operating on a time constraint," said Bennings, maintaining a big smile.

"Aren't we all," said Padilla, not amused.

"If I don't make a phone call at exactly ten o'clock, after I brief you, they're going to kill my sister too."

Margarite Padilla's eyes went big, and her jaw dropped slightly.

"Smile," said Bennings, "because everyone's watching us."

Madam Secretary swallowed, then smiled the big smile she was famous for.

"It was no car accident. My mother was murdered yesterday. A few hours ago, a hit team stormed my family's house in California. Rick and Maria Carrillo, my parent's best friends, were like an uncle and aunt to me. They were shot dead in our house. My sister, Staci, was kidnapped . . . and then tortured."

"Oh, my lord!"

"Keep smiling."

"Who did it?"

"Viktor Popov. Former KGB general, now one of many Mafia dons operating in America and Russia. I've been meeting with him as part of my defense attaché cover. Mostly we just sat around and shot the breeze."

"Then why did he go after your family?"

"He offered me two hundred thousand dollars to marry his niece, get her a visa, and take her to the U.S. I refused in no uncertain terms."

"And for that he's killing your family? You're sure it's him?"

"He showed me video. I watched his henchmen break my sister's bones."

Padilla gasped.

Kit turned them away from another couple and led them toward an empty patch of dance floor.

"Okay, I'll call Ray Cormier and—"

"No," he said with quiet authority. "You get the FBI or law enforcement into this and Staci is dead."

"But we have to notify—"

"I'm notifying you. That's it. I'll fly to California tomorrow. I know that the FBI could eventually find her. But she'd be dead by then."

"I can't authorize you to—"

"I'm not asking you to authorize anything. I just wanted to tell you what I was going to do. You can have me detained or arrested before I leave the premises tonight. I'm giving you that option, but I'm not asking for anybody's permission to save my sister."

Padilla digested this. She forced a laugh, then waved to another couple across the floor. "What is it exactly you're going to do?"

"I'm going to marry Popov's niece early tomorrow morning. She'll be on the flight with me to L.A."

"But you said she doesn't have a visa."

"I'll be at the embassy at nine in the morning with her passport, and I need to be in and out damn quick if I'm going to make the flight."

"I can't . . ." began Padilla, then she stopped once her eyes met Bennings's. They exchanged the look of two people who shared deep, important secrets. Bennings held her gaze until she finally looked away and cast her eyes downward.

"Remember how we used to joke about all of the 'I can't,' 'we can't,' 'no can do' colonels in D.C.? The worthless ticket punchers afraid to do *anything* or it might screw up their chance to become a general? I hope you haven't become like them." There was no accusation in his voice, but his words held a kind of gentle resolve.

Padilla looked up and smiled even bigger. "I have more enemies than any colonel ever had. There are tens of thousands of political types in Washington with the long knives out who would just love an excuse to stick me in the back. If I give them an excuse, it will happen, and then the black world of special operations will lose its biggest supporter inside the Beltway. The question is, what does Popov really want you to do? No one pays two hundred thousand dollars to a soldier to marry a girl."

"Exactly." Kit's eyes flashed. This was the conclusion he'd been waiting for Padilla to arrive at. He stood ready, willing, and able to go

rogue, but maybe, just maybe, he could keep Padilla in his corner, at least for the time being. "I mean, why the marriage at all? Popov could get her into the States. He doesn't need help with that."

"I think the marriage is extra insurance. More leverage against you. If your sister dies in captivity, they lose your cooperation. But if they have evidence of you committing a federal offense—taking the money—a crime that would get you court-martialed and thrown in prison, then they have an ax over your head."

"And maybe they want her traveling with me. They might have a tracking device in her things."

"I'm sure they'd want to keep an eye on you," said Padilla.

"I've been thinking about all of my conversations with him, but I can't figure out why he targeted me."

"Does Popov know about you and Sinclair?"

"That was my first concern, but I can't see how. He thinks I'm an attaché spy, and not a very good one. I don't know why he picked me, but regardless, I'm screwed. My career, if not my life, is over, based on what I intend to do."

"Take on Popov and his entire organization."

Bennings nodded.

"I'll personally order the head of the consular section to issue a visa. I'll tell her a . . . a . . ."

"A least untruthful lie?"

"Least untruthful lie" was a term originally used by the director of national intelligence to describe a lie he told while under oath to the U.S. Senate regarding NSA surveillance of American citizens. "Yes, exactly," said Padilla. "A least untruthful lie. You're learning diplomatic speak."

Bennings relaxed a little. Padilla was providing him a bit of support. It wasn't much, but enough to get the ball rolling, and for that he felt profoundly grateful.

"I'm sorry that Sinclair and I didn't get the third mole, Madam Secretary. But we have a good idea who it is. I appreciate you putting your trust in me for that kind of sensitive mission."

"You did good work here." Padilla stopped smiling and pursed her lips together. "This wouldn't have happened if I hadn't sent you to Moscow."

Bennings didn't respond. There was no turning back the clock; there was only going balls to the wall.

"I'll be going AWOL, most likely," said Bennings. "So maybe there is one call you could make for me. A secure call to Larry Bing."

"Your old commander at the Activity."

"When everybody is calling for me to be skinned alive, could you let him know that everything is not as it seems?"

She nodded. "I'm so sorry about your family."

"Secretary Padilla, just so we're clear. I'll do just about anything to save my sister. I'm not going to be too concerned with what's legal. She's all the family I have left. So either have me arrested or wish me luck, because I have a call to make."

CHAPTER 12

Dennis Kedrov took in the clear Wyoming sky and enjoyed the crisp breeze on his face; the day was shaping up to be a beauty. He wished he could get in eighteen holes of golf somewhere. He flicked his Turkish cigarette, stepped under the camouflage netting, and leaned over the open tailgate of a covered pickup truck to inspect the bomb.

The explosive device was a type of shaped charge called a linear shaped charge. Dennis had used them before to take down buildings. This one was large, about the size of a railroad tie, but a couple of feet shorter. The unit had an inverted-V profile running along one side. The V profile focused the force of the explosion in one direction, forming an axlike blast that would cut anything in its path to a certain depth. Dennis had decided to go with a big bomb to make sure they hit the target.

"Okay," said Dennis, satisfied. "Get it in the hole."

Workers carefully slid the device onto the tines of a small Bobcat front loader, which then slowly carried it near a fourteen-feet-deep, six-feet-in-diameter hole carved out of rock-hard earth, where dowser Irene Shanks had once placed pink plastic flags.

The camouflage netting over the hole had to come down to allow the rest of the operation to proceed. Dennis wasn't too concerned, since the spy satellites wouldn't be overhead for another couple of hours. Still, there was no time to waste. A tracked mini crane maneuvered a small boom above the bomb. Workers connected thick canvas lifting straps cradling the device to the boom. The crane then lifted the unit into the air and pivoted it over the cavity.

Within seconds, the linear shaped charge was lowered into the hole, with the V profile pointing downward, so when the bomb exploded, the force of the cutting blast would be directed deeper into the ground.

Dennis looked on pleased. The whole process had so far gone without a hitch, and he expected that when the deceptions were complete, he would be spending plenty of time on the golf courses of his choice.

"It's done," said a worker.

"Fill in the dirt and tamp it down carefully," said Dennis, removing a yellow golf ball from his pants pocket. He casually tossed the ball into the air and caught it one-handed. "Then erase any trace that we were ever here."

Kit Bennings sat on a hard wooden chair in a drab Russian government office. On the other side of a battered table, Yulana Petkova sat erect and businesslike. She wore a light blue blouse under a simple gray pantsuit. The clothes looked good but weren't expensive. Her off-brand purse and black heels matched well, and the costume jewelry was of the latest trend. Yulana, like many Russian women, went to a lot of trouble to look good. Of course, in Yulana's case, she could be wearing a dirty bedsheet and sandals or be barefoot with tattered overalls and it wouldn't have mattered, since she was drop-dead gorgeous.

She could easily be draped with real jewels or the finest furs and designer fashions, but that would require her to sell out or sell herself or marry some rich jerk she didn't love, so she wore what she could afford to pay for from her modest government salary.

Her long, thick, jet-black hair with just the slightest wavy quality framed her face as it fell almost to her waist. Pale white blemish-free skin looked stark next to her hair, and natural aqua eyes tented by thin, finely arched eyebrows were the kind of eye color one might find on Polynesian girls. Yulana's long, fairly thin nose and full soft-pink lips completed an exotic look that had turned many a head, even in Moscow, a city rich with beautiful, well-appointed women.

And like with many Russian women, her demeanor was tempered by a tough undercurrent. It was like an electrified third rail running along the tracks that was best left untouched. Was it the stereotype of the morose, depressed Russian showing itself? Or was her face betraying the suggestion that she didn't want to be here any more than Bennings did? Or was her dark expression simply the result of her life experience? Of heartbreak, betrayal, and hard work and a longing for escape to something, anything better than whatever it was that held her in its clutches. Maybe for Yulana, it was a little bit of all of the above; she looked as though she could literally feel her inner hard edge, as naturally as she could feel a pebble in her shoe.

At least he looks sober, thought Yulana, when she first glanced at Kit Bennings. That was the first and so far only time she'd looked at him, when they were first introduced a few minutes earlier. She didn't bother to stand, offer her hand, or smile. She gave him a quick glance of acknowledgment and then returned to the distractions of her smartphone. For her, the good news was that he wasn't old, ugly, or fat. Still, she hoped she wouldn't have to spend too much time with him; if he were a drunk who tried to get fresh with her, especially since they were about to be married and he might have some false ideas about what kind of intimacy that granted him, well, she'd been there plenty of times before and knew how to reduce a man to a ball of screaming pain in the fetal position.

A government clerk with a file folder, and two of Popov's thugs entered the room. The clerk wordlessly handed Kit's and Yulana's passports back to them, then gave each of them an official document from the folder.

"Congratulations. You are now married," said the clerk in Russian. To Yulana, the clerk's tone sounded like he had just pronounced a death sentence. And maybe he had.

From the corner of her eye she observed as the stocky thug, who was holding a manila envelope, handed a large wad of U.S. hundred-dollar bills to the nonplussed clerk. The clerk took the money without counting it and left the room.

Yulana watched the stocky thug put the manila envelope on the table and slide it over to Kit, as the other thug recorded the payoff with a video camcorder.

"Open and count," commanded the stocky thug.

Bennings gave him a hard look but then did as he was told. "Fifty thousand," said Kit. Yulana didn't know it, but Popov had cut the original bribe offering by three-quarters.

"The boss told me to tell you you're not even worth this much."

"Tell Popov he can shove it up his fat Russian ass." Kit tossed the envelope of large bills at the stocky thug, who caught it in front of his face. "We all know this isn't about money."

Yulana flashed a slight look of surprise. *The American doesn't want the money?* She felt intrigued and struggled to hide her interest.

"If you don't take the money, we don't have a deal." The way the thug said this indicated there was no negotiation on the point. He threw the envelope onto the floor at Bennings's feet.

Yulana stoically watched as Bennings hesitated, then reached down for the envelope. He stuffed it inside his jacket.

The man with the camcorder turned it off, then tossed a cell phone at Bennings, which he caught in the air.

"We'll contact you in Los Angeles," said the taller thug.

After the two men left, Bennings stood, pocketed the cell phone, and turned to her. "We need to get going," he said in perfect, Moscow-accented Russian.

She stood up without looking at him and moved toward the door. The threshold had been crossed; she wondered if in a week from now, she'd still be alive.

The stop at the embassy to get Yulana Petkova's visa was quick and per-functory. Secretary of State Margarite Padilla had come through; they were in and out in twenty minutes, and Yulana hadn't spoken a word.

The car Kit had hired for the morning spent two harrowing hours in chaotic traffic for the ride from the embassy to Sheremetyevo Airport. Ninety minutes after checking in, the Aeroflot nonstop on an Airbus A330-200 to Los Angeles was wheels up. So far, Yulana Petkova had spoken exactly zero words to Kit Bennings.

Yulana ordered a vodka and peach juice from the vacuous, dye-job-blond flight attendant in the quasi-military style Aeroflot uniform. Service on Aeroflot generally ran from fair to poor, just as customer service all over Russia lagged far behind Asia and the West. The idea of taking good care of paying customers was still a foreign concept to the Russians. Kit had had nothing but bad experiences flying Aeroflot, but the airline flew nonstop from Moscow to Los Angeles, so here he was.

He ordered the same drink as Yulana and knocked it back quickly. Unable to sleep or relax, he'd been absentmindedly fingering a key that he wore as a pendant on a silver chain around his neck. His father had worn the key for most of his life and had passed it on to Kit about a year before he died. The key opened a strongbox in the attic of the Chino Hills family home, where important papers and irreplaceable mementos were kept. The steel box held nothing of tremendous monetary value, so the key was more symbolic, a passing of family responsibility from one generation to the next.

There had been nothing sexist in his father's gesture: Tommy Bennings bluntly told Kit he got the key because he was the oldest and for no other reason. Staci was as sharp as they came, and Kit had considered passing the key to her, especially after all of the close brushes with death he'd had in the last few years. But he'd kept the key and taken his responsibility to the remnants of his family very seriously.

But now only Staci was left, and he couldn't pass the key to her if he wanted to. Assuming she was still alive.

Bennings scratched his head, his mind stale from internally reviewing scenarios he might have to use in the quest to free Staci. He and Buzz Van Wyke had already worked out some diversionary tactics to employ at LAX in case there was a Russian welcoming committee waiting for them, so at least that much was taken care of. And although he was worried sick about his sister, his thoughts turned to his seatmate and new wife. Feeling frustrated in general, he decided he'd had enough of her pretense.

Yulana sat in her seat with earbuds plugged in as she watched an out-of-date film the airline was so generous to provide. He reached over and pulled her earbud plug out of the jack. She flashed him a look of irritation and tried to pull the cord free from his grasp. But instead, he yanked hard and the earbuds flew out of her ears.

She welled with anger, her flashing eyes tore into him, but she didn't speak, didn't make a sound. Her gaze leavened into one of annoyance, as if Kit were insignificant.

"You're not deaf and dumb. You ordered the drink. And now that we've cleared Russian airspace, it's time we had a chat," he said in Russian.

"And what could I possibly want to say to you, soldier boy?" she asked, irritated, in perfect English.

"Tell me about your real relationship to Viktor Popov."

"No."

"But you're not his niece."

"Did he say I am?"

"Yes."

"Then I am his niece."

"You know, sorry, my mistake, he didn't say niece. He said cousin. He said you were a *kissing* cousin." Yulana wasn't the only one who looked irritated, and Bennings was baiting her.

"You think I'm coming to America to be Popov's lover, or to be a prostitute?"

"Your words, not mine."

"Why is it that so many men, when they feel threatened by a woman, have to make themselves feel superior by reducing the woman to the status of 'whore'?"

"I don't feel superior to anyone, but that doesn't mean you're not a threat. I don't know what your role is in this, other than to spy on me, but it would be better for you to just tell me."

"I'm spying on you?"

"This cold-shoulder business, the silent treatment, is a bad act to make you appear disinterested."

"Believe me, not being interested in you is no act."

A little exasperated, Kit said, "I didn't mean romantically interested. This isn't a game we're playing, lady. This is life and death, and most people show some interest in that."

He bore his eyes into her and got nothing in return; he could have been staring into a dry well.

"Tell me what you know. Why did Popov target me for the fake marriage?"

She'd make a good poker player and betrayed no reaction as she said, "I'll tell you nothing."

"We'll see about that," he said, with more than a little bit of threat to his tone.

A hint, the briefest hint of fear, flashed in her eyes.

"So let me give you something to put in your first report," said Kit. "Very soon I intend to dance on Viktor Popov's grave. And I will kill all of his people who were connected to what happened to my family. Viktor will understand this, because it's what he himself has done to the men who murdered his daughters."

Yulana's eyes widened just a bit.

"So if I learn you were involved, believe me, I'll have no problem blowing your brains out. Right into your peach juice and vodka."

Yulana looked at him for a long time. Her mask of intractability softened. There was slightly less judgment in her gaze now. "What happened to your family?"

"Don't pretend you don't know." He tossed the earbuds into her lap and looked away. "I liked you better when you didn't talk."

CHAPTER 13

Until recently, the international terminal at Los Angeles International Airport had long been one of America's greatest embarrassments. Buzz Van Wyke remembered all too clearly how the departure and arrival gates and corridors and concourses for hundreds of thousands of visitors either setting foot on or leaving American soil created one big dingy, shabby, uninspiring, hard-to-fathom letdown. The subtext for arriving passengers had been: *Hey, we let you into our country, so don't complain. What did you expect, luscious colors, convenience, modern amenities, clean toilets not marred with gang graffiti? Yes, we're purely functional, out-of-date, and tawdry, but the sunshine and palm trees and movies stars are outside, so keep walking, please.* Similarly, the underlying message to departing passengers had been *Good-bye, and we don't really care if you come back.*

Even today, with improvements in place, a country as small as South Korea has an international airport that puts LAX to shame. Yes, L.A.'s departure area is now a fabulously chic and artful juxtaposition of metal and glass—graceful curves meeting sharp angles, all designed to optimize the gorgeous light of Southern California. Towers of LED screens called "Portals" interactively display continuous shapes and forms; a quasi-retro design theme informs some common area café chairs and tables; faux wrought-iron rails and light fixtures add nice arty touches. The ubiquitous designer shops hawk their overpriced wares and branches of local high-end trendy cafés tempt the traveler with everything from caviar and champagne to gourmet tacos.

But the departure terminal is actually quite small for a major international airport, the concourses narrow, and there simply aren't enough seats. Departing passengers waiting to board super-jumbos must line up in the concourse walk space, blocking the path of any other travelers. After tens of millions of dollars, things are much better, but LAX just can't seem to get it right.

Despite renovations elsewhere in the international terminal, the seediness of the old arrivals hall remained, and that suited Buzz Van Wyke just fine. He liked the feeling of Third World bus depots, so he felt right at home in the cramped mess.

Buzz had just bought a lousy cup of overpriced coffee, which he nursed when he wasn't chewing on the stem of the Savinelli "413" smoking pipe given to him by his late wife. Dressed in chinos, a T-shirt, and a light khaki jacket, Buzz casually counted the surveillance cameras and airport police officers present as he leaned on an aluminum luggage cart he'd paid five bucks to rent. The airport police had been absorbed by the LAPD years ago, but the officer sitting behind a high desk at the top of the ramp where arriving passengers trudged up to meet family and friends seemed more interested in the smartphone he was trying to keep from view than he was in scanning the crowd for potential threats.

None of the airport coppers Buzz watched looked even vaguely concerned about their situational awareness. They were phoning it in, perhaps letting the unseen crew watching the security cameras do the heavy lifting.

Buzz casually glanced about fifty yards across the hall, where Angel Perez scanned a brochure at a kiosk, as he twirled his lucky green-handled screwdriver in one hand like a drum major twirling a baton. The screwdriver was "lucky," because he had once used it to successfully diffuse a dirty bomb that was rigged to explode. A twenty-eight-year-old, barrel-chested Puerto Rican American with longish, unruly black hair, who was as intense as Buzz was laid-back, Angel was a brilliant gadget geek and backyard mechanical engineer /inventor. He was also one of the smartest close-quarters combat fighters on the planet. There was something kinetic about him, as if he were always in motion, even when standing still. He tended to speak his mind bluntly without editing himself, and that was one of the reasons both Buzz and Kit liked working with him: they could count on getting Angel's unvarnished opinions, every time. Kit and Angel had first gotten to know each other when they were Rangers together in Afghanistan.

Angel and Buzz communicated with encrypted two-way radios that looked like cell phones, because speaking into your sleeve or having an earpiece was just too obvious in such a crowded space.

"Buzz, there's an Asian girl over here that I'd have to rate as a nine point six," said Angel, in his usual rapid-fire delivery.

"You've got a hot girlfriend, *mijo,* remember? You told me that if you ever looked at another woman again to please just shoot you," said Buzz. "Or was I supposed to call Yumi Nakamura in D.C. before I pulled the trigger?" Nakamura was a Japanese American lawyer for the DEA whom Angel had been seeing for over a year.

"Buzz, I'm a seventh son of a seventh son!"

"Meaning?"

"I'm not sure, but it should be worth something. So please cut me some slack."

Buzz chuckled to himself. He was almost as proud of Angel Perez as he was his own kids. Angel was a self-made man who grew up in extreme poverty in Puerto Rico. At age three he was taking things apart to see how they worked. At age five he was building his own toy tanks and jeeps from scrap metal. The United States Army gave Angel a more formal education, and he'd been repaying them with his blood and loyalty ever since.

"Angel, forget about the eye candy. What do you have for me?"

"First of all, it would seem that none of my goodies have been discovered." The "goodies" Angel referred to were small, easily concealable smoke bombs that had sticky tape on one side. A slick operator could easily attach such a device to most surfaces. When detonated, it made a sharp report, then released an enormous amount of colorful smoke for its small size. This morning, when large crowds were arriving from Asia, Angel had donned a blond wig and a facial prosthetic that defeated facial recognition software. He stealthily planted dozens of the mini smoke bombs, set to detonate remotely, under chairs, tables, sinks in the men's room, and elsewhere. That the devices hadn't been found was testament to the fact that cleaning people don't look under things.

"Good," said Buzz. "What else?"

"The two bruisers standing together by the arrivals board have to be cops."

Buzz casually clocked the two men. He didn't know it, but the bigger Asian one was San Bernardino County Sheriff's Detective Bobby Chan.

"Detectives investigating the Chino Hills shoot-out?" asked Buzz.

"That would make sense. Kit's neighbor told the cops he was flying in today, remember? They probably want to talk to him real bad," said Angel.

"But he doesn't want to talk to them, just yet."

"I also made a deuce in black leather jackets. Sitting over by the low wall. Russians, without a doubt. Where do they get their taste in shirts, anyway?"

"Maybe they watched *Goodfellas* too many times." Buzz casually glanced toward the men. "Got 'em. Which means we have a quartet. Might be too far for you to see, but check the pair over my shoulder, far back corner of this poor excuse for a café behind me."

Angel, who wore jeans, sneakers, and a loose-fitting brown shirt, seemed to casually glance at the second pair of men while still holding the phone to his ear.

"So four mob guys and two deputies, plus airport police and all the cameras. Plus maybe more mobsters in a van or SUV in the parking structure or circling the airport. In other words, no problem."

Buzz considered the layout for a moment. "I'll slow down the two behind me. You delay the leather jackets. The deputies are the wild card."

The longest part of the customs-clearing process was the last check after you got your bags, which was really no check at all. Since his body was still on Moscow time and he hadn't slept on the plane, hadn't slept at all since he heard of his mother's death, by all rights Bennings should be exhausted.

But the adrenaline kicked in as he started to lead Yulana up the ramp into the arrivals hall, because he knew what was coming. He pulled out his U.S. cell phone and called Angel. It was 3:37 in the afternoon, Pacific time.

Angel answered his cell without saying hello. "Boss, welcome home. We are a go and can handle the Russkie greeting committee, but there are two big county-mounties, plainclothes, that might be here looking for you."

"Understood. Stand by," said Kit into the phone.

Yulana had only brought one rolling suitcase, and Kit took it from her and hefted it by the handle. Before she could say anything, he said, "Take off your shoes."

"What?!"

He drilled her with one of his stares. "Take off your shoes and do exactly as I say."

She stared at him for a few seconds, then took off her heels and held on to them. They walked farther up the ramp, slowly, being passed by throngs of Russian citizens hurrying to begin their Southern California vacations.

"On my mark . . . five, four . . ." said Kit slowly into the cell phone.

As Kit's eye level came even with the floor level of the arrivals hall, he saw scores—check that—hundreds of people waiting to meet friends or loved ones.

"Three . . . two . . ."

He locked eyes with Buzz Van Wyke. Now it would be a race.

"One . . . zero!" said Kit into the phone.

He quickly pocketed the cell and grabbed Yulana's arm as small bangs sounding like gunfire began echoing throughout the hall. Screams rang out; Kit saw the airport cop at the high desk leap to his feet, looking confused. Then all hell broke loose and the hall quickly filled with colorful smoke.

"Run!" shouted Kit to Yulana, pulling her along. But she resisted. "Run with me or I'll kill you where you stand!"

She looked frightened, perhaps as much from the pandemonium as from Kit's grasp on her arm and his intimidating eyes. So they ran together right into the mass of panicked, smoky confusion, barely able to see.

CHAPTER 14

Several of Angel's smoke bombs had gone off right under the seats of the Russian thugs sitting by the low wall. As the men stood, they were enveloped by smoke but started to calmly move toward the ramp. Until Angel blocked the way. He held an ASP collapsible steel baton and with more than a little relish, thrust the unopened unit into the first thug's solar plexus. He assumed these men took part in the carnage at the Bennings family home, and hoped he'd have a chance to do more than just hit them with a baton.

"Vete pa'l carajo so cabrón!" said Angel. Go to hell!

He then swung right as hard as he could and caught the second man in the neck. They both went down, and Angel scrambled away in a green-yellow-pink haze.

Angel bolted to the other side of the hall, to give Buzz backup. Angel's father had died shortly after he was born, and Buzz had become something of a father figure to him. It blew Angel's mind that Van Wyke still lived in the large home in Kennsington, Maryland, where he'd raised his three kids. As a widower, Buzz lived alone in that house, but maintained it was full of nothing but good, happy memories, and that he'd never move. Angel had visited Buzz there often. As much as he respected him, Angel was worried about how his older friend would fare with two Russian bears.

He spotted Buzz through the smoky air just as he slammed his luggage cart hard into one man, tumbling the Russian ass-over-teakettle. Buzz then grabbed the startled second guy's left arm and lifted it, then punched hard with an Alpha Hornet compliance tool into the man's armpit. The Russian thug screamed and staggered backward, disappearing in the smoke.

Angel nodded approvingly from about ten feet away, then turned and ran in the other direction.

A shrill alarm added to the mayhem in the arrivals hall. Kit led Yulana as fast as he could away from the closest exit, which was jammed with panicked, screaming, choking hordes running for their lives, trying to get out . . . but not without all of their luggage, thank you very much.

Kit angled for the northern exit, where fewer people usually congregated. From the corner of his eye he saw a big Asian guy moving fast for a man of his size, bearing down on him from his right side. He pegged him for being one of the county detectives, and since Kit didn't want to fight a cop, this would come down to being a footrace, after all.

In football, it's called "clipping," and at first, Chan didn't know what hit him, as Angel performed a perfect clip from behind. The big Chinese American detective went sprawling, and Angel rolled next to him. As Chan tried to stand, Angel grabbed his legs, babbling in Puerto Rican Spanish like a maniacal, terrified little boy.

"Acho men! A juyir, man! Mui a la loco apretao!"

"Settle down, sir, settle down!" said Chan, irritated. He spoke Mexican Spanish, but wasn't sure what this person was saying; some gibberish about a madman chasing him, or something. Chan yanked himself free of Angel's grasp and moved toward the exit, but Detective Ron Franklin, an athletic black man in his mid-thirties, sprinted past him and reached the door far ahead of Chan.

Franklin barreled through the sliding glass doors, into the sunlight, and caught sight of Kit Bennings and Yulana Petkova getting into the side doors of a white panel van on World Way South as airport police cars with sirens blaring screeched into the drop-off lanes.

Franklin cut through the herd as fast as possible, but throngs of terrified people blocked his path.

"Franklin!" called Chan, emerging from the arrivals hall.

Franklin turned back to the big detective and yelled, "They're in the white van!" Franklin then shoved and pushed through the crowd. "Police officer, stand aside!"

He accidentally knocked an old Asian lady down but kept moving. He finally broke into the clear, and with Chan huffing and puffing right behind him, ran up to a white van stopped in traffic. Franklin flung open the side door.

But the van was empty, except for the driver, who, unknown to the policemen, just so happened to be a navy SEAL.

"Where are the man and woman who got in here?!" demanded Franklin.

"Hey, what the hell! Close my door!" said the driver. "Are you crazy?"

Franklin noticed the van had side doors on *both* sides. "They went out the other side!" he said to Bobby Chan. The men ran around the van in time to see two more identical white panel vans driving away, rounding the bend toward terminal 4. Then the van they'd just looked into pulled away, too.

Chan looked at Franklin. "You sure about this?"

Suddenly Franklin didn't look so sure. "Well, I . . ."

Just then Chan spotted two tough-looking men in black leather coats who had jogged up. The men stopped when they saw the detectives.

"You two!" yelled Chan, taking a step toward the men. "Police! Get your hands up!"

As one of the Russians reached inside his jacket, Chan drew his weapon in a flash and leveled it at the men. Franklin did the same.

"I said hands up! Kneel down! Get on your knees!" The two men reluctantly complied. "Lace your fingers behind your head."

Airport cops came running up. Chan flashed his ID as Franklin cuffed the Russians. A quick search found they both had concealed firearms. The airport cops called for backup, which arrived in seconds.

"This is your jurisdiction so it's your bust," said Chan to the ranking airport officer, "but I'd like a word with these guys."

"Not a problem," said the officer.

Franklin examined the men's IDs. "Yuri Rugov and Vitaly Dubinin." Franklin looked to Chan. "So what the hell is going on?"

"Wish I knew," said Detective Bobby Chan.

Kit Bennings allowed himself a real smile, not the fake ones he'd used at the embassy party. He sat on the hard steel floor of a panel van driven by Buzz Van Wyke's navy SEAL son, Randy.

"You okay, Major Bennings?" asked Randy Van Wyke, who looked a lot like his dad, except Randy had hair and a short blond beard.

"Roger that. You're Buzz's son, Randy?"

"Yes, sir. Honor to meet you."

"Believe me, the pleasure is all mine. Thanks for your help, because those cops almost nabbed me." Kit checked his watch. "Nothing like making an entrance. Or in this case, an exit. Right, Jen?"

Kit turned to face First Lieutenant Jennifer Huffman, who sat across from him, next to a bewildered Yulana Petkova. "Pixie-ish" was the word—to Huffman's great displeasure—that best described her. At age twenty-seven she stood five feet two with boots on, weighed a hundred pounds dripping wet, wore her sandy blond hair cropped short because it was easier to keep clean that way, and still bore a chip on her shoulder about not being allowed to try out for the Special Forces Qualification Course due to her gender. She was cute yet at the same time quite androgynous.

Much more important to note, Jen Huffman was a brilliant IT specialist who always traveled with at least three laptops. She'd been both a white hat and a black hat hacker in her past and made miracles happen with a computer. Oh, and she was a germaphobe to the extent that she made Lady Macbeth's hand washing seem tame.

"I'm so sorry about your loss, and everything else, Kit," said Jen, as she squeezed hand sanitizer onto her hands from a small bottle.

"Thanks. And thanks for being here. How did you arrange it?"

"Simple. I took leave, same as Angel. I'm yours for three weeks, if it takes that long," said Jen, with a slight northern accent that betrayed her Minnesota upbringing.

Jen was in the Activity for one reason and one reason only: Kit Bennings had gone to bat for her. After a stint at NSA, she'd been assigned to the 3rd Special Forces Group Headquarters and Headquarters company, where her skills were not being utilized, when Kit first met her. He staked everything on convincing Col. Larry Bing to bring her aboard.

The problem was that the army had revoked her security clearance after learning that at age fourteen she'd hacked into Bank of America and defaced some of their Web pages. The FBI had tracked her down and she was convicted of a misdemeanor under the Computer Fraud and Abuse Act of 1986. Because she was a minor, her record was sealed. By age sixteen she was a contract-hacker *for* the FBI. At eighteen, she joined the army and got slotted right to NSA. When she left the No Such Agency, a jilted lover dropped a dime on her about her hacking arrest, and so she lost her clearance.

Bing eventually got her clearance reinstated and she'd been one of the Activity's best IT people ever since. And she never forgot that Kit Bennings was the reason for it all.

"We'll catch up later, Jen, but would you mind taking care of our Russian guest?" Kit crawled up into the front and sat next to Randy Van Wyke.

Jen tugged on blue latex gloves as she looked at Yulana. "Please don't take this wrong, but I need you to strip naked."

Two of the white vans turned south onto Pacific Coast Highway, drove through the tunnel under runways and taxiways, and then turned west onto Imperial Highway. The vans pulled over, and Jen bounded out with Yulana's suitcase, purse, and other effects. She got into the other van with the items, and they sped off. The van driven by Randy, with Kit and Yulana as passengers, made a U-turn at the first intersection and drove in the opposite direction.

Kit returned to the back of the van and sat across from Yulana, who now wore jeans, sandals, and a pink shirt. Her jewelry was gone, all of her things were gone.

"There were personal items in my luggage," said Yulana.

"Your belongings will be carefully checked. Anything we deem safe will be returned to you."

Yulana started to say something, then stopped.

"Want to tell me where the tracking devices are?"

She shrugged. "I can tell you that they gave me the suitcase."

"What else?"

"A makeup compact. Just those two things."

"Anything else you can tell me?"

"That I don't want to be here." She looked at him sadly. "Not at all."

She hung her head, and Kit thought he heard soft sobs. But he tuned her out. He'd deal with her and whatever her truths were later.

Bennings knew he'd just achieved a small victory in his war with Viktor Popov. They were in America now, not Russia, and "the Bear" had just been stung. He prayed Staci would not be hurt as a result, but he had to become proactive, to fight back. He'd been off-balance and on his heels in Moscow, reduced to taking orders not only from a Mafia don but from his minions.

So this little business here today was a message to Popov that he was no longer in total control. And for better or worse, Kit had Yulana. Whether or not she was a bargaining chip remained to be seen. The SEALs had to get back to Coronado later that night, but with Buzz, Angel, and Jen, he had a pretty good team. And one way or another, he intended to win.

Still, this was no time to get cocky. The action today reminded him of history, history from WWII. America was at a low point after Pearl Harbor, the fall of the Philippines, and other defeats. America needed a victory, and so an all-volunteer group of army aviators

called Doolittle's Raiders launched a dangerous, daring aerial operation to bomb Japan. Not much damage was done to the Japanese, but
the attack gave Americans a much-needed morale boost, while dent-
ing Japan's aura of invincibility. And the raid made the Japanese feel
vulnerable and caused them to commit more forces to the protection
of their mainland than they would have liked.

And like the Doolittle Raid, today was just one small skirmish in
an all-out war. Bennings had much to do and hoped there would be
time to do it before the cell phone in his pocket would ring with a call
from the Russian Mafia don who had already turned his life upside
down.

CHAPTER 15

Viktor Popov sat at a table in West Hollywood's Plummer Park, playing chess with an elderly Russian gentleman who had been playing chess in the park—the heart and soul of Los Angeles's Russian immigrant community—every day for twenty-two years. As the men played chess, Russian American teenage boys shouted catcalls at teenage girls who strutted through the park in groups. Old women gossiped and bragged about their grandchildren. Moms and dads brought their kids to play on the swings and slides as they sipped Cokes and ate Russian pastries.

A lot of the folks in the park were here only because in 1974, Congress passed legislation designed primarily to force the Soviet Union to allow its Jewish citizens to emigrate. Most of them went to Israel or the United States. The Soviets didn't like what America had done, so in a duplicitous gesture—a master stroke of *maskirovka*—the KGB emptied the gulags and prisons of the most undesirable criminals, crooks, and killers. The convicts had the word "Jew" stamped on their passports, whether they were Jewish or not, and the United States opened its arms to them, not knowing their true past.

Thus, an invasion of hellish thugs, mixed in with the good folks, landed on the shores of America. And for reasons lost in the fog of time, many of those Russian immigrants gravitated to West Hollywood, when it was still a funky, loosely regulated, unincorporated part of Los Angeles County. And just as with every other location where the Russians settled, the cancer called the Russian mob soon infected the body of the community.

Viktor Popov noshed on a take-out plate of dumplings and ke-babs from Traktir on Santa Monica Boulevard and sipped homemade infused vodka in a plastic cup. He'd arrived in Southern California several hours earlier, after flying on an executive jet into Santa Monica Airport, where the city had raised landing fees in an effort to discourage pilots from actually using the historic facility. The city of Santa Monica wanted to close their airport and develop the land—similar, thought Popov, to how the city of West Hollywood wanted to develop "Little Russia," including Plummer Park, with a new general plan. West Hollywood and Santa Monica were already two of the most overregulated, overdeveloped cities on the planet, but there's no accounting for greed and power-grabs. *And people think I'm a crook,* thought Popov.

In short order Viktor won the chess game and shook hands with his opponent, who moved to another table, smiling. A number of Popov's bodyguards were discreetly posted around the park, and they nodded when Mikhail Travkin, wearing a conservative but expensive suit, approached from the parking lot and sat down close to his boss. With soft brown eyes, pale skin, and a receding hairline, Mikhail looked the picture of corporate success: quiet, smart, and ruthless. Only in his early thirties, he understood the digital world and how to steal from it better than most. Mikhail was Viktor's top man in Los Angeles. And his nephew. A cautious number cruncher with an MBA as well as an engineering degree, he was the heir apparent to his volatile uncle's empire.

"There's been a problem," said Mikhail softly.

"Okay, but first? You see the guy playing tennis without a shirt on? Black bikini shorts? Only a Russian would play tennis looking like that."

"So?"

"So he's selling drugs out of his gym bag. If he's working for one of our friends, just gently let them know their guy shouldn't be selling drugs in a park where young children play. Look," said Viktor, pointing to some babushka grandmas pushing their grandkids in strollers, "there are little kids right there. But if the guy is a freelancer, make sure he *never* comes back."

Mikhail nodded solemnly.

"Now what's the problem?" asked Viktor.

"Bennings had friends waiting at LAX. They created a panic with smoke bombs, and he got away with Petkova. The Feds think it's some kind of terrorist dry run, and it's all over the TV news."

"And your men?"

"They took some hits, so their pride was hurt. And Vitaly and Yuri were arrested for carrying concealed weapons."

Viktor looked sharply at Mikhail.

"They're out on bail," said Mikhail.

"Not very smart carrying a gun into an airport. This isn't Chechnya."

"I agree. And there was something odd. They were questioned by sheriff's detectives from San Bernardino County."

Viktor took another sip of vodka.

"The detectives were probably there for Bennings. You should have considered that possibility, Mikhail. There was no need to send an armed group to the airport."

Mikhail nodded slightly. "Yes, Viktor, you're right. Shall I send Vitaly and Yuri out of town until our deceptions are complete?"

Viktor shook his head. "No. Put them on stakeout duty. That's their punishment. Their job is to be *seen*. Understood? I want Bennings to see them so he suspects I can find him anywhere, but they are not to make contact or to follow him."

"I understand, but . . . this brings me to my big concern: Bennings's behavior."

"He's trying to establish some control. He's back in his own country and feeling like he can take charge." Viktor didn't seem particularly surprised or disturbed by Bennings's "escape."

"I understand using him was always a calculated risk, but he's dangerous," said Mikhail. "The FBI will be investigating what happened at the airport. Bennings doesn't mind taking a big chance. That's reckless, and it draws too much attention toward us. Maybe we should hurt his sister some more and let him see it."

"No, I don't want him to rage emotionally more than he already has. And just who ordered the sister to be beaten, anyway?"

"She knocked Lily unconscious during the snatch. So Lily got some payback."

"You authorized that?"

"Of course not. She acted on her own."

"Explain to Lily that I'm unhappy with what she did. Very unhappy. So she's out of any operational role and demoted to babysitting the woman for the duration of the deceptions. And no one is to touch the Bennings girl unless I say so. Is that completely clear, Mikhail?"

Mikhail nodded. "Yes, Uncle."

"Bennings doesn't know enough to hurt us yet, and the upside to using him is very considerable. I just need to remind him how weak his position really is. Release the tape to the big shot in Washington, D.C."

Mikhail pulled out his tablet phone and sent a one-character message. "Secretary of the Army Fitzgerald will have the tape within minutes."

"I imagine that will cause quite a disturbance in Washington. Now what about Dennis?" asked Viktor.

"He's ready in Wyoming. The area has small earthquakes almost daily. When the right seismic activity registers, he'll blow the charge."

"Good. Very good."

CHAPTER 16

The L-shaped shopping center in El Monte, in the San Gabriel Valley of Los Angeles County, had seen better days, but not by much. There had never been a well-known grocery or drugstore "anchor," and half of the storefronts now stood empty. Double Lucky Donuts and Saigon 88 Noodles suggested changing demographics in the previously Caucasian, then Hispanic, city. The Vietnamese-owned noodle joint and the Cambodian-owned donut shop were the closest shopping center tenants to Commercial-Industrial Applications, which was the end unit.

Almost no one paid attention to the initials of Commercial-Industrial Applications. And almost no one actually ever entered the locked premises, whose windows were tinted too dark to see through. But this early spring evening, with a scent of night-blooming jasmine floating in the cool air, the secret safe house had plenty of activity.

Kit Bennings, Angel Perez, and Yulana Petkova stood by at the rear entrance as Buzz Van Wyke entered a ten-digit code on a keypad. A *click* sounded, and then a steel panel slid open revealing biometric security devices. Buzz leaned forward and looked into an eyepiece where his iris was scanned for a match. Lastly, he slid his index finger into a narrow glass trough about four inches long.

"Finger vein scan?" asked Kit.

Buzz nodded. "The CIA has more safe houses around the country than you can shake a stick at. This one is seldom used but gets checked every week. We're good to squat here for a few days."

"How did you get the entry code and your data into the system?" asked Bennings.

"If I told you, you'd become party to a federal crime."

"I think I already am," said Bennings with a smile as the group entered.

The first order of business was to give Yulana food and drink and lock her in an interrogation room. A cot, chair, and some magazines had been placed in the room. It was the perfect place to keep her for now.

Good-byes were said and thanks offered to Buzz's son Randy and the other SEALs, who had to get back to Coronado, pronto.

So the men settled in. Buzz took Kit into a small communications room to show him all of the sophisticated comms, but more important, he briefed him on the closed-circuit TV coverage and alarm systems that kept the safe house secure. The entire facility was heavily reinforced, and Kit immediately felt better.

As they stood in the communications room, a video monitor showed a taxi pulling around to the back door.

"That should be Jen," said Kit.

They watched the video feed as Jen Huffman got out of the cab holding a suitcase and backpack.

"I'll let her in," said Angel, moving toward the rear door. Earlier, Jen had been dropped off at a hotel, where she checked out all of Yulana's belongings for bugs and trackers and disabled the two that she found. One was hidden in a makeup compact, the other in the lining of the suitcase.

After Jen squared away her gear, Angel grabbed four beers from the big fridge in the large, well-stocked kitchen, and he and Buzz gave the nickel tour to Jen and Kit. Jen hadn't seen the place yet, because she'd flown in to LAX from D.C. shortly before Kit and Yulana had arrived.

The safe house was pretty impressive. A bunk room comfortably slept eight. There were two soundproof interrogation rooms, the small communications room, a phony reception room with desk and chairs, a conference room with a table that sat ten, and a common room with sofas, a TV, and, Kit noted, an old acoustic guitar leaning in a corner. The place had toilets and showers, discreet parking in the back, steel-reinforced walls and doors. A gun room had a gun safe with weapons and ammo the SEALs had loaned to Buzz. A cache of orange-colored Czech-made Semtex plastic explosives sat in a corner—something the CIA must have forgotten about. Other goodies and gadgets were stashed in the conference room.

"Here's the coolest thing," said Angel, leading Kit, Buzz, and Jen through a gray steel door into a storage room. "I want to make one of these for my house."

Angel pressed a hidden switch, and a section of the suspended ceiling opened up as a ladder dropped down. "Escape hatch to the roof. If you stay low, you're out of sight, and it's an easy run on the roof all the way to the other end of the shopping center, where they have a rope ladder rolled up."

"Your black-budget tax dollars hard at work," joked Jen.

"I don't think we'll be needing it, but anything's better than a tunnel," said Kit. The others looked at him for clarification. "Never mind."

"Kit, I want to park one of the vans at the other end of the mall, in case we do need to use it," said Angel.

"You're joking."

"I agree with Angel," said Buzz, nodding. "As long as the Russian woman is with us, I want to take every precaution."

"Okay, Angel, do it."

Kit held out his can of beer, and they all touched cans.

Kit, Angel, and Jen sat with pens, papers, and laptops at the conference table as Buzz drew four circles on a whiteboard while holding his pipe.

"According to my contact at the FBI's Organized Crime Unit, Viktor Popov is one of maybe forty Russian mob bosses in the United

States. He's considered small potatoes, so the Bureau, which has had very limited resources directed at gangsters since the war on terror ramped up in 2001, never went after him. Besides, Popov still has friends in D.C. who remember all the good intelligence he gave them back in the late 1990s. Rumor is he's still giving them the occasional intel nugget.

"The big Russian outfit here in L.A. is an offshoot of the Odessa Mafia. Popov demurs to them and pays them a percentage of his action. And since he does things they don't do, mainly high-end hacking, he's not stepping on their toes, although his guys did knock off an armored truck once for twelve million."

"Where's his headquarters?" asked Jen as she used a small can of compressed air to blow dust off her laptop screens.

"Good question," responded Buzz. "Nobody knows."

"He doesn't own a restaurant or nightclub . . . maybe hang out in a social club?" asked Angel.

"No, nothing like that at all. He owns several legitimate businesses and possibly launders money through them: a moving company, a construction outfit, heavy-equipment rental company, some electronics stores. But I say 'possibly' because he's not really a cash criminal."

"A what?" asked Angel as he twirled his green-handled screwdriver.

"Drugs, prostitution, gambling, and extortion generate cash, but Popov doesn't do any of that. All the high-tech rip-offs his people do? The money is just electronically transferred overseas and disappears into an unending series of shell companies. And that's only if he steals *money*. As you all know, after I retired as a marine aviator and before I became a contract employee of the CIA, I was, among other things, an investigator for the Treasury Department's Office of Terrorism and Financial Intelligence. It can take months just to trace one transaction. And by the time you do, the money is gone."

"So Popov is . . ." began Jen without completing the thought.

"Popov is first and foremost an information broker. He steals data, blueprints, technological secrets and sells them on the open market."

"Kind of like a freelance industrial spy," said Jen.

"Yes, but he'll hack the bank accounts of private citizens, too, as long as there's money to be gotten."

"I guess my account is safe then," joked Angel.

"Popov falls in the cracks between being a spy and a thief," said Kit, who was already aware of most, but not all, of the background information Buzz had been presenting.

"Exactly. Very few people in his organization even know they work for him. He uses six-person cells of hackers, and it's rumored they move from location to location every few months. He also uses highly trained analysts, former Russian intelligence people, to sift through all the stolen information and rate its value on the open market. The analysts work out of large RVs, those big ones the size of a bus."

"So his operation is very decentralized."

"Very." Buzz touched his pipe stem to a circle on the whiteboard. "In this circle are the hackers and analysts." Buzz wrote WORKERS in the circle with a black marker. "They are the worker bees, the desk jockeys. They don't know anyone else in Popov's outfit except members of the security team—which is this circle." Buzz indicated a circle and wrote SECURITY/SOLDIERS.

"So Popov has thugs protecting his hackers and analysts. And spying on them, too, I would imagine," said Kit.

"Yes, and he has many of what I just call 'soldiers,' otherwise some other mob could easily move in and take over. Those soldiers fall into the security circle."

"What's the next circle?" asked Jen, who used a cleaning wipe to finish tidying up her laptops.

"Special operations." Buzz wrote SPEC OPS inside the circle. "An example of that would be the crew that took down the armored truck. They do specialized, high-value crimes, and they are very, very good. But again, they're insulated from the rest of the organization."

"And the last circle has to be Popov and his upper management. So who is his top person in Los Angeles?" asked Kit.

"A young guy named Mikhail Travkin." Buzz wrote POPOV/TRAVKIN in the final circle. "He's Popov's nephew. Has graduate degrees from both Stanford and MIT, paid for by Uncle Viktor."

"Mobsters with business degrees and Ph.D.s in physics and engineering—that's the Russians for you," said Kit.

"I heard that Russian mob guys will shoot you just to see if their gun works," said Angel, with his usual rat-a-tat-tat delivery.

"They are smart, ruthless, and have a business sense that puts them in a class by themselves," said Kit. "But everyone has a weakness. Maybe we can locate the nephew. He could lead us to Popov." Bennings ran his fingers through his coarse hair and scratched his head, as he often did when lost in thought. After a moment, he looked up. "Thanks, Buzz, that was good information. We'll just have to develop more details, like locations, on our own."

"Popov has been seen occasionally in West Hollywood, where thousands of Russian immigrants live, but his people are under orders to avoid places frequented by their fellow Russians."

"West Hollywood has dozens and dozens of places where Russian immigrants hang out," said Kit. "We'd need an army to put every location under surveillance."

"Good luck keeping a Russian away from a steam bath," cracked Angel.

"It's funny, Angel," said Buzz. "Popov himself is old school, but his entire organization is very young. They don't care about the old ways. They have assimilated into the American Dream."

"Yeah, except they're not earning their piece of the American Dream, they're stealing it," carped Jen.

"The Russians are the hardest-working crooks you'll find," cracked Angel.

"*If* we can find them. Popov told me himself he has multiple passports under different names, so he could be anywhere in L.A. Meaning Staci could be anywhere." Kit rubbed his eyes. "Jen, when Popov calls me on this cell," Kit held up the cell phone the thug had tossed to him in Moscow, "can we track his location?"

"Maybe. I'll need about an hour to set up." Jen took the phone and left the room.

Buzz looked directly at Kit. "We need to talk about your Russian bride."

"My loving wife?" Kit joked sarcastically.

"Why don't we just blindfold her, drive her to the beach, and turn her loose?" asked Angel.

"If we do that, how will we find out what her role is?" asked Kit.

"I think the two tracking devices explained what her role is."

"It's possible she's being blackmailed, similar to myself."

"For what purpose?" asked Buzz.

"I don't know that anymore than I know what *my* purpose is in this whole thing," said Kit, feeling frustrated. "Believe me, it's driving me crazy."

"Smells like you're being set up as a patsy...maybe her too," said Angel.

Kit nodded. "I've considered that. The bottom line is, we know a lot about Popov, but we know squat about what his plans are." Worry lines etched themselves across his forehead as he fingered the key he wore on a thick silver necklace.

"We don't have time for some masterful interrogation, so let's just waterboard her."

Kit and Buzz raised their eyebrows.

Angel continued, "Some say it's torture, some say it's not. To me, torture is what those Islamist terrorists did in that Kenya shopping mall attack; they pulled the fingers off of hostages with pliers, they gouged out people's eyes, and ripped off their noses and ears. They castrated men and dismembered women. That's torture. Waterboarding won't kill your Russian wife, it doesn't do permanent physical damage, but it's damn uncomfortable—intolerable. That's why people talk, because they want it to stop."

"But Angel, we don't have much of a baseline of truth. She could lie through her teeth and we wouldn't know."

"She's expendable, or she wouldn't have been sent with you," said Buzz. "So I seriously doubt she knows what Popov's plans are. That suggests there's little of real value she could give us, so waterboarding or any other interrogation technique would be a waste of time."

"Okay," said Angel quickly, "then maybe she's a disinformation agent. She as much as admitted she had two tracking devices, but so what, we were about to find them, anyway. She might even be an assassin playing a role, just waiting to deliver a killer line."

"I don't trust her, either, guys," said Kit. "But for now, she's not my priority. It doesn't hurt us to keep her on ice until we have a bigger picture."

The ringing of a cell phone sent them all to silence. Then Kit realized it was his old U.S. phone. He checked the number. "It's Larry Bing. Angel, your stopwatch. Time one minute so the call can't be traced."

Angel nodded and engaged the stopwatch feature on his chronograph.

Kit pressed the green button and put the phone on speaker. "Colonel Bing, this is Major Bennings, on speakerphone."

Colonel Larry Bing commanded the Activity. Like Bennings, he was rock hard, fair to a fault, and cared about his people; that generated a lot of loyalty in the ranks. Unlike Bennings, most of the battles he fought weren't with the enemy but with the feckless, the small-minded, the yes-men and yes-women, the sycophants and the sellout bureaucrats and the general officers in and around D.C. who only cared about CYA—covering your ass—and not about kicking the ass of America's foes.

"Damn it, Bennings, you are in a world of bull crap. I wanted this call to be about my condolences on the loss of your mother, but I just got my butt chewed out by Secretary of the Army Fitzgerald, who has a video of you taking a cash bribe to marry a Russian woman. And the suggestion is she's a spy. A spy who you apparently brought with you to America."

"Thank you for the condolences, sir."

"Be quiet! The fact that I am getting called on the carpet and I'm not even your commanding officer anymore should impress upon you, Major, just how angry the army is right now."

"I understand, sir."

"So here is the message I was told to deliver if I got hold of you. You have two hours from right now to turn yourself in to Colonel Spano, the CID commander at Fort Irwin. You will stay put there until this can be sorted out. Two hours, or you will be declared AWOL, understand?"

"I'm on emergency leave, sir."

"Your leave has been canceled. CID officers have been ordered to find and detain you, although you didn't hear that from me."

CID officers worked for the army's Criminal Investigation Command. Some of those investigators were hard-nosed, top-flight snoops and were essentially cops for the DoD. Kit hadn't expected them to come after him so fast.

Angel gave Kit the cutthroat gesture.

"Yes, sir. Thank you and good-bye."

"Kit!!" snapped Colonel Bing, who then softened his tone as he said, "Keep your head down and watch your six."

"Will do, Colonel."

Kit terminated the call, popped off the back cover, and pulled the battery and SIM card from the phone.

"Damn," said Buzz.

"Popov leaked the video of me taking the money in Moscow. Probably as a response to our little escapade at LAX," said Kit. "He didn't expect me to do that, and so he's countering. I take this as a good omen."

"Good omen?!" asked Angel. "The secretary of the army wants your head on a platter."

"The only time I ever beat Popov at chess was when I attacked wildly with my queen. He anticipated certain strategies, but I just winged it."

"Well this ain't chess, partner," said Buzz.

Kit exhaled audibly, then closed his eyes for a moment. "You guys have a chance to check with the morgue?" he asked softly.

"Yes," said Buzz. "Your sister was kidnapped before she could make funeral arrangements. So your mom's body is still there."

"I want to go see her."

"What about Jen's trace when Popov calls?" asked Angel.

"I doubt that he'll call tonight. He turned up the heat by releasing the video of me taking the bribe, and now he wants me to sweat."

"Let me call a funeral home, have them handle everything about your mom," offered Buzz.

"Not yet. I just got an idea. Jen can hack the morgue's security video and take it down. Then we're all going to the morgue—you guys and Yulana too."

"What!?"

"Kit, you have the Russian mob, the San Berdu cop-shop boys, CID investigators, and probably the FBI looking for you, and they all know that your mom is at the morgue."

"I'm hoping it's the Russians waiting for me. We'll grab one and find out for ourselves just how decentralized the information in Popov's organization really is."

Buzz chewed on his pipe stem, then nodded. "It's risky, but until we find Travkin, it's one of the few moves we have."

"I get it," said Angel. "It's the reckless-queen-with-no-strategy strategy."

"I'm making this up as I go along." Kit smiled. "But first . . ." Kit reached into his backpack and produced four identical cell phones. "These phones are sterile and encrypted. Starting now we only use these. We all give our other phones to Jen and let her check them for tracking software that might have been installed." Kit slid his old cell phone with the battery and SIM taken out to the middle of the table.

"Second, and I mean right now, we 'acquire' some different vehicles. Then we go out to play."

CHAPTER 17

The facility and parking lot on South Lena Drive in San Bernardino were surrounded by a wall of tall, bushy trees, like sentinels keeping bad things out. Or in. The brown stucco building trimmed with green tile and capped with a green tile roof almost looked inviting. Rose-bushes, jacaranda, palm trees, and bougainvillea adorned the grounds. You'd think the place was a resort, not the county morgue. If your body has to get taken to a cold slab somewhere, this was a pretty nice place.

But it's never nice to look at a dead loved one.

Yulana hadn't wanted to come, but Yulana wasn't calling too many shots these days. So she stood silently next to Kit as he gazed at his deceased mother on the stainless-steel roll-out tray in a very chilly room.

She noticed Kit's eyes were moist, but he didn't cry. And he didn't say a word.

When she shifted her eyes to Gina Bennings's lifeless form, it was Yulana's eyes that grew moist. She bit her lip and then burst into tears.

She watched Kit, who looked surprised, stare at her quizzically. She then broke down into a ragged, emotional crying jag that convulsed her body. Through tear-blurred eyes, she saw him boring his eyes into her, as if seeking some kind of answer.

She didn't care anymore what he or the other Americans

thought. She only cared about one thing, but she couldn't dare tell anyone, couldn't trust anyone. She was on her own in the worst kind of way, held against her will in a foreign country with no money, no family, no friends, no coworkers; not a single soul existed whom she could turn to for help. She felt more like a Ping-Pong ball than a pawn; she was part of a game that was batting her around from one side to the other.

As more tears rushed from her eyes, she knew that no matter who won the game, a cold slab in a chilly room was the most likely fate for her and for the only one she truly loved.

She wiped away tears. Bennings's gaze had softened. He looked different somehow. Not kindly, but . . . understanding. Not that it mattered. Yulana Petkova was sure her unfortunate fate was sealed. So she didn't protest as he took her hand and led her out of the room.

Yulana struggled to keep up with Kit as he quickly crossed over the lighted fish pond on a small concrete walkway toward the Chevy Tahoe 4x4 in the dark parking lot. The Tahoe had a heavy steel front grill guard and a heavy-duty rear bumper—extras that looked like they meant business.

"We're about to meet some of Viktor Popov's employees," said Kit, with an edge to his voice.

The two vehicles containing Russians had been spotted by Buzz when he reconnoitered the place on a motorcycle. Two late-model sedans sat parked in the very dim light near the two entrances. It was hard to see the occupants, but they were there.

In the Tahoe, Kit pulled out his favorite knife, a Gerber DMF automatic folder with a tanto blade, and gunned the truck toward an exit. "Get in the back quick and hold on!"

Frightened, Yulana scrambled over the console into the rear seat as the Tahoe neared the exit. Kit heard the dark sedan start its engine and watched as its headlights came on. At the last second, he swerved violently and sent the SUV flying into the sedan broadside at about 35 mph.

The sickening crunch was heard blocks away.

Kit used the Gerber to puncture the Tahoe's air bags instead of waiting for them to deflate on their own. He didn't stop to admire his handiwork but threw the big SUV into reverse and floored it.

He blew a rear tire bouncing over a median but accelerated to almost 40 mph in reverse toward the second sedan. The Russians started to pull out in an attempt to get clear, but Kit slammed the rear of his truck into the trunk of the sedan, which went flying head-first into a tree.

Kit shook his head to clear his senses, then keyed his encrypted two-way radio: "Talk to me."

"Got a live one," said Angel Perez.

Kit bounded out of the Tahoe as he pulled a silenced Kel-Tec Sub-2000 from a shoulder rig. He unfolded the uniquely designed weapon and it became a subgun that fired .40 caliber pistol ammunition. The two dazed occupants saw him, drew their pistols, and started to raise them.

"Drop your weapons or I'll shoot!" yelled Kit in Russian, as he took aim.

The men didn't comply but instead wheeled their guns in his direction.

"Drop them, now!"

As the two Russians sighted on him, Kit fired bursts into each man.

He quickly returned to the Tahoe, and Yulana looked at him with true fear in her eyes.

Good. It's about time you became afraid, Yulana, because this is no game.

He grabbed her wrist and pulled her out of the wrecked Tahoe as Angel sped up in one of the white vans. Once again, they piled into the back of a van, this time joining a bound-up Russian, and then they were gone.

Buzz and Angel took the captured Russian into the safe house for interrogation. Yulana was now a nervous wreck, and she was a smoker, so Kit drove her in a Honda Accord toward Koreatown. The drive would help him relax, and he wanted time alone with her, while she was seemingly vulnerable, to take a crack at her hard shell. He doubted she knew anything that could help him find Staci, but he wanted some truth as to how she fit into the picture. So he stopped in a liquor store to buy vodka, cold sake, and cigarettes. Then he took her to Koffea.

Koffea, on South Berendo in L.A.'s Koreatown is so big it would impress a Texan. Off-street valet parking is only a buck, but a simple cup of java with no refill, like at almost all Korean coffee joints, is *très cher*. It's not so much that you're buying coffee as it is you're renting the seat. Koffea, with soft K-pop on the speaker system, is generally quiet, so a lot of students show up to study. There are many different rooms, nooks, crannies, and open spaces, so even when they're busy, there are plenty of tables to be had. Kit led Yulana out onto the back patio, where recessed fireplaces warmed against the light chill in the night air.

The steaming green tea and cold glasses of water came quickly. When the waitress left, Kit dumped their water into a potted plant, pulled a pint of Stoli from his jacket pocket, and filled her glass with vodka. He slid a pack of Marlboros and a lighter to her, and she quickly lit up, inhaling nicotine deeply into her lungs. The ashtray was a small celadon bowl filled with damp coffee grounds, and she nervously tapped ash into it, then took a long hit of the vodka. As she drew deep intakes from her cigarette, he surreptitiously removed a small bottle of Kikuyoi sake from another pocket and poured it into his water glass. He took a sip, savoring the taste, then ignored her as she smoked in sullen silence and calmed down.

Kit jotted notes on a pad for twenty minutes as they sat at the round marble table without speaking. Her aqua eyes, the color of a Caribbean lagoon, held no sparkle. Dark circles pooled below them. A droop of sadness pervaded her entire face. She was so beautiful . . . and so perfectly miserable. Kit thought back on something Larry Bing had taught him when dealing with reluctant allies: "Sometimes to get truth, you have to give a little."

So he turned to Yulana and looked her right in the eyes.

"Viktor Popov offered me two hundred thousand U.S. dollars to marry you and bring you here to America. I refused. So then he murdered my mother. To force me to marry you. And he kidnapped my sister, Staci. They were kind enough to show me the video of how badly she's been beaten. He'll kill Staci if I don't do what he says, but I don't know what it is he wants. I'm only sure it's something bad.

"I was a diplomatic attaché working at the embassy in Moscow. Why did Popov target me to marry you? You're so beautiful, he could have found some American guy to do it for nothing, for free. What is it that I can do for him that someone else can't?

"As you've seen since we flew in . . . I'm fighting back. Partly because I understand that even if I do everything he says, he'll still kill my sister and probably me too. But I'm also fighting back because when you do nothing, a cancer will just grow and grow. And for some reason the cancer called Popov has infected my life. We live in a very corrupt world, you and me. We can't right all the wrongs; all we can do is take care of our own as best we can. So I choose to take aggressive action to fight the cancer called Viktor Popov."

She studied him for a long beat. "You cannot defeat this cancer," she finally said, stubbing out her cigarette into the coffee grounds.

"Cancer is beaten or sent into remission all the time."

"You think you can defeat the Russian Mafia?"

"Of course not. But I think I can kill Popov and stop whatever it is he wants to do. I absolutely think that's possible."

"You and your three friends?" she asked sarcastically.

"We all have special skills."

"Do you have nine lives? Popov has dozens, *hundreds* of killers working for him. He's rich, powerful, friendly with the other rich and powerful Mafia dons and spy chiefs and military generals. He seems to know everything about everyone all the time. How can you beat him?"

"I haven't figured that out yet. And it won't be easy. But I'm going to do it."

"Or die trying?" she asked.

"Or die trying."

She said nothing, just looked away and nervously bit her fingernail.

Kit removed a photo from his pocket and placed it in front of her. It showed a smiling, very happy Yulana holding a laughing three-year-old girl. "You said you had some personal things in your bag you wanted back."

She quickly grabbed the picture and held it tightly.

"If they killed your mother. And if they will kill your sister even when you do what they ask, then . . ." Tears ran down Yulana's cheeks.

"Then you don't think there's any hope for your daughter. Popov has her in Russia, right? That's why you cried when you saw my mother. You thought it could be your daughter lying in a morgue somewhere."

"She's only three years old," she said, trying to choke back tears.

"Then you're lucky. Popov is an evil man, but I can tell you this: he'll never harm a child, especially a toddler. He might try to kill *you*, but he won't harm your little girl."

"I wish I could believe you."

"Believe what you want."

She looked up at him sharply. "I didn't ask for any of this!"

"Maybe not. But at least you know why you are here. Don't you?"

She guiltily averted his eyes.

"Unlike me, you know what Popov wants you to do. And because you love your little girl, you'll do it. But deep in your heart, you believe it's hopeless, that you're both doomed."

She looked at him like a deer caught in the headlights.

"I'm here to offer you hope," he continued. "But I need your help. I need to know what you know. Anything that might be important."

Yulana wasn't sure what to think; she looked like a woman racked with confusion and doubt. "So you want me to believe you're a good guy in this war?"

"I'm a good guy who is willing to fight dirty to win. Because if you don't fight dirty, you lose."

"Okay, then Mr. Good Guy. Let me go free."

Without pausing, Kit pulled an envelope from an inside jacket pocket and gave it to her. "Your passport, your return ticket to Moscow, and three hundred dollars. *Udachi*. Good luck."

She looked shocked, not sure whether this was some kind of

cruel joke. She checked inside the envelope, then gave Kit a long pen-etrating stare.

"I should warn you, though: You remember the video they took at the marriage office, where they made me count the money?"

She nodded as a frown set upon her lips.

"Popov sent it to the chief of all the American army. So there are many people looking to arrest me right now. And the American gov-ernment thinks you, Yulana Petkova, are a Russian spy. That means they're looking for you too. And the airport is the first place they'd start to watch. Your name will be red flagged. You might want to get to Mexico somehow. Maybe you could fly out of Mexico City. But Cuba would be safer, much safer. So, personally, I'd try for Havana."

The frown stayed on Yulana's lips. She downed the last of her vodka, pocketed the cigarettes and lighter, and walked out clutching the envelope.

Kit watched her go. Without a doubt, he now believed that Yulana Petkova had been trapped, just as he had been.

He sat quietly for another few minutes, finished the sake, then rang the buzzer for the waitress. He paid the bill and walked outside, fumbling in his pockets for the valet claim check, but couldn't find it. He found it in his wallet while walking toward the Mexican valet.

"Sorry, Señor, I know the pretty lady come with you in the black Honda. She say she cold and you coming right out, so I bring the car up, but she jump in and drive away." The valet looked nervous; he knew he'd made a mistake.

"Don't worry about it," said Kit handing him the claim check and a tip. He glanced into the lot to confirm that the car was indeed gone.

He turned away from the valet and scanned the street, but there was no sign of Yulana. His face twisted into a frown as he walked briskly to Sixth Street and then headed west. He knew a Korean soju joint with a hip crowd in the refurbished Chapman Market complex just up ahead. He needed to put a little distance between himself and Koffea and get off the street, just to be on the safe side. He'd misjudged Petkova; she not only took the opportunity to run, she stole his car.

CHAPTER 18

Just as in Korea, where every square foot of level space is fair game to park something on, Koreatown mall parking lots are so jam-packed they have security to direct the chaotic flux of vehicles into seemingly illogical parking configurations. As he threaded through the parking lot of the historic Chapman Market Courtyard complex crowded with trendy young Koreans and Korean Americans, Bennings fished out his sterile cell and called Buzz.

"Good news on this end," said Buzz.

"Our friend was chatty?"

"Very."

"Great. Listen, I'm in Koreatown and I need somebody to pick me up," said Kit.

"What happened?"

"My lovely Russian bride . . ."

Just then a horn honked. Kit turned around and saw Yulana behind the wheel of the Honda, snaking along in a single-file line of luxury cars. She gave him a wave.

"Disregard that. I'll be back soon for the debrief." Kit ended the call, backtracked toward her, and got into the passenger seat.

He and Yulana exchanged a long look that told him he'd made a new ally.

"Thanks for coming back," he said.

"I almost lost you," she said as she pulled a fifth of Grey Goose from a paper bag. "I like drinking this better. It will help me tell you some things."

He nodded.

"So where do we go now?" she asked, inching the car forward.

He checked his watch. "We'll head back. If that's okay with you."

"Yes, it's okay," she said, easing the car forward, out of the parking lot and into street traffic. "But do I have to stay locked in that room?"

"I'll make it nicer for you."

She nodded. "If I flew back to Russia, I think Popov's men would just grab me again. Going to the police in Moscow would not help me at all. The SVR might help me because I know state secrets, but they couldn't return Kala, my daughter, to me." She looked over at Kit. "So I'm going to take a chance that maybe you can."

"I'll do my best, you have my word on that. And since you already pointed out that it's just me and my three friends and we don't have nine lives, then you know that it won't be easy."

"The story of my life is that things are not easy. So . . . what to tell you? Well, believe it or not, I'm an engineer. My degree is in engineering physics, but because of politics and my refusal to sleep with my chief, I was transferred to a poorly funded department. I've been working as a research-and-development scientist in Samara on special projects." She sighed. "Can we just stop somewhere?"

They were sitting at a red light at Sixth and Vermont. "Turn right. There's a restaurant right there, open all night."

She pulled into a Denny's and parked in back. After shutting off the Honda, she opened the Grey Goose and took a hit right from the bottle. "Sorry, it's not polite to drink from the bottle. Reminds me of when I was a teenager." She offered him the bottle. Just to put her more at ease, he pretended to take a drink.

"So you lived and worked in Samara. A lot of sensitive engineering takes place there. Can you tell me what kind of research you do?"

"Any emerging technologies. We look at everything and evaluate how it might be weaponized."

"So you're a black-projects engineer, like our people in DARPA, the Defense Advanced Research Projects Agency."

"Yes, but without the generous funding DARPA has. They don't even provide toilet paper in our restrooms."

"They probably would provide toilet paper if your bosses weren't stealing the money," said Kit.

"Yes, perhaps. One thing is . . . please, don't ask me to betray my country by giving you any specifics. I won't do that."

"I understand."

"Well, what else? My husband is a civil engineer. He's an abusive drunk, so we divorced two years ago. I have lived in an apartment with my daughter since then."

"How do you know Popov?"

"I don't. I've never met him. I know who he is, only because of what I heard from the older engineers. His wife used to be a department chief at a weapons complex in Samara. In the 1990s, when the country was in chaos, Popov and his wife and their thugs looted the arsenal of EMPs, electromagnetic pulse weapons."

Kit already knew this from having read Popov's dossier. There are many different types and designs of e-bombs, EMP weapons, or directed energy weapons, but they share common results: the affected target areas, subject to extreme magnetic fields, would be, technologically speaking, sent back one hundred years. Computers and most if not all data on them would be destroyed. TVs and fluorescent lights would glow even if turned off—and never work again. Anything electronic would be rendered useless, forever. Only some diesel engines would survive, but all other vehicles would never start again. Batteries would become warm and ruin cell phones and any device that used them. Telephone lines would pool into mush. Air-conditioning, elevators, refrigerators, cars, trucks, hair dryers, radios, and anything that needed a battery or electricity would be destroyed.

Cascading blackouts would also likely result, knocking out power for potentially tens of millions of people, hundreds if not thousands of miles away from the original target, because, unlike wise consumers, electrical substations and generating plants don't have surge protectors. And once the grid went down in a big way, it would not be so easy to bring it back up.

So while humans aren't killed by e-bombs—thus making the devices nonlethal weapons—the way of life of the targeted humans is killed.

"The e-bombs Popov stole . . . were they nuclear?"

"Nonnuclear. They sold them on the black market, is what I was told. Every last one in the entire Russian arsenal! Can you imagine?"

"Yes, I can. Lots of arsenals all over Russia were being emptied out and sold in those days. Luckily, I believe most of the EMP weapons ended up in the hands of the CIA and not terrorists."

"Well, Russia has a nonlethal weapons program, as America does, of course, but now all of our EMP weapons are part of our nuclear arsenal."

"The nuclear explosion provides the energy for the EMP effects," said Kit.

"Correct. Nonnuclear EMPs rely on conventional explosives to initiate the reactions. Anyway, when I first went to work after I got my university degree, I was schooled in the use, construction, and operation of the old, nonnuclear EMPs. And I studied the American designs, too. I learned on nonworking models. We were going to restock our arsenal but never did because they were not dependable devices. At least our EMPs weren't. Generals like to know exactly what will happen when a weapon is employed, but with our e-bombs, there was little consistency. The U.S. nonnuclear EMP arsenal is more advanced than ours ever was, but no funds were forthcoming for us to restart the program. So I was transferred to the R and D unit where I now work."

"Okay."

"One night about two weeks ago some men came to my apartment. They took me and my daughter, Kala. They said if I wanted to see her alive again, I would do exactly what they said. They said I was to marry an American soldier, travel to America, and perform some work that I was trained in. I was instructed to tell you nothing, nothing at all . . . or Kala would die."

She looked at Kit nakedly. There was no disguising the fact that her revelations put her daughter at even greater risk. Kit didn't speak but nodded his understanding. "My sister, your daughter. We'll get them back, one way or another," he said.

Yulana smiled a little sadly; he knew she had no choice but to hope he was right.

"The one thing that seems to connect me to Popov is the EMPs. But I don't know, I'm just guessing," she said, resigned.

The gist of the scheme clicked into place in Kit's mind like an unwelcome revelation. He saw the connections now, including his own.

"They need you to work on some kind of device, Yulana."

"Do you think Popov has found one of the old Soviet nonnuclear EMP bombs?"

"Maybe." Kit said it, but he didn't believe it. He had his own connection to e-bombs. A few years back, Kit had led a Red Team, as part of a security training exercise, that had broken into an arsenal of EMP weapons stored at Sandia National Labs in New Mexico. He'd gotten in rather easily, actually. And that must be why Viktor Popov needed the services of Kit Bennings.

Sandia. Popov wants me to steal an electromagnetic pulse bomb from Sandia, and Yulana's job is to make sure it detonates. But what does he want to hit? What is the target?

Bennings picked up the bottle of vodka and took a swig for real.

CHAPTER 19

A stiff breeze blew cool dry air over the desert floor, gifting Las Vegas with the kind of temperature more common to midwinter than late May. Endless sunshine, mild temps, and clean air comprised an allure almost as compelling as the nonstop party atmosphere of the Strip; the notion that anything was possible in this city was an idea for many—especially the desperate—that constantly bubbled to the surface.

Fantastic fun, if not outlandish riches, were just waiting to be had with the roll of the dice or the push of a slot button, and starting life over with a winning hand was par for the course for those who chose to make the attempt. At least that was the bill of goods sold in slick marketing campaigns to the gullible.

And so the transient population of the city was never a low figure.

Siegel Suites on Tropicana west of the Strip and the I-15 freeway catered to a transient clientele. Furnished, one-bedroom "suites" with utilities included rented by the week or month. Prostitutes in town for a few weeks, pimps, drug dealers, cons, criminals, and others living on the lower margins made the roach-infested complex home.

The units looked presentable on the outside but were often shabby on the inside. It was the perfect location to remain low-key, where residents didn't pry or ask questions of their neighbors. The perfect place to stash Staci Bennings with a two-person babysitting detail.

The Russian man, the one called Gregory, had fallen asleep at the kitchen table. Again. He sat slumped, his head tilted back over the edge of the straight-backed kitchen chair. The blue-eyed blond woman, Lily, was outside smoking somewhere on the third-floor walkway.

They were in Las Vegas. Staci was sure of that. Maybe a mile west of the Vegas Strip. She had caught a glimpse of the horizon the night they first carried her up to the apartment. They were somewhere due south of the Rio, which had been lit up with purple and red lights, and the Palms, with the electric rainbow on the roof. She had recognized those buildings.

Staci was confined to the living room, where she slept on the ratty, filthy sofa at night and watched endless TV shows the rest of the time. All of the windows were blacked out, and she had to ask permission to use the grungy toilet or the kitchen area. The bedroom was used by Lily and Gregory to sleep in shifts. The TV droned on with some late-night program that wasn't that funny and featured celebrity guests who weren't particularly talented.

Staci's swollen and discolored wrist was broken and still throbbed with stabbing pain. Her puffy left knee hurt almost as much, but maybe she only had ligament damage. These injuries were courtesy of Lily, administered while Staci stood drugged and held from behind by Gregory.

At least Gregory had given her aspirin, elastic bandages, and mentholated cream. She had to apply the bandages herself; her captors wouldn't help her. Staci understood that Lily wanted to kill her, and she also understood that since she could clearly identify both of them, they probably would. Unless she could get them first.

If she had a weapon she could kill Gregory right now as he slept; he was supposed to be awake, watching her. But the room had been sanitized. There were no pots or pans, cutlery, no heavy objects or blunt instruments. If her wrist wasn't broken, she could sneak up behind him and choke him to death, and then take her chances with Lily. But Staci knew she was too badly injured to put up much of a fight. And they both carried weapons.

So what other options did she have?

The phone. Gregory's cell phone lay on the round kitchen table just inches from his hand.

But who could she call? She remembered few phone numbers by heart. Her fiancé, Blanchard, was half a world away in the concrete canyons of Tokyo. Kit! Surely Kit would be in Los Angeles by now. She would send a text to his U.S. cell phone, the same number he'd had for over ten years. One of the few numbers she remembered.

As she stood, excruciating pain coursed through her knee and she almost cried out. Slowly, carefully, and as quietly as she could, she limped to the table. She held her injured wrist against her chest; there was no way she could use that hand.

Gregory, who had had four shots of vodka, as he did every night, snored lightly. She'd watched him like this before, when he sometimes would wake suddenly, for no reason. Was he going to wake? She could worry about it or she could just do it.

Staci's hand trembled and she stopped breathing as she picked up the phone. She tried to remember if his keypad was set to make a sound when he inputted characters. *Yes, it was,* she thought. So she first went to SETTINGS, then GENERAL, then PERSONALIZATION and silenced KEYPAD TONES. Then she went to MESSAGES, CREATE NEW, and entered Kit's number. Then she typed, "Vegas S of Rio/Plms nr Strip 3fl 2Russ hrry Stci." She started to hit SEND but thought of something to add: "dnt rspnd." She hit SEND. Then she went to the SENT FOLDER and deleted the message.

Gregory snorted and stirred. *Is he going to wake up?!* Damn, what kind of beating would it be this time? Staci started to replace the phone, then waited. But Gregory still slept.

She couldn't call 911, since she didn't know where she was. They could trace the call, but she would have to leave the line open for that to work and she couldn't risk it: Lily would return any minute. So she called home. She assumed no one would pick up and she would leave a message.

Her hand shook by the time the answering machine finally beeped. As quietly as possible she whispered "Las Vegas, south of the Rio and Palms, third-floor apartment or hotel. A dump. Help, Las Vegas . . ."

Footsteps outside the door. Lily!

Staci ended the call, then clicked on MENU. More movement outside the door! Her hand shook as she clicked on LOG, then RECENT CALLS. Damn, there were too many pages to click to do this! And just then, Gregory stirred.

She clicked DIALED NUMBERS. There was the call! But now she had to select OPTIONS just as she heard the sound of a key going into the lock.

Screw it, she thought, and with determination, using just one hand, she clicked DELETE. But then she had to confirm the choice and clicked YES. Then she pushed the red button and put the phone back on the table.

The door started to open slowly, and Staci ran back to the sofa and slumped onto it just as Lily entered the room and Gregory woke up. Her face was turned away from them and she held her breath as tears streamed down her cheeks from the knifelike pain that stabbed her knee.

She took a slow breath, careful not to reveal she was awake. A sense of victory washed over her, the seeds of hope had been delivered, until she remembered . . . she hadn't gone back to SETTINGS and turned the KEYPAD TONES feature back on. The next time Gregory used his phone, it would be silent.

CHAPTER 20

A double homicide in the parking lot of the county morgue was a first. Generator-powered mobile light towers turned the scene from night to day, so it was easy to spot Sheriff's Detective Bobby Chan finish off the last of a 7-Eleven hot dog as he arrived on-site. The smiling coroner didn't seem to mind that the deed was done in his own front yard, probably because he could walk from his office to the crime scene.

"Chan!" called out Detective Ron Franklin, who had been working the scene. He stood next to a sedan wrapped around a palm tree.

"Talk to me Ronnie; the wife won't," said Chan, approaching.

"You've been divorced for over five years, Chan."

"And she's still not talking to me. Go figure."

"Our dearly departed buddies here won't be doing much talking, either." Franklin was holding the dead men's wallets and waved them toward the bodies still in the car.

Chan looked in through a broken-out window. "Well, well, it's déjà vu all over again. The same two Russians we busted this afternoon. These guys have been working too hard. Stress can kill, you know."

"LAPD didn't even hold them overnight."

Chan shrugged. "If they had a clean record and a good lawyer, then it's 'Adios, see you in court.' The jails are overcrowded, no room for the bad guys anymore."

"This ties right into the Bennings investigation."

"It would seem so. These guys are shooters. They wanted to get him at the airport but missed. Then they tried again tonight, but Bennings *didn't* miss. Kind of makes me think the Russians pulled the hit in Chino Hills."

Franklin nodded. "But we still don't know what the beef is about."

"The stiffs here look all mobbed-up to me, so I guarantee it's something to do with money." Chan looked back to the dead Russians. "I'm going to tell the coroner that I'm reclassifying the death of Gina Bennings as a probable homicide. Looks like the Russian mob went after Major Bennings and his whole damn family."

"The registration address of both cars is a PO box in Beverly Hills. And the dead guys have identical residence addresses on their driver's licenses—a storefront in West Hollywood."

"Find out who their lawyer was that got them sprung so fast today. Might lead somewhere," said Chan.

"Hey, Bobby," warned Franklin as he took in the sight of two men with buzz cuts and wearing cheap dark suits approach.

"Remind me again," said Chan quietly to Franklin. "Is polyester in or out?"

"Excuse us, Detective Chan?" said the stocky one with a bald head.

"That's me," said Chan, eyeing the two men warily.

"We understand you're the lead investigator into the murders at the Bennings house in Chino Hills."

"And you are?"

"Agents Flood and Bates, U.S. Army Criminal Investigation Command." Bates, the stocky one, handed Chan a business card.

Bobby Chan held up the card into the light. "Seven Hundred and First Military Police Group, Field Investigative Unit." The two men definitely looked military and not like regular coppers to Chan. "What can I do for you?"

"We're looking for this man, Major Kitman Bennings." Flood

was a tall black man who didn't look a day over twenty-five. He handed Chan a color printout of Kit Bennings wearing his army uniform.

"Never met him. But I've seen his ass in gear." The soldiers looked confused. "I saw him run out of the international terminal at LAX this afternoon."

"So he eluded being taken into custody?" asked Flood.

"I didn't say that. I said I saw him run out of the terminal."

"Was he alone?" pressed Flood.

Chan stared at the agent and smiled. "Now don't go getting existential on me," said Chan. Flood and Bates exchanged a quick, confused look. "Alone in a crowd of thousands? Well, let's see; my partner and I were there, some Russian thugs were there. . . . Where were you guys, the wrong terminal?"

Flood and Bates looked like they were finally getting the idea that Chan was screwing with them. "Do you have any leads as to the major's location?" asked Bates.

"I'm rich with leads. Poor with time. So if you'll excuse me—"

"Did Major Bennings have anything to do with the killings here tonight?" asked Flood.

"Now that's a good question." Chan didn't elaborate.

"Sir, the clerk inside said Bennings left minutes before the shots were fired."

"The clerk inside heard shots?"

"He, well, no, he said—"

"You know, fellas, about twenty years ago I was on lunch break and stopped at my bank. Was it Wells Fargo? Wells Fargo sucks, but then, all of the big greedy banks suck. Anyway, I used to go there a lot because there was a real pretty Asian girl working as a teller. I mean, she was smoking. So . . . you know, I'd go in and get change for a quarter, whatever. It was pretty pathetic."

Bates and Flood both started shifting their feet and looking down.

"Anyway, one day, a few minutes after I left, the place was robbed by a guy with a shotgun. But I promise that even though I'd just left,

I didn't have anything to do with the armed robbery. I did marry the clerk, though."

"Sir, could you tell us . . . ?" Bates started to ask.

Chan looked at the business card again. "Quantico, Virginia, huh? You know, Franklin, almost nobody lives in Quantico, but the big marine base is there, the FBI Academy, FBI Lab, all kinds of important stuff there." Chan handed the card to Franklin, who pulled out his seven-inch tablet computer.

"What do you want Bennings for?" asked Chan.

"He's AWOL, sir."

"Really? Let's see, he's a defense attaché in Russia, he flies from Moscow to L.A., arriving here about three-thirty this afternoon. He's on leave because of a death in the family, and nine hours after he arrives he's AWOL?"

"That's right, sir."

"You boys flew all the way from Quantico to pick up a soldier who is obviously on leave, who you now say is AWOL? Why didn't a CID team just drive in from Fort Irwin? That's only ninety minutes from here."

Flood and Bates looked at each other but stayed silent.

"Sounds to me like something secret is afoot, Detective Franklin."

"Sounds that way," said Franklin.

"Want to explain to me what's really going on?" asked Chan to the army investigators.

"Sir, it's classified."

"Got it," said Franklin looking at his computer screen. He started to read, "Field Investigative Unit conducts investigations involving sensitive matters and other investigations of interest to senior army leadership requiring exceptional levels of discretion." Franklin looked to Chan.

"You two are just like the FBI guys that are investigating the kidnapping of Staci Bennings. It's all one way. You don't answer any of *my* questions, you don't tell *me* squat, you just want me to hand everything over to you. You two grunts want me to give you a person of interest in a murder investigation so you can bundle him onto some base where I don't have any access to him. Well, heck, yes, that sounds like a great deal to the San Bernardino County Sheriff's Department Homicide Unit, San Bernardino, California."

"Detective Chan, it would behoove you to—"

"Behoove your sorry asses out of my crime scene! Franklin! Escort these two no-neck imbeciles out of here and pass the word that nobody is to give them so much as directions to a slit trench."

Franklin stepped forward. Flood and Bates hesitated, then walked to their vehicle. Bobby Chan watched them go, then looked again at the photo of Kit Bennings that he held in his hand.

"Curiouser and curiouser."

CHAPTER 21

Dennis Kedrov's laptop alarm beeped. He'd been dozing in the backseat of the black Yukon parked under camo netting about one hundred yards from the bomb site. His laptop screen provided the only light in the vehicle, and the USGS, United States Geological Survey live earthquake Web site showed a readout of a real-time earthquake in the vicinity measuring 1.5. Not much of a quake, but big enough, so Dennis flicked on a flashlight and spotted the detonator. The unit was connected to an ultrathin wire that ran out the window and off into the darkness. He carefully picked up the detonator and pressed the button.

The earth rumbled and shook. It was too dark for him to see it, but dust shot several feet into the air all around the blast site. A depression in the soil of about six inches suddenly formed in a jagged, seventy-five-foot-diameter circle, with the bomb's location as the epicenter.

Under a partly cloudy sky with starlight filtering through in soft dollops of illumination, Dennis smiled as he retrieved as much of the detonation wire as he could. He quickly collapsed, folded, and stored the camouflage netting into the back of the Yukon, then drove away into the darkness.

·   ·   ·

The AT&T Global Network Operations Center in Bedminster, New Jersey, does exactly what its name suggests: it manages all aspects of the communications giant's global network. Over 140 large video screens comprise a massive, curved wall giving network managers 24/7 monitoring of all networks, including broadband, Internet, data, and telephony.

One of those wall-mounted screens suddenly depicted a flashing red light on a network route. The location was southwestern Wyoming.

A chiming alarm sounded at Georgia Anderson's workstation, snapping her out of a daydream that had something to do with a tall red-haired man she'd seen working out at her gym.

"Damn!" she said out loud, sitting up straighter in her chair and brushing hair away from her eyes.

Anderson quickly brought up multiple screens on the large flat-panel monitor at her sleek oak computer console. Her slim fingers flew over the keyboard, pausing only to place a headset boom mike on her head. She brought up pages showing color-coded graphed readouts of data traffic flow.

"What?" Georgia said aloud, to herself. She couldn't quite believe what she was seeing. She keyed in GPS coordinates and brought up the latest satellite imagery of the problem area. She saw nothing out of the ordinary but quickly checked a few other Web sites.

Georgia nervously pushed a telephone button to call an immediate supervisor, a man who had less time on the job than she did and who knew less than she did. "Ben, it's Georgia. I know you're seeing what I'm seeing, but I can confirm it's a complete break."

Georgia tried to rein in the anxiety in her voice but couldn't. This was big. No, *huge*. The biggest problem she'd ever handled and maybe the biggest she had heard of since she'd been working for AT&T. "The entire cable bundle must be severed...." She paused to listen to a question she couldn't answer. "I don't know how, but there was a small earthquake in the vicinity just before we lost all signal. I suggest you run this up the chain, quick, and contact Langley, the

White House, Fort Meade, DHS, and any other three-letter agency on your emergency-call-sheet list. Any affected agencies will probably want to divert their traffic onto our southern cable."

Almost breathless, Georgia nodded and pushed a button ending the call. She then went to work sending "STATUS RED" e-mail alerts out to supervisors of emergency repair crews and other technicians, with the exact GPS coordinates of the break. They would bust their butts to get on scene, ASAP. As she sent the e-mails, Georgia doubted that she'd have time to hit the gym and look for the red-haired guy anytime soon.

CHAPTER 22

Yulana Petkova slept soundly on a cot that had been placed in Interrogation Room #1 along with a few other items to make her "quarters" more comfortable. The lone surviving Russian thug pulled from the wrecked sedan by Buzz and Angel also slept soundly—on the floor of Interrogation Room #2.

At three-forty-five in the morning, Kit, Buzz, Angel, and Jen were all tired, but no one mentioned that as they fortified themselves with snacks in the conference room.

"The bad news is that our Russian friend in the other room has no idea where Staci is being held," said Angel.

"But he admitted he was part of the raid on your mom's house. He claims he's never met Popov but that he met Popov's nephew, Mikhail Travkin," said Buzz.

"I've already hacked into law enforcement databases. Travkin is clean. I'll have to dig deeper to see if there's something on the guy," said Jen, eating a chocolate donut with one hand as she swabbed down her keyboards with a cleaning wipe in her other hand. "But we already know his address, so that's good."

"How'd you get that?" asked Kit, perking up.

"The Russian we grabbed in the parking lot," said Angel, "has a hooker girlfriend who used to service Travkin at his condo on

Wilshire Boulevard in Westwood while the wife and kids were out shopping."

"Good work," said Kit, rubbing his eyes from exhaustion. If only he could have slept on the flight in from Moscow. "We move on Travkin tomorrow to get to Popov."

"We've already sketched out a plan," said Buzz, opening a folder.

"Before we get to that, I need to fill you in about Yulana." Kit recounted to them events at the coffeehouse and some of the other discussions he had with her, emphasizing that she was being blackmailed due to a kidnapped family member, the same as him.

"She's a black-projects scientist? She looks more like a fashion model," said Jen. "She's so pretty, I hate her."

"She could be lying about all of this," said Angel.

"You're right. She could be the best actress in the world and be selling me a bill of goods. But I don't think so. I asked her some very specific technical questions about EMP weapons as we drove back here a little while ago, and she answered them all accurately. In fact, she corrected me a few times."

"If what she says is true, then . . . ?" Buzz looked concerned as he chewed on the stem of his pipe.

"Then I'm thinking it's about an EMP bomb, Buzz. You guys remember hearing about those Red Team security exercises against supersensitive facilities that I ran a few years back?"

"I heard your team gained access to a navy facility that stored nukes," said Jen, smiling.

"We got into the facility, but not into the bunker where the nukes were. And we got into plenty of other places too. But we did it in a way that didn't embarrass the local security pukes or the generals or admirals in charge. I always made sure that most members of my team got captured, looking foolish. And we focused on follow-up training. We didn't want to tell them they were doing things wrong, but we tried to make them *see* what they were doing wrong."

"So what does that have to do with Popov?"

"Not many people know this, but my Red Team gained access to a storage building at Sandia National Labs in Albuquerque. That building was full of nonnuclear EMP and directed energy weapons."

Angel whistled a "holy cow" kind of whistle. "You actually got inside?"

Kit nodded. "We could have cleaned the place out, Angel. Taken whatever we wanted."

"EMPs—Yulana's specialty," said Jen.

The group shared serious looks all around.

"So your mission will be to steal an e-bomb from Sandia," said Buzz.

"That's the best guess I have right now. Otherwise, why does Popov need me?" asked Kit.

"Why would he need an e-bomb?" asked Jen.

"Maybe he wants to sell it," said Angel, twirling his green-handled screwdriver out of nervous habit. "Or he's doing this for the SVR or GRU because they want our technology."

"Popov has no loyalty to the Russian intelligence agencies. His biggest complaint in life is that he's a millionaire, not a billionaire. He's bitter that he didn't become one of the new oligarchs of Russia. He wants money and lots of it."

"But he won't become filthy rich selling one or two American EMP bombs," said Buzz.

"So how do you get rich *using* an e-bomb?" asked Angel, pointing the tip of his screwdriver at Kit.

"That, Angel, is the billion-dollar question."

Kit ordered everyone to sack out for a couple of hours in the bunk room. He then set up his laptop in the common room. Using Darknet software, he attached a digital photo of Yulana to an urgent encrypted message and sent it to a friend in D.C. still assigned to the Activity; he asked the friend to fly to Albuquerque *today* with certain sensitive equipment and other items and to personally bring it to a private mailbox address. Since the man was like a brother to Bennings, Kit knew the delivery would be made.

He reclined on a sofa in the common room, but sleep eluded

him. He spent a couple of minutes pressing the migraine pressure point on his hand; all of the recent stress and lack of sleep was like an invitation for a migraine to show up. Since meds didn't work for him, all he had was the acupressure to try and keep a migraine from kicking in. He got up and crossed over to the acoustic guitar he'd spotted earlier in a corner of the room. He quietly tuned it and then played a muted rendition of Sleepy John Estes's "Worried Life Blues."

As he plucked the strings, he thought of his mom, of Staci, of Rick and Maria Carrillo. For Staci's sake and in honor of the dead, he had to win, had to be the best he'd ever been, had to cover every base, every angle, had to become bigger and stronger and smarter than he'd ever been.

But something was bothering him, something lapping at his memory. What was it, what had he missed? A vague thought or notion, a suspicion about these recent events nagged at him like a pain that came and went, that the doctors couldn't identify. What were the questions that he should be asking that he wasn't? What was the obvious connection to Popov he hadn't yet made?

Bennings mentally hit rewind. As he relaxed and free-associated, a question popped to the forefront: How had Popov learned of his successful Red Team penetration of Sandia? Only about a dozen people in the world could link him to that.

Many of the pricey high-rise condo buildings on an exclusive stretch of Wilshire Boulevard in Westwood, California, have a helipad on the roof. But in one particular building, access to the two massive penthouses was gained only via a private elevator. Visitors first had to get past the discreetly armed guards—former LAPD officers—in the lobby. After being buzzed through a heavy security door, a private elevator awaited. The elevator was controlled by an operator in the penthouse security station.

Mikhail Travkin's condo took up one-half of the top floor, Viktor Popov's the other half.

The evening had been mostly social until a few hours earlier, when Popov and Travkin sat down to business, accompanied by plenty of food and drink.

Now, in the wee hours of the morning, with the penetrating scent of eucalyptus from the branches sitting in a plastic bucket full of water, Popov and Travkin lightly dozed as buxom young masseuses rubbed down both men in Popov's nearly authentic *banya*. Travkin called it a sauna, because he grew up in the United States, and a sauna was a sauna.

The soft chime from his small tablet phone awoke Mikhail. His thin lips curled into a snarl and he shook his head, squinting as he read a text message.

"Viktor, we must speak." Mikhail turned to the masseuses and gestured for them to leave.

"What now, Misha? I was just dreaming something lovely."

"Two of our men are dead, one is missing. At the morgue where Bennings's mother is."

"That's not good news," said Viktor sitting up.

"No, it isn't."

"Their orders were not to initiate contact with Bennings, not even to follow him. We don't need to follow him, just make their presence known. Did they disobey orders?"

"Unlikely. I made it very clear they were to take no action."

"So Bennings murdered them?"

"I believe so. Uncle, I have always taken your counsel, but this time, I ask that you take mine. We cannot afford this unwanted attention. Dead Russians point to us. Eventually, connections will be made by the authorities."

"It's not good, I'll go that far."

"That's not far enough to go. The FBI, the police, the army investigators are closing in on Bennings. What happens when they catch him? Do you really think he won't mention your name and that you kidnapped his sister?"

"Allegations are cheap, Mikhail. They can prove nothing."

"Correct, you and I personally have nothing to worry about. Our deceptions, however, are something else. I'm ordering a team to take them all out—Bennings, his friends, the Petkova woman. It would have been nice to use the major, but the risks have grown too high."

"We can still—"

"Uncle. The men are already in place. We can't risk the whole operation based on the belief that Bennings will deliver. We thought he would stay docile because we held his sister. I can only deduce he is more callous than his evaluation indicated. We *must* do this, Viktor, to secure what has long eluded you, what has been denied you. Forget Bennings, we have Doctor Rodchenko. The end result for us will be the same."

Mikhail had never stood up to Popov before, and Travkin could almost read his uncle's mind. This was a shift in their relationship. He watched closely, reading the irritation on Popov's face as the older man appeared to consider what this meant for their relationship.

"I have grown attached to the Bennings outcome, mainly because of its allure and because so much has gone into engineering events. But great generals must be flexible and be ready to pivot and change strategies as events dictate," said Viktor. After another moment of seeming reflection, he nodded his acquiescence. "I won't oppose your decision, Mikhail. Perhaps we have reached the end of the line with Major Bennings. But tell your men not to kill Petkova. She may still be useful."

"Thank you, Uncle," said Travkin, although he had no intention of telling his men to spare Yulana Petkova. Better they all died now.

CHAPTER 23

Bennings had been dozing on the sofa in the common room for less than ten minutes, with the guitar still in his lap, when a soft but shrill beeping from the alarm control panel in the communications room woke him. The alert was a proximity alarm. *Maybe a dog or a cat sniffing at the door?* But since you don't install expensive alarm systems to ignore them, he got up and crossed to the bank of CCTV security monitors in the small adjoining room.

In a flash he snapped alert, not quite believing what he saw. Men dressed in black and wearing balaclava masks stood at both the front and back doors. *SWAT? An FBI Special Response Team? CID?* The men quietly examined the door and doorframe, as if checking for alarms or the construction of the door itself.

Kit quickly checked monitors showing views of the front and rear parking lots. At least a dozen vehicles surrounded the shopping-center safe house. He estimated thirty or more men stood holding weapons in the predawn dimness. He zoomed in a camera and saw men in front of a dump truck, attaching something to the bumper. Check that; there were *two* dump trucks, front and back, and the items being attached to the bumpers were battering rams.

He zoomed in on a group of men, looked at their faces, jackets, and shirts. They were thugs. Russian mobster soldiers. And they were about to attack.

Bennings bolted into the bunk room, flipping on the lights. "Thirty Russians outside, ready to break down the doors! Grab only what you can carry including guns and ammo! We go up to the roof in half a minute. Move!"

Buzz, Angel, and Jen scrambled off their cots, instantly alert.

Kit still wore his holstered Kel-Tec Sub-2000, and he grabbed his day pack and bolted into the room where Yulana slept. He rousted her and stuck the barrel of a SIG SAUER .45 pistol against her forehead. She stared at him incomprehensibly, blinking aqua eyes as wide as saucers. "We're about to get hit by Popov's army. If you tipped them off, I promise I will slit your throat."

He pulled the Russian beauty to her feet, grabbed her purse, and dragged her out.

Buzz and Angel hustled into the hallway wearing packs and carrying HK MP7A1s. Kit joined them holding on to Yulana.

"Where's Jen?"

"Getting her laptops!"

The building shuddered as the loud crashing sounds of the two steel doors getting knocked from their hinges rang out a warning that the fight was on.

Kit thrust Yulana at Buzz. "Take her and get to the roof!" Kit spun and bolted back toward the common room.

Buzz and Angel both gave Yulana hard looks.

"I didn't tell anyone! How could I? I don't know where we are!" protested Yulana.

"You have come and gone a couple of times, and we haven't had you blindfolded. You could have seen street signs, the name of this shopping center," said Angel, grasping his green-handled screwdriver like an ice pick.

"You slipped away from Kit earlier tonight, didn't you? And called Popov," said Buzz.

"I didn't!"

"You lying bitch. If it wasn't for Kit, I'd kill you right now."

"Please do it!" She grabbed Angel's hand and brought the tip of the screwdriver to her throat. "Please! I beg you." Tears streamed down her face. "Because then Popov won't kill my baby," she cried.

Buzz grabbed her. "Listen to me! Did you get an inoculation before you came here? A shot somewhere in your body?"

"Yes, they said I had to for the U.S. visa. Right here," she wiped her eyes, then reached back to touch the area between her shoulder blades.

"Crap, she's been chipped!"

Angel spun her around and held her tight as he pulled down the back of her blouse.

"They told me there would be a bump for a week or so."

"There's a bump, all right. They injected you with a tracking device. This will hurt, so scream if you want," said Buzz.

Yulana whimpered but didn't scream as Buzz used his pocketknife to slice open her skin. He used the tip of the knife to pry out a tiny cylindrical device about a half inch long. He dropped it to the floor and crushed it with his boot.

Kit and Jen were in the common room, firing their suppressed weapons at Russians just outside the rear doorway, and at another group that had broken down the front door and now controlled the reception area.

Since the Russians also used suppressed weapons, it was a strangely quiet gun battle: bursts of soft *puffts,* followed by sounds of bullets shattering wood, plastic, and plaster and pinging off metal.

The gunfight might have been be a semisilent one, but the only question in Bennings's mind was how to pull off a retreat, and fast. Jen would have to make a break out into the open, exposed to cross fire from two sides just to get to his position at the entrance to the hallway. As he quickly slid a new magazine into the subgun, he silently berated himself for underestimating Popov's organizational reach and abilities. Kit had instantly become complacent in the CIA safe house, and as a result, was about to have his ass handed to him. Only hours earlier he'd told Yulana it wouldn't be easy to defeat the

Mafia don—an understatement to say the least—since he was right now fighting for his life and the lives of his friends.

Dimi, formerly a driver, had replaced Lily as operational leader of Popov's soldiers. Travkin had made the change after Popov ordered Lily demoted. It was a decision welcomed by the rank and file.

Dimi stood next to a black Yukon talking into a radio.

"We need flash bangs!" a man's voice pleaded.

"You need a pair of balls!" spat Dimi into his radio. He then gestured for more men to enter the building as he unwrapped a piece of bubble gum. "What are you waiting for, an invitation?" he yelled, and then popped the gum into his mouth. "Get in there!"

The fight in the common room intensified. A few Russians went down, but more of them streamed into the room.

"Jen, pull back, now!"

Kit laid down covering fire, holding the subgun with one hand and his SIG with the other, firing simultaneously in different directions as Jen fast-crawled toward the hallway. He stood, offering himself as a target, then fired a long burst. Bullets tore in all around him as Jen scrambled past. Once she was clear, he dove into the hallway, sprang to his feet, and reloaded while running for the storage-room door, half expecting to have his legs shot out from beneath him.

As Jen made it to the gray steel door, Kit spun around and fired at Russians who'd appeared at the hallway opening. The Russians ducked for cover, but as he turned to enter the storage room . . .

. . . the biggest Russian goon he had ever seen simply exploded through the hallway wall, splintering drywall and showering Kit with paint chips and dust. The goon teetered right next to him, having pulverized the wall between Kit and the reception room.

Bennings wheeled the subgun, but the goon grabbed Kit's gun hand in a viselike lock. As Kit raised his weak-side hand holding the SIG, the goon grabbed that hand too. The man was incredibly strong and slammed Kit's body against the wall, then pressed in close. His huge hands clamped harder around Kit's hands and started moving both gun barrels toward Kit's head.

The Russian's plan was easy to fathom; he was going to force Kit to shoot himself with his own guns.

Bennings glanced down the hallway; a couple of thugs had taken aim, waiting for the outcome of the grappling contest he now found himself in with the Russian poster boy for steroid abuse. Sweat broke out on his forehead as he looked his maniacal assailant in the eye; it was like looking into a soul of pure murderous lust. It reminded him of the look on the face of the woman who had broken his sister's bones.

Staci. Staci's favorite martial art was aikido. She was so good at avoiding his attacks when they sparred together, he used to bust up laughing. He could almost hear her voice say, "Merge with the momentum of the attacker rather than resisting, then redirect the force."

Aikido while pinned to a wall? Why not? thought Kit, so he instantly relaxed the resistance in his arms, allowing the goon's force to point the gun barrels at his head. But this change in physical dynamic was a feint, and Kit then pivoted his strong wrists sharply, causing the gun barrels to change direction, as he pulled both triggers.

Rounds shattered the front teeth of the goon, then tore into his brain. Bennings squeezed his eyes closed against a spray of spittle and tooth chips and blood as he shoved off from the giant, then he hosed the hallway with suppressing fire. The storage door opened behind Kit; Jen had come looking for him.

Russian thugs returned fire, but most of their rounds only found the body of the giant who swayed unsteadily, still on his feet even though he was already dead.

Jen grabbed Kit by his upper arm, pulled him into the storage room, and slammed closed the gray steel door just as rounds impacted on the other side. She tripped the door lock.

Bennings was dripping with sweat and breathing heavily. "Damn, we're getting our asses kicked," he said.

"I dunno, looked to me like you nailed that big guy."

"Close enough for government work," said Kit, who weakly managed a wink.

Jen started up the ladder.

"I left them a special surprise," she called down. "So get your butt up here, quick."

Bennings didn't need to be asked twice. He hurried up the escape ladder into a dim attic space. Faint light filtered in from a hatch that led to the flat roof. He retracted the ladder and pulled up the ceiling panels, closing them and erasing evidence of their escape route.

He clambered onto the roof, and Jen helped him close and lock the hatch. Buzz, Angel, and Yulana, barely visible in the first light of dawn a hundred yards ahead of them on the roof, were running in a low crouch. The exterior walls of the structure came up four feet higher than roof level, keeping them out of sight of anyone on the ground as long as they stayed low.

He and Jen exchanged a look, then took off running.

Dimi hustled into the safe house, where his men were busy searching the place. He moved toward the gray steel door and watched as some men used pry bars on the door. He was about to say something when other men ran up with sledgehammers and went to work.

Just then, the Russian who was taken prisoner from the morgue parking lot was brought to him, still in handcuffs.

"Dimi! Get me out of these cuffs."

Dimi glanced down at the handcuffs. There was no warmth in his voice when he asked, "What did you tell the Americans?"

"Nothing! What could I tell them? I don't know anything!"

"Everybody knows something." Dimi turned to another thug. "Put him in the Yukon."

Dimi turned to look as the gray steel door gave way. Men charged in to find . . . an empty storage room. "Dimi!" one of them called.

Dimi hurried into the room and cursed. "Look for false walls, trapdoors! Everywhere! Quickly! This is taking too much time!" He looked to the ceiling and fired a burst into the ceiling tiles. "Check up there too! Hurry!"

Dimi crossed back into the hallway and grabbed a man. "There's an empty business next door. Take most of the men and check," said Dimi. The man ran off, ordering others to follow him.

Dimi scanned the common room and saw a large laptop sitting on the coffee table. He reached for it.

Kit and Jen made it to the opposite end of the roof of the L-shaped shopping center. Running in a crouch for a long distance can make one remember forgotten muscles, and the remembrance isn't a particularly fond one. Kit looked over the edge of the wall and saw that Buzz, Angel, and Yulana had already dropped down on a rope ladder and were getting into the white van parked just below.

Jen looked at her watch. "Boom."

Just then, a tremendous explosion ripped the dawn. They felt the building shake under them.

"You rigged the Semtex left behind by the CIA?" asked Kit.

She nodded grimly. "I didn't like the way they woke us up," said Jen, and it didn't sound like she was joking.

They chanced a peek over the top of the facade wall and saw that the entire end of the shopping center that held the safe house had been demolished; smoke and dust rose, rubble rained down.

Fifteen or twenty Russians had been knocked to the ground just outside the blast area. Anyone who'd been inside was now south of the frost line.

"We could take out a few more of those bastards," said Jen, hoisting her MP7.

"Every cop in the county will be here in minutes. Let's go. Popov wins this round."

CHAPTER 24

Louis Kraminski, the bearded, seventy-two-year-old longtime manager of Wheels Up Aviation at Chino Airport, ate breakfast at Flo's Airport Café every working day of his life. Flo's was kind of a classic Southern California greasy spoon; if Louis didn't feel like Salisbury steak, he'd get the huevos rancheros. A lifelong aviation nut, he'd arrive like clockwork at 6:45 A.M., and at 7:30 he'd leave Flo's and make his way through a security gate to get onto the airport proper and open the doors for business.

Over six hundred aircraft were based at Chino, which is a somewhat historic, general-aviation reliever airport serving private, business, and corporate tenants. Wheels Up owned and maintained six executive jets. A collection of other aircraft owned by the Bennings and Carrillo families were flown less frequently. The business model was simple: corporate or private clients would call to book a jet to their chosen destination. Wheels Up provided the jet and arranged for a pilot and any additional crew to staff the plane. Business had been good.

But now . . . the airport gossip had been so thick, what with the FBI and sheriff's and army investigators nosing around after the murders of the Carrillos and the disappearance of Staci Bennings, that Louis felt almost sick to his stomach. The Carrillos and Bennings and

Wheels Up Aviation had been his family for more than twenty-five years, since his wife had passed away from breast cancer at age forty-five. But today he wasn't at all sure what to do, especially if Staci Bennings didn't return soon.

Louis trudged out of Flo's at 7:33. As he crossed the asphalt parking lot toward his pickup, a horn honked. A man with a gray-haired buzz cut waved at him and stopped his white van just feet away. "Louis!" said Buzz Van Wyke from behind the wheel, smiling, like he was greeting an old friend.

"Morning," said Louis taking a step toward the van. Lots of clients remembered Louis, but it wasn't always so easy to remember all of the clients.

The driver lowered his voice. "I've got a message for you from Kit."

Louis registered surprise, then shuffled up to the van, a bit wary. "And who would you be?"

"He's a good friend, Louis," said Kit crouched down behind Buzz. Kit and Louis could see each other through a small space between the driver's seat and the window.

"Kit, are you okay?" asked Louis, excitedly stepping closer to the van.

"I'm fine."

"I'm so sorry about what happened to your mom and sister, Rick and Maria. . . ."

"We'll all get through this. Don't worry."

"The police, the feds searched the facility, like we're some kind of criminals. They come every day. They're watching the company. Probably there now."

"Just ignore them. But right now, I need your help," said Kit.

"Name it."

"You know the business as well as anyone. Open every day and run things as best you can."

"Okay."

"As soon as Julio comes in this morning, have him gas up the twin Cessna and tow it over to Dave Tallichet's old hangar. Tell him to put it inside, that Mike Matthews is going to borrow it to fly to Cable Airport. You got it?"

"Got it."

"Sorry to ask you to lie to Julio, but you can't let him or anyone else know you saw me and that I'm taking the plane. Okay?"

"Okay. But Kit, what about Staci?" pleaded Louis. Louis had been looking after Staci like he would his own daughter for the last several years. "Kit, I'm so worried about her I can't sleep."

"She's alive. And I'm going to find her. I promise you that."

"There's the old man," said CID Agent Flood, watching through binoculars as Louis Kraminski unlocked the doors to Wheels Up Aviation. Flood polished off the last of a maple donut, then found a paper napkin in the messy rented sedan.

Kraminski's cell phone and the company phone lines and e-mails were being monitored, without a court order, thanks to Flood's buddy in the NSA. The same cyber-spook had taps on other phone lines, including Detectives Bobby Chan's and Ron Franklin's. And minutes earlier, the contents of Chan's work computer had been e-mailed to the CID agents. Agent Bates was right now examining Chan's case files.

Bates looked up from his laptop as other Wheels Up employees followed Louis inside. Bates sniffed. "You know what it smells like in here?"

"Donuts?"

"No. Ass."

"Well, that would be your ass, not mine," said Flood.

"So what do you think about this aviation connection? Maybe Wheels Up was ferrying dope for the Russian mob and they had a falling out?"

"Makes sense to me. The Russians got screwed over, so they decided to kill everyone connected to the company. That's how Russians operate."

"So what's with Bennings and the Russian chick from Moscow?"

Flood shrugged. "Maybe she works for a different mob."

Bates nodded as he checked his computer. "Your NSA pal just sent me an audio file. From the tap on the Bennings house."

"But no one's in the house," said Flood.

"Answering machine, remember? Somebody left a message."

Flood and Bates had already conducted an extensive illegal search of the home in Chino Hills. Bates opened the file and played it once, then turned the volume up all the way and replayed it. The voice was just barely audible: "Las Vegas, south of the Rio and Palms, third-floor apartment or hotel. A dump. Help, Las Vegas . . ."

The two agents looked at each other. "Could that be Bennings's sister?" asked Flood.

Bates reached for his cell phone and punched in a number.

A small convoy of AT&T utility trucks and repair vehicles snaked their way on a dirt track toward the blast site in Wyoming north of Interstate 80.

The lead pickup truck was driven by the crew's foreman, Chuck McNair, and he skidded his vehicle to a stop when he saw the seventy-five-foot-diameter depression in the ground.

McNair put on his hard hat and walked to the edge of the depression. Soon other men joined him.

"Damn, what do you make of this?" asked McNair to no one in particular.

"Somethin' like a sinkhole," said a worker.

"Sinkhole?" said Danny Jones, a lanky technician with a mocking tone. "I didn't work as an EOD guy in Iraq, but that looks to me like something blew up underground. Like some bomb was buried and they blew it."

"Who's 'they'?" asked the worker.

"Hell, how do I know?" asked Jones. "The Taliban? I mean, crap, take a look. The main northern fiber-optic communications cable is toast. Who would do that except terrorists?"

"Okay, just everybody settle down. We don't know that a bomb went off." McNair started to take cell-phone snaps of the depression, then quickly sent them onward over his phone.

The 1969 Cessna 401A holding five occupants taxied within one hundred yards of CID agents Flood and Bates, who sat parked outside a steel hangar at Chino Airport. The army investigators had no idea Kit Bennings was the plane's pilot. No flight plan had been filed and the transponder was switched off. Bennings had even refused to tell his team where they were going and why. Three and a half hours later, the Cessna touched down at Moriarty Municipal Airport outside of Albuquerque, New Mexico.

The Albuquerque safe house was a vacation rental near Kirtland Air Force Base that had been hastily arranged by Kit over the Internet during the flight in. Two Nissan Pathfinders, rented using a phony name but a working credit card, sat parked in the driveway.

By about two in the afternoon, Kit, Buzz, Angel, Jen, and Yulana had stashed what little gear they had left and reconvened in the living room. They all looked exhausted.

"Okay, we're here in Albuquerque, but why are we here, since Popov and Travkin are in Los Angeles?" asked Jen.

"Because Sandia is here, right, boss?" asked Angel.

"Popov has yet to explain what he wants Kit to do." Buzz chewed on his pipe, thinking, then looked to Yulana.

She shrugged. "I don't know why we're here, either, but the mountains are beautiful."

"So I guess it's unanimous," said Buzz. "Why did we come here?"

Before Kit could answer, his phone rang, startling him.

"That's not your sterile phone ringing. Do you have another phone?" asked Jen.

"That's my satellite phone." He checked the incoming number . . . *Staci!* "It's Staci's sat phone calling."

Kit signaled to the group. They all saw the anticipation on his face and fell silent. He answered and put the call on speaker.

"Go ahead," said Kit.

Silence on the other end, then . . .

"You are no longer needed. Your participation has ended. Should you or your friends do anything in a public way, any more killings, attacks, any action that draws attention from the authorities, I will kill your sister without hesitation. If you so much as get a parking ticket, she's dead. Go to ground, hide, hunker down, whatever you want to call it. Stand down or she dies, and I mean she dies horribly. Do you understand?" said Viktor Popov.

"It was *you* who attacked *me* this morning, General." Kit practically spat out the words with venom. "And you accuse me of bringing attention from the authorities? You order *me* to stand down?!"

"If you want to see—"

"Shut up, you pathetic old man! You call me using my sister's phone because you think that will intimidate me, make me afraid for her safety? *Sosi hui, dolboeb,*" spewed Kit, with utter contempt. *Suck my d***, f***head.* "If anything happens to my sister, if anyone so much as *touches* her from this moment on, I guarantee that you and your nephew, Mikhail Travkin, Travkin's wife, Natalie, and his children, Petra and Ivan, your wife, your children, your children's children, all of your soldiers, all of the computer geeks working out of those big RVs, and your analysts and special operators, like the people who robbed the armored truck . . . *all* of them will be killed. You and your family will be hunted to the ends of the earth by me or by others loyal to me, and your deaths will be brutally cruel." Kit said it with a hate, a rage, a vehemence that came from a very dark place within him.

"I know what you want, Popov. I tortured Yulana into talking before I killed her. You want me to steal an EMP device from Sandia National Labs. That would be easy for me to do. Which model do you want?" Silence on the line. "Which one?!" demanded Kit.

"An RT-Seven," said Popov.

"I could easily get an RT-Seven, so maybe we'll make a trade. But let me think about it. Oh, and don't call me. I'll call you."

Kit hung up. He let out a big exhale, and everyone just stared at one another. No one spoke for about a minute.

"Just to clarify, I would never harm a hair on the head of any wives or family members or innocents. But *he* would—look what he did to my mom and to Staci. So I talked strong to get his attention, using the kind of threats he would use if he were in my position."

"Yeah, we understand that. But, Kit . . . he said you were out, that he didn't need you. That means he has an alternate plan," said Buzz.

"Could he have one of the old Russian EMP bombs?" asked Angel.

"Or maybe," Yulana said, "he has built one. It's possible to do it cheaply. If Popov has a weapons scientist, he could easily construct one. But it would likely be crude, not precise, and do more damage over a wider area."

"Kit, it sounds like Popov was dead set on using you to steal an RT-Seven e-bomb, but you became so troublesome and problematic, he decided to move ahead without you," said Buzz.

"We still have to stop him," said Angel.

"*Someone* has to stop him." Jen looked troubled.

"What do you mean, Jen?" asked Kit.

"We've just flown eight hundred miles away from a guy who most likely has an e-bomb, and who could detonate it at any minute. And we don't know the target. I hate to say it, but we need to consider getting some agencies engaged in this."

"You're absolutely right," said Kit. "I'll call Padilla and brief her on most everything that has happened, leaving your names out of it. I'll ask her to immediately get all of the appropriate agencies involved."

"Where does that leave *us*?" asked Angel.

"Out of a job," said Kit. "Buzz, Angel, Jen, I owe you a debt that will be hard to repay. But here is where we part company. One of the reasons I flew us all here was to get you three away from a number of crime scenes and an army of Russian killers. We are all very lucky to be alive after what happened at the safe house."

"But we're just getting started! We need to go after Travkin," groused Angel.

"Angel, I'm so far off the reservation, the Feds may decide to wipe me. You three can simply no longer be involved with what I'm doing. You could lose your careers, be sent to jail, or worse.

"Yulana and I have loved ones being held hostage, so the stakes are different for us. I was hoping to find Staci first." Kit looked downward and his voice choked a bit. "But I'll proceed under the assumption that the Russians won't harm her any further. Popov will take my threat seriously, at least until I'm dead."

The choices and circumstances were rotten, and the looks on the faces of Buzz, Angel, and Jen reflected that.

"Regardless of what the Feds will do, Yulana and I are going to steal an RT-Seven from Sandia. I'll set up a trade with Popov, except it won't be a trade, it'll be a trap."

Kit's team exchanged concerned, skeptical glances; they clearly disagreed with him on this point.

"You're going to ask the secretary of state's permission to steal a device?" asked Buzz.

"No. I won't even beg forgiveness after I steal it."

"Boss, that kind of crime gets someone locked up forever, regardless of how good the intentions might have been," said Angel.

"Stealing an EMP weapon would be crossing a whole different kind of line. Even if you got Staci back, the SECSTATE couldn't protect you. You'd never see another day of freedom," said Jen.

"And if I don't try, neither will Staci."

CHAPTER 25

Mikhail Travkin stood with his uncle Viktor Popov on a corner terrace of Mikhail's penthouse apartment, above the tantalizing backdrop of billions of dollars' worth of West Los Angeles real estate. Traffic on the streets below had shifted into gridlock afternoon rush-hour mode.

"All of my fears about how this could go wrong have been realized," carped Mikhail, pacing on the expensive outdoor carpeting. He internally berated himself for a series of blunders, and almost all of the mistakes had to do with his not standing up to his uncle on key decisions.

"All of your fears? What do you know of fear?"

"He knows about our entire organization. The hackers, the analysts." In Travkin's analytical mind, the percentage for success had taken a hit.

"He doesn't know locations," said Viktor.

"He'll find out! He mentioned killing my wife and children and he knows their names! He knows that you wanted him to steal an EMP device! How has he learned so much so quickly?"

"Calm down and forget about him for now. Don't answer if he calls. When we're ready, we'll talk to him. We can contract out his murder to the Haitians or a biker gang or—"

"Uncle, if he alerts the police or the FBI, the whole deception is not worth pursuing."

"With what proof, what evidence can he give them? And he has no credibility; he's a wanted man! Perhaps we can plant a large amount of cocaine at the aviation company in Chino. The police will easily convince themselves these killings were about a drug feud and that Bennings is more dirty than they already suspected."

"He doesn't need proof. Can't you see that? All of the fingers would point to us if an e-bomb is detonated, and the full weight of the American system will crush us!"

"No, because we'll be in Russia by then. When Bennings calls back, we set up a trade—his sister for the RT-Seven. After we have it, they will both be killed."

"Please forget about the American bomb!"

"I can't! If you're going to fly over the Alps, do you want to do it in a Gulfstream Five, or in an ultralight plane you built in your backyard? Dennis will soon be in Las Vegas. After he certifies the operation there, send him to Albuquerque with his best men."

"Have you lost your mind? Everything you propose is high risk, high profile."

"Everything *I* propose?! Was it me who ordered thirty men to kill Bennings this morning?! It was your idea, your order, and you failed in the worst possible fashion! Don't make me do something unpleasant, Nephew. I take your counsel from time to time. I don't take your orders. I am the don, this is my *maskirovka,* and we will proceed as I say."

Mikhail looked for a long time at his uncle and then blinked. Mikhail was smart and ruthless, but he'd known too much privilege. He knew very well that he'd never had to fight for what was his; not really. And was he really going to have to fight his uncle? Because . . . had Viktor forgotten? This elaborate deception, potentially the greatest theft the world will have ever seen, had been his idea. *Mikhail Travkin's brainchild!* The largest theft, monetarily, in the history of mankind, was within easy grasp. And the most elegant heists are those where the victim doesn't even know they've been robbed!

My God, they stood on the threshold of a staggering criminal achievement, a crowning glory to Viktor Popov's career that Mikhail had gifted to his uncle, the man who, in spite of his callous, imperious nature, had been amazingly good to him, had made him who he was today.

The names Popov and Travkin would be regarded as demigods by their fellow *vor v zakone*. They'd become . . . untouchable.

But here Viktor was now claiming the deception was his idea and not Mikhail's. Why? Why would he do that? So he could justify not having to listen to anyone else? Holy Jesus, Viktor had become so blinded to an outcome that he couldn't see he'd taken a wrong turn.

Perhaps his uncle had made him what he was today, but as Travkin looked at the old man, he realized it would be up to himself to make whatever it was he would become tomorrow. Decisions faced him, decisions that could not be made with a calculator or by constructing an elegant algorithm.

Mikhail's mouth felt dry and he swallowed, but the taste was not good.

"It has always been my plan to permanently relocate back to Russia after we explode the device," said Popov. "That won't be so bad, considering the billions we'll make."

Mikhail didn't look so sure about anything anymore. "You often cautioned me, Uncle, not to spend my money before I made it."

Mikhail watched as Viktor stopped short and regarded him with a penetrating glare. "Perhaps your tone of caution is wise, Mikhail." There was a long silence as the two men stared at each other. "Let us be cautious: send all of the technical people—the analysts, the hackers—on flights to Moscow immediately. *Immediately!* And you, your wife and children too."

Travkin looked at Popov for a long beat. This was not the time to fight. Perhaps there was another way. "Yes, Uncle."

Buzz squinted into the late-afternoon sun as he piloted the twin Cessna 401A on the flight toward California. Angel dozed in the right seat, while Jen sat in the back checking out the contents of her backpack.

Kit had asked them to leave the plane at a friend's hangar at Montgomery Field in San Diego, then fly back to their homes before more trouble ensued. Instead, the three of them, once they were airborne, had decided to fly to Van Nuys Airport in L.A.'s San Fernando Valley and look into how they could track Viktor Popov through Mikhail Travkin.

As Jen inventoried her backpack, she found two of Kit's cell phones: the one given to him in Moscow by Popov's men (the one she had hoped to put a trace on) and Kit's old U.S. cell phone. The batteries and SIM cards had been taken out of both phones so they couldn't be triangulated and used to locate Kit. Bennings still had one of the new sterile phones they were all using, and he had his encrypted sat phone.

Jen, Buzz, and Angel all wore headsets so they could talk to one another in the noisy compartment.

"Buzz, what's our approximate location?"

"Coming up on Prescott, Arizona, why?"

"I've got Kit's old cell phone. If I turn it back on, maybe we could lead anyone trying to find him in the wrong direction. Then toss it out of the plane before we get to L.A."

"Good idea."

The intercom had awoken Angel, and he turned around and watched from the front as Jen slipped the battery into Kit's phone and booted it up. A window popped up showing there were several new text messages, so Jen clicked to view them. The very first message she checked was the one sent from Staci Bennings in Las Vegas.

Jen's eyes went wide as she read. "Holy cow!"

"What is it?" asked Angel.

"A text message to Kit that you're not going to believe," she said, handing him the phone.

Angel read the text carefully: "Vegas S of Rio/Plms nr Strip 3fl 2Russ hrry Stci. dnt rspnd." He looked at Jen in disbelief, then read his interpretation of the text aloud. "Las Vegas, south of the Rio and Palms Casinos. Near the Strip. Third floor. Two Russians. Hurry. Staci. Don't respond." He handed the phone to Buzz, who quickly scanned the text.

"Ladies and gentlemen, this is the captain," said Buzz. "Brace for a change of course."

Buzz banked the plane sharply to the north and increased air speed to maximum.

The call to Secretary of State Margarite Padilla could have gone worse. Bennings sold her on his version of events, leaving out key facts and any mention of the participation of Buzz, Angel, Jen, or the navy SEALs. He glossed over the smoke-bomb diversion at LAX saying that no one had been hurt. He parsed his words carefully and truthfully insisted that he had nothing to do with the explosion in El Monte and that he was running for his life when the building blew. He admitted killing the men at the morgue in self-defense.

Bennings argued that facts suggested Popov intended to use a Russian-made e-bomb for some unknown purpose on an unknown target.

He urged her to convince the FBI to apprehend Mikhail Travkin at his Wilshire Boulevard condo and to raid all businesses known to be owned or controlled by Popov. Lastly, he maintained that Yulana Petkova was not a spy and that he wouldn't be turning her or himself in, just yet, in spite of the secretary's insistence.

He knew his revelations constituted mostly bad news and put Padilla into a tougher position than he'd already put her in. But at least armed thugs weren't trying to shoot her dead. Padilla was a smart lady and a seasoned D.C. insider. She'd survive. He wasn't so sure about himself. The nagging notion that he'd finally bit off more than he could chew and was on something of a suicide mission had become a thought that he couldn't shake.

Detective Bobby Chan and a uniformed sheriff's deputy stood in the bottom of a deeply shaded arroyo just off Carbon Canyon Road. Small pieces of wreckage from Gina Bennings's car lay strewn around the slope.

"The front end was wedged right here," said the deputy, pointing to an indentation in the soil.

Chan took short steps, walking slowing, scanning carefully. He used a SureFire LED flashlight like a searchlight over the dirt.

After watching Chan for over ten minutes, the deputy finally spoke up. "What is it you're looking for?"

"Whatever doesn't belong," said Chan.

Chan stopped and looked up. He scanned the steep bank of the arroyo leading up to the road. A patch of white caught his eye.

The deputy saw it, too. "Plastic grocery bag?"

"I don't think so," said Chan.

Chan climbed the grade, not the easiest thing for a heavy guy with bad knees to do. He stood over the object, then carefully used tweezers to pick up a white cotton glove. The deputy climbed up next to him.

"Would any of the first responders have been wearing cotton gloves? Or the coroner's staff or anybody?"

"Hell, Detective, you know the answer to that is 'negative.' Not cotton gloves."

"Just wanted to hear someone else say it." Chan placed the glove into a plastic evidence bag and winced from the pain in his knees—college football injuries—as he climbed out of the arroyo into the soft light of late afternoon. Traffic ran heavy as commuters made their way home.

Chan got to his unmarked vehicle just as Ron Franklin pulled up and bailed out of his unit.

"Bobby, get this. That big explosion in El Monte this morning? The Feds are covering something up. Word is there was a big shoot-out and a bunch of Russians got blown to pieces."

"Well, well. But no word on Bennings?"

"Nothing." Franklin noticed the evidence bag Chan held. "Find something down there?"

"I remain ever hopeful. The crime scene techs found long blond hairs in the Bennings house. And this is a small glove, maybe for a female. I'll bet whoever wore this did some sweating. Check the DNA in this against those blond hairs."

"Sounds like a long shot."

"At least it's a shot." Chan looked over at the traffic-choked Car-bon Canyon S turn. "You know, since we're so close, let's take one more look at the house."

Chan and Franklin spotted two men in a sedan on stakeout near the Bennings house. The detectives boxed in the car with their own units and ordered the men out of their car, even though the pair in dark suits had shown their CID ID. All four men stood in the street.

"Where are your two buddies from Quantico—Flood and Bates?"

"Las Vegas," said the shorter CID agent, without thinking. His partner gave him a "shut up" stare.

"Why'd they go to Vegas?"

Both CID men remained silent. Off Chan's sly gesture, Franklin began playing the role of the good cop. "Look, we've turned up some new intelligence. We're willing to share, if you'll give us something in return."

The CID guys both smirked. "You don't have anything we need," said the shorter one with the loose mouth.

Chan got a funny feeling from the remark and their attitude in general. He pulled out his phone like he was going to make a call, then peered through the open driver's window. A manila folder thick with files sat on the seat. A printed report on top of the folder caught Chan's eye. He leaned in through the open window and read a few lines of copy . . . and recognized the words.

They were *his* words.

Angry, Chan flung open the driver's door. . . .

"Hey, you can't go in there!" said the shorter agent as he grabbed Chan's arm.

It happened so fast, Franklin wasn't sure he saw it. All 285 pounds of Bobby Chan went into fast motion, and within seconds, both CID men lay sprawled on the pavement.

"Cuff them," he growled.

Chan retrieved the files from the vehicle. In it were copies of all of the reports Chan had generated on the case. "They have all of our reports, Ronnie. Every last one of them. And some stuff from my computer that I've never shown anyone."

"What?!" exclaimed Franklin as he finished handcuffing the men.

And then Chan saw something else. Transcripts.

"Seems they've been listening to all of our phone calls too. Including calls we made to friends and family." He held out a transcript for Franklin.

Franklin flashed angry. As he took a step toward Chan, he "accidentally" slammed his foot into the face of the shorter CID agent. "Oh, sorry."

He grabbed the transcript, then "accidentally" slammed his foot into the face of the second CID man. "Wow, sorry. I am so clumsy today."

The two detectives stood there reading as the CID agents lay bleeding on the street.

"Gambling junket coming," said Chan as he read a transcript.

The black detective looked at Chan for clarification.

"Staci Bennings is being held prisoner in Las Vegas."

CHAPTER 26

Cautiously emerging from a crushing housing, jobs, and economic collapse that hit it harder than virtually any other municipality in the United States, Las Vegas was growing again. And the only viable direction left in which to grow was southward. So the number of empty parcels of land on South Las Vegas Boulevard all the way down to South Pointe Hotel and Casino were diminishing rapidly.

Near the Antique Mall of America, sprawling new four-story condo complexes painted in earth tones blended in well with the windswept desert that was never far off.

A corner property near Agate Avenue looked ripe for development. The boarded-up one-story cinder-block motel with a metal A-frame roof sat far back from the street, its asphalt parking lot crumbling and overgrown with weeds. A high chain-link fence with padlocked gates surrounded the U-shaped structure. Surely the old abandoned eyesore would be removed and something modern and attractive and functional would emerge, although there seemed to be no activity at this site.

No visible activity, anyway.

It was still daylight when Dennis Kedrov had finished settling into his room. He entered the chow hall that had been feeding three meals a day to thirty men for the last three months: construction

workers, security, IT technical specialists, and Dr. Nikoli Rodchenko and his two assistants. One wing of the motel housed the
workers; the other wing comprised Rodchenko's lab and the tunneling operation.

So, in classic *maskirovka* fashion, a very old, modest, and seemingly condemned structure fronted for a very sophisticated operation.

Dennis, the leader of Popov's Special Operations Group, was in
Las Vegas for only one night before heading to Albuquerque, but he
wanted to have fun, so he toasted the blue-collar workers at dinner
with bottles of Russian Standard he'd brought with him. Smiling as
always, his already rosy cheeks now bright red from the vodka flush,
he joked with the men easily as he toyed with his yellow golf ball. The
workers' tasks were finished, and later tonight a bus would drive
them back to Los Angeles and their regular jobs working in Popov-
owned construction companies.

Dennis made his way to the table where Dr. Rodchenko and his
team sat.

"All is well, Doctor?"

"Yes, yes. The device is operational. There's nothing left for me to
do until you people are ready to act."

"Good."

"Please tell the truth: How much longer? We have been held like
prisoners here, not even allowed to go outside."

"Once I certify that everything is ready, the call might come any
time. So please be patient and stay rested."

Dennis smiled, rose from the table, and gestured to the IT specialists to follow him outside, past an armed guard. He looked up
into the diffused light of sunset as the group walked across the
open area to the other wing of the old motel complex.

Dennis walked through a door that had once led to a motel
room but now opened into a large gutted area of the structure. The
roof and exterior walls remained, but interior walls from half a dozen
motel rooms had been ripped out, and the big space was now filled
with generators, tunneling equipment, tools, and dirt. Lots of dirt.
Small front loaders had moved out most of the soil from the tunnel-

ing operation and spread it out onto the four-acre plot behind the motel. This work had been done only at night, using heavy equipment that had special mufflers installed, thus creating almost no noise.

A thin woman in her forties with dark circles under her eyes showed Dennis the seven-foot-diameter hole that dropped down thirty feet into rock-hard earth. A small steel ladder bolted to the side of the hole led to the bottom. Communications, electrical, and other cables ran from equipment in the complex into the hole and tunnel beyond.

The woman didn't speak, just gestured for Dennis to descend into the hole. He did so without hesitation.

In moments he was at the bottom and followed the cabling into a small lighted tunnel, crawling on all fours. There was only enough room for one person to move in one direction at a time, and an uneasy feeling of claustrophobia enveloped him as he crawled the eighty-yard length of the passageway.

Finally emerging into an eight-by-eight-foot space large enough to stand in, Dennis shook hands with Alex Bobrik, a wiry, bespectacled engineer about fifty years old. "Sorry to keep you waiting, Alex."

"Welcome to the underworld," said Alex, smiling.

Dennis glanced around the small room carved from the ground. An ice chest, toolboxes, laptops in hard cases, and shiny aluminum crates were stacked neatly in the space. Dennis noticed cabling was wound onto small wooden spools, a telephone handset attached to a thin line, and a bucket with the lid sealed that functioned as a toilet.

"So this is all of the equipment you will need?"

"Yes. We have already taken everything inside several times and practiced positioning it for the actual event. Then we brought it back here. So we are ready and now just standing by. Would you like to see the room?"

"Just to look inside, not to go in. So I can assure the boss we are complete."

Three walls of the room they stood in were dirt; the fourth wall was poured cement, meaning they had tunneled right up to the exterior wall of some underground structure.

"We used a concrete saw to cut out this doorway," said Alex. He pointed to a small panel, about three by three, with two handles attached to it. Alex bent down and easily pulled the panel out of the cement wall. Suddenly, a flood of cool air scented with ozone filled Dennis's nostrils. The hum of machinery murmured in the super-still air.

"The panel is made of wood but painted to look like cement to fool any workers on the other side. It's not a perfect ruse, but since the room is dim and seldom inspected, we should have no problems," said Alex as he stood up.

Dennis got down on his hands and knees and peered through the small opening into the room beyond.

"Beautiful," he said.

Less than seven miles away on West Tropicana, CID Agents Flood and Bates walked out of the office of Siegel Suites. No Russian-sounding names were on the guest register, and the manager and front-desk clerks were fairly certain that no one with a Russian or European accent had checked in recently. The names connected to the dozens of third-floor units in multiple buildings got extra scrutiny. And no one had recognized the eight-by-tens of Staci Bennings that the agents showed them. So the CID boys had no idea they stood about fifty yards from her location.

"What now?" asked Flood.

Las Vegas police detectives were already helping to check the hundreds of possible third-floor units in the city that might be the location indicated by Staci Bennings in her telephone message.

"We keep looking until we find the bitch," said Bates, irritated. Neither of the men wanted to be looking for the woman, but CID brass wanted the army to have Staci as a way to get to her brother.

Staci Bennings slumped on the sofa pretending to watch TV. She was scared, very scared, because from the corner of her eye she watched one of her Russian captors, Gregory, playing a video game on his cell phone as he sat at the kitchen table. She faintly heard the sounds from the game; he was playing video golf.

Staci's elation from having sent the text and voice messages had quickly faded. Help had not come. And the seconds ticking by were like dimmers ratcheting down her hope for rescue. Perhaps someone was looking for her, but she felt like the needle in the proverbial haystack.

And now, here sat Gregory playing with his phone. What would happen when he noticed the keypad tones were shut off? He had yet to make a call or send a text, but surely he would, and soon.

And then, almost as if he had been listening to her thoughts, Gregory turned off the game and placed a call. Staci steeled herself, waiting to see the reaction, the suspicious look sent in her direction. She waited for him to stand and charge across the room and lunge at her.

But nothing happened. He began chatting amiably in Russian, probably to a woman. He hadn't noticed a thing.

Then Staci sensed something. She felt a presence and turned slightly toward the bedroom.

Lily Bain stood in the doorway, staring at her with a wicked smile, as she sensuously rubbed gun oil onto the frame of her pistol.

CHAPTER 27

Time was the enemy now. As soon as Buzz, Angel, and Jen had gone, Kit took Yulana to an electronics store and she picked out various tools and parts. They both bought new outfits—the fastest shopping trip in history—at a Ross Dress for Less clothing store, and Kit bought one hundred pounds of lead pipe, two identical three-feet-long steel toolboxes, and a hand dolly at a building supply store. Next stop was a private mailbox facility on Albuquerque's Central Avenue, where Kit picked up a large Pelican case that had been dropped there by his friend from the Activity within the last hour. The case contained a slew of gadgets and just-generated fake IDs and other esoteric items that might be needed for the operation tonight.

From there it was a short drive to the Chili's restaurant on Central near Eubank. Old habits die hard, and the happy-hour crowd in the packed bar area was full of mostly male black-projects scientists from Sandia getting their drink on and ogling the waitresses as they watched TV sports and talked shop, often while table-hopping.

The setting was much the same four years ago when Kit had pickpocketed security badges from the tipsy scientists. And as Kit had learned as a Red Team leader probing security arrangements at sensitive facilities, there was always an organizational impetus *not to change,* even after management had been shown the errors of their ways. He was counting on that dynamic to work in his favor tonight.

"All eyes will be on you," said Kit to Yulana as they stood just outside the front doors. He held a brown briefcase that had been in the Pelican case. The briefcase had a button recessed in the handle. "I'll be pretty much ignored."

"I'm not sure how good I will be."

"You'll be fine. Just remember what I told you. But please unbutton one more button of your blouse."

She did so, revealing even more cleavage.

"You look gorgeous. Just don't start flirting until we find the right group."

They entered Chili's and squeezed into the raucous bar area. Yulana led the way, and that seemed to ease the process. Entire tables full of men stopped their conversations and just stared at her: the pale skin, aqua eyes, and unruly long black hair almost had a mesmerizing effect on some of the men—and maybe a few of the women too.

Kit scanned the standing-room-only crowd searching for faces but looked like he was coming up empty.

"Which way?" she asked.

"I don't see them. Go right."

She worked her way around to the other side of the bar, toward the rear door.

"There," he said. "The last table before the exit."

Three men and a woman sat in a booth against the windows. They were sharing an appetizer. Kit sent a round of drinks—doubles—to their table anonymously. The more the scientists drank, the better. He ordered an iced tea for himself and a vodka martini for Yulana. They stood near the bar, pressed in by people from all sides.

She took a sip as soon as the drinks came.

"Wow," she said, looking at him. "That's good."

"No offense, but I think it will help loosen you up."

He watched in awe as she guzzled the martini.

"I think you're right. But can we just do it? I don't want to get nervous thinking about it."

He nodded slightly, ceaselessly amazed by how much Russians can drink, and they moved to the targets.

"No table here, either," said Yulana loud enough for the four scientists sitting in the booth to hear. "Is this place always so crowded?" she asked, smiling, making eye contact with each person at the table.

"It's because everyone knew you were coming," said Al Lara, standing as he extended his hand. "Al Lara."

"Elfi Korhonen."

"Have a seat, Elfi. We can squeeze you in."

She hesitated, then, "Okay," said Yulana/Elfi, sitting next to the female scientist.

As she sat down, Kit "accidentally" bumped into Lara, pretending to have been pushed by someone in the standing-room-only crowd.

"Excuse me. There are a few drunks in here, I think," said Kit, having filched Lara's BlackBerry during the physical contact.

"There are a few at this table," joked Al.

Al sat back down so that Yulana was the meat in a sandwich. Kit remained standing. "I just flew in from D.C., and I hate flying. I need to relax and have a few drinks," said Yulana. "That's my cousin, Peter. He lives here."

Yulana had indicated Kit, and he gave a wave and a nod to everyone.

"Sorry we don't have a chair for you."

"No problem. I've been sitting all day," said Kit as he surreptitiously pushed the button in the handle of his briefcase. Electronics inside the case enabled him to "image" any magnetic keycards and magnetic strips used on many security badges. While he did this, Yulana/Elfi introduced herself to the others at the table.

"What were you doing in Washington?" asked Al. Al Lara was Kit's main target. Divorced, forty-five, and always on the make, he was the head of Sandia's nonlethal weapons R&D directorate. Kit learned years ago that Al was sloppy with security and often took his Sandia-issued laptop home with him.

"I'm posted to the Pentagon. I was born in Finland, but I'm a U.S. Army first lieutenant. I joined as a pathway to get my citizenship."

Everyone congratulated her, but only Al touched her arm as he did so.

"So what do you do at the Pentagon?" asked Al, slurring his words slightly.

"I could tell you, but then I would have to kill . . . myself!"

Everyone laughed.

"To be honest, my job is boring."

"Let's see some ID," said Al. He said it lightly, but even though he was drunk, a part of him was still being careful.

"You show me yours, I'll show you mine," said Yulana, reaching into her purse.

"Promise?" Al practically shouted.

The female scientist shook her head in amused embarrassment.

Yulana/Elfi fished out some identification and handed Al an army ID that had just arrived an hour earlier in the black Pelican case.

"Damn, she really is a grunt. A ground pounder. A grunting pounder—"

"Al!" admonished one of the male scientists.

"I want to talk about cars!" Yulana/Elfi laughed. "I don't have one yet."

"Cars?" asked the female scientist.

"I love cars! Peter has a white SUV, but that's boring, I think. What kind of cars do you guys have? And what color?"

"White Toyota."

"Silver Honda."

"Since you're Swedish, I have to say Vulva," joked Al.

"That's *Volvo*, Al, and she's Finnish."

"Then I'd like to start her engine and cross the finish line," cracked Al.

"Stop joking! What kind of car?" asked Yulana/Elfi.

"Black Beaver," said Al, looking at Yulana's hair.

"He means black *Beamer*—a BMW, and I have a boring white SUV," said the female scientist, a bit exasperated with Al's behavior.

Yulana pointed out the window at a passing car. "What is that one?"

As they all looked out the window, Kit swiftly dropped a tiny tablet into Al's drink. The scientist would sleep soundly tonight, unable to answer any late-night phone calls from Sandia's security team if they should happen to call his home landline.

"Excuse me," interrupted Kit. "Elfi, I'm just going to put my briefcase in the car. I'll be back." Kit left through the rear door.

He found all four vehicles in the parking lot and casually pointed his briefcase at them as he passed, constantly pushing the button recessed into the handle. And he stealthily took photos of the Sandia decals on a certain black BMW.

Kit unlocked the rented Pathfinder and sat behind the wheel. Seven minutes later, Yulana strode out of the front door and a group of guys yelled catcalls as she breezed past.

"I told them I was going to the toilet," she said, getting into the SUV.

"And Al didn't try to follow you?" Kit joked.

"He tried."

"I don't blame him." Kit held her gaze. "You did great, by the way."

Yulana smiled at him. For the first time. And for the first time, he smiled at her.

As Yulana kept her smile going, she thought, *This man Bennings, he will save my daughter.*

The technology to remotely capture all of the information on a target computer's hard drive has been around for a long time. That's why the infamous NSA whistleblower Edward Snowden didn't have to personally hand over digital secrets to the Chinese or Russians after he fled America. Those foreign intelligence agencies simply had to use equipment to "image" his laptops from a distance; he was possibly completely unaware they were taking the information—every last 0 and 1—from his computers.

Bennings had "imaged" the contents of Al Lara's Sandia laptop even though it was locked in his car, a car primarily made of plastic, not a medium that defeats electromagnetic function.

And while Kit Bennings wasn't in Jen Huffman's league, he still knew how to do a few things digitally. As he sat at the kitchen table of the vacation rental near Kirtland Air Force Base, he hacked away. Within an hour, Kit had sent "URGENT" messages using Al Lara's e-mail box to the security post at Sandia and to a small detachment of the 898th Munitions Squadron of the Air Force Materiel Command, directing them to take certain actions concerning a Model RT-Seven EMP bomb, serial number 55327VL, that was securely stored at Sandia Labs.

E-mails from a honcho such as Al Lara tended not to be ignored, but security would confirm it with a phone call, which is why Kit had pickpocketed Lara's BlackBerry. He expected a call to come anytime now.

To better sell the ruse, Kit had attached a fake but very authentic-looking e-mail from the CIA's Directorate of Science and Technology asking Al Lara to grant all cooperation to its two scientists as part of a snap inspection of the bomb in the clean room of Building 27A.

Al's e-mails to security and to the 898th apologized for having overlooked the CIA request and not scheduling it sooner.

With the e-mails sent, Kit reconsidered the plan. *What the hell—it just might work.* Since the directed-energy and EMP weapons at Sandia were now held in an underground bunker with the kind of state-of-the-art overkill security systems that truly kept the bad guys out, Bennings had decided to make the theft a little simpler and have the military deliver the e-bomb right to him. Sometimes audacious is the best way to go.

As he sat at the kitchen table trying to remember what he'd forgotten to do, Al Lara's BlackBerry rang. Yulana silently watched as Kit quickly stuffed into his cheeks the cotton balls he'd earlier laid out on the table. He turned the volume up high on a digital music player, and with a gruff slur answered the phone. "Lara."

"Sir, this is Lieutenant Saputo at—"

"You got my e-mail?"

"Yes, that's why I'm calling. Sir, this is highly—"

"Complain to the CIA. Just make it happen." Kit terminated the call. *That should do it.*

The irony, of course, was that Sandia National Labs, which was owned by Lockheed Martin and managed by them for the U.S. Department of Energy, had made running Red Teams something of a specialty for themselves, training other agencies or companies in how to do it right. And they maintained their own ongoing Red Team, constantly probing their own vulnerabilities. But politics, as it always does, trumps everything, even security. The egos and tempers of those at the top, upper management pukes who expect rules to be bent at their whims—people who can make or break the careers of those lower on the food chain—often had the effect of cowing subordinates into violating procedures, even inviolate ones.

Hubris was a wonderful thing to exploit.

CHAPTER 28

Bennings had cloned the electronic keycards of Al Lara and the female scientist from Chili's. He'd printed out a decal and bumper sticker with a bar code that mirrored Lara's.

Armed with terrific fake credentials, Kit and Yulana easily accessed the sprawling, campuslike area of Sandia National Labs, located within Kirtland Air Force Base.

Sandia had come into existence from Z Division, the supersecret nuclear assembly, testing, and design apparatus of Los Alamos National Laboratory during World War II. With the advent of a nuclear weapons testing moratorium in the 1990s, the focus of Sandia's ten-thousand-strong personnel roster shifted in several nonnuclear directions, although they still remained closely connected to America's nuclear weapons program.

Bennings and Petkova drove unescorted to Building 27A. He opened the rear hatch of the SUV and brought out the hand dolly. He muscled his toolbox with both hands—it contained a hundred pounds of steep pipe—and set it on the dolly. Yulana's toolbox contained real tools and went on top of his. Yulana closed up the SUV, Kit tilted the dolly back and wheeled it to the entrance where they used their cloned keycards to enter.

Bennings had deliberately chosen a lab designed for unclassified work, so no biometric scan was necessary to gain access. The only workers present were those on a cleaning crew, who weren't doing much in the way of cleaning; they pretended to get busy when Kit and Yulana showed up, and pretending to be busy was good enough for most government or government-contracted work. The cleaners quickly moved to another part of the building, no doubt in search of privacy.

Bennings found the clean room. He and Yulana donned clean-room garb over their clothes: lab coat, cap, and booties. As he entered the clean room behind her, he noted the overhead security cameras. She quickly prepped a worktable and two rolling polished-aluminum carts.

They lifted her toolbox and placed it onto a cart. Then they pretended his toolbox wasn't heavy as together they heaved it onto the other cart. They opened the toolboxes and positioned the carts in such a way as to screen the cameras from seeing the switch they intended to make. Kit turned on the handheld radio clipped to his belt under his lab coat, connected the earbuds, and placed one of the earbuds into his right ear. The radio was another item from the Pelican case and was calibrated to monitor the frequency of the Sandia guards.

He checked his watch and was almost overcome by the temerity of what he was attempting to do. Yes, he had breached Sandia before, but he did so with ten days of prep, eight operators, and generous resources. Tonight was a rushed, last-minute cowboy operation flying on a wing and a prayer, with a Russian who seemed to enjoy large quantities of vodka. He started to have serious doubts about the entire plan and absentmindedly pressed hard on the migraine acupressure point on his hand.

But it was too late to start second-guessing now, and Yulana was watching, so he put aside his concerns and gave her a reassuring look.

"Stay relaxed, and in an hour, we'll be driving out of Albuquerque," he said with all of the assurance he could muster. In his heart he didn't believe it and felt certain there was something terribly important he'd forgotten to do. But what, what had he forgotten?

He heard radio traffic in his earbud. It was exactly 12:15 A.M., and the security escort had arrived outside. The bomb was here.

Two Humvees and a specially rigged two-and-a-half-ton truck pulled up to the cargo bay of Building 27A. Soldiers from the 898th set up a special trolley and rolling jigs. They carefully removed a crate from the truck bed using a roll-out assembly, and by cranking a wheel, lowered it onto the trolley. The crate was made from some kind of nonmetallic composite material and was about the size of a steamer trunk.

The exterior roll-up cargo door of Building 27A was akin to a jumbo-sized garage door, and it slowly rose open. Soldiers wheeled the trolley through the doorway and into a large two-story-tall air lock, where Bennings stood waiting in clean-room garb.

Sergeant Simms, a lanky veteran noncommissioned officer, was in charge of the bomb transport detail, and Kit could tell the man wasn't happy. Having spent many years in the army, Kit read Simms like a book; the sergeant was worried that this was one of those un-scheduled last-minute deals that had a tendency to screw up easily. Simms held a clipboard as he approached Kit.

"You're Doctor Gned?"

"That's right, Sergeant," said Kit, holding up the photo ID he had generated.

"May I see your CIA ID, sir?"

"Of course." Kit handed over a CIA identification—another item that had arrived in the Pelican case—to Simms, who copied down information from it.

Simms handed back the ID. "Sign here, please."

Kit took the clipboard and signed "Dr. Rick Gned."

"If you and your men will wait outside, I'll get this done as fast as I can," said Kit, smoothly assuming the role of ranking authority figure.

"Sir, due to the last-minute and irregular nature of this inspec-tion, I have to stay with the weapon."

Damn! Kit hadn't anticipated this. He couldn't allow the sergeant to stay, or there could be no switch. He had to be careful how he handled his response.

"No offense, but I don't want you in my clean room, Sergeant. Still, I understand your orders. I'll tell you what: you, and only you, can wait here in the air lock. You can watch through these windows in the inner roll-up door here. That way you can keep eyes on the device if you feel that's necessary."

Simms thought about it. "That sounds okay, sir."

Kit pushed the green button, and the exterior roll-up door closed, so only he and Simms now stood in the air lock. When the exterior door had closed, Kit crossed to a different control panel and pushed the button to open the interior roll-up door—an equally large cargo door with four rectangular eight-by-twelve-inch windows.

As the door rose they could see Yulana waiting in the clean room next to the rolling carts. Although she stood a good thirty yards away, Simms looked to be momentarily distracted by the sight of Dr. Petkova.

"Oh, and Sergeant, if you haven't already, turn off your cell phone and two-way radio so we don't have any unwanted interference with the inspection. If you have to have your electronics on, then you'll need to wait outside the building with your men."

Simms liked the whole situation less and less. He tugged on his ear as if thinking about the options.

"How long will your inspection take?"

"That's classified, and you're wasting my time with all of this. Why don't you just wait outside, so you can keep your phone and everything else on," said Kit pretending to be irritated.

"It's okay, sir. I'll wait here in the air lock."

Kit watched as Simms turned off the electronics. Kit then wheeled the trolley holding the crated weapon into the clean room and closed the interior roll-up door, leaving Simms in the air lock, where he wouldn't be able to hear them. Kit pulled the trolley over to the carts where Yulana waited.

"Good thing you're covered up with the clean-room gear. Otherwise, he'd never stop looking through the window."

The small windows in the roll-up door were about five feet high, and Simms stood bent over in the air lock looking into the clean room.

"How can we do this if he's watching?" asked Yulana.

"I'm hoping his back will start hurting from bending over and he'll lose interest. In the meantime, I'm trying to come up with plan B."

The sergeant appeared to be standing still as stone, observing from the other side of the glass as Kit opened the crate. The small device, which looked like a conventional type of bomb dropped by an aircraft, rested on rubber-padded mounts. It was only about three feet long and weighed one hundred pounds. A GPS guidance system was enclosed in the rear next to four stabilizer fins.

"The bomb was designed to be worked on without being taken from the crate," said Yulana. "I can simply remove the housing panels and do my inspections and the alterations we discussed."

"I think we'd better take it from the crate and position it next to my toolbox. Make a big show of it, like the bomb is heavy and it takes two of us to move it, okay? Then you can go to work."

She nodded. They took up positions at either end of the bomb crate and carefully lifted the unit, exaggerating its weight, and making it look to Simms or any security watching on camera that it took two people to move the bomb.

With the device securely on the cart, Yulana went to work. Kit checked the lead pipes he had already removed from his toolbox and had hidden under towels on one of the aluminum carts. But if Simms didn't stop watching, there could be no switch. No switch, no trade for Staci's life. Kit started sweating under his clean-room garb, even though the room was quite cool. He used his right thumb to press hard on the pressure point on his hand; he didn't get migraines often, but when he did, they were killers. The balls-out stress of the last few days had opened the door for one of his debilitating head-bangers to make an appearance—headaches so bad he could barely walk. Acupuncture worked best to fend off the symptoms, but this was hardly the time to go looking for a doctor of Oriental medicine.

Yulana completed her work. From the corner of her eye, she saw Sgt. Simms looking at her through the small window in the roll-up door. Even if the man were a weapons engineer, he stood far enough away that there was no way he could know what kind of adjustments she had just performed. She carefully replaced the bomb housing panels and then looked to Kit. "I'm finished," she said. "The bomb functions check out, so if someone tests it, the results will be good. I changed the GPS identifier and modified the guidance system so that we hold the key to track the bomb. The U.S. government has now lost any tracking capability of this device. And as we discussed, I installed a remote kill-switch. It will be up to you or me to deactivate the weapon."

"How?"

"By sending a special code using the GPS carrier signal."

"And we can do that from any computer connected to the GPS system?"

She nodded. "I've been thinking . . ." She looked to the bomb, then to Kit. "Why does Popov want an RT-Seven? This is old technology. Very old in terms of EMP devices, even for Russia."

"It's not just old, it's ancient," said Kit.

"Boeing Phantom Works has developed a microwave missile called a CHAMP—Counter-electronics High-powered Microwave Advanced Missile Project. A burst of high-powered microwaves will knock out the electronic systems and computers of a targeted building. *A single building.* And the weapon won't cause chain-reaction blackouts."

"So Popov must *want* the rolling blackouts, the chain-reaction failures of electrical substations that will cause large areas to lose all electrical power."

"Because he's hitting multiple targets?" asked Yulana.

Kit nodded. "He must be. But there are other ways to create rolling blackouts. You don't have to go to the trouble of using an e-bomb."

"Unless you needed the effects of the e-bomb at the *first target*, but not the subsequent targets," she said. "Does that sound plausible?" Yulana was feeling more and more at ease with her give-and-take with Bennings. Somehow he made her feel comfortable, even in the middle of a high-tech heist that could get them both sent to Death Row.

Kit looked like a man having an epiphany. "You, Doctor Petkova, are brilliant. There are *two* targets. I'd kiss you, but Simms is watching, and I think he's already jealous."

"If we get out of here, I'll give you a rain check."

He flashed her a small smile, then nodded. "Popov always was three steps ahead of me at chess."

"He made the mistake of putting us together, forcing us to marry with the assumption we'd remain at odds. So he's not invincible, is he?" she asked, smiling. "If he always beat you at chess, play a different game with him. Play *your* game with him."

Kit locked eyes with her. "You're right. I have to game Popov in a new way."

"Anyway, what's next? The soldier sometimes looks away for a few seconds, but he always looks back."

"What's next is a command performance starring *you*, in the reprisal of a role you play very well."

CHAPTER 29

Sgt. Simms watched as the woman walked in his direction but then crossed to the "man door," the door that accommodated personnel traffic when it wasn't necessary to open the roll-up cargo door.

Damn, she's beautiful. He'd never seen a scientist so good-looking.

Simms watched with anticipation as the doorknob turned, the door opened, and the woman sort of poured through it. Sweet Jesus, she was a fox, even though she was a doc. He called all of the scientists "Doc"—since most of them had Ph.D.s and always called themselves doctors. Doctors of Bull Crap, is what Simms thought most of them were. But this woman was . . .

"Sergeant, you didn't check my ID yet. And I need a break from that jerk, Doctor Gned."

Well, *hello.* Maybe she didn't have her head up her butt like all the others did. Simms watched her pull off the translucent white cotton hair covering, and then a cascade of thick, jet-black hair fell down all the way to her waist. *Hot damn.*

She popped open all of the snaps of her lab coat and produced her CIA ID from the front pocket of very tight blue jeans.

"Yes, ma'am, I'll check you out." Simms crossed over to Yulana at the man door, meaning he was no longer able to look into the clean room through the small windows in the roll-up cargo door. He knew the camera jockeys were probably watching from the overhead eye in the sky—even the air lock had a security cam—so he would have to be quick. But maybe not too quick.

He took his time and studied her name. "I can't place your accent, Doc."

"Finland. I've been an American citizen for over ten years but can't lose my accent."

He handed her ID back. "I don't mind if you don't mind," he said, smiling.

"Sergeant, do you smoke?"

"Yes ma'am, but—"

"Call me Elfi."

"We can't smoke inside the building, Elfi."

"I know that," she said with a grin. "Can you give me one for later? Doctor Gned is a nonsmoker and he won't stop anywhere for me to buy cigarettes."

"Sure, Elfi." Simms produced a pack and gave her a smoke.

Yulana opened her lab coat wide, and Simms's eyes riveted instantly to her cleavage. She tucked the cigarette into the front pocket of her tight blouse. The fact that she wasn't wearing a bra was not lost on Simms.

"You need another one?"

"Okay. Twice is better than once," she said, smiling.

Simms had to swallow. He was thinking, trying to calculate how he should handle this. *This girl might be in play.*

Unless this was some kind of trick—another Red Team drill, this one using a smoking-hot woman. "Excuse me one second." Simms backtracked toward the windows in the roll-up door.

"Too bad we have to fly back to Washington tomorrow. I wouldn't mind going out and having some fun."

Simms shot a fast glance into the clean room. It was such a quick look, Bennings could have been playing air guitar nude and Simms wouldn't have noticed.

"Which hotel are you staying at, Elfi?" said Simms as he crossed back toward her.

"The Hilton, but the bar there is boring." She smiled the big smile, and Simms fell in love.

As soon as Simms left the window, Kit chanced making the switch. Any security officers watching the cameras were probably right now watching Yulana in the air lock, but still, he was careful to keep his movements screened from camera view.

He strained to lift the bomb up about eight inches above the cart; Bennings could do hundred-pound barbell curls with no problem, but he strained, because the position was awkward. He eased the unit into his toolbox and then used the towels as packing materials. He quickly loaded the lead pipes into the weapons crate and closed the lid. The switch took just under ten seconds.

He secured the toolbox. Kit gritted as he used both hands to manhandle his toolbox, which now contained the bomb, onto the hand dolly. He placed Yulana's toolbox on top of his, then tilted the dolly and wheeled it over to the roll-up door. He then returned and quickly pulled the trolley with the weapons crate over to the door. He hit the button, and the interior roll-up door began to rise.

In the security office, three men crowded in close around one particular monitor.

"Come on, zoom it in farther."

The guy with the joystick did exactly that, and Yulana's figure filled the screen.

"Damn, Sarge! Get the hell away from my future ex-wife!" joked one of the men.

"This babe is CIA? I work for the wrong company."

"Can we detain her? I'll do the pat down."

"Pat down? I'm thinking a body cavity search."

Kit needn't have worried; he could have emptied out the entire clean room and no one would have noticed.

·   ·   ·

With the hand dolly and trolley now in the air lock, Kit closed the interior roll-up door. He and Yulana discarded their clean-room garb into a plastic bin.

Simms looked like a salesman who'd been interrupted before he could close a big sale.

"Sergeant, appreciate all of your help." Kit pressed the button to open the exterior roll-up door and heard the sudden footsteps of men outside. Was there a problem? Or were the men outside merely startled by the door opening?

"I need to check the weapon, sir."

Kit sighed and looked at his watch. "Don't tell me you opened this crate in the storage facility to 'check it' before you brought it here."

"Well, no, sir." Simms shifted on his feet. Yulana moved away from the soldier.

"Because this weapons crate can only be opened in a clean-room environment, which this air lock is not. Now I am well aware of how your unit was decertified in 2010 for its sloppy practices. They wouldn't let you people handle nukes anymore, isn't that right? Because of bad practices. That was a big scandal, wasn't it?"

"Umm, yes, sir."

"Well, I'm not here to get you decertified again. But don't be opening the weapons crate unless you're in a clean room, understood?"

"I'm not aware of any regulation that we have to open the crate in a clean room, Doctor." It wasn't a direct challenge, but Simms stared at Bennings, waiting for a response.

"The regs were amended for the RT-Sevens about a month ago. You can confirm that with your CO." Kit said it casually enough so it didn't sound like he was parrying the sergeant's remark. It was pure bluff on his part, but being in the military himself, he knew how difficult it was to keep up with the minutiae of constantly changing regulations. And he knew the chances of the CO being awake, much less on duty, at this hour were slim at best.

Still, Bennings was sweating under his clothes. A quick glance at the overhead camera reminded him they were being monitored—a certainty considering Yulana's presence. Simms had become the unanticipated monkey wrench in his plan. He now calculated that he might have to subdue the sergeant, overcome the troops outside, and just make a run for it. Kit could feel the odds of success rapidly slipping away from him.

The exterior roll-up door was all the way open now. The soldiers outside were readying the jigs to reload the bomb crate onto the truck. Yulana took another step toward the open door. Kit crossed to the hand dolly that held his toolbox that, unbeknownst to the soldiers, contained the RT-Seven EMP bomb. He didn't want to move the toolbox until he had to, since it weighed a hundred pounds. If they saw how heavy the box was, it would raise suspicion, although suspicion seemed to have crept in all by itself.

"No disrespect, sir, but if we ever have to use one of these weapons, we won't be opening the crate in a clean room."

Damn, Simms wasn't going to let this go. "That's different, soldier. Now get this thing out of here. I want to go home," snapped Bennings. Intimidation was the only play Kit had left, short of getting physical.

"Home? I thought you two were at a hotel."

"First we go to the hotel, Sergeant, then we get to fly home. To Langley," Kit said, working hard to sound exasperated.

"Sir, I have to check the weapon. I don't want my unit to be decertified again, and for all I know, you are testing me right now in some kind of Red Team drill."

No doubt about it now, this was going to be a race to get off the base. Kit's SIG rested snugly tucked into an inside-the-pants holster, and it suddenly felt heavy.

"We're heading back to the hotel," said Kit, pretending to lose his patience and speaking loudly enough so all of the other soldiers could hear. "You've been watching the device for almost an hour. You haven't taken your eyes off it. But if you have to check it, then close the exterior door, put on some clean-room garb, open the interior door, take the weapon inside, close the interior door, and *then* you can check it. Understood? Otherwise, I'm going to write your ass up and have a talk with your CO! Now good night."

What happened in the next few moments would determine just how ugly this was going to get.

Simms stared hard and looked like a man trying to make a decision. If he shouted an order for his troops to stop them, Kit would put the bomb down and come up with his gun. No way he would shoot innocents, not even to save Staci's life, but he could surely bluff if he had to.

But the soldiers had weapons, too, and might not be shy about using them. He doubted they'd shoot Yulana, but he had no doubt they'd send lead downrange in his direction.

Yulana moved out first and had the tailgate open as Kit tilted the hand dolly and wheeled it over the the SUV.

Yulana turned to face Simms, and took a stop toward him as she removed a cigarette from her blouse pocket. "Sorry for the trouble, Sergeant. Can I got a light?"

Thank God she was creating another distraction. Bennings quickly slid her toolbox into the SUV. As Simms gave her a light, Kit turned his back to Simms and the soldiers so they couldn't see him strain as he lifted his bomb-laden toolbox into the vehicle. The soldiers watched closely, not because they were suspicious, but because they couldn't get enough of Yulana.

And Simms didn't say a word.

Bennings hoisted the dolly inside, closed the hatchback, and then he and Petkova got in without speaking. As they drove off in the Pathfinder, Kit checked the rearview mirror. It looked as if Simms advised his men to stand by, and he closed the exterior roll-up door, remaining in the air lock alone.

CHAPTER 30

Sandia wasn't a huge facility, but it would take at least a couple of minutes to get to the Eubank Boulevard gate. Kit clutched the two-way radio, put an earbud in his ear, and turned the volume up.

"If he follows procedure, we should have just enough time to get off base. But if he pops the lid to the crate right there in the air lock, we're screwed."

"Either way, as American people say, we are in deep doo-doo now," said Yulana, looking worried.

"Yes, we are." Kit tromped on the accelerator, driving dangerously fast toward the gate as he continued to listen for Simms to call in an alarm to dispatch. His face muscles tightened. *Did Simms follow his orders or not?*

At the time he was standing in the air lock with Simms, he thought the mention of the 898th's decertification was a good idea to put the sergeant on the defensive, but it instead made him pricklier, more of a stickler for procedure . . . as long as Bennings was standing there. But as soon as Kit and Yulana drove away, what would Simms really do? Then Bennings asked himself what *he* would do.

"The sergeant hasn't radioed in a problem, and the gate is around the corner. But, damn it, if it was me, I'd just pop the sucker open."

"Maybe he didn't use the radio."

Kit slammed on the brakes and they skidded to a stop just short of rounding the corner, so they were still out of sight from the gate guards, but just barely. "You're right. He'd use a landline. You don't want to put out on the radio a big screwup unless you have to."

He threw the vehicle into reverse and spun a 180-degree turn-around.

Kit pressed the TALK button on the radio. "Dispatch, this is unit——" He hit the squelch button, causing feedback to cover up the fact that he didn't have a radio handle to use. "Three, repeat, three drones now landing inside the base on the west side of Building sixty-seven. They are all painted black. Some kind of electrical interference——" Kit hit squelch again and then turned the radio off.

"Diversions," said Kit as he looked at Yulana. "I forgot to set up any diversions in case we had to make a run for it."

Having been alerted by Sgt. Simms to secure the gates and stop the couple in the Pathfinder, the guards at every gate that wasn't already closed had raised up the pneumatic posts from the ground that comprised impenetrable vehicle blockades.

All gate guards at Sandia placed loaded magazines into their M4s, as frantic radio traffic squawked about intruders with a stolen bomb and drones and mobile units being dispatched to Building 67.

The perimeters of most sensitive facilities are not as formidable as one might think; they are designed to keep the honest people out, not the bad guys in. So Kit raced the Pathfinder off-road across an expanse of brown grass and slammed through eight-foot-high chain-link fencing topped with concertina wire.

He fishtailed onto Eubank Boulevard and floored it heading north. Just as he looked into the rearview mirror, the headlights of a vehicle came on and it pulled onto the road behind him, accelerating fast.

"Who the hell is that?"

Yulana looked back. "Police?"

"If it's the police, where are the flashing lights?"

Kit made a screeching right turn onto Southern Boulevard, and the vehicle following did likewise. He saw that it was a dark SUV with tinted windows.

"It can't be."

"Can't be what?" asked Kit.

"Popov," she said, making the word sound like a curse.

Kit's mouth opened, but no words came out.

"It's the Feds, it has to be FBI, or . . . maybe plainclothes Sandia security."

But as he thought about it, why couldn't it be Popov? The Russians had to suspect he might come to Sandia to steal the weapon, and Sandia wasn't that big. But, surely . . .

Kit wrenched the wheel at the thought and veered up Elizabeth Street to Central Avenue, where he hung another wide right, glancing off an old Ford, which then spun out.

The dark SUV relentlessly followed and closed ground.

Did Yulana borrow the sergeant's phone while she was out of my sight and call someone? Someone who was standing by in the vicinity, just waiting to pounce? The thought almost made him physically sick.

An oncoming sedan suddenly veered across the double yellow lines of Central right at them. More of Popov's men. Kit careened left into oncoming lanes and then tried to correct, but he was traveling too fast. He lost control, and the Pathfinder skidded sideways and exploded through the storefront of a large indoor flea market.

Shattering glass and splintering wood rained like a downpour in monsoon season, as the Pathfinder tore a new path through antique furniture, old appliances, and funky jewelry displays. Miraculously, the vehicle didn't flip.

Bullets pinged into the driver's compartment. *Definitely not the Feds or security.* Yulana threw open her door and rolled out onto the concrete floor of the flea market. Kit reached into the backseat for his backpack and the Kel-Tec subgun. He felt a burning sensation in his upper arm; he'd been shot.

The incoming grew more intense, so he kicked his door open, scrambled out, and found cover behind an old Kenmore fridge.

As he put on his backpack, he quickly counted eight different muzzle flashes closing in from the darkness. Eight killers. He had to backpedal *now*! Just as he began to lay grazing fire, he saw movement to his left. He wheeled and was about to fire, when Yulana, wild-eyed with fear, crawled toward him.

"What do we do? We can't leave the device!" As soon as she got the words out, a fusillade of lead tore in all around them.

"It's too late. If we stay, we die. Come on!" He pulled on her arm and they retreated.

Had Yulana betrayed him? He wanted to give the woman whose hand he now held as they ran in the darkness the benefit of the doubt; he couldn't assume she'd been nothing but a spy after all they'd been through. But as they crouched low and moved deeper into the market, a different thought consumed him. *How could a scientist operate as slickly as she did? Was she working for Popov after all?*

He pulled up next to some old stoves and laid down covering fire. The bolt locking back on his weapon told him he was out of ammo. Sounds of killers bumping into furniture on both sides of them meant they were being flanked. He had only seconds to decide: make a break for it alone, or bring her with him?

He looked into her eyes. Could she possibly fake the kind of fright on her face right now? *No*, he decided, and so he pulled her along, running flat out in the dark.

They crashed out of a rear door to the flea market. Moonlight revealed old refrigerators next to the door, so Kit heaved and pushed one onto its side, blocking the door from opening. Almost instantly he heard voices from inside the building as men tried to open the door. Kit pulled Yulana along, threading through piles of rusty stoves, broken tables, and clunky office furniture stacked into towering piles.

Voices closed in, looking for them. At the six-foot-high rear wall, he boosted her up, and she climbed over easily. But when he tried to follow, searing pain from where he'd been shot stabbed through his arm and into his shoulder as he struggled to pull himself up. Gritting his teeth as he grimaced, he finally got a leg onto the ledge and spilled over the top of the wall.

He landed on the arm where he'd been shot and winced in pain. Yulana sprang to her feet like a cat, then helped him stand up.

They'd dropped into a mobile-home park. A big Hispanic guy, alerted by the sound of gunfire, had just come out of his trailer holding his car keys, keys to a faded blue 1965 Chevy sitting in the driveway. Kit and Yulana stumbled out of the darkness toward the man.

"Keys," said Kit, pointing the gun into the man's face. The gun was empty, but the Hispanic man didn't know that.

The man looked at the gun, looked at Yulana, then looked at Kit and his bloody arm. He didn't appear to be either frightened or impressed. He finally tossed him the keys and said, "Try not to wreck it. And don't get blood on my upholstery! It's custom tuck-and-roll."

"If they don't kill me, I'll return it with a cash bonus," said Kit, dead serious.

"Who's they?"

"Russian Mafia. There's a whole bunch of them on the other side of your wall." Kit's eyes dropped for just a moment to the man's waist. A chrome-plated .357 Magnum revolver was tucked into the front of his pants. As Bennings's eyes met the Hispanic man's, Kit's demeanor morphed into pure bloodlust killer mode. His eyes now looked . . . deranged? Psychotic? He bore them into the man as a warning not to go for his pistol.

Perhaps the Hispanic man had spent time in jail, or perhaps he'd just rubbed elbows with the criminally insane, but he seemed to recognize the power behind Kit's gaze.

"The Russians are some bad mothers," said the man. He wasn't afraid, and he looked hard at Kit, sizing him up. He then gestured with his head, "Better get your asses out of here."

Kit and Yulana piled into the car, and when Kit turned the key, it rumbled to life with the kind of sounds that made street racers all warm and fuzzy. So what if it didn't look like much? It was a four-on-the-floor and ran like a lizard.

Ran, in fact, all the way to the outskirts of Albuquerque, using mostly side streets.

They stopped at an all-night convenience store for snacks and simple medical supplies. Back in the Chevy, in the backseat, Yulana bandaged his arm as he ravenously consumed ready-made sandwiches and energy drinks.

"The bleeding is not so bad," she said, finishing.

"Your turn."

She looked confused.

"The cut on your back from when Buzz took out the chip," said Kit.

She turned her back to him and lowered her blouse. He rubbed antibiotic ointment into the nasty gash where Buzz had used his pocketknife to cut out the tracking chip. He then gently applied bandages.

"Okay, you're golden. Until we can get you stitched up proper so you won't have a big-ass scar."

She turned around to face him and slowly buttoned her blouse. Somehow Kit pulled his eyes from her and fished a tablet computer from his backpack. He logged into a GPS software program.

"The key is K-I-T-1," she said.

He smiled. "If I can't remember that one, then I'm hopeless." He entered the key, and the signal popped up on the screen. His eyes narrowed and mouth tightened into a frown.

"The bomb is on the move. And I mean it's moving; it must be on a plane, probably a small jet."

He looked up at her. So at least his instincts regarding Yulana were correct; she was on his side after all. The GPS tracking was working perfectly. He felt guilty for having suspected her after all she had done. It was the sole positive thing he could latch onto on a day that had seen radical swings of momentum.

"What a rotten piece of luck. Popov has the e-bomb! We barely got out of Sandia before the bastard grabbed it. It's like winning a gold medal, but it gets snatched before you make it to the reviewing stand."

How would he explain this to Padilla? To anyone?

"No, it's worse than that," he went on. "I've lost my bargaining chip to get Staci back. And I've got no one to blame but myself."

As he watched the device continuing to head west on the tablet screen, his eyes grew heavy. He hadn't slept in days and couldn't think clearly. Blood loss was minimal, but he felt woozy, anyway. A thousand thoughts were rushing through his brain, when Yulana leaned in and gently stroked his cheek. He snapped out of his hyperactive thought process and was suddenly calmed as he lost himself in the sweet depths of her eyes.

She tenderly touched his hand. Bennings felt a powerful desire to take Yulana Petkova right there in the backseat of the Chevy. He let that desire wash over him for about two seconds before forcing his cerebral nature to take over again. *Stay focused on the mission,* was a concept drilled into his brain, so he pulled his hand away from hers.

"You know what I want to do with you right now?" he asked.

"I can guess."

"I want to go steal a plane."

She showed slight surprise, then broke into a smile. "Yes. That's what I was thinking, too."

CHAPTER 31

Kit Bennings flew VFR, visual flight rules, under the stars in a Beechcraft Baron stolen from Double Eagle II Airport on the west side of Albuquerque. Yulana had watched in amazement as Kit used a simple screwdriver to get them past the door lock and into the cockpit. As with most planes, the pilot's operating handbook was conveniently left in the aircraft. She and Bennings had quickly reviewed it and then engaged the master switch, magneto switches, fuel selector, boost pump, and starter switch and were in business, no keys needed, thank you very much. Within minutes they'd become airborne. She'd smiled when she thought of how many laws she'd broken since she met Kit Bennings.

After getting the feel of the plane, Kit programmed in the rest of the flight and engaged the autopilot. The cockpit of a Beechcraft Baron was quiet enough that they didn't need to wear headphones in order to communicate. He looked tired; Yulana wasn't sure whether she should let him sleep or keep him talking.

"Do you trust the autopilot?"

"I'd trust it more if I had used it before. So I think I'll skip taking a nap."

Okay, so keep him talking, she thought. "Do all American defense attachés know how to steal airplanes?" she asked.

"This one does," he cracked. He looked over to her, as if formulating a question. "Can all Russian female scientists manipulate men so easily?"

"All women know how to fake it with men. You must know that."

He laughed. "Sorry, I'd forgotten."

She paused, then, "So there is no real Mrs. Bennings?"

"There was, a long time ago. The marriage lasted five years. I can't blame her, because I was deployed so much. So she found comfort in the arms of—"

"Another man?"

"My best friend."

"Ouch." She hesitated, then, "Did you love her?"

"Yes, ouch, and yes, I loved her. Deeply. So I lost my two best friends."

She thought about that. "How sad for you. It was different for me because I never loved my husband and never thought of him as a best friend. I was dating him for intellectual, rational reasons. He seemed like a good Russian man, and I thought he might perhaps make a proper life mate and father. You see, I'm an engineer—I don't care about money, I care about stability, I care about things working properly. My friends kept pushing me to marry, but I resisted since I wasn't at least ninety percent convinced.

"But then he refused to use a condom one night. We'd both been drinking. He forced the issue and hit me. It was the first time, but not the last. I should have ended it then, but I got pregnant and we married. He gifted me with a beautiful daughter and taught me a bitter lesson about self-respect, so I choose to only feel sorry for him and not to hate him.

"But I've never been in romantic love, like you have. So I'm jealous. I'd very much like to experience that kind of love. Unless . . ." She hesitated, unsure if she should say the words. "Unless I'm not capable of feeling such a thing."

"In my experience, Russians are a passionate people."

She shrugged. "It's a stereotype. But I do cry when I listen to sad songs. There are many black American singers I like, who sing with such strong feelings. When Luthor Vandross sings 'Dance with My Father,' I always . . ." Almost on cue, a tear formed and rolled down her cheek. She looked at Kit and smiled. "Can you see the Russian tears?"

She looked at him through teary eyes and saw his demeanor soften.

"There were no other men for you?" he asked.

"Men have always shown interest in me. And the interest of course is for sex. They don't care about what's inside, about my personality, about what I like or don't like. And when they find out I'm smarter than they are and that I'm not interested in casual sex, they fade away quickly."

"My mom used to say that there was somebody out there for every person, and I believe that. Don't worry, you'll meet somebody good," said Kit, as they exchanged a look.

"Your mom raised quite a son. Even if you are a spy."

Kit smiled. "When I was twelve years old I wanted two things: to play blues guitar and to be a spy. So I took music lessons and read espionage novels, watched James Bond movies. I wanted to visit all of the old Asian colonial capitals and be involved in danger and intrigue. I mean, how many twelve-year-olds have posters of Singapore and Rangoon and Jakarta and Hong Kong on their bedroom walls? So I joined the army to see the world. Now, at age thirty-five, I've been to all of those capitals—as a spy—and have learned to play guitar."

"You got what you wanted."

"But what I learned, is that the most important thing in life is your family. Everything else is just details."

She looked at him, shocked by the notion that she was developing strong feelings for this man Bennings.

Angel Perez snored as he lay sprawled on the sofa in a suite at the Venetian on the Las Vegas Strip. Across the room, Buzz Van Wyke slept soundly on bedding placed on the floor. The door to the bedroom was closed.

Angel's sterile cell phone rang. Both men woke quickly, but Angel fumbled around in the dark, trying to find the ringing phone. He picked up after four rings and sounded as if he'd been in deep sleep.

"Hey boss man, good to hear from you," said Angel, putting the phone on speaker as he tried not to sound groggy.

"Well I'm glad somebody's getting some sleep," joked Kit. "I'm on speaker with Yulana in the cockpit of a Beechcraft Baron I just boosted in Albuquerque."

"No fair you get to have all the fun. Hey, don't be jealous, but we're living large here. It's been at least an hour since we racked out," said Angel, checking his watch.

"'We' doesn't mean you're all still together, does it?" asked Kit, surprised.

"Indeed we are, in beautiful Las Vegas," called out Buzz loudly so he could be heard on the speakerphone. He then rapped on the closed bedroom door. "Jen, get in here!"

"Vegas? You were all supposed to go home. I don't need to remind you that it's way too risky to be involved with me. Especially after what just happened."

"Don't worry about us," said Buzz. "Now what just happened?"

"Calls in the middle of the night usually don't bring good news," said Jen as she shuffled into the room.

"You're right about that, Jen." Kit then filled them in on all of the recent developments.

"Yulana and I have been monitoring the bomb's location with GPS," added Kit.

"The device was on a jet that landed at North Las Vegas Airport a few minutes ago," said Yulana, checking Kit's tablet computer. "Unfortunately, the signal was just terminated."

"Don't worry, we'll get the signal back," said Angel.

"I think you're right. But when we do, we might not have much time to act," said Kit. "By the way, why did you all go to Las Vegas?"

"Let's save the good news till last," said Buzz, winking at Angel and Jen.

"Kit, unless Popov's bomb expert is working in a shielded room, we should get the signal back when he checks out the device to confirm it's operational," said Angel. "Yulana, do you have any idea how long that will take?"

"Not more than an hour," said Yulana. "My concern is that Popov's people have already inspected the device on the flight to Las Vegas. If they have switched off the GPS targeting signal, they don't need to turn it back on until just before dropping the bomb. Perhaps as little as three or four minutes."

Buzz, Angel, and Jen looked at one another with great concern at this sobering consideration. "Let's hope that's not the case," said Buzz.

"Since the bomb requires an airborne delivery system, North Las Vegas Airport could be where Popov's HQ is located," said Kit.

"I can look into that. And it will be easy to find out which private jets landed there tonight," said Jen.

"Kit, since you're in a hot plane, there's a small airstrip next to the casino in Jean, Nevada, near the California border on Interstate Fifteen. I'll drive there now to bring you guys into town," said Buzz.

"Good idea. Now what's this good news you mentioned? And why are you all in Vegas?" asked Kit.

"Staci's here," said Buzz. "She was somehow able to send a text message to your old cell phone that you gave to Jen. We have a general idea of where she's being held, apparently by a couple of Russians. I hired a half-dozen private investigators who will resume knocking on doors looking for her as soon as it's daylight."

Kit visibly perked up like a bankrupt man who'd just won the lottery. It was exactly what he needed to hear to help him keep going in spite of all the recent developments. "That's fantastic news!" he said excitedly. "Awesome!" Smiling, he looked to Yulana and reached out and squeezed her hand. "Buzz . . . how did . . . what . . . I mean how . . . ?" Kit was so happy he couldn't get words out.

"I'll give you all the details when you land. Hopefully, we'll have her back in the next twelve hours," said Buzz.

"Buzz, Jen, Angel, you guys are—"

"Are forgiven for disobeying your orders?" joked Jen.

"Listen, since we learned Staci was being held here, I started thinking that Popov's target was here," said Buzz.

"Makes sense," said Kit. "Las Vegas is a target-rich environment, of both a civilian and military nature."

"Is he hitting casinos?" asked Angel. "That's where the big money is."

"Buzz, rent us a hangar and helicopter at McCarran Airport. We'll set up an HQ there."

"Great minds think alike. I did all of that as soon as we touched down yesterday."

"That's why you make the big money," joked Kit. "Hey, if it doesn't look like Popov is using North Las Vegas, call the fueling operations at all of the other area airports. Maybe even talk to the gas jockeys in person. Ask if they're fueling any airplanes belonging to Russians."

"Got it."

"Just to clarify, it sounds like Popov could use the bomb today," said Jen.

"I expect he'll use it as soon as he can. Which means I'd like to have more than six people looking for Staci."

"I'll make it happen," said Buzz.

Sheriff Jim McCain called Detective Bobby Chan into his office for a 5:00 A.M. meeting about the government spying on his officers. After listening to Chan's version of events, McCain didn't speak for a full ten minutes. He paced behind his desk, looked out his office window, and jotted some notes onto a yellow legal pad. He made one phone call that Chan couldn't hear, even though he tried to eavesdrop. Luckily, the big Chinese American detective had some snack crackers stashed in his sport coat, and he munched on them as he watched the sheriff.

Jim McCain was a smart former lawyer, but Chan wasn't sure how the sheriff would play this to maximize any potential benefit— not to the department, but to McCain's reelection prospects. He'd surprised Chan by ordering the CID agents to be charged with assaulting an officer and resisting arrest. Other charges were "pending." Chan was shocked McCain had even gone that far.

The sheriff finished his call and waved Chan over to sit in front of his large desk.

"My brother-in-law, Harry Davenport, is a hotshot Phoenix lawyer and a former federal prosecutor. He's setting up a conference call with General Duffy, who's the top guy at the army's Criminal Investigation Command back on the East Coast, where it's . . ." McCain checked his watch. ". . . eight twenty-two in the morning."

"So he's the boss of our perps," said Chan.

"Yes."

The desk phone rang. "This is the call." McCain picked it up and put it on speaker. "Sheriff McCain here."

"Jim, it's Harry. We have General Duffy on the line."

"Sheriff, Mr. Davenport has apprised me of the situation there in great detail," said General Duffy, whose voice sounded thin and strained, possibly from ill health. "Your department is making some very serious allegations, and I promise I'll look into it immediately."

"You'll look into it immediately?"

"Of course," said General Duffy.

"And what else, General?"

There was a pause, then, "What exactly are you getting at, Sheriff?"

"What do you need to look into? You have incontrovertibly damning evidence on your desk in front of you of a federal crime committed by your CID officers. I want something done right now. Today."

"These things take time, and you know that, Sheriff." Duffy managed to muster a bit more substance to his voice with the remark.

"Sorry, but I'm short on time. So I want to know everything you have on this investigation. I want to know all about Major Kitman Bennings. I want to know why the Russian mob killed two people in his family home, and probably his mother too. And I want any names connected with your investigation. I want your associates at the FBI to give us everything they have on Staci Bennings's kidnapping, because, like you, they have frozen us out. If you don't cut me in on the action, you will experience repercussions."

"Sheriff, I think I'll have to have some people come and talk to you." This time, Duffy's voice had strengthened to the point that he sounded threatening.

"Why don't *you* try talking to me in a meaningful way. Did I forget to mention that we have arrested your two agents who committed the federal crime?"

"I believe I forgot to mention that to the general," said Harry Davenport.

"I have to ask you to please release them at once," said General Duffy.

"Actually, I was thinking about using them in the press conference."

"What press conference?" asked Duffy, sounding angry.

"The one I have scheduled for two o'clock this afternoon, about eight hours from now, in time to make the evening news nationwide. The one that will explain how the U.S. Army illegally used the NSA to spy on police detectives conducting a murder investigation."

"That would be very unwise of you," said Duffy.

"How so? I'm in a tight reelection race, and the army and FBI are actively, willfully hampering my department's ability to solve multiple homicides."

"There are issues here, that you are simply not cleared to be privy to. I'd suggest exercising some patience and self-control until we can resolve them."

"Or you will do what?"

"I'm not going to do anything," said Duffy, modulating his tone. "But you're going to be getting some visitors. And if the NSA has taken liberty with your officers' personal and work communications, and I'm not saying they have, then they could probably do the same to you. Everyone has skeletons," said General Duffy matter-of-factly. "And you certainly wouldn't want any of yours surfacing right now, during an election. So I'm asking you to exercise good judgment until we can—"

"You know what the problem is with the federal government? No one ever gets held accountable anymore. The IRS scandal, Benghazi, the trumped-up WMD excuse President Bush used to justify invading

Iraq, no-bid government contracts awarded to companies owned by big campaign contributors . . . Whether it's a Democrat in the White House, or a Republican, everything just gets papered over and no one gets fired.

"The only way to get some 'justice' is to have leverage. And my leverage is going public with you, General Duffy, threatening to smear me by illegally using the NSA to dig up dirt from my past."

"I did no such thing!"

"I've got it on tape."

"If you are recording this conversation, that would be illegal and will get you into very serious trouble if you try to—"

"The sheriff isn't recording you, General. I'm recording you," said Harry Davenport. "In Arizona and in Virginia, where you are now, one-party consent to recording a conversation makes it perfectly legal."

"I'm in California," said Sheriff McCain, "where two-party consent is required, but I gave my consent to be recorded. So screw you."

The sheriff slammed the phone down.

Bobby Chan sat there almost speechless. He'd never realized Jim McCain had a pair of brass ones. He looked at the chief and said one word: "Wow."

"That's what I like about you, Chan, you're so eloquent. Here's the deal: we've been dealt a hand, and I'm going to play it as best I can. I'm playing hardball to kick your investigation into a higher gear. And hopefully, that helps both of us.

"Just so you know, Harry Davenport is right now calling the secretary of defense," continued McCain. "He's demanding General Duffy's resignation *today*. We're also demanding the name of the NSA systems analyst who spied on you and Franklin, and I want to read in the national media *today* that he or she has been fired for abuse of authority. They can lie about the specifics, but I want him or her fired. And I'm demanding that those two agents from CID who spoke to you at the morgue . . ."

"Flood and Bates," said Chan.

". . . Flood and Bates, be in my office before six P.M. today. They will be stopping in to personally apologize to me on their way back to Quantico, because they are off this case, and their military careers are essentially over."

"To be honest, I'm not sure I see the feds agreeing to any of your demands," said Chan.

"Did I mention that my hotshot brother-in-law graduated from Harvard Law?"

"And . . . ?"

"And the secretary of defense is his old frat buddy and former rommate."

Chan nodded as he smiled. "Sheriff McCain, if you will authorize a Code Three patrol escort all the way to the Nevada state line, Franklin and I can be in Vegas in less than three hours. Since CID is desperate to find Staci Bennings, we need to find her first. And wouldn't it be great to skunk the FBI's kidnapping detail?"

"Go make it happen, Chan."

CHAPTER 32

The private security vault off of South Rainbow Boulevard was not to be confused with the twenty-four-hour-access private-security-vault businesses from Las Vegas's past. Those joints were located in mini malls next to nail salons and catered to a certain type of client who wanted ready access to their "goods," at least, that is, until those small private vaults were mysteriously robbed and the contents of many vaults emptied. Strangely enough, few police reports were filed, possibly because that would entail listing what had been stolen.

Mainichi was a leading Japanese auction house that had chosen South Las Vegas as the location for their ultrasecure, state-of-the-art U.S. storage facility. While their two-story building resembled most of the other boxy, terra-cotta–colored buildings in the light-industrial complex, as a private vault holding everything from expensive modern art to valuable electric guitars to priceless artifacts and gems, the building was quite different from its neighbors.

Elaborate fire-suppression and environmental systems were built into the windowless steel-and-concrete structure with a three-membrane roof. A ten-foot-high steel fence surrounded the property, and the only gate was manned 24/7 by an armed guard. Over sixty high-resolution CCTV monitors watched the exterior and interiors of the building. Motion sensors, intruder alarms, and compartmentalized access complemented biometric scanners and electronic access control. A minimum of eight armed guards, all former police or military, were on duty at all times and supplemented regular staff members in keeping the valuables secure.

Aside from temporarily securing valuables that would soon be auctioned, Mainichi's storage clients ranged from moneyed locals to visiting billionaires, who often placed tens of millions of dollars' worth of goods for safekeeping. One famous casino tycoon alone had a collection of diamonds in his Mainichi private vault worth $500 million. And he just kept adding to it, as security guard Jerry Kotsky, Viktor Popov's inside man, had reported many times during the last three years.

Dennis Kedrov inhaled smoke from his Turkish cigarette as he watched men raise tenting up and over the flatbed semitrailer. The long truck had just backed into the old motel's U-shaped courtyard on South Las Vegas Boulevard. The load on the flatbed was already covered with tarps, but now that everything was under a huge tent, the cargo could be unwrapped.

The cargo was a lightweight R66 helicopter built by Robinson in Long Beach, California. Special hard points—bomb attachments— had already been installed on the helo's undercarriage.

Satisfied, Dennis flicked his cigarette, made his way out of the tent, and crossed toward Dr. Rodchenko's makeshift lab. But before he reached the door, Viktor Popov emerged, followed by three bodyguards. And Dennis knew Viktor well enough to see that the man was not happy.

"So we have the best of both worlds. An American bomb and a Russian bomb," said Dennis, smiling.

"How long will it take to load the bombs onto the helicopter?" asked Viktor, all business.

"From the time we open the shielded crates to when the helicopter lifts off, will be less than three minutes."

"That's satisfactory. But I've made a slight change of plans. There is a large empty parking lot one mile south of here. Just before zero hour, truck the helicopter and the bombs there. We'll load the bombs in the parking lot, and I'll take off from that location, not here."

"That brings more risk to us," said Dennis cautiously.

"When Doctor Rodchenko examined the device on the flight from Albuquerque, he confirmed there was no tracking device installed. He needed to keep the GPS guidance-system unit turned on in order to complete his systems check, but doing that might have given the location to anyone looking for it."

"So the Americans might already know the bomb is in Las Vegas?"

"Possibly. But I won't switch on the GPS guidance system until the last minute."

"Once you do that, the Americans might scramble jets from Nellis Air Force Base—"

"Doubtful. It's a two-minute flight for me to the target. I'm not worried about being shot down."

"Then we are almost ready," said Dennis.

Viktor nodded but showed no joy in that acknowledgment, only concern.

"It's been a long time coming to this day," said Dennis. "So much money spent, so much preparation. Now we are ready to push the button, but you don't look happy."

"I'd be happier if Major Bennings had been killed by you in Albuquerque, as you promised me he would," said Viktor coldly.

Dennis casually lit another cigarette. He exhaled and smiled slightly, his ruddy cheeks like two ripe crab apples. "You gave me a last-minute assignment, Viktor, against a target whom you did not truly identify to me. You said Bennings was a defense attaché. You neglected to mention he was a member of the most elite intelligence unit in the American military's Special Operations Command. He has worked in incredibly dangerous areas *prior* to the arrival of SEAL Team Six or Delta Force. Do you understand the level of operator that represents and the skills he possesses? If you had explained this to me, my approach would have been much different, because someone such as Bennings is truly a hard target."

"Then I suppose I overestimated your abilities," said Popov.

Dennis's already red cheeks flushed darker crimson with a combination of anger and embarrassment, but he didn't speak.

"One of the reasons I ordered his sister kidnapped was to keep him from going to the authorities," said Popov. "But now, my concern is not so much the authorities as it is Bennings himself."

"Is that why Mikhail has left the country?"

Popov nodded. "My nephew is more prudent than I am. He has chosen to prepare for a worst-case scenario for this deception, and I gave him my blessing to do so."

"As I have told you before, since I never lie to you, I must repeat that your nephew is a coward. He can order men to kill, but he could never do it himself. This makes him weak."

"You're right. Mikhail is a numbers man, always hedging his bets. But it's good to have such people in the organization. You and I are warriors, Dennis. Today, we will either succeed spectacularly or fail abysmally." Popov looked intently, eye to eye with his top henchman. "Now that you know your adversary, prepare for another meeting with Bennings. I don't think we've seen the last of him." Popov stepped in very close to Dennis and thrust his finger in the blond man's chest. "And next time, if you don't kill him, you better die trying."

CHAPTER 33

The MD 530F helicopter sat parked in front of an end hangar at a private terminal of McCarran Airport, right off South Las Vegas Boulevard. The big sliding door of the steel hangar was closed, but an old Dodge diesel pickup truck stood idle inside.

Also inside were five people who were anything but idle. Jen worked her magic at a folding table covered with laptops, weapons, maps, and communications gear. Yulana sat hunched over a different table working a laptop. Angle started a portable backup diesel generator to test it, then quickly shut down the loud machine. Buzz made notes as he talked on a cell phone. Kit stood looking at a huge map of Las Vegas taped to the back wall.

Kit checked his watch and turned to the others. "Okay, everybody. Can we have a sitrep now?"

Everyone disengaged from what they were doing, and Kit and Angel moved closer to the tables.

"First and foremost, the search for Staci," said Kit, looking toward Buzz. "We have eighteen armed searchers working in pairs. They're coordinating with each other. All either retired cops or former military. They all know the risk, but they obviously don't have the big picture." Buzz crossed to a highlighted area of a Las Vegas city map that was tacked to an easel. "The challenge is that there are hundreds and hundreds of possible third-floor locations in the area Staci described in her text message."

"Could the Russians have moved her?" asked Kit.

"Too risky to move her, don't you think?"

"Probably. But just so you all know . . ." Kit made eye contact with each of them. "If Popov doesn't make his play by tonight, I'm joining the search for Staci."

Angel started to say something, then he looked over to Buzz, who in turn looked to Jen. It was Jen who spoke up. "Kit, we could use you here, but we all understand how you must feel. Anytime you want to join the search, just go. We'll handle this end."

Kit looked at his team for a long time. "Thank you."

"I have to say, though," said Buzz, "that we might not be the ones who find Staci."

"Meaning?" asked Kit.

"I have a friend in Metro PD, Criminal Intelligence Bureau."

"Buzz, how do you make all these friends?" asked Angel.

Buzz chuckled. "It's called being old and having spent your entire life working in intelligence and federal law enforcement. Anyway, I checked in with her when we started looking for Staci yesterday, and she told me there were two guys from army CID already working with Metro detectives trying to find her."

"CID?" Kit looked puzzled. He'd managed to get a short nap in the truck after Buzz had picked up him and Yulana at Jean Airport, but he felt like he could sleep for an entire day. He rubbed his red eyes. "Staci must have left messages on other numbers and they found one. Or they hacked my phone account. Shouldn't it be the FBI trying to find her, not CID?"

"Kit, I think everybody and their brother is trying to find Staci right now. And that's not a bad thing."

"There's probably one or two folks trying to find us, too," said Angel.

"You think?" said Kit smiling. "Okay, I feel good that we're doing what we can for Staci. Jen, what do you have on the jet?"

"The plane that carried the e-bomb from Albuquerque was a

Citation XLS, tail number N313XXX. It took off from North Las Vegas Airport shortly after it arrived. Its present location is unknown, but it belongs to a shell corporation suspected of being controlled by Popov.

"Chances are no one on the ground saw anything," continued Jen, "and there's zero indication that Popov is using North Las Vegas as his HQ. There's no sign he's here at McCarran, and no evidence he's working out of Henderson Airport, either."

"For all we know, he's going to use a drone to drop the bomb. So he could operate it off some remote paved road," said Angel.

"Or take off from a dirt strip if he's in a crop duster," said Kit. "But that might be good news. If he has farther to fly to the target, the better chance we have of stopping him."

"When the GPS signal returns, I can neutralize the bomb, regardless of its location, anywhere on earth. Which is what I recommend," said Yulana.

They all nodded. "That's good news," said Buzz.

"What if they've installed some other guidance system? A different GPS guidance system that we can't track?" asked Kit.

"Possibly, but that would be a gamble to use an untested guidance system. Too much chance of failure, so I don't think so," said Yulana.

Kit nodded. "Okay, but we have to proceed on the assumption that when Popov goes airborne he'll be carrying both bombs. I would if it was me."

"And I should remind all of you that if he detonates the Russian EMP device we assume he possesses, then those of you who will be responding on the ground must realize you will be heading into chaos," said Yulana. "Everything operated with electricity will stop working. Traffic lights will go out. All lights. Backup generators may come on, if they are diesel, but the devices they power may already be worthless. No phones or radios will function. Anything that has a battery, from children's toys to your laptops and iPods, will be ruined. Car and truck engines will stop and never run again. Except for some older diesels. Any aircraft flying in the target zone will likely crash."

"That's the big question: What is our target zone?" asked Buzz.

"Look at the military targets he could hit," said Kit, turning to the map. "Nellis Air Force Base, the Nevada National Security Site, the drone operations at Creech Air Force Base, the Tonopah Test Range . . ."

"And then there's the really secret stuff, a little farther north," joked Angel.

"I don't believe he's going after a military target," said Jen. "How could he benefit? And remember, just because the power and communications go out doesn't mean that bullets won't fire from soldiers' guns. He doesn't have enough thugs to overpower our security forces at sensitive facilities."

"It's got to be a casino," said Angel.

"Popov would need a small army to physically remove the cash from a casino. When he steals money, he does it electronically," said Buzz.

"Except for that armored-truck heist," said Jen.

"Actually," said Kit, "that's not quite true."

"What do you mean?" Buzz looked quizzically at Kit.

"I went back and did some research into that caper you told us about. The truck wasn't full of cash. The cargo was gems. Diamonds. Everyone assumed it was cash because it was an armored truck that had just done a bank pickup, but there was very little actual money in the truck. The jewelers who lost the gems didn't want publicity."

"Okay, so maybe not a casino," said Angel. "Unless one of them has some big diamond collection on display or something."

"The Wynn Casino has tens of millions of dollars in fine art, but I haven't heard about any diamond collection," said Jen.

"The thing about Popov is that he's primarily an information broker. What valuable information could he obtain by exploding the e-bomb?" asked Kit.

No one had an answer.

"Could it be information kept on computers in Faraday cages?" asked Jen. "That could explain hitting a military or government target."

"A Faraday cage," said Yulana, "is supposed to protect sensitive electronics from electromagnetic pulses. But the truth is that Faraday cages don't always work when an e-bomb is detonated. Popov would know that."

"And just to complicate our little puzzle further, don't forget that Yulana figured out there are most likely two targets," said Kit. "The first target requires the effects of an EMP weapon for the takedown, while the second target only requires a power outage from a rolling blackout."

Buzz, Angel, and Jen all shook their heads.

"Whatever it is, it has to be a big score," said Buzz. "Huge. Gargantuan. Popov would not risk having the full might of the U.S. government come after him for detonating an EMP device on our soil unless he stood to gain . . . hundreds of millions of dollars. Minimum." They all exchanged looks.

"That's more than I make in a month," cracked Angel, breaking the solemn mood.

"A little more than you and me combined, Angel," said Kit smiling. "We're going to have to live with the fact that we don't know the target yet. So we keep working the phones. Everyone is ready? Everyone knows their responsibilities?"

They all nodded.

"The truck and helicopter are loaded with goodies," said Angel. "All of the weapons have infrared or thermal sights, in case we roll at night. And if Jen loses power here in the hangar when we're out in the field, I rigged the generator to come on automatically."

"Some of my local contacts who are well connected introduced me to the people who really run this town," said Buzz. "And I'm not talking about the mayor or any politicians. I had a conference call with a few people and gave them a friendly, unofficial heads-up that there might be a big heist coming down soon, and I suggested they may want to tighten up their security. What does this get us? Right now, nothing. But if Popov pulls off a robbery that affects these people, we'll have some new friends in this town who will go to bat for us."

"Always good to have more friends," said Kit. "Thanks for all the good work, everybody."

The impromptu meeting over, Kit reached into a bag from the Coffee Bean & Tea Leaf and grabbed an extra-large green-tea latte as Yulana joined him.

"Doctor Petkova," said Kit, as he fished out another paper cup of tea and handed it to her. "I want you to know that I haven't forgotten my promise to you. About Kala."

Just the mention of her daughter's name caused Yulana's eyes to moisten. "I'm trying hard to keep believing that maybe . . ." A tear rolled down her cheek. Kit gently brushed it off with his hand.

"Popov's hackers stole a lot of money from my mom, but the family fortune that they obviously didn't know about was untouched."

"Family fortune?"

"You didn't know you married well?" he asked with a small smile. "I bring this up only to tell you that . . . Buzz helped me make some arrangements. Put some money into an escrow account. If something happens to me before I can do it myself, I'm putting out a contract in Moscow."

"To kill Popov?" she asked, a bit confused.

He smiled. "Not that kind of contract. It's to find and rescue Kala. There are private security companies staffed with veteran operators that specialize in that kind of thing. So if something happens to me, well, I don't want you to give up hope."

Kit took a sip of the lukewarm tea drink and then set it down. But he couldn't set down the heavy weight that sat on his shoulders, the weight he'd been carrying since this whole mess began. He flinched slightly as Yulana took his hand and held it.

"First we have to find Staci," she said.

Kit slowly nodded. "I don't think they'll kill her as long as I'm still alive."

"So promise me you won't get killed."

"Promise," said Kit, smiling wearily. "But in case the man upstairs has other plans, if possible, could you make sure that my sister gets this?" asked Kit, indicating the key he wore around his neck. "It has special meaning to my family."

"I promise."

CHAPTER 34

Bobby Chan and Ron Franklin didn't bother checking in with Metro PD. They simply started inspecting hotel or apartment units that seemed a likely prospect. But their idea of "likely prospect" was different from CID Agents Flood and Bates's purely methodical, grid approach. It was the difference between employing veteran detectives using only their instincts to spot potential terrorists in airports or employing the TSA and their politically correct dogmas to spot terrorists. One way was effective, the other created jobs and bureaucratic fiefdoms.

The San Bernardino detectives ruled out condos and any upscale apartment buildings. Most hotels were held in abeyance for now. Their first priority was lower-rent establishments—the "no questions asked" type motels or hotels and "no contract, no lease" apartments that catered to a more-transient and lower-end crowd. And unlike the CID boys, Chan and Franklin not only asked at the office, but they personally knocked on every suspect third-floor door.

They grabbed burgers from Wendy's and ate as they walked the interior and exterior hallways or walkways of sketchy buildings close to, but west of the Strip and south of the Rio and Palms. Their feet hurt, but they never complained; they just kept moving.

.   .   .

"Would you rather that Major Bennings have been killed at the CIA safe house?" asked Secretary of State Margarite Padilla.

"Yes, I suppose so. Then we wouldn't be wasting the president's time having this emergency meeting. And a highly destructive American weapon that could send one of our cities back to the Stone Age wouldn't be in the hands of a Russian gangster," snapped John Stout, the DCI—Director of Central Intelligence—the top boss man of the CIA.

To say the meeting was contentious was to put a positive spin on it.

The secret Presidential Finding that had allowed Padilla to use a CIA SAD officer and an operator from the Activity to run the Moscow op that uncovered U.S. moles had been an irritant to Stout for the last six months; but now, with that secret finding out in the open, others in the room who considered counterintelligence to be their fiefdom unleashed a firestorm of resentment. National Security Adviser Bob Shay, the FBI director, and others were steaming because they hadn't been informed of the action and they would always fight fiercely for control of their perceived turfs, or for, at the very least, being kept in the loop. File that one under big egos, ruffled feathers, and interagency rivalries.

"Viktor Popov apparently has a Russian-built e-bomb that he was going to use if he couldn't get one of ours," said Padilla.

"Do you have some evidence to back that up?" asked Stout.

"No, she doesn't," said Shay, answering for her, "but there's plenty of evidence that her man Bennings and his Russian bride stole the bomb from Sandia. And shot up half of Albuquerque."

"Thanks for answering for me, Bob, but would you mind saving the second-guessing until after I finish the brief?"

"I think we got the gist of it, Margarite," said President Jason Lane. Thin and savvy, Lane appeared intently focused on the issues at hand. "The secretary of state didn't authorize Bennings to steal the bomb, so keep the sniping down, people. The question is what to do now."

"We throw everything we've got at finding Bennings and his

most likely collaborators," said Stout. The DCI signaled his aide, who distributed dossiers on Buzz Van Wyke, Angel Perez, and Jen Huffman to everyone in the room.

"Wouldn't our efforts better be served by focusing on Viktor Popov and *his* collaborators?" asked Padilla. "Unless you're protecting a source, John."

"That's out of line." Stout gave Padilla a look that suggested he intended to get even with her. And soon.

"Well, John, the CIA has a history of protecting Popov, doesn't it?" asked Secretary of Defense Dan Bartok. Bartok was the old college buddy of Sheriff McCain's brother-in-law and was already taking action regarding the spying mess created by the two CID officers and their NSA pal.

"I wasn't the DCI then."

"No," said the president, "but you're the DCI now, and neither the CIA nor FBI uncovered this plot, did they? Why did I hear about it from a lone operator working undercover for the State Department?"

"Sounds to me like the lone operator is in on it. Maybe that's why, Mister President," said Stout.

"Considering what happened to Bennings's family, that's cynical, John. Even for you. We're here right now because Major Bennings has been keeping the secretary of state apprised of developments," said the president, not bothering to hide his displeasure.

"So Secretary Padilla makes a mess and we have to clean it up, is that it?" asked Shay.

President Lane slammed his coffee cup down, breaking it. "The next person who bitches about turf issues and doesn't focus on protecting the country will be removed from this room . . . and will *never* return, as long as I'm president. I want to hear constructive comments and potential solutions only, is that clear? Save the butcher work for some other meeting."

Silence fell over the room. The president wasn't known for such outbursts, and so Stout, Shay, and others knew they'd have to proceed in a more . . . clever fashion.

"Clearly the focus should be on finding Viktor Popov and his men," said Padilla.

"Agreed," said the president.

"We should quietly raise the DEFCON level and security threat level nationwide. Deploy agents or local officers to every airport in the country," suggested Bartok.

"We should close the airspace over the Las Vegas Strip and all military and federal sites in Nevada," said Shay, trying to sound helpful now.

"We'll need armed jets over Las Vegas and other sites in Nevada flying continuous sorties. If the e-bomb's GPS gets activated, we will have a very short shoot-down time," offered Stout.

"We'll need to move more fighter squadrons into the area," said Bartok.

"Alert FEMA and the governors of every state within five hundred miles of Las Vegas to ramp up their disaster response agencies," suggested the FBI director.

"I disagree with most of what's being suggested here." Donna Ibrahim, the president's chief of staff, was perhaps the craftiest political player in the room. Her remark garnered sharp visual reactions from everyone. But no one spoke, because they all respected just how sly, conniving, and totally amoral she was.

"Elaborate on that, Donna," said President Lane.

"First, we're talking about a nonlethal weapon that will cause no loss of life. Second, the bomb's target zone is very small and would affect relatively few people. Third, there's a very good chance the target is civilian and does not threaten national security. So since there's no evidence that Popov possesses a Russian bomb, and since Bennings can deactivate the Sandia bomb if the GPS signal becomes active, we should take only very discreet actions.

"Forget about going public in any way, and don't notify any states or governors that they may have a crisis on their hands—that would leak out to the press almost instantly. Instead, we implement a covert, full-court press to hunt down Viktor Popov and his gang's leadership and terminate all of them, unofficially, of course. Popov's entire U.S. organization must be dismantled, regardless of whether they are legal entities or not. This will send a message to the Russians not to try anything like this again.

"We should announce a training exercise and close all airspace over military installations and sensitive federal sites in the Southwest. And yes, have twenty-four/seven armed jets patrolling with secret orders to shoot down any intruders.

"We tell the Sandia folks that a secret CIA Red Team stole their device and to keep their mouths shut about it. We tell Albuquerque PD a training exercise went awry, to cover up the shoot-out there. The shopping mall explosion in El Monte is easy: since Russian gangsters were the only fatalities, we have DEA sell it as a drug beef. The LAX smoke-bomb business we call another Red Team exercise. And by the way, why *didn't* the local yokels find those devices before they went off? Put some public pressure in the press for LAPD to tighten up at LAX.

"As for Major Bennings and his team, they must be captured and extensively debriefed. Bennings should then be promoted, given some medals, and forced to retire from the army. But make it an honorable discharge, and let him keep his pension."

After a few moments, a number of people in the room began to nod in agreement; not Stout or Shay, but a consensus had emerged.

Padilla had a slight smile on her face as she stared at Ibrahim. A bigger snake you couldn't find in D.C., but the woman had hit on a plan that would probably satisfy most in the room. And it protected the powers that be while leaving the public with their asses hanging out, making it business as usual in Washington.

Bennings would only lose his career, not his freedom. That was more than he expected he would get when he made the decision to go rogue. Of course, his freedom was contingent upon his not being killed by Viktor Popov.

CHAPTER 35

Two pickup trucks, a couple of big "bucket trucks," and a lowboy semitrailer carrying a giant, 87-ton D10 bulldozer, turned as a convoy from South Rainbow Boulevard onto West Post Road just north of the 215 freeway on a beautiful Las Vegas night, with the faint scent of desert sage wafting in a slight breeze.

The convoy pulled over and parked a half block from Rainbow Boulevard.

Dennis Kedrov, wearing a white hard hat, sat in the passenger seat of the lead pickup. A pile of weapons on the floorboard was covered with a dirty blanket.

Dennis lit a Turkish cigarette and marveled at how well built the road was for such a lightly traveled street. It would not be so in Mother Russia, where too many hands reached in, hands like his own, so there was seldom enough money to do simple things right.

He would surely miss America, but with the bonus money he was about to earn, the south of France would do just fine. He already had his eye on a couple of chalets.

Alex Bobrik bent down in the small underground room, grabbed the handles, and eased the wooden panel out of the concrete wall as his two assistants watched. Alex crawled through the opening into the room on the other side of the wall, and his assistants began passing electronics and the other gear to him that had been stacked and was ready to use in the long-awaited deception.

An orange-pink sunset painted the horizon above the Spring Mountains. The Vegas Strip ran calmer with a quiet interlude before the controlled chaos of the evening's diversions. One in a seemingly constant stream of blue-and-red Southwest Airlines jets roared in low at McCarran Airport and touched down on runway 1L.

In a private hangar not far from where the Southwest flight just landed, Yulana dozed with her head on the table next to a laptop; the tips of her fingers, which twitched slightly as she slept, rested on the now-dog-eared photograph of her and her daughter, Kala.

Kit stirred from his own nap and checked his watch. He rubbed his eyes, grabbed an untouched cup of cold tea, and crossed over toward Jen and Buzz, whose tired eyes scanned laptop screens. Angel slumped in a chair as he made adjustments to the guts of a handheld radio using his lucky green screwdriver.

"Any word on Staci?" asked Kit.

Buzz shook his head.

"I'll hang around another hour. Then I'm going to join the search." Kit looked over to Yulana. "She's got to be worried sick about her daughter, but you should have seen how she handled herself in Albuquerque."

"Life-or-death stakes. People do things they never thought they could do," said Buzz.

"Kit, there's something here you need to see. It's about your family, and about you."

Kit's face grew serious as he walked around behind Jen. "What you got?"

"News item from the Internet," she said, as Angel joined the group.

Jen clicked PLAY and the video of a Los Angeles TV news reporter appeared on the screen.

"San Bernardino County Sheriff Jim McCain held a press conference today and announced that the death of a Chino Hills woman was

now being classified as a homicide and is linked to a recent multiple murder and possible kidnapping in a Chino Hills home.

"Gina Bennings, age sixty, was found dead in her car at the bottom of an arroyo off of Carbon Canyon Road.

"Forensic evidence now links her death to the grisly scene of a gun battle in her home, where Rick and Maria Carrillo were shot to death by unknown assailants. The fingerprints of Gina Bennings's missing daughter, Staci, were found on a tranquilizer dart at the scene, and detectives now believe she was tranquilized, kidnapped, and remains missing.

"Here's what Sheriff McCain had to say about the strange case":

"I'd like to reassure the citizens of Chino Hills and all of San Bernardino County that they are not in danger. While I can't get into details, my department has a good idea of who the perpetrators are, and now that we are working closely with the FBI and the army's Criminal Investigation Command, we expect a breakthrough very soon.

"My detectives would very much like to talk to Major Kitman Bennings, who disappeared after arriving in Los Angeles two days ago. He is not a suspect in the murders or kidnapping. In fact, he's exactly the opposite. There is concern that he might be a target and might now be suffering from some kind of emotional breakdown.

"General Stoakes, the newly appointed commander of CID, asked me to make clear that no charges will be filed against Major Bennings for any actions he has committed during the last seven days, if he reports for duty at any army post in the next twenty-four hours. That is an ironclad guarantee of amnesty and a good-faith public gesture on the army's part to help solve the horrible tragedy that has befallen the Bennings family. That's all I can say for now."

"So a very unusual case continues to develop here in San Bernardino. I'm Roberto Riviera, Fox 11 News."

Jen clicked off the video.

"Politics, politics, politics. They're worried about me. That's nice to know," said Kit.

"The army sent a message through the sheriff granting you blanket amnesty." Buzz looked Kit in the eye.

"They want the bomb back," said Kit.

"Whatever their motivation, we all hope you take the offer seriously."

"There's nothing I can do to change the fact that my military career is over. They may not bring me up on charges, but I'm toast."

"Toast sounds better than thirty years in a military correctional facility," said Angel.

"I think they're more scared of what *you* might do than of what Popov might do," said Jen.

"They should be. Because I'm not giving up till my sister is safe, and until I've evened a score with Viktor Popov."

CHAPTER 36

Popov watched from the shadows as technicians attached two bombs—one Russian, one American—onto hard points on the R66 helicopter's undercarriage. This was done in the open in the unlit parking lot off South Las Vegas Boulevard. And as Viktor had predicted, no one noticed. A traffic cop could have pulled up and called it in, and the whole deception would be in the toilet. But no one in glitzy Las Vegas noticed a black helicopter with no lights and no markings sitting on a truck in the rear of a dark, empty parking lot.

The rotors were untethered, the tie-downs removed. The copter would lift off right from the bed of the lowboy trailer.

Popov's already hulking form looked even larger due to the bulk of a slim black parachute he wore snugly over his black flight suit. The technicians smiled at the boss, but he only scowled. He turned away from them, and as a throwaway afterthought said, "See you in L.A." They had no way of knowing that, win or lose tonight, he had no intention of ever returning to Los Angeles.

Popov stepped up onto the trailer and climbed into the cockpit. The first thing he checked was to make sure the transponder was switched off. Three minutes later he was airborne, flying dark as he gained altitude while heading northwest. One minute from the target, he activated the American bomb's GPS guidance system.

. . .

Jen Huffman's laptop alarm beeped, and she snapped to, ultra-alert. One of her screens displayed a map of the Las Vegas area and showed a "+" marker moving slowly.

"I've got it! I've got the bomb. Heading northwest, approaching the Two-fifteen freeway."

Yulana, who had just made herself some tea, scrambled to her laptop.

"Yulana, we're on!" said Kit, as he slipped on the shoulder holster holding the subgun.

"One second," she said, diving into her chair. The computer had gone into sleep mode, so she pressed ENTER to bring it back to life. As the others looked on anxiously, she had to wait several seconds for her software program to refresh. "One second," she said again, with anticipation.

When a new page finally popped onto the screen, her fingers flew over the keyboard. She hesitated, shot Kit a quick look, and then pressed ENTER. She exhaled. "It's done. The American EMP weapon should be deactivated."

"Let's pray you're right," said Kit. "Okay, we roll!"

Angel began to muscle open the heavy sliding steel hangar door, and Kit and Yulana ran through the opening, toward the helicopter, as Buzz climbed behind the wheel of the diesel pickup.

Kit switched off the transponder and started the chopper. Buzz backed the truck out. Angel closed the hangar door and then jumped into the truck cab with Buzz.

The pickup drove off at the same time Kit lifted the copter into the Vegas night air. He stayed low, just high enough to clear the hangars, then flew westward as close to the deck as he could. Within seconds he was off the airport. Chances were, no one from the far-off tower would have spotted the lights-out takeoff, and chances were also good that on this busy night full of incoming air traffic, the controllers wouldn't notice any image the airport's BRITE radar might paint of the MD 530F, as long as he flew at minimum altitude.

Jen remained in the hangar and adjusted her radio headset as her eyes excitedly flashed across four laptop screens.

"We're on, fellas," she said into the headset boom mike as she rubbed her hands together in anticipation.

Bobby Chan and Ron Franklin stood in the office of Siegel Suites on West Tropicana going through the folders connected to all third-floor tenants. The company made color copies of driver's licenses of all adults staying in each unit and also took Social Security card, credit card, and other documentation. But somehow, all of the paperwork didn't keep the riffraff out.

Chan stopped when he got to the folder of Lily Bain. He stared at her photo. "Hey, Franklin, here's a Blondie." Chan looked at the other documents in the folder. "Shacked up with some guy named Gregory. Remember the long blond hair we found?"

"She looks kind'a hard," said Franklin.

"She is kind of hard," said the desk clerk.

"What do you mean?"

"I was working when she checked in. Pegged her for just another working girl. We get loads of them here. She had a fresh welt on the side of her head like somebody had hit her a good one."

Chan and Franklin looked at each other.

"She have an accent?"

"When you came in, you said you were looking for Russians, but I don't know what that sounds like, except from the movies. She could have been a foreigner, I guess, but her ID was all American."

"What about Gregory?"

"He stayed in the car. She brought the ID in, so I never seen him."

"You get a look at the car?"

"Tinted windows and it was night. Didn't see a thing. But my girlfriend, JoAnn, lives just down from them on the third floor. She's long-term, comes for six months every year, but she's about to go back to Michigan for the summer. JoAnn keeps an eye on everybody 'cause she's scared of being robbed again. She might know something."

"Can you give your friend a call? We can meet her in the laundry room, ask a couple of questions."

Popov had reached his intended altitude and released the bomb stolen by Kit Bennings from Sandia National Labs. He heard radio traffic from Las Vegas air traffic controllers demanding certain unidentified aircraft identify themselves. *Idiots,* he thought. In Russia, jets would have already been scrambled to shoot him down.

He wouldn't be able to see the small aboveground explosion, and the actual effects of the device were invisible, but the affected area on the ground would go instantly dark. So he circled at a safe distance, watching for a patch of black to emerge from the light. It was a metaphor for his life, as Viktor Popov was a man who created darkness.

But this time, as he stared downward, it was the light that won out.

Jen Huffman relayed the GPS coordinates of the EMP device to Kit and Buzz simultaneously. "This is weird, but the signal is stationary. Wouldn't the GPS unit be destroyed on impact?"

"Apparently not. Give me the location," said Kit.

"Two blocks east of South Rainbow and just north of West Post Road, but, wait and I'll tell you what's in the immediate vicinity.... Looks like half a dozen different companies—Consolidated Janitorial, Good Times Catering, Mainichi Auction House. That might be it. Private storage vaults!"

"That's it," said Kit. "Buzz, you copy?"

"Copy."

"Hey, Yulana. Congratulations! The little boy didn't go boom," said Angel.

"But I'm worried about his crude Russian cousin," she said.

Alex Bobrik and his two assistants sat patiently waiting in the subterranean room below AT&T's PIC. PIC was an unofficial nickname used by telecom workers when referring to the "central office," a physical location where local communication lines are merged with interexchange, or long haul lines.

The basement room where Alex and his team waited housed a main repeater station for AT&T's southern fiber-optic trunk line. A massive three-foot-wide bundle of fiber-optic cables—there were thirty thousand individual fiber-optic cables in the bundle—ran vertically up from an opening in the cement floor and entered a gigantic relay switch. The bundle ran out of the other side of the switch and disappeared back into the cement floor as it continued its journey across the United States, all the way to Los Angeles.

There was no more space left for data on this cable bundle, since the recent severing of AT&T's northern fiber-optic trunk line in Wyoming had caused all available room to be given to customers with the biggest clout—the big banks and the U.S. government.

The Russian technician with dark circles under her eyes adjusted some sort of electronic collar that had been placed around the cable bundle. The collar was connected via inch-thick black cables to some kind of portable device about the size of a microwave oven, and Alex's laptops were connected to that device, which the Russians had nicknamed, the "toaster."

Alex checked his watch, but what they were really waiting for was a radical change in the reading of the voltmeter Alex held, a change that would signal the power was out at the AT&T facility, out due to rolling blackouts that would soon plague the entire city and hence would not draw any suspicion to the PIC itself.

When the power went off, however briefly, Alex could make an "electronic splice" and begin stealing some of the most closely guarded secrets of a host of major banks, stock exchanges, brokerage houses, Fortune 500 companies, and the United States government, including secure communications from POTUS—President of the United States— and some of America's intelligence agencies.

And the best part was that the thefts would go unnoticed until long after the catastrophic damage was done.

CHAPTER 37

Dennis Kedrov checked the time on the dashboard clock as he rolled the yellow golf ball around in his hand. He knew something was wrong. He could see all of the lights still on for blocks ahead.

Each of the trucks in Dennis's convoy had very heavy, specially constructed boxes made of lead. Those boxes held all of the men's electronics: watches, cell phones, two-way radios, flashlights, laser sights, and thermal optics. This was precautionary, since they were parked just outside of the estimated zone of effective damage. The trucks' diesel engines would not be affected, he had been told, even if they were inside the zone.

He shook his head and smiled. *Bennings has outwitted Viktor Popov!* Dennis knew it was true, and a part of him was thrilled by the revelation. Yes, his boss would simply now drop the Russian bomb, and if it worked, the plan would still go forward. But Popov had not planned well at all. The American should never have been approached. This should have been a Russian *maskirovka* operation exclusively from start to finish. What in the world had gotten into his boss? But then, Dennis knew the answer, and had already begun taking steps to protect his own interests. Clearly, former KGB General Viktor Popov was well past his prime.

And when crime lords are past their prime, upheaval generally follows.

"Tak chto, dorogiye priduki, my zakonchili igrat'?" So, dear assholes, *are we finished playing?* Popov scowled as he released the Russian bomb and sent it hurtling toward the airspace above Mainichi Auction House.

He nosed the helo into a radical descent but kept a wide birth of the target area to escape the effects of the bomb.

Jerry Kotsky checked the wall clock in the security duty office of Mainichi Auction House. He checked the wall clock because his watch, along with certain other items, right now rested in a lead box disguised to look like his lunch cooler.

Any second, he thought. The night-shift lieutenant sat at the duty officer's desk filling out paperwork. The female officer at the CCTV monitor station had a bank of sixteen monitors in front of her, but she was cycling through other camera views, doing a good job of keeping an eye on things.

Then suddenly the room went dark. Pitch black. All of the monitors shut down, every last LED light was gone. Jerry literally could not see the fingers just inches from his eyes.

"What the hell?!" exclaimed Jerry.

"What's going on, what happened?! Where are the emergency lights?" asked the lieutenant. "The backup generators?"

"I can't see a thing," said Jerry as he bent down in the utter, complete blackness and found his cooler, then flipped open the lid.

"Damn!" yelled the lieutenant.

"What now?" asked the female officer.

"My cell phone is red hot. I was going to use it as a flashlight," said the lieutenant.

"Mine too, call nine-one-one."

"Yeah, no kidding, if I can find the phone. Use your radio to call and have everybody check in. Jerry, grab a flashlight."

"My flashlight isn't working," said Jerry.

"The battery is hot on my radio," said the female officer. "Radio check, radio check."

There was no answer.

"Press the squelch button."

"I tried, but it's not working," she said.

"What the hell is happening? Jerry, you're a smoker, where's your lighter?" barked the lieutenant.

"One second."

Jerry found the HK45 Tactical pistol in his cooler with a suppressor attached and a thermal sight. He felt for the button, and the thermal sight lit up.

"There's no dial tone for the phone. Damn! The lighter, Jerry!" said the lieutenant impatiently.

"Here, let me light you up." Jerry stood and fired two rounds into the lieutenant's head, and was fascinated by how the blood splatter looked through the thermal sight, which showed temperature variations of surface objects.

The screams of the female officer suggested that even with the suppressor attached, she must have seen some muzzle flash, so Jerry found her in the sight as she stumbled toward a wall, and he shot her three times.

He turned on a flashlight that he'd also removed from his cooler and put one more round into her head. He then crossed to his special cooler and equipped himself with the rest of the gear from within: two-way radio, two cell phones, extra flashlights, ammo magazines, and night-vision goggles. He put the goggles on, turned off the flashlight, and *voilà!* He could see but no one could see him. He opened the door and moved into the total blackness of the hallway, looking for targets.

"What the heck is going on? Did you guys knock out the power?" yelled the Mainichi front gate guard. He had come out of the guard shack and called out to a worker in a white hard hat who looked like he was from the power company, although it was hard to see in the dark, with the only light coming from the moon and stars.

Smiling as big as ever, Dennis Kedrov walked up to the guard on the other side of the massive steel gate.

"The phone is out, the radio won't work, and my cell phone exploded," said the guard in disbelief.

"Some kind of super blackout," said Dennis, looking closely at the gate. "Don't think your electric gate is going to open anytime soon, either."

"How will I get home?"

Dennis then casually shot the guard three times in the chest. "Don't think you're going home, except to see Jesus."

Dennis signaled with a flashlight to the men who had just driven the lowboy trailer up to Mainichi, and the D10 bulldozer roared to life. The tracked dozer drove off the trailer, pivoted, and quickly bore down on Mainichi's front gate. With it's scoop lifted to use as a battering ram, the bulldozer, whose engine produced 700 horsepower, easily knocked down the gate and drove on toward the building itself.

Dennis's men swarmed in, flanking the bulldozer, as other men drove down the dark street in both directions and blocked it with their big bucket trucks.

A guard stepped out of Mainichi's front door and stood still, shocked by the sight of the dozer closing in. He reached for his weapon but was cut down before he could remove it from his holster.

Dennis spoke into his two-way radio over the roar of the dozer's engine. "Camel, this is Tiger, copy."

"Tiger, scratch two inside."

"Camel, scratch two outside. So three more inside."

"Hit the first waypoint; I'm clear," said Jerry.

The bulldozer operator had a GPS unit taped to the windshield. Jerry had long ago provided GPS waypoints—very specific saved coordinates—so the D10 made for the first waypoint and drove right through the reinforced wall of Mainichi Auction House.

"Scratch two more inside," came the radio traffic from Jerry in the building.

"Roger. One remaining inside," said Dennis.

. . .

"The Sandia bomb landed in the vacant lot just behind Mainichi. I'm still reading the GPS signal," said Jen into her headset as she monitored developments from her post inside the hangar at McCarran Airport. "Could the bomb have survived impact?"

Kit and Yulana both wore headsets in the MD 530F, as they cautiously approached the target area. "That's possible, Jen. Intact, unexploded bombs that have been dropped from airplanes during past wars are uncovered fairly frequently. Buzz, are you copying this traffic?"

"Affirmative," said Buzz

"Before you and Angel leave the area, try to get the remnants of the device," said Kit.

"We'll try," said Buzz into a handheld radio, as he slowed the pickup truck on West Post Road. "We're coming up on a roadblock."

Angel swept the area ahead of them using the scope on an M4 rifle. "I'm counting three armed men next to the truck."

Kit used forward-looking infrared optics to scan the Mainichi compound as he hovered the helicopter. "Jen, call Metro PD and tell them a bulldozer is knocking down the walls to the building right now," said Kit. "Buzz, take out that roadblock; I'll get the roadblock at the other end of the street."

"Look!" said Yulana. "There's another helicopter."

"We got a bird touching down inside the fence at Mainichi. I'll bet it's Popov, here to take the loot," said Kit as he nosed the copter in for a landing between one of the truck blockades and the Mainichi building.

CHAPTER 38

Buzz crouched, hiding in the truck bed, as Angel drove the battered old truck with salsa music blaring from the radio right up to the bucket truck blocking the road. Popov's men shined lights into his eyes and yelled, "Go back!"

Angel smiled and waved and blabbered on in rapid-fire Puerto Rican Spanish. He stopped the truck and slowly got out, making sure to keep his hands visible to them but without drawing attention to that fact.

"I must to go clean!" said Angel with a thick accent. "I good clean for my boss!"

The Russians didn't have orders to kill people, just not to let them pass. The burly leader stepped forward, hiding a gun under his jacket. "Come back in one hour. Big problem here right now."

"One hour?" asked Angel, looking to the faces of the three men he clocked at the blockade. "Okay, I go back." As Angel turned from them, the Russians relaxed.

But Angel had a gun under his jacket, too, and he simultaneously pulled it and spun, and in less than two seconds, literally, he had shot all three men in the head.

Buzz popped up from the truck bed with an M4 to cover Angel, but he'd gotten them all.

"Good shooting, as usual, *mijo*. Grab the keys from the truck and let's go!"

Angel pulled the keys from the ignition of the bucket truck and then climbed into the pickup, as Buzz slowly rolled past and onward toward Mainichi Auction House.

A hundred yards away, Buzz stopped the truck, and he and Angel moved forward on opposite sides of the street. They immediately came under fire from thugs guarding the front gate area.

Just as Popov got out of the R66, Dennis realized his men were engaging targets on the street, so he ran to his boss.

"Viktor, it seems there's another player at the roulette table tonight. Please take cover."

Popov looked over with a scowl. "Bennings."

"I would think so."

"Where are the diamonds?"

"Give me sixty seconds." Dennis sprinted in through the huge, gaping hole in the building's wall and disappeared into the dark cavern.

Dennis held a small night-vision monocular to his eye as he ran. He followed the booming thunder of the D10 smashing steel and concrete, but he already knew where it was going; he'd memorized the blueprints and waypoints for the attack. He rounded a corner and came upon the dozer as it smashed through another wall.

"Stop!" yelled Jerry to the driver. "That's good!"

Using a gargantuan bulldozer to access the diamonds was kind of an on-steroids version of a smash-and-grab jewelry store heist. Jerry and several thugs lit up the large private vault with portable lights and quickly went to work emptying dozens of slide-out, velvet-lined trays of fine diamonds from a standing cabinet. They dumped the contents of each tray into a black valise on a table as Dennis watched.

In seconds the job was finished. Dennis stepped forward, closed the valise, and handed it to one of the thugs. "Run fast and get this to Viktor. All of you go with him!"

Dennis motioned for the dozer operator to come down from the cab. "Follow them!"

"What about me?" asked Jerry, the inside man.

"A one-million-dollar bonus. Ride with me in the bulldozer, you can—"

"Jerry!" called a voice from the darkness.

As Jerry and Dennis turned, three shots rang out, all hitting Jerry in the chest. Dennis emptied his gun at a dark form, which then fell into a pool of light.

"You didn't scratch the last guard, Jerry."

Jerry lay on the dust-covered floor, gasping for breath. Dennis stood over him and reloaded his gun. "You could have had a million dollars, my friend." Dennis then put two rounds into Jerry's head.

Dennis climbed into the cab of the idling D10, grabbed the controls, pivoted the beast, and powered it right through a wall.

Kit left the helicopter idling and ducked under the spinning rotor blades as he waved to the men at the blockade just up the street. "*Bystro! Idi syuda, speshite!*" Kit called out in Russian. *Quick, come here! Hurry up!*

Starlight provided the ambient lighting, and the three men from the blockade ran forward in the dimness. As they got close, Kit leveled his Sub-2000 at them. "Stop! Drop your weapons!"

But one of the men wanted to be a hero and raised his gun.

The shoot-out was over in a couple of seconds, and all three men lay dead.

Yulana scrambled over to Kit and looked without compassion at the dead men.

"Sorry you had to see that," said Kit.

"Men such as this came in the middle of the night to take my daughter," she said coldly. She bent down and grabbed a pistol from a dead man. "Maybe you don't trust me quite yet, but I think I should have a gun."

"All you had to do was ask!" Kit smiled. "Hey, do me a favor, go grab the keys out of that truck. I don't want Popov's other rats to drive away before the police arrive. Then wait for me here, okay?"

Kit ran off toward the Mainichi building. Buzz and Angel were still exchanging small-arms fire with men at the front gate. Then Kit heard an engine whine and could make out the R66 lifting off from inside the compound.

"Damn!" Kit stopped in his tracks. He aimed carefully and fired three-shot bursts at the rising helicopter. As he reached for the radio on his belt, the D10 bulldozer exploded though an exterior wall of the Mainichi building, sending chunks of concrete, plaster, and grit flying everywhere. The yellow behemoth belched black diesel exhaust as it hurtled across a small grassy area, then crashed through the steel fence and careened onto the street.

"Buzz, disengage and grab the RT-Seven," said Kit into the two-way.

"Roger that!"

Kit loaded a new magazine without taking his eyes off the bulldozer, and fixed on the blond man in the lighted cab; the man turned on a spotlight and swung the beam, illuminating Kit like a Broadway star delivering a solo.

"We have cascading blackouts now hitting the city!" crackled Jen's voice over the radio.

"I could use a little blackout right now," mumbled Kit to himself. He fired a burst but missed the spotlight. The blond dozer operator then lifted the huge steel scoop and accelerated.

Kit turned on his heels and ran like hell. "Get into the copter!" he yelled at Yulana.

She saw him running forward with the dozer chasing him, so she moved quickly into the cockpit, which sat facing the charging bulldozer.

Good thing I didn't shut the bird down! Kit didn't waste time with the seat belt. As he looked up, the tracked yellow giant, with its steel teeth glistening on the scoop, hurtled closer. Kit twisted the throttle to maximum power as he yanked up the collective.

The MD 530F lifted straight into the air as the scoop rose high on the D10, trying to catch the helo. The raised scoop of the skittering dozer missed the rising helicopter's skids by inches.

Kit pushed the cyclic forward, and the copter tilted forward and accelerated as it found altitude. He'd last seen Popov heading north and so directed the bird northward, pushing it to its limits. Popov's R66 was a slower aircraft, and Kit scanned the sky for his prey.

Kit put on his headset and shot Yulana a quick look. "Any idea who the blond guy was?"

"Yes: a crazy man. Did they get what they came for?" she asked, over the headset.

"Probably. But unless he has more tricks, Popov can run but he can't hide."

"Vegas PD is rolling up in force to Mainichi. They're already chasing down men on foot," said Jen over the radio.

"Jen, have you hacked into the BRITE radar display from McCarran?" asked Kit.

"Roger. He's painting pretty weak, but I have him at your eleven o'clock, heading northeast, crossing Russell Road at Jones Boulevard right now."

"Got him!"

Kit eased the cyclic stick to the left as he closed the gap between him and Popov.

"The rolling blackouts are heading toward the Strip," said Jen, over the radio. "What do you think the other target is?"

"Maybe he's going there right now."

CHAPTER 39

The electricity was still working on South Las Vegas Boulevard near Agate Avenue. Security lights illuminated the old boarded-up motel compound that secretly functioned as Viktor Popov's headquarters.

Next door to the motel was an AT&T facility surrounded by a barbed-wire-topped, ten-foot-high chain-link fence. Huge wooden spools held cabling as thick as your fist and sat stacked in the parking lot, next to parked utility trucks, bucket trucks, and mobile generators mounted on trailers.

A bone-colored two-story, cement-block, L-shaped building suggested little about the contents inside, although a square, four-story-tall microwave tower rose up from the roof.

But who notices microwave towers anymore? The whole AT&T complex, in fact, was hard to notice in a city like Las Vegas. So much screams for attention in Sin City, so many glittery, sensual, over-the-top visual distractions assault the senses, that the unassuming easily goes unnoticed.

Unless you were a communications techie or geek. Or a thief looking to steal some copper or a mobile generator or maybe the Keys to the Kingdom.

Alex Bobrik tried to relax as he sat on an overturned plastic crate in the subterranean room. The constant harmonics of the humming electronics and the soft glow of dozens of LED lights felt soothingly reassuring in a kind of bizarre, postindustrial way. His back ached like crazy from all of the tunnel crawling and now from sitting frozen in place, one hand holding the voltmeter connected to a junction box, the other hand just inches from a metallic red toggle switch on his electronic toaster.

His assistants sat quietly; there was nothing to say. The unspoken fear for all three people was that something would go wrong and Popov would have them killed. Or something else could go wrong and the American authorities would catch them and put them in prison for a very long time.

If everything went right, then, well, maybe, they could get back to the safety of Moscow, and their families would be left alone. Yes, they were being well paid, but they weren't here for the money; they were here for the lives of their loved ones, although they had never once spoken about it with one another.

The voltmeter in Alex's hand dipped dramatically, and the room went dark. Alex instantly flipped the red toggle switch, and a series of green lights began to appear, first from the toaster, and then from the electronic collar around the fiber-optic trunk, and then from Alex's and his assistants' laptops.

"We're in! We've got it! We've got all of it! We have spliced into America's cerebral cortex!" whispered Alex with considerable elation.

The toaster and electronic collar were Alex's inventions, and like a lot of Russian technology, they were crude, rugged, and effective. Popov had approached him three years ago with an offer he couldn't refuse, so he'd been working eighteen-hour days ever since. The toaster and collar were game-changing technological breakthroughs that might never see the light of day, but so what? He had done it. Before now, it had not been possible to splice into more than one strand of a fiber-optic trunk at a time. His modest equipment had just accessed all thirty thousand of them.

After only a few seconds, the lights in the room slowly came back on, softer now, since they were powered by the backup generators.

"Begin the data transfer from the first two fibers to our two fibers," said Alex.

His assistants got busy. One of Popov's shell corporations had long ago leased space on two of the strands on the southern trunk. Data was now being copied, without anyone's knowledge, from randomly selected fibers to Popov's leased fibers. It would take the geeks back at Popov's facility in Moscow about ten minutes to determine what kind of data they were looking at and from which company or institution it came from.

Ten minutes to check two strands meant one hour to check twelve strands, and there were thirty thousand strands. It might take weeks or months to find all of the dedicated strands of the big banks, the big brokerage houses, the global corporate behemoths, POTUS, and other supersensitive government entities, but chances are they would be found.

Technicians rarely inspected the room where Alex and his co-workers now sat. Once a month, if that. So with an inspection having just recently been performed, Alex comfortably concluded they could obtain the data from over eight thousand strands in the coming four weeks without fear of interruption.

And since Popov's men had the AT&T site under close surveillance, Alex would have plenty of time to pull his gear and retreat back into the tunnel without a trace if an inspection team showed up. Once the inspectors left, the Russians would have to engineer another blackout before they could splice in again.

The problem with doing so was that any blackout that was location specific to the PIC would result in AT&T reinspecting the facility pronto. But with tonight's chaos from the e-bomb and the cascading blackouts all over town, AT&T technicians would be busy for many weeks dealing with a host of critical issues elsewhere.

Although it frightened him to possess such knowledge, Bobrik knew more then he was supposed to know about the deceptions. His lips formed a smile just thinking of the brilliant audacity of the plan: the theft of a half-billion dollars' worth of diamonds was merely a feint, a smoke screen for the real theft, which was now transpiring unnoticed. What brilliant *maskirovka*! It made the deceptions employed by Vladimir Putin to annex the Crimea appear clumsy.

Alex marveled at the possibilities he had just presented to Popov's hackers. They could not only steal data, they could *change data*! Or intercept or override communications! Stock market manipulation, anyone? Now that was real power. One was only limited by imagination in terms of what damage could be done by changing data. The economic and intelligence implications were staggering.

Since there was also a massive amount of garbage data on the thirty thousand lines—from universities, cities and townships, countless state government agencies, entertainment and news organizations—it might take some time for Popov's Moscow team to hit real pay dirt.

And although he wasn't privy to the whole operation, Alex assumed the Mafia kingpin had buyers standing by, ready to shell out billions for certain information. If Popov could sell data that would enable a crooked enterprise to scam $20 billion from Bank of America, well, paying him only $1 billion for the info, plus a 10 percent—$2 billion—commission was a good deal. Or perhaps Popov himself would scam the $20 billion.

Calculating conservatively, Alex concluded that this deception, in a very short period of time, would make Viktor Popov the richest person in the world.

Georgia Anderson sat at her workstation in the AT&T Global Network Operations Center in Bedminster, New Jersey. The tempo of activity in the massive room seemed normal, but Georgia was right now running down information on something very abnormal. Las Vegas was being rocked by cascading energy blackouts, and that didn't happen every day.

She had checked very carefully and was certain there had been no indication that the southern fiber-optic trunk line had been compromised. Since the severing of the northern cable, she and three other employees had been tasked specifically to closely monitor any and all issues related to the southern trunk. She could order the immediate inspection of any PICs in the blackout areas, but the radio traffic she'd monitored suggested that the AT&T crews were already shifting into emergency mode and had their hands full.

So Georgia Anderson sent an e-mail requesting an inspection of the AT&T facility on South Las Vegas Boulevard, "as time permits."

Her brain told her that was the sensible thing to do, since she could see from the log that the building had just recently been inspected, but her gut didn't like the Vegas event coming on the heels of what happened in Wyoming. There had been nothing in the press or on TV news, but scuttlebutt ran rampant that terrorists had blown the northern trunk. A massive effort to make repairs ASAP was under way, and upper management was supposedly conducting a top-to-bottom reevaluation of how to better secure the fiber-optic trunk lines.

Georgia thought about that as she tasted her lukewarm hazelnut-flavored coffee. She had lots of ideas about making the thousands of miles of trunk lines more secure, but it would cost big bucks. Meaning her ideas were nonstarters. So she just stared at the huge monitor depicting the map of the entire trunk line and looked for anomalies as she sipped her coffee.

Bobby Chan and Ron Franklin stood in one of the laundry rooms at the Siegel Suites complex on West Tropicana. An open window allowed the sweet smell of hashish to waft into the dirty room, which needed new linoleum, paint, counters, and machines. Other than that, the laundry room was fine.

JoAnn Lennox, the friend of the front-desk clerk, wore tight stretch pants in spite of being about fifty pounds overweight. Chan wasn't exactly a poster boy for a weight-reduction program, either, but he tried to hide his obesity behind a sport coat. Lennox flaunted her flab with a come-and-get-it-boys insouciance. Chan and Franklin waited as she studied the 8x10 photo of Staci Bennings.

"No, never seen her. Cute, though," she said, exhaling cigarette smoke.

"So tell us about the blonde in three-fourteen," said Chan.

"I try not to smoke in my place, so I step out onto the walkway in front of my unit to light up. Or I'll sit at the open window and blow the smoke out. Anyway, the blonde smokes, too. She must go outside twenty times a day to have a smoke."

"Ever talk to her?"

"I gave up trying. She'd see me, but look away. Made it clear she didn't want to talk."

"So you never heard her speak?"

"Well, one time I had my window open and she was smoking and then started to pace a little as she talked into her cell phone. She was talking some kind of gibberish."

"Gibberish?"

"A foreign language."

"Russian?"

"Don't know. I never had a Russian man."

"What about the guy with her, Gregory?" asked Franklin.

"Never seen him."

"Do they have a routine? You know come and go at certain times? Or could she be hooking, bringing guys into the room?"

"Nobody goes in and out except her, from what I've seen. She don't look happy, that's for sure. She leaves the complex three times a day to buy food, that's it. McDonald's in the morning, tacos for lunch, In-N-Out Burger for dinner."

"All those fast-food joints are within a block of here."

JoAnn nodded. "Usually within an hour after she's brought the food back, she puts a trash bag outside the door."

"She leaves it there?"

"Until the next time she goes down the stairs."

"Was there a bag of trash outside her door just now when you came down?" asked Chan.

"Sure was."

CHAPTER 40

Popov intended to fly over the Strip and skirt to the north of McCarran Airport as he headed east. He didn't even care that the airspace over the Strip was Class B airspace, the most restricted category. He was flying low, and the R66 was such a small bird, he doubted the McCarran radar had been painting him since he took off from Mainichi Auction House. A van was waiting for him at a large plot of barren land off of Boulder Highway. He would then be ferried to Perkins Field in Overton, Nevada, an uncontrolled public airstrip where the Citation XLS sat fueled and ready. The Citation would fly him into Mexican airspace and embark on a hopscotch journey back to Moscow.

Moscow would be beautiful this time of year, and the thousands of glittering diamonds that filled the black valise at his side would fetch at least double their U.S. prices in the Russian capital. So the half-billion-dollar heist would actually be a billion-dollar job when all was said and done.

He liked the word "billion." He knew that soon, the long overdue distinction would be his: his wealth would be measured in billions. Tens, no *hundreds* of billions. Popov had never spoken the words, but this deception could easily make him richer than a dozen Bill Gates.

He flashed angry when he thought of how Bennings had nearly ruined everything with the rigged EMP weapon. And the major must have somehow tracked the device through the GPS guidance signal, which probably required the assistance of Yulana Petkova. Using Bennings had been one of the biggest mistakes in his life, a mistake made just when he was on the threshold of his biggest success, of fantastic riches. Was it self-sabotage on his part? Did he subconsciously choose to work with the American knowing it would bring on disaster? Was he unconsciously trying to punish himself for the thousands of misdeeds that comprised his life of crime and killing?

It wouldn't be the first time Viktor had shot himself in the foot, so to speak. The pattern had existed throughout his life, of being on the brink of some great achievement but then finding a way to snatch defeat from the jaws of victory and do some stupid thing that ruined everything. It was only pure ruthlessness that had allowed him to become a KGB general; somehow, he hadn't sabotaged that aspect of his life.

Bennings! Why did he have to walk into my life three months ago? If the major hadn't shown up in Moscow, the deceptions would have proceeded using Rodchenko's bomb, a bomb that Viktor now knew worked just fine.

Hopefully, Dennis had made him suffer before killing him. And that whore, that *gryaznaya shlyukha,* filthy slut, the scientist Yulana Petkova obviously didn't love her daughter or she wouldn't have helped the Americans. So . . . so her daughter, much as he hated to think about it, would be disappeared. He'd deal with that later, in Moscow, after things settled down.

Thinking of Petkova's daughter reminded him he must call Lily Bain from the Citation jet and tell her to kill Bennings's sister and dispose of the body in such a way that it wouldn't be found.

Time to start tying up loose ends, which is why Dr. Rodchenko and his team were right now being driven to the Citation. They would accompany him as far as Havana, where they would perish in a tragic boating accident while enjoying a few well-deserved days in the sun.

Movement to his left caused Viktor to turn his head, and he was startled to see . . .

. . . another helicopter flying dangerously, crazy dangerously, close to his port side, the left side! The cockpit lights were on, and he clearly saw Kit Bennings holding the cyclic stick between his legs with one hand, while the other hand held a submachine gun nosing out of a small window opening. Orange muzzle flashes erupted from the gun, and, while he couldn't hear them, Popov knew the bullets were ripping into his R66.

He jerked the cyclic right, and his copter veered sharply starboard as he pushed the collective down with his left hand, sending the bird into a steep descent.

So, it's up to me, thought Viktor. *Okay, I flew helicopters before you were born. Let's play.*

He made a radical descent, leveling out just fifty feet above Las Vegas Boulevard—the heart of the Strip—as thousands of pedestrians gaped in awe, thinking it was some kind of free show.

Yulana tried to grab a handhold that wasn't there.

"What are you doing?" she said, louder than necessary.

"I'm trying to follow him."

"But shouldn't we be in the sky?"

There was no argument from Kit on that point. As they zoomed over the Strip at 140 knots, Popov suddenly banked left just north of Harmon Avenue and threaded his way between two towers of the Cosmopolitan.

Bennings went clammy as he focused every ounce of concentration on closely following the R66, but hopefully not into a casino high-rise.

Popov emerged over the Bellagio's front pool just as the computer-controlled fountains erupted in an orgasm of white froth to the sounds of "Viva Las Vegas."

The R66 flew so low it sliced through the columns of water, and Kit had no choice but to do the same, electrifying the tourist throngs. The helicopters banked hard right, crossed the Strip, and threaded the narrow space between the half-scale replica Eiffel Tower at Paris Las Vegas and the hotel's high-rise tower.

They continued to bank hard right, splitting between more

buildings before cutting back south over the Strip and then into the gracefully curving concrete and steel canyons created by the crescent-shaped high-rises of Aria and Vdara. They flew so close to the structures, Kit felt certain his rotors would chip window glass.

And then, the Strip went dark.

"No!" screamed Yulana, covering her eyes.

The world outside the cockpit went black as a dungeon. All lights flicked off, save for car headlights on the streets below. Kit instantly backed off the throttle and maintained the mental picture in his mind of the building in front of him, until . . .

. . . Backup generators kicked in all along the Strip and threw enough light for him to avoid slamming into a tram station stop. At a much slower speed, he gained altitude, carefully, but there was no sign of Popov in the R66.

Popov had flown a few blocks from Aria when two chip lights came on in the R66's instrument panel—indications of imminent catastrophic failure of both the main gearbox and the engine. Oil pressure was plummeting, and the controls felt sluggish in Popov's hand. Bennings's gunfire had done damage. Viktor had to put the bird down right now.

So he fought the controls and made a rough landing onto the roof of the closest building, and one of the tallest buildings in Las Vegas—the Palazzo Resort Hotel Casino. He shut down the helicopter and looked out. The electricity was off, but cell towers operated with four hours of battery backup, so he pulled out his cell, and made a quick call.

"There he is!"

Yulana spotted the black copter on the all-white roof of Palazzo, just below them. As Kit descended, they saw the cockpit door open and Popov climb out holding the black valise.

"Jen, Popov landed on the roof of Palazzo. We're going in after him," said Kit into his headset boom mike.

"Look, he has a black case," said Yulana.

"He's got the stolen goods, Jen. Notify Metro, and then you better clear out of the hangar, PDQ."

"Roger that," said Jen.

"We copy, too," said Buzz. "We've got the RT-Seven. It landed in a soft, sandy area that was wet, probably from a leaking water main, so it's fairly intact."

"Roger and out," said Kit, concentrating on his landing. Careful to avoid rooftop clutter from air-conditioning units, crane booms, or antennae, Kit set the MD 530F down. Hopefully, the roof would support the weight, but it was too late to worry about that now.

He slammed a new magazine into his Kel-Tec Sub-2000 and tore out of the cockpit.

CHAPTER 41

The rooftop steel door was locked! *"Sookin syn!"* screamed Viktor Popov as he spun away from his means of escape. *Son of a bitch!*

He had a weapon, but it was inside his flight suit and he couldn't remember which pocket he'd put it in. The valise felt heavy as he stumbled off the steel stairway and jogged toward the roof's edge.

From the corner of his eye he saw Bennings and Petkova running toward him. *Damn, I'm getting old. No, be honest: I am old. Too old for these kinds of games anymore. Oh, well, it almost worked. I can only blame myself for the curse of Bennings.*

"Stop right there, Viktor."

Popov slowly turned; he stood less than two yards from the roof's edge. The garish glow from billions of watts of light below shone dim now as the Strip sucked its juice from emergency generators. Likewise, his own hopes had dimmed considerably, and like much of the city right now, Viktor was reduced to operating on a backup plan.

Regrettably, he couldn't hold on to the valise and still do what he had to do. A simple bungee cord would solve his dilemma, but he didn't have one.

Bennings had the subgun pointed at Viktor's heart. "I have no problem killing you."

"You have shown me, Major, that, like me, you have no problem killing, period."

"You kill innocent people. That's just one of the differences between you and me."

"If you had taken my generous cash offer, nothing would have happened to your family."

"This might not be a good time to remind me of what has happened to my family."

"We all have to die sometime. Better to die rich," said Popov as he flung the valise at Bennings, then turned and ran the two yards and dived off the edge of the roof into the dimness below.

Yulana gasped, but only because she didn't understand he was wearing a parachute.

Kit ran to the edge and looked down toward Sands Avenue. In the subdued illumination he caught a fleeting glimpse of a floating black shadow that quickly disappeared around the corner of the building. Kit folded and holstered his subgun, then spoke into the two-way radio as he picked up the black valise.

"Buzz, Viktor has—"

Kit and Yulana were suddenly bathed in the beam of a ten-million-candlepower searchlight from a Metro PD police helicopter overhead.

"Freeze! Police!" came a disembodied voice over the helicopter's public address system.

They stood still, but Kit took his finger off the radio's transmit button.

"Sounds like you have company," said Buzz, over the radio.

Kit looked to Yulana and made a slight gesture with his head toward the MD 530F. They both took a step toward the helicopter, but then half a dozen Metro coppers charged through the steel rooftop door that Popov had been unable to open and pointed pistols at them. The cops couldn't see as Kit pressed the transmit button on his radio.

"Don't move. Just drop the bag!"

"Okay. Please hold your fire."

Kit dropped the bag.

"The man you want just jumped off the roof, and he was wearing a parachute," yelled Kit.

"Drop the radio!"

Kit knew Buzz had heard the exchange of key information. "Okay, I will. Don't shoot. Looks like it's time to go to plan B."

He dropped the radio and faintly heard Buzz say, "Copy."

The Vegas officers closed in quickly. "You're the man we want. Now get on your knees!"

CHAPTER 42

The wall-mounted air conditioner for room 314 droned on as Ron Franklin gingerly approached the door and grabbed the trash bag sitting outside. He retreated with it to the end of the walkway, where Bobby Chan stood waiting.

Franklin held the bag open while Chan routed through it.

"Three empty drink containers, three nearly empty bags of fries, and three burger wrappers."

"Unless Blondie is pregnant and she's eating for two, I'm betting there are three people in there," said Chan.

"And one of them is Staci Bennings."

"We're exposed here. Let's go downstairs and I'll call Metro for backup."

Just then, the power went out and the whole neighborhood went dark.

"What the hell?!"

There were no backup generators in this neck of the woods, just moonlight and spillover from headlights on West Tropicana. Chan pulled out his cell phone and used it as a flashlight. The detectives took a couple of steps toward the stairs.

Then the door to 314 opened. Lily Bain looked down. There was enough light for her to see that the trash bag was gone. She then looked over to Chan and Franklin, who still held the trash bag.

It's not that cops have a certain look to them, but many of them do have a certain vibe, a certain presence. The way they walk, the way they carry themselves, the look in their eyes. When Lily's eyes met Chan's, she slammed the door shut.

"She made us!" said Franklin.

"Forget backup, we're going in now or she might cap the girl!"

They charged forward, and Franklin slammed his full weight into the flimsy, warped door, which popped right off its hinges. He went sprawling onto the floor of the small front room.

Staci Bennings screamed a bloodcurdling, torturous scream of pain as Lily Bain dragged her deeper into the room toward the bedroom doorway. The scream sent chills up Bobby Chan's massive arms as he stepped inside.

As time stretched into slow motion, muzzle flashes lit up the kitchen area with what Chan instinctively knew to be brief tableaux of the last moments of life and the first moments of death. But for whom?

He swept the room with a short burst of incredibly bright, blinding light from his SureFire. Franklin lay on the floor dazed, maybe shot.

Gregory held a smoking pistol as he stood at the kitchen table, so Chan drilled him with three rounds from his .40 caliber Para Ordnance P16.

Chan saw Staci Bennings elbow Lily Bain in the face, then spin away. He lit Lily up with his light as she raised her pistol in Staci's direction. Strangely, the blonde flashed something of a cutie-pie smile.

It wasn't him shooting in the dark, it was some other being, some vengeful angel of justice that pulled his trigger seven times, sending all seven rounds home to center mass, but since she just stood there, motionless, the angel fired Chan's weapon three more times, head shots this time, and Lily Bain's mutilated corpse collapsed into a twisted heap in the first seconds of death.

Chan knew he'd been shot—it was hard to miss a big fat guy standing in a doorway—but he walked in shadowy light toward the sounds of sobbing.

"It's okay, Miss Bennings. We've come to take you home."

"I'm sorry I screamed. Can you help me stand up? My knee is destroyed."

A light came on behind him. Franklin stood holding a small LED, shining it to the floor and not in Staci's face—a face the coppers could see had two black eyes, a broken nose, smashed lips.

"My wrist is broken, too."

"Blessed Mary, mother of God, what did they do to you?" asked Chan, bending down. He felt the burning now, in his left side, and his shirt felt sticky with blood, but he ignored it.

"This is Detective Franklin, we need an ambulance at . . ."

Chan tuned out Franklin, who was calling in the shooting. He glanced around the room shrouded in inky blackness. "You want to wait for the paramedics, or you want me to carry you out of this dump right now?"

"Can you please take me now?"

The big man lifted her as easily and gently as if she were a newborn. And maybe, somehow, she was.

Middle-of-the-night phone calls never bring good news. The secretary of state answered it, anyway.

"Padilla," she said, trying not to sound too groggy.

"Your man Bennings has caused quite a stir in Las Vegas," said DCI John Stout. "The EMP weapon he stole from Sandia was detonated over the city about forty-five minutes ago."

"Are you certain?"

"We don't make mistakes."

Like hell you don't. "Bennings said Popov had a Russian-built e-bomb."

"I recall you had no proof of that, but we have very good video of Major Bennings and the Russian spy Yulana Petkova stealing the RT-Seven, don't we? And the damage was limited to a two-square-block area. A Russian weapon would most likely have left a significantly larger footprint."

"That's speculation. And neither of us, John, has any proof right now telling us exactly which weapon was used," retorted Padilla. "What's the situation on the ground there?"

"Fluid. But the public will never learn an e-bomb was detonated. The bad guys hit a private storage vault and apparently made off with a massive trove of diamonds. I'll brief the president first thing in the morning."

"What about Major Bennings?"

"He was captured. Holding the diamonds. He's being detained at Nellis for now. I'll be demanding the army rescind the offer of amnesty. Good night."

Padilla turned off the phone and shook her head. There would be no return to sleep, even fitful sleep, so she got out of bed, pulled on a robe, and padded down the stairs of her Georgetown home toward the kitchen.

CHAPTER 43

Bennings knew that army units sometimes trained at Nellis Air Force Base, but he had never taken part in any training there. The army had their own small post tucked away at Nellis, which Kit hadn't been aware of. He was aware of it now.

He sat with his hands handcuffed behind his back at a Formica table. His position made the flesh wound to his upper arm hurt, but just a little. Bright fluorescent lights shone overhead in a drab room that looked like it was strictly for meetings, not for interrogations or prisoner detention. Yulana had been taken to a different room.

All of his belongings had been taken from him, but the thing he most needed now was a handcuff key. He'd been in the room for seven minutes and was fairly certain there was no hidden video camera observing him. So he stood up and walked to a table against the wall that held some basic office supplies, but he didn't see what he was looking for.

He crossed to another table on the other side of the room. A few magazines, a file folder, some kind of report stapled together and then some pages held with a paper clip. He turned his back to the pages, slipped off the paper clip, then returned to his seat.

Within two minutes he'd picked the handcuffs' lock with the paper clip. He quickly rifled the drawers of a desk and found scissors and a roll of duct tape, which he pocketed.

The angle of the door orientation to the room and furniture arrangement was such that a person entering the room would have to step inside before seeing that Bennings's chair was empty. So he moved to the side of the door and waited. With luck, one of the MPs who had brought him here would come in to check on him before the serious boys in black suits arrived. He needed to get out, sooner rather than later. He decided to wait five minutes before forcing the issue and venturing out into the hallway.

One minute later the door opened.

Most people are right-handed. So most people use their right hand, their gun hand, to turn a doorknob and push open a door, meaning their gun hand is engaged.

Kit reached around, grabbed the hand on the doorknob, and wrenched it into a wristlock while pulling the body into the room. He had a female MP, a brunette lieutenant, and as she went down to the floor, he pulled her 9mm Beretta free from its holster.

"Don't make a sound," he whispered while standing over her, applying the painful wristlock with only his right hand. Using his left hand, he eased back the slide on the Beretta, confirming there was a round in the chamber.

He quietly closed the door, tucked the pistol into his waistband, and bent down. GANZ was the name emblazoned over the breast pocket of her pixelated digital camouflage BDU blouse.

"Lieutenant Ganz, I'll ease up on the wristlock if you promise not to make any noise. I just want to talk with you quietly, okay? Do we have a deal?"

"No deal. If I talk to you, it will make trouble for me."

"Tell them I pointed a gun to your head. I'm not going to do that, but you can tell them that."

"Sorry, no," said Ganz through gritted teeth. She looked to be about thirty, with blue eyes and fair skin. It occurred to Bennings that she was too pretty to be in the army, meaning she probably suffered a lot of sexual harassment.

Since she wasn't struggling or making noise, he eased up on the wristlock. "Okay, we don't have a deal, but I need you to stay quiet."

She didn't say anything. Good. "Have you served overseas?" he asked. Better to start her off with some easy questions.

"Afghanistan."

"As an MP?"

"Civil Affairs."

"All right, so you're halfway smart. Tell me why I'm here."

He could see in her eyes that she was gauging an answer, so he pressed harder on the wristlock. "Don't scam me, just speak the truth as you know it," said Bennings as he drilled her with his most intimidating stare.

"Agents are coming to take you into custody."

"CID?"

"CIA."

Bennings's eyes narrowed. "I thought I was being given amnesty."

"I don't know anything about that. My MP unit is here for two weeks of desert training. We were supposed to train overseas, but because of budget cuts, they sent us here. Urgent orders came in tonight to do a prisoner transfer of you and Miss Petkova from Las Vegas PD and detain you both here."

"How long before the agents get here?"

"Any time."

"Where's Miss Petkova?"

"The next room. To the right."

"My belongings?"

"Front desk."

"How many of you on duty?"

"Five. So why don't you just give me back my pistol and we'll forget this happened? You can't get away. You're on an army post, and we have orders to shoot both of you if you try to escape."

Kit registered surprise. "Orders to shoot us? That's interesting, since we haven't been charged with a crime."

"They said you're spies, that you're a traitor. And a murderer."

"The CIA lied, Lieutenant." Bennings's eyes darted around the room, his mind racing. Then a sobering thought rocked him. It ran all the way to Padilla and the power politics played by the president's closest advisers and cabinet members. A radical decision had been made; Padilla was clearly no longer able to protect him.

Bennings hadn't been applying pressure to the wristlock, but now he released his grip entirely.

"They want me dead," he said, with quiet certainty.

Ganz looked at him quizzically.

"How many members of your MP unit are here training?"

"About fifty," she said.

"So if I'm so dangerous, why are there only five of you watching the two of us?"

She hesitated, then: "Those were the orders."

"And why would I be held in an office and not in the brig? There's a brig on this post, right?"

Ganz nodded reluctantly. "They specifically told us to put you in an office. I'm not much on questioning orders from my commander."

He looked at her for a long beat, as if deciding how to play the lieutenant. "Want to know why it was so easy for me to get out of the handcuffs? It's because they want me and Miss Petkova to escape. So they can kill us. They must already have snipers in place."

He took a step toward the windows and took a quick, careful peek behind the blinds. "These windows actually open," he said as he leveled a penetrating gaze at Ganz. She seemed more unnerved now than ever. "Calm down and think about it. Vegas PD had us in jail. Why couldn't the CIA just pick up two spies, two dangerous murderers, there? Wouldn't that have been safer? Why did your unit bring us all the way out here and stick us in unsecured offices, offices with windows, with no armed guards in the room watching us?"

She looked like she didn't know what to say.

Bennings paced the room, not bothering to watch her closely. It was almost unbelievable, but his execution had been ordered due to the turf wars Padilla had been fighting. Padilla had told him the agency and other outfits were furious that the president had allowed her to secretly run the mole counterintelligence op in Moscow; face and power had been lost, and influence had shifted. And his going rogue and stealing the Sandia bomb with a Russian national hadn't exactly helped his position. No doubt the political-appointee dolts at Langley truly thought he'd gone bad and was teamed up with a Russian agent on some kind of mission to wreak havoc and possibly imperil national security.

And no doubt they'd concluded that if he were killed "escaping," his guilt would be sealed, Padilla would be severely damaged, and the president would be unlikely to authorize any more secret operations that encroached on agency turf. Bennings understood it wasn't personal on their part, but being on the receiving end of a bullet fired by your own government made it a bit personal for him.

"If what you say is true, why wouldn't the CIA take you into custody and just shoot you on a desert road and say you had tried to escape?" she asked.

"Because they want to make it look like army MPs did it. Keep the blame away from themselves."

She thought about that, then shook her head slowly. "You might be telling the truth. I don't know. But I know what my orders are."

Bennings quickly rolled up his right sleeve and showed her a series of tattoos. "Recognize these?"

She squinted to see better, as she moved her eyes up his arm. "Seventy-fifth Ranger Regiment, Special Forces Command . . . Is that ISA? You were with the Activity?"

He tilted his head and looked at her a bit strangely. "Not many people recognize that one. Good on you." Bennings looked at her sharply, as if he'd made a decision. He removed the Beretta from his waist, spun it so the grip faced her, and held out the gun for Ganz to take. She looked shocked to see the prisoner, who had just turned the tables on her, offer her weapon back. "So whose side are you on, Lieutenant? The army's, or the CIA's?"

She paused, then: "I'm a soldier." She reached out, took her sidearm back, and stuck it in her ballistic nylon holster.

"That makes two of us." He extended a hand and helped her to her feet. He took a step as if to cross behind her, then lashed out with his left arm, wrenched her into a bar-arm choke hold, and applied symmetrical pressure using a V configuration of his forearm and upper arm on the sides of her neck. After fifteen seconds, she went still, and he let her drop to the floor.

CHAPTER 44

Recovery from a carotid restraint hold is generally quick; in Ganz's case, about thirty seconds. Time enough for Bennings to handcuff her arms behind her back and put duct tape around her legs and over her mouth.

"I need a couple of minutes to think this out," Bennings said loudly, as he unbuttoned her camouflage BDU blouse. He checked the inside of the garment, then looked at her bra; something didn't look right. "So just be quiet for a minute, okay? Don't talk." He was speaking for someone's benefit, but it wasn't Ganz.

As Ganz came to, her eyes went wide and she began to squirm as she realized her predicament. Kit quickly straddled her to keep her from rolling away. Careful not to touch her breasts, he used scissors to cut the front of her bra in half. Her breasts were now exposed, but he paid no attention to them. It was the "wire," the transmitter and microphone attached inside the bra, he was interested in. And the .380 subcompact semiauto Velcroed inside one of her breast cups.

He snipped the wire of the transmitter, neutralizing it; now no one could listen in on the conversation. He took the .380 and then quickly covered her breasts by rebuttoning her BDU blouse. He moved off of her, kneeling next to her. "I apologize for cutting open your bra.

If you were really in the army you could get me into all kinds of trouble for that. But you're not in the military, are you?"

Ganz's eyes were like saucers.

"Let me guess: your Beretta has a broken firing pin. I was supposed to take it from you, thinking it was actually a functioning gun. It's why I gave it back to you, and it's why you holstered it. You couldn't use it on me if you wanted to. Right?"

No doubt about it now, Ganz was scared. She looked like a lady who knew she was in a world of trouble.

"You're good, and you're probably former military, but there were a couple of different things that gave you away. You said 'Special Forces Command,' but it's Special *Operations* Command. And you recognized the old ISA logo. Chances of a female first lieutenant knowing that logo are slim—ninety-nine point nine-nine percent of the army doesn't know that logo—but a CIA assassin who had read my dossier would know it."

He performed a quick search of her cargo pockets and found a Gerber folder with a nasty serrated edge—a gutting knife, which he opened.

"Now we're going to have a quiet, honest chat." He slowly moved the tip of the knife under her right eye and pressed slightly. "The first time you lie, you lose your eye. Another lie, another eye. You also have ears and a nose, so think carefully before you speak."

Ganz swallowed hard, and Bennings tore off the tape from over her mouth. "Who do you work for?"

"I'm a contract player."

"For . . . ?"

"Name a three-letter agency. American or foreign. You know how it works."

Bennings indeed knew how it worked. Thousands, maybe tens of thousands of such "contract players" rented themselves out as freelance operators around the world. Allegiances were murky at best, but Bennings knew all too well it wasn't just in the arena of contract players where allegiances were murky.

"When I said 'for'? I meant who are you working for tonight?"

"Langley."

"How many of you?"

"Seven."

"So all five of the 'MPs' who picked us up from Vegas PD, plus two others?"

"Yes."

"And Petkova and I are both to be killed while escaping?"

"Yes. Preferably shot by real army MPs. Two platoons of MPs have set up choke points all around the post. If we radio them that you've escaped, their orders are shoot to kill."

Bennings nodded. Crap, it was one thing to have police detectives and CID agents trying to track him down, but when killers are dispatched by the intelligence service of the nation you serve, well . . . He let out a big exhale.

"Listen carefully," he said with a ruthless intensity. "If you want to see tomorrow, you will get me and Petkova out of here. Alive. In one piece. Right now."

"I can do it. I know exactly how to do it." She swallowed again. He could see in her eyes that she really wanted him to believe her. The question was, would she lead him into a trap. "Bennings, I don't know the truth about what you did to piss off the Company, but this was nothing personal."

"Oh, it's all personal, girl," said Kit, as he used the knife to cut the duct tape that had bound her legs. "Everything I'm doing these days is personal."

Using the .380, Bennings subdued the fake MP who was in the room with Yulana. He got duct taped to a chair. A few minutes later, Bennings and Yulana, wearing MP uniforms, overcame the fake MP at the front desk. Yulana retrieved their belongings while Kit cuffed and gagged the contract killer and liberated the man's Generation 4 Glock 21 and some other goodies.

"What about the other four CIA killers?" asked Yulana.

Kit looked at Ganz. She hesitated, then said, "Might be better to make a break for it now."

Kit nodded. "They have to know something's going down. Your wire's been silent for too long. Any idea where they are?"

"Two of them will be in a green SUV somewhere outside, for Command and Control. But the other two...?" Ganz didn't finish the question.

"So we run for it. But just to be clear," he said with a raw edge to his voice, "if we don't make it, you don't make it." His look told her that he meant it.

Ganz nodded, then led them down a different hallway, where they broke into a run. They rounded a few corners and ended up in a custodial room, then through a utility door out into the open air. They ran balls-out across a patch of grass to the corner of another building.

After leapfrogging from building to building in the darkness, Ganz stopped at the door of a small motor pool. "There are quads inside. I saw them earlier." Kit quickly jimmied the padlock, and the group filed in. A dozen tricked-out 4x4 ATVs used as patrol vehicles on the post sat gassed and ready to go. Steered with handlebars like a motorcycle, the small, four-wheeled "quads" had fat off-road tires and could drive just about anywhere. They were designed for one person plus cargo but could seat two in a pinch.

"I always wanted to ride one of these," said Yulana, looking them over.

"Careful what you wish for," said Kit.

"You'll have to stay off road to avoid the choke points manned by the MPs," said Ganz, trying to sound helpful.

"Someone from your team will have called in our escape by now," said Kit with sharp certainty.

"Probably. So the MPs will shoot if they see you. But they're only set up on real roads, since we assumed you'd steal a vehicle and drive off post. We parked Humvees all around the building where you were being held."

"So as long as we stay dark and off road, we might make it," said Kit. He glanced at Ganz, who looked scared to death that he was going to kill her right there.

"Since I've never driven one of these, I'll follow you," said Yulana. She then looked with contempt at Ganz. "But what about her?"

"Her? She's my lucky hood ornament."

Ganz was still cuffed, but Bennings once again duct taped her mouth and then lifted her in a sitting position onto the cast-aluminum front cargo rack, where he lashed her down tight with rope and bungee cords like she was a piece of luggage.

He then moved off to a tool cabinet and began searching for something. The waiting made Yulana nervous.

"Kit, you're taking too long."

"You're right, but we'll need one of these."

He pocketed a tool, then crossed to the garage door. The creaky door made a lot of noise as Kit pulled it open. He then ran to his quad, and they started the engines, which ran surprisingly quietly, since they had special mufflers installed to make them somewhat "stealthy."

Kit drove out, followed by Yulana, and crossed the road under the yellowish glow of a streetlight. They headed north. After traveling less than one hundred yards, gunfire erupted from the darkness to their right.

Kit saw the muzzle flashes and heard a man yell, "They're over here!" He didn't bother to return fire, he just bent lower, and as he gunned the throttle, the ATV shot off into the dry desert night, its stillness now punctuated by staccato bursts of innocuous-sounding pops, which were anything but innocuous. Whoever was shooting was employing an ineffective technique called "spray and pray," firing blindly at a target in the hope of making a one-in-a-million shot.

Bennings glanced back to make sure Yulana was on his tail, as the lights of the post and the gunfire quickly faded behind them.

The northerly escape was a feint, and Kit soon led them due west. The going was slower since they couldn't use their lights, but the brilliantly starry sky provided enough soft light so they could negotiate the dry washes and arroyos as they avoided any roads.

Now Kit's main worry became helicopters that could launch from Nellis. Or drones. Had the CIA contractors brought their own mini drones? His neck craned toward the sky whenever he could risk taking his eyes away from the terrain in front of them.

Twelve minutes elapsed before they came upon the eight-foot-high chain-link fence that separated the army post from Nellis proper. He and Yulana stopped their quads right up against the fence.

Kit silently dismounted and went to work with the tool he found in the motor pool—a pair of snips—to cut an opening in the chain link. He worked feverishly, and in less than two minutes, he'd cut an opening large enough to drive through.

He heard Yulana get off her quad and then say, "Oh, my God!"

Bennings spun around to see her gawking at Ganz, who sat perfectly upright, lashed to the cargo rack.

Perfectly upright, and perfectly dead.

"Aww, crap." Kit stood up and moved in close. Ganz had taken a round to the side of her head. A one-in-a-million shot that found an unintended target. "All right, we leave this quad here," said Kit quickly. "You sit behind me on your quad."

"But . . ."

"But what? Believe me, they'll find her body soon enough. And the bullet that killed her was meant for you or me. They're probably launching helicopters right now to track us down and make us as dead as her."

"I'll tell you 'but what'?" exclaimed Yulana, getting emotional. "I expect Popov and his men to try and kill us. But I don't expect American soldiers or the CIA to try. How can we continue, how can we even dream of living through this, of saving my child, your sister?"

As he looked at her, he realized she was on the verge of falling apart. He crossed to her and gently held her.

"Only we can kill the dream, Yulana. As long as we're alive, as long as we're free, if we can take one more step, then the dream can live within us. I refuse to quit living the dream of freeing my sister and your daughter and stopping Popov. I simply refuse." He took her hands and placed them against his chest. "Look how far we've come in the last few days. Think of what we've done! When you got off that plane at LAX, would you have thought any of it possible?"

She smiled as tears streamed down her cheeks. "No."

"Okay. So then think about where we might be two days from now. Think about what we might achieve. It's up to us to keep dreaming, to not give up. You will have Kala happy and laughing in your arms again. That's my dream for you."

She wiped away tears and nodded. "It's a good dream. I like it."

He hugged her with true tenderness, then gently led her to the quad. Kit climbed on and revved it to life. She took a last look at Ganz, then got on behind him. He drove through the opening in the fence and onto Nellis Air Force Base.

Now that he was on more-familiar turf, it only took nine minutes until they stopped on Blytheville Drive, where a bunch of vans sat parked outside a storage building.

In a matter of minutes, Kit had a blue panel van hot-wired, and they drove off base toward the lights of the Strip, shining brightly once again.

CHAPTER 45

Chan and Franklin convinced Metro PD to place Staci Bennings under "Jane Doe" at Sunrise Hospital & Medical Center. They were protecting her from a possible Russian Mafia reprisal, but they also didn't want the FBI or CID aware of her rescue. At least not yet. Not until they could ask some questions.

They planned to drive her back to San Bernardino in the morning, but tonight they dozed in chairs in her room. Both detectives had sustained lucky gunshot wounds; Franklin had been grazed in the shoulder and Chan had a through-and-through bullet wound in the flabby left side of his considerable waist. They were both very fortunate.

Staci awoke and saw her guardians fast asleep. Her broken wrist was in a cast, her knee wrapped and in a brace, her nose bandaged. She didn't like drugs, but the pain meds helped a lot. She manipulated the electric bed to put herself in a sitting position and then swung her legs over the side and onto the floor. With some agonized effort she stood and pulled a sheet from her bed.

She softly whispered, "Thank you, God. Thank you, God," as she draped the sheet over Bobby Chan. She found a blanket and limped over to the other side of the bed, where she draped it onto Ron Franklin.

"Thank you, God."

Tears streamed down her cheeks, and she whimpered softly as she stood at the foot of her bed.

Chan woke up, disoriented for a second. He noticed the sheet covering him, then saw Staci Bennings standing a few feet away, crying.

The big man silently stood and crossed to her, then gently embraced her. She grabbed him tightly, buried her head into his chest, and cried.

Margarite Padilla sat at her kitchen table scanning news Web sites— *The Huffington Post, Drudge Report, the Hill, Politico*—on her tablet computer as she swigged coffee from a red St. Louis Cardinals mug.

A cell phone rang from within her purse, but her look said it wasn't a cell phone she wanted to answer.

"This better be good," she said into the phone.

"The EMP bomb from Sandia is in a white Dodge pickup on the second level of the parking structure at Hooters Casino in Las Vegas," said Kit as he drove the blue van toward downtown.

"I just got a call from the DCI who told me the weapon you stole detonated over Las Vegas earlier tonight."

"Negative. A Russian device detonated. I warned you about it."

"The DCI insists the Sandia bomb was used."

"It's at Hooters. Send a team to pick it up. It's . . . not exactly in the same condition as when I borrowed it, but maybe you could use it to embarrass the DCI."

Padilla almost allowed herself a smile. "That's the smartest thing you've said in a while. So Popov used his bomb for a diamond heist?"

Bennings quickly explained how Popov had parachuted from the Palazzo and how he was caught holding the stolen goods.

"All of this for diamonds?"

"Negative again. But the clueless political hacks in top management of the CIA might believe that."

"If you think the robbery was a diversion, then what's the real target?"

"I'm working on it."

"You're in custody at Nellis!"

"Not exactly."

"What's that supposed to mean?"

"I was there, but opportunity knocked."

"Bennings, they were going to give you amnesty."

"My job isn't finished yet, Madam Secretary."

"Yes, it's *finished*. This has gone far enough," she said with cold authority. "The DCI keeps talking about 'your man Bennings.' That was true in Moscow, but not anymore. You are off the reservation, soldier. I am ordering you to turn yourself in. Don't call me again until you do."

"Why? Because it's inconvenient for you? Because you might have to assume some responsibility you'd rather not by having 'your man Bennings' in play? I risk my life, but we mustn't interrupt your high tea at the Mayflower, is that it?"

"You are out of line!"

"No, *you* are out of line!" yelled Bennings as he pulled the van over to the side of the highway. "I volunteered, as a soldier, to give my life for my country. I did not volunteer my family to give *their* lives. This is not finished!

"People like me work long hours for lousy pay in places that could get us tortured and killed. We don't get public acknowledgment, we have to spend months or years away from our loved ones, but we do it out of service to our country.

"Whether we succeed or whether we fail, we don't expect any support from all of the spineless, inside-the-Beltway, power-hungry political appointees, bureaucrats, and hatchet men and women that make up so much of Washington. We all know better than to expect much support from the D.C. sewer system. It would be nice, however, if you all would sometimes put politics and your own self-promotion aside and do what's good for the country. In this instance that means stopping Viktor Popov, a man the CIA still loves because of all the free intelligence he's given them and continues to give them, a man whom the FBI couldn't locate if he was using their toilet on Pennsylvania Avenue!

"Here's a CRITIC, a critical intelligence message, for you, Padilla.

I'm the guy who is going to stop Popov! Do I have to tattoo a reminder on your ass that my mother was murdered because you sent me on a job I didn't ask for or want? I spent nine months of my life to find two moles the agency couldn't locate, and you will reap the hosannas in the power circles, won't you!? And all it cost me was my mom and sister!"

"I have taken a lot of heat trying to provide you with political cover," Padilla said defensively.

"*You* have taken heat *trying* to give me cover? I got news for you: when you have secret operatives in the field, you don't *try* to give them cover, you do it! You have tacitly approved everything I've done. Own it!

"Oh, and by the way, seven CIA contract killers masquerading as army MPs tried to wipe me and Petkova at Nellis about thirty minutes ago. Stout tried to take out 'your man Bennings.' And how was your day?"

Kit angrily threw the cell phone out the window onto Interstate 15.

He sat there for two minutes, regulating his breathing and settling down.

"There's a small army looking for Staci. You and I helping wouldn't make much difference, so our next stop is Moscow," he said. "We have unfinished business."

CHAPTER 46

Since there wasn't enough room for a piece of paper between the Russian neoclassical buildings crowded onto Nikolskaya Street, in Moscow's city center, the best way to tell one solid old structure from the next was to examine the subtle changes in paint schemes and the slight differences in architectural details.

Even though the neighborhood had been run-down when the Soviet Union collapsed, Popov had wisely bought the building on the assumption a renaissance would eventually take place. He was correct. The GUM Department Store was just down the street. In the bad old days of communism, the lines were long for jars of borscht and loaves of bread sold from mostly empty shelves. Now GUM is a jewel of a shopping center purveying Armani and Yves Saint Laurent and the best designer goods from around the world. So Popov's investment had paid off, but instead of selling the three-story Nikolskaya building for a tidy profit, he undertook massive internal renovations to make it his Moscow headquarters.

Over the last ten years, fortified with heavy-duty electrical wiring, fiber-optic cabling, a high-end HVAC system, and other improvements, the solid, sturdy building had evolved into a Tier 4 data center exclusively for Popov's Russian black hat hackers. The servers were kept in an environmentally controlled room, while the hackers worked in shifts in a third-floor room. The entire third floor of the modestly sized building was devoted to the hackers and their needs: dining room/kitchen with a cook available 24/7, game room with pool table and arcade games, chill lounge, showers, and small individual bedrooms. The well-paid hackers had never before been confined to the premises, but they were now confined for the duration of the deception, so Popov had made it as comfortable for them as he could.

The second floor contained Popov's luxurious personal bachelor quarters (his family lived in a huge dacha outside of town) and his offices. His personal staff of four stayed busy taking care of myriad business concerns.

Security goons inhabited the ground floor. A minimum of sixteen men stood duty at all times, working twelve-hour shifts: one in the back parking lot, one at the iron driveway gate to the street, two on the roof in a disguised guard shack, two on duty in the CCTV room / security center, two at the rear entrance—the only entrance—to the building, and one man each on the second and third floors. The rest functioned as rovers and relief for the other posts. The men rotated posts every hour to help break up the boredom.

Popov's corner office had views out onto Nikolskaya through two-inch-thick ballistic glass, coated with a special film to prevent laser eavesdropping. Likewise, ballistic ceramic sheets had been placed between layers of the floor, ceiling, and walls of Popov's second-floor quarters when the building was retrofitted.

Viktor Popov felt safely ensconced back in his Moscow office, surround by an impressive collection of Imperial Russian porcelains, Fabergé silver and gold pieces, Imperial porcelain Easter eggs, silver and cloisonné bowls and cups, gold Russian Imperial military plates, and a gorgeous "Virgin and Child" enameled religious icon. He felt so good, he decided to have a cigar, which he rarely did unless there was cause to celebrate.

"Mikhail, we pulled off a half-billion-dollar heist. Not quite as impressive as what Wall Street does to the American taxpayer, or what Mr. Putin has done to our fellow Russians, but still, we did it, and with flair," he said, relishing the first few puffs.

Travkin, wearing a trendy Hugo Boss suit, sipped some cranberry juice. He wasn't feeling as ebullient, since they didn't have the diamonds, and he was smarting from the ongoing debacle that had befallen their operations in America via a series of FBI and IRS raids on most of their U.S.-based business operations.

"I'm glad you are here and safe, Uncle, but I'm not sure it's time to celebrate yet. We've been badly damaged—especially in the eyes of our fellow thieves-in-law, who now perceive us to be weak and in chaos."

"Sometimes it's good to be underestimated. The money flowing to us, Mikhail, will turn everything around. Now, what have you heard?"

"Bennings and Petkova were taken into custody by Las Vegas police on the rooftop where you crash-landed. They were then turned over to military police. Some of our friends in Washington heard rumors that they escaped from custody. And now other friends are telling us there is a massive manhunt for both of them in southern Arizona and northern Mexico."

"And the diamonds?"

"Recovered by Las Vegas police."

"Meaning half of them have disappeared by now."

"I'm not sure the police will steal any, considering who they belong to. And that could become a problem for us, as we have discussed many times."

"The Italians won't come after me in Moscow. We'll plead ignorance. After I've made some money, I'll make a substantial peace offering to smooth things over."

Travkin nodded, then slowly took another sip. "Will he come for you?"

"Bennings? If he really escaped to Mexico, he might try. But the Americans will do everything they can to locate him. And they can do a lot. Still, if the U.S. authorities can't find him, maybe the Russian authorities can. He and Petkova will be traveling under false identities, so get their photos to every port of entry, every unit, department, bureau, division, detachment, and office that might be appropriate. Make the reward for apprehension three million rubles."

"And Petkova's child on the second floor?"

One guest suite housed three-year-old Kala Petkova and a nanny who stayed with her twenty-four hours a day.

"She'll be on a train to Siberia very soon, maybe tomorrow," said Popov dispassionately.

Travkin couldn't tell if he meant that in a literal way or as code that the little girl would be terminated. If Popov ordered him to have her killed, he'd pass it on to a man he knew who would have no problem with the task. But he hoped the child was really going to Siberia.

A knock sounded at the heavy mahogany door, and a female voice inquired, "Viktor?"

"Come in, Sasha."

Sasha was a tall redhead with a narrow face, bright blue eyes, and other pleasing attributes; she worked as Viktor's executive assistant. "One of the strands we have intercepted carries data for a small bank in Chicago. The hackers say we can take it right now for fifty million dollars."

"That's exactly ten percent of five hundred million. Which is the peace-offering figure I had in mind for the Italian," said Travkin.

"The man will get his diamonds back from the police, but . . . why not?" said Popov, pouring a shot of vodka into an emerald-encrusted, solid-gold shot glass. "Transfer the fifty million into one of the Panamanian accounts. Be prepared to send it on soon." Popov gestured for her to leave.

"Yes, Viktor." She turned away and quietly left.

"So, we haven't hit any of the big targets yet?" asked Popov.

"Not as of twenty minutes ago," said Mikhail. "But there is already over seven billion dollars confirmed, waiting to be transferred to us, just for the data from a few of the target strands we will acquire."

"That's a nice number," said Viktor, seemingly lost in thought. He put down his cigar. "Go call the Italian and get his bank account information. We'll make peace. To peace and enormous riches, Nephew. We're turning a new page."

As Popov reached for his glass, Travkin pretended not to notice and walked out of the room. Viktor Popov lifted his glass and drank alone.

CHAPTER 47

Herb Sinclair got out of a taxi two blocks from his flat in Moscow's Nagorny District. It was just after midnight and he felt a little tipsy, but very satisfied with the sex from the young woman he'd had tonight; her perfume lingered in his nostrils, and that made him smile.

He casually looked about for a tail, then performed good countersurveillance as he took twenty minutes to walk home. He knew that nothing about him stood out, and that he looked like any other middle-class, middle-age Russian man heading home after having a few drinks and some fun.

He avoided a couple of broken vodka bottles in the poorly lit, narrow concrete stairway of his apartment building. Russian pigs, he thought. Four doors greeted him on the small second-floor landing; his was the first one on the right. Unlike the others, his door and locks were strong. He unlocked all three locks, twisted the doorknob, and took a step inside.

Something sticky from the doorknob was now on his hand, and he wiped it on his pants. Damn kids! No wonder they all grow up to be drunks. But then a jolt of fear stabbed Sinclair, and he froze before fully entering the dark room; something was very wrong. He reached inside his jacket for his gun.

"Herb, it's me, Kit Bennings. Close that door, quick."

But Sinclair was still going for a gun.

"Pull a gun and I'll shoot you where you stand. Slowly bring your hand out from your jacket."

Sinclair carefully brought his hand into the open.

"Now close the damn door."

A light came on in Herb Sinclair's apartment.

Kit Bennings sat in an easy chair with a suppressed automatic pointed at Sinclair. Yulana Petkova sat in a straight-backed chair across the room, also holding a suppressed pistol. A body covered by a blanket lay on the floor near her.

"What in the hell have you done?! Are you insane?"

"Relax, Herb," said Bennings, almost casually.

"Relax?! What are you doing here? Who's she? Who's the stiff? Five years of deep-cover penetration and you've just blown everything!"

"You've been blown for some time now," said Bennings, as if Sinclair were insignificant.

"Bennings. The word is out. You've gone rogue. You are in such deep trouble. And coming here, like this?" He shook his head. "Whatever your problem is, I won't help. Take it outside right now. You walk out that door and I'll give you three hours before I call it in. And I'll do that only because you saved my life once."

"Sit down, do it slowly, and keep your hands where I can see them." The tone in Kit's voice had sharpened. He flashed Sinclair a look that indicated he wasn't joking.

Sinclair took a big step forward. "Sit down, my ass! You—"

Kit fired a round into an armoire behind Sinclair, shattering wood. Sinclair stopped in his tracks.

"The next one goes into your shin or your knee. Now sit down, slowly, hands where I can see them."

Sinclair sat down. Bennings took a long pull on a bottle of Dos Equis that he'd liberated from the fridge in the kitchen. He stared for a long time, knowing it made Sinclair even more unnerved.

"Where can I find Viktor Popov?"

"Popov?" Sinclair looked incredulous. "How do I know where he is? You're the one who was meeting with him every week."

Kit fired again, putting the bullet into the leg of the wooden chair Sinclair sat on.

"You are so dead, Bennings."

"You're the one who's dead, Herb, if you don't come clean."

"Come clean? You shoot me and there is no rock on planet Earth the Special Activities Division will not look under to skin you alive."

"But I've already poisoned you, so if I shoot you, it'll only be in the shin or knee to get your attention."

The blood drained from Sinclair's face, and his jaw dropped slightly. Bennings held up a vial, and Sinclair's eyes riveted on it.

"You poisoned me?"

Kit nodded. "This is the antidote for the greasy stuff that was on the doorknob when you came in. Pretty exotic toxin, absorbs through the skin. Your body will start to ache, you'll break out in a cold sweat, vision will start to blur . . . but you have some time yet."

Sinclair's visage had been a mask of righteous anger, but Kit saw an unmistakable crack of uncertainty now spread across his face like a windshield that was slowly shattering.

Kit gestured to Yulana, and she pulled the sheet from the body on the floor. Sergei Lopatin, the handsome guy who had been romancing embassy employee Julie Rufo, lay still on the floor.

"Remember Romeo here?" asked Kit.

"Is he dead?"

"Put it this way: he's finally eligible for that management position he always wanted."

Sinclair's eyes darted around the room, but they looked unfocused, like he was trying to concoct a plan but couldn't think straight.

"Sergei was a bad guy, who you set up to be a patsy. You kept selling me on the idea that the communications specialist at the embassy, Julie Rufo, was our third mole, giving up the store to handsome here.

"Sergei talked quite a bit. He was FSB but secretly worked for Popov. He told me where to find Viktor. He even told me Rufo was no mole, that his job was to romance her so as to throw suspicion on her. You were going to generate dummy evidence against her. But then, I'm boring you with stuff you already know."

"I don't know what you're talking about, and I don't know that asshole, except from having surveilled him with you."

"I know otherwise."

"Screw you, dead man."

"Check the time, because are you really going to commit suicide?"

Sinclair didn't look so good. He was obviously feeling something inside, and he apparently didn't like what he felt. A sheen of sweat had broken out on his forehead, and he gritted his teeth as if from some inner pain.

"I didn't come to Moscow for you," said Kit. "You're not important to me. Go over to the Russians—I don't give a damn anymore. The agency has already tried to whack me, so screw Washington. I want Popov. Give me what I want and you can walk out that door."

"You said Sergei gave you the information you need."

"I want confirmation from you."

Kit could see Sinclair was wavering. The veteran CIA officer slowly removed his glasses, ran a hand across his eyes, and blinked.

"The symptoms are becoming more pronounced, aren't they?"

Sinclair looked very ill. "My mouth is dry. I need a drink."

"Later. Right now, you need to talk to me."

"Yes, I have information on Popov. And a thousand other Russians in this town. That's no secret, it's my job to know things."

"When did you start working for him?"

"I don't"—Sinclair almost doubled over from sudden, stabbing pain—"work for him."

The poison was clearly working, but Sinclair had yet to incriminate himself. Kit knew there wasn't much time, but he couldn't appear rushed. "So what's the arrangement, then? Did he approach you? Did you approach him? Moscow is one of the most expensive cities in the world, and Christians in Action dumped you here. They expect you to survive on scraps, don't they? Five years undercover on, what? A GS-12 pay grade? Sure, sure, there are bonuses and other perks and expenses they cover, but damn, those five-hundred-dollar-an-hour hookers you see a couple of times a week, I mean, that starts to get expensive. The girls are part of a pool that services Popov's hackers—Sergei here told me about that. Anyway, hell, just going out for dinner and drinks costs—"

"What did you dose me with, asshole?!"

"Relax, I have the antidote right here. What was I saying? Oh, yeah, I remember how you complained that those Langley suits have been making their careers on your back. For five years they've kept squeezing and wringing every last drop from you, wanting you to do more and more with people you didn't even know, risking your cover, because what were you to them? Just a cipher. A file number."

"And so you decided to start selling some of what you knew. Or did Popov roll you up and give you no real choice but to sell out?"

"Give me that antidote!"

"Why? Decided you want to live, after all?"

"Give it to me!"

Kit just looked at him. Sinclair was one tough bastard. Even in death. "Where is Popov's HQ?"

"Nikolskaya Ulitsa, number nine, right off Red Square."

"Is Yulana Petkova's daughter there? The three-year-old they kidnapped to blackmail her mom?"

"Yes, that's what I heard."

He's speaking faster now, thought Kit. *He's weakening, he knows he's out of options. I've almost got him.* "What's the real target in Las Vegas?"

"I don't know."

"Liar!"

"It's about information. Some massive database he will exploit . . . sell access to. He's already raking in money from it. He'll make billions. Megabillions."

Sinclair winced and held his stomach. Sweat dripped from his chin as he blinked his eyes.

Kit lifted a travel bag from the end table next to him and heaved it toward Sinclair.

"We found thirty million rubles in your mattress. Where's the rest? Numbered account in Dubai? Vanuatu?"

Sinclair squeezed his eyes shut from the pain. And maybe from the questions.

"How much did you sell out for? How much?!"

"Five million U.S. Now give me the damn antidote."

"You sold me out after I showed up here in Moscow. You told Popov I ran a Red Team against Sandia, didn't you? How else could he have known that? That's not in my two-zero-one file, because I didn't use my real name. Even when I took the army's Red Team Leader course at Fort Leavenworth, I was using an alias. But you knew it, Herb. You knew I ran the Red Team against Sandia."

"Lots of people knew that."

Kit shook his head. "No. Very few people knew, and they're not the kind of people who would talk." Kit fixed Sinclair with a penetrating gaze as if he could read the man's thoughts. "Before I came along, Popov was going ahead with his plan to use a homemade Russian EMP weapon. But thanks to you, he saw the chance to use me to get a much more dependable device. I'd already broken into Sandia, it would be easy for me to do it again. All he needed was some leverage to force me to act."

"Yes, I told him about you! But I didn't know he would hurt your family," said Sinclair through gritted teeth.

"You're the third mole, Herb. It wasn't someone inside the embassy. It was the guy outside the embassy who was spying on our people better than the Russians were spying on our people. You asked Popov to order one of his men to seduce Rufo. Sergei didn't get the assignment until after you and I identified the first two moles. The idea was for you and me to eavesdrop on her passing a secret to Sergei, and that would have been a wrap. But if Sergei couldn't turn her, you'd just falsify some kind of communications intercept. We'd ID Rufo as the third mole, I'd go home, our secret investigation would close, and your risk of exposure as the real mole would end."

Kit took another sip of Dos Equis.

"You pushed Popov on the idea of using me to steal the e-bomb. You desperately wanted me out of Moscow. You were afraid."

A wall of pain surrounded Herb Sinclair; he knew it was over. Tears rolled down his cheeks. Kit looked on with no satisfaction as the CIA legend crumpled in front of his eyes.

"I asked seven times for them to bring me in from the cold. They wouldn't, so to hell with them. I was already on my own, I figured I might as well cash in. It was a hell of a ride while it lasted. Need someone to blame? Blame the suits at Langley."

He wretched, then stood on wobbly legs.

"Antidote. And then I'm walking out that door."

"I won't stop you, I told you I wouldn't. But I did . . . what's the word the politicians use when they're forced to admit they told a bald-faced lie? I 'misspoke.' See, I *did* come to Moscow to kill you. There is no antidote."

Bennings reached over to the end table and turned off a tape recorder that was hidden by a piece of paper. He pocketed the recorder as Sinclair fell to the floor in the throes of death.

He retrieved the heavy bag of money and crossed to Yulana. "If we live through this . . . college tuition money for Kala."

CHAPTER 48

Larry Bing, commanding officer of the Activity, had gone out on a long limb to help Kit Bennings and Yulana Petkova acquire what they needed to get out of the United States and into Moscow. Even though Bing had gotten a heads-up from the SECSTATE days before telling him Bennings was a "special case" and not to believe allegations he might hear about the major, he provided help without tapping army resources or active personnel, just to be on the safe side.

Hence, Kit Bennings and Yulana Petkova had been well equipped for the confrontations with Sergei Lopatin and Herb Sinclair. And thanks to Angel Perez's doings, CIA/FBI/CID were scouring the Mexican border area for the fugitives. Angel had driven the van Kit had stolen off of Nellis Air Force Base all the way to Gila Bend, Arizona. There, he had used Kit's ATM card at a dive that didn't have security video, and then he abandoned the van, making sure to leave a few other incriminating items inside.

That diversion had given Kit the confidence to use the goth decorated apartment in Moscow—the one connecting his old apartment via tunnel—as his and Yulana's temporary safe house. They'd already made a round-trip using the tunnel to retrieve weapons and other gear from his real apartment.

They had also stopped at Herb Sinclair's workshop and found a secret room crammed with esoteric electronic equipment he used for his snooping.

And they found a weapons cache and small-scale supply depot. The SAD counted on Sinclair to be able to support a wide range of missions on a moment's notice, and so they had invested heavily in creating a unique, well-stocked storeroom of items, ranging from the nonlethal, like CS gas, to the very lethal, such as plastic explosives and poisons.

Kit and Yulana had gathered quite a few pieces of gear that might come in handy for the incursion at Popov's HQ. Kit also found thermite grenades, nasty little canisters that created superintense heat and were used to destroy weapons and materiel. A thermite grenade could melt right through the engine block of a truck. Herb had had them in case he needed to destroy his electronic spy gear in a hurry. Kit had packed twenty-three of them into a backpack to make sure he could demolish Popov's computer servers.

So right now, at 2:37 A.M. Moscow time, as they sat on the dilapidated couch in the goth safe house while listening to Buddy Guy belt out "Damn Right, I've Got the Blues," Kit sent an e-mail containing a "key" number to one of Margarite Padilla's private e-mail addresses. Then he used Darknet software to send the audio file of Herb Sinclair's interrogation and confession into the ether. Pieces of the heavily encrypted audio file would be distributed to many "points." When Padilla submitted the key number to Darknet, the program would go out and gather up the pieces of the encrypted audio file and reassemble them for her.

He was telegraphing his presence in Moscow by sending her the audio file, but knowing how Padilla operated, he knew he had fourteen to sixteen hours before the CIA would come looking for him. And the unmasking of the third and most important mole—a CIA agent at that—would cut him a lot of slack and be more ammo for Padilla to use against the DCI, John Stout.

Kit checked his TAG Heuer chronograph and rubbed the pressure point on his hand. The migraine he'd been keeping at bay with hand reflexology during the last few days was on the verge of taking root; he was experiencing an "aura" precursor—a slight blurring of his vision, a symptom he knew well. Stress, lack of sleep, having been shot . . . made him so run-down that all the acupressure in the world couldn't keep this migraine away. It would probably hit him full force in the next hour or two.

"Three forty-five in the afternoon in Las Vegas," said Kit. "One call to make before we go."

"Have a drink with me first, then make your call." She poured vodka into two small glasses and handed one to him.

"You're a bad influence on me, do you know that?"

"*Nyet,* I'm a good influence," she said matter-of-factly. "I can't believe all of this has happened." She shook her head. "I'm just a research scientist, but now I feel . . ."

"Different?"

She nodded. "Even if we find Kala, what can I do then? How can I go back to my old life? I don't know what to think anymore."

"We'll get Kala back, and I'll get my sister back. That's the meat of it. Don't worry about the rest."

He smiled, toasted with her, and pretended to take a sip of the vodka. The truth was, he felt far from sure he could free Kala, considering Popov was holed up in a veritable fortress, but there was no good in sharing his doubts with Yulana.

Angel snoozed on a couch in a three-bedroom suite at the Venetian. Buzz sat on the terrace in a pair of shorts reading the paper. Jen had four laptops going on the kitchen table, as usual, when her sterile cell phone rang.

She wiped it down with a cleaning wipe before answering: "Go ahead." The tone of her voice and the look on her face suggested she didn't know who was calling.

"I'm closing in on Popov's headquarters here in Moscow."

"What?!" She held the phone away from her and yelled, "Buzz! Angel!" She waved the men toward her and put the phone on speaker.

"Whatever Popov hit in Vegas gave him a massive info dump.

He's got a data center set up staffed by hackers that are evaluating the information. Information he can sell for billions," said Kit.

"Billions?" asked Buzz.

"And he pinched it during a blackout," said Angel.

"What did you say?" asked Jen.

"I said he pinched it, which means he stole it."

"A 'pinch' means something else to telecom people. Kit, give me a second, I might know what they hit." Jen's fingers flew over one of her keyboards.

"Jen, what is it?"

"This is not good," she said scanning her monitors. "America has two main fiber-optic trunk lines that go coast-to-coast, maintained by AT&T. Buried underground all the way across the country, in trenches that are anywhere from fifteen to thirty feet deep. But the trunks, which are literally as big around as a tree trunk, have to come up into facilities nicknamed PICs—repeater stations—you know, like a huge relay switch to keep the information going. I didn't realize it, but the southern trunk runs right through Las Vegas."

"What kind of data is on these trunk lines?" asked Kit.

"The cream of the crop: government agencies, including three-letter agencies, the big global banks, stock exchanges, investment houses, credit unions—I mean, we're talking all of Wall Street and some of the most sensitive stuff coming out of D.C., including the White House and their hotwires."

"Jeez Louise," said Angel.

"But AT&T must monitor the signals closely so bad guys can't tap in," said Kit.

"They do. And I don't think it's possible to intercept all of that traffic simultaneously. There are something like thirty thousand fiber-optic strands that make up one trunk. AT&T has good system scans. A bad guy would have to physically splice in to each and every fiber-optic strand, one at a time, and if that happened, an alarm would go off at AT&T."

"If they did the splice during a blackout?" asked Buzz.

"No alarm."

"What if Popov figured out how to splice into the whole trunk—all thirty thousand strands—during a blackout?" asked Kit.

"He'd have the whole enchilada!" said Angel.

"Yes and no. If Popov is somehow intercepting the contents of the entire trunk, there would have to be equipment in the PIC right now. But they couldn't know which of the thirty thousand strands had the golden data, because ninety percent of the traffic on the trunk would be of no resale value. It would take time to find the ten percent, the three thousand strands that have high-dollar or intelligence value."

"But I thought you said they might have intercepted the whole thing?" asked Angel.

"Even if they have, how could they transmit out what they've spliced into? They'd have to have thirty thousand fiber-optic strands to send the information to Moscow, and they don't have that. They could only be transmitting out and examining the contents of a few strands at a time at most. At most."

"How much time does it take to examine each strand, Jen?" asked Kit, rubbing his temples.

"Fifteen minutes or so is my guess. Maybe less if there is a lot of data traffic on it."

"Where in Las Vegas is the PIC?"

She zoomed in the map on her laptop screen. "South Las Vegas Boulevard, just a few miles from us. The Russians will be set up in some kind of basement room where the fiber-optic trunk comes up out of the ground and runs into a huge relay switch, then goes out the other side and back into the ground on its way to the next repeater station."

"Recon the PIC first. The Russians might be watching it. And think about how they gained access—I mean, how could they be set up in there without the AT&T technicians knowing it?"

"Sounds like we need to get in there, pronto," said Buzz.

"While you're doing that, we're going to hit Popov's hackers here."

"Who is we?"

"Yulana and me."

"That's suicide!" protested Angel.

"Kit, be reasonable," said Buzz. "Let us hit the PIC first. If the Russians are there, we grab them and we'll all be heroes. Then the Company can help you take down Popov's HQ."

"You're forgetting the CIA tried to wipe me at Nellis, Buzz. But even if they loved me, in a million years, they would not go in hot to take down a target in Moscow, a block from Red Square. It's up to us," said Kit emphatically. "Jen, how many strands could they have intercepted so far?"

Jen did the numbers, then took on a sober tone. "I'd say about five hundred."

Kit shook his head. "That just reinforces to me that we have to hit them right now. How do we know the data they've gotten so far will be in the computers at Popov's headquarters? Couldn't they have sent it elsewhere?"

"Yulana could confirm that," said Jen. "There will be a separate room for the computer servers. I'll explain it to her. But you will need to destroy the servers."

"I know."

"You got a plan, boss?"

"You know my plan, Angel. The aggressive-queen, no-strategy strategy."

"We forgot to tell him about Staci!" said Jen.

Buzz had heard through his Metro PD contact about the shootout and rescue at Siegel Suites. The press were playing along and had withheld Staci Bennings's name. Jen had even managed to speak to Staci briefly on the phone.

"I didn't forget," said Buzz.

Angel and Jen both looked at him quizzically. "Forget Yulana. Kit is going to try and take down Popov's headquarters by himself. It's great news about Staci, but if we told him, it would have taken some of his edge off. And right now he needs all of the edge he can get."

CHAPTER 49

Yulana offered vodka, but Kit shook his head in refusal. He got up from the couch and crossed to where his Fender Stratocaster rested in a stand. The guitar had been given to him by his mom, Gina, when he was in junior high. So he picked it up and held it, maybe for the last time. Holding the Fender brought back lots of memories, almost all of them good. Holding it also brought him pain from the gunshot wound to his upper arm. He could feel it bleeding again, probably as a result of the scuffling he had had to do with Sergei Lopatin before the man died.

"You can play guitar?" asked Yulana.

"Badly," he said as his gaze shifted to the table where all of the weapons and other gear were laid out. From being lead guitarist of a high school blues band, to having been raised with privilege and love and financial support and opportunity, the twists of fate that comprised his life had lead him to this very night, standing in a Moscow safe house full of exotic weapons of death, with his future, his very life and the lives of others near and dear to him, on the line. What a long strange trip it had been.

He held no regrets, since you can't change the past, making regrets a waste of time. So he gently put down the guitar and crossed to the table, where he began to methodically check each piece of equipment, stuffing them into pockets, pouches, and packs. He eased a futuristic-looking, sound-suppressed, P90 submachine gun into a special large shoulder holster, then put on a light jacket to cover it. He'd culled together a nice, sophisticated arsenal but held little hope he could actually penetrate Popov's HQ and free Kala. He gave himself a 30 percent chance, especially if the migraine hit; his migraines could be incapacitating—blistering pain, vomiting, and vision affected to the point he could barely see.

Yulana joined him at the table and set down both shot glasses.

"Okay, so we drink when we come back," she said.

"You stay here. Wait for one hour after I leave. Then take a taxi out to that hotel across from Domodedovo Airport. I'll join you there for breakfast with Kala."

"No. I'm coming with you."

He stopped his preparations and gazed downward. He didn't want her to come with him, because he didn't want her to die.

"Your government thinks I'm a spy, so they will not help rescue my daughter," she said emphatically. "They won't even help *you* move against Popov. And the Russian police won't help rescue Kala, either. Popov is too powerful."

"I have the element of surprise, so this should be easy. You'd just slow me down," he said, avoiding her gaze.

"Like I have slowed you down until now?" She touched his arm.

"This is different."

"You are a poor liar. You don't even need to go, do you?"

"What does that mean?" he asked.

"Your friends will stop the information theft in Las Vegas. Five hundred strands . . . not good, but not the end of the world. And if you want to kill Popov, you don't need to invade his fortress; you told me yourself he takes breakfast at the same hotel every week. You are only going for one reason: to save Kala."

He didn't answer and wouldn't meet her eyes. He picked up an ammunition magazine, but she tore it out of his hand and pulled him into her arms. Her lips insistently found his, and for many long moments they lost themselves in hot desire. Then he broke off the kiss and looked into her mesmerizing eyes.

"I've got to go."

"*We* have got to go." She said it as an absolute.

"Yulana, I . . . I don't want you to be . . . injured."

"You don't want me to get killed, is what you were thinking. But I won't allow you to change the game on me now. We are both in this until the end!"

He looked into her eyes, searching them to measure her resolve. "It won't be like Sandia. People are going to die. Lots of people."

She picked up a glass of vodka from the table and downed it. "Do I have to find my own gun again, or will you give me one this time?"

He looked at her for a long beat and could see it was useless to try to dissuade her from coming. "If you really want to do this, then you'll be carrying a lot more than a gun."

Scaling a three-story Russian neoclassical building on Nikolskaya Street is doable, as long as you're a hardened, well-trained special operator. Even though he carried over seventy pounds of gear in a backpack and distributed on his body, the many hand- and footholds, outcroppings of cement blocks, window ledges, drain spouts, and conduits made the climb possible. Not easy, but possible.

In the darkness at 04:33 A.M., Kit made it to the roof of a building three doors down from Popov's headquarters. In a city known for its wild nightlife, the street had finally quieted down around four o'clock.

His gunshot wound hurt like hell, and physical exertion exacerbated a migraine's symptoms. Bennings promptly threw up. He felt like crap-on-a-stick, and part of him wanted to just sprawl on the roof and call it a night. But that line of thinking lasted about three seconds. He blinked his eyes, trying to focus as he looked over toward Popov's lair.

Since there was no space between the buildings, the approach would be straightforward. Using low-light binoculars, Kit spotted the two rooftop guards in a fifteen-foot-tall cement tower topped by a cupola. Popov had turned the classic architectural feature into a security post.

Kit silently eased off his backpack and left it on the neighboring roof. He then crept up to the tower, where the guards sat inside on high stools, smoking, chatting, and listening to Russian pop at a low volume. Kit sprang into the room and slammed the butt of a marine KA-BAR knife into the skull of the biggest guard. The other guard, a thin guy, was too shocked to even speak, and Kit swung the other way, catching him in the jaw with the butt of the knife and knocking him down. He then pounced, pressing the supersharp blade against the guard's throat.

"Help me and you will live. Do you understand?" asked Kit in Russian. The adrenaline now pumping into his system helped him concentrate.

"*Da.*" The man was so frightened he could barely speak.

"The three-year-old girl, Kala Petkova—which room is she in? Which floor?"

The thin man hesitated, and Kit pressed the knife harder against his skin.

"Second floor. In a private room across from Popov's suite. She has a nanny in there with her. Room number is eight."

"If you're lying, you'll pay with your life." Kit lifted him to his feet and pulled him outside. "Let's take a little stroll on the roof. You will explain to me, floor by floor, room by room, where everything is in the building. Do that, and I won't kill you."

The man nodded. Kit guided him out of the tower, and they began to walk a grid pattern on the roof.

"The computer servers. Where is the room with the computer servers?"

The man led him to the northeast corner of the roof. "Here," said the guard. "A corner room."

"Right under here? On the third floor?"

"Yes. Right below us here."

Yulana had never been to Popov's building before, and there was some risk she might be recognized by the men who had accompanied her when she met and married Bennings just a few days previous, although it now seemed like a lifetime ago.

So her hair was up in an asymmetrical ponytail, and a baseball cap rode crooked and low over her forehead. Bright red lipstick and heavy eye makeup altered her looks but didn't change the fact that she was perfectly gorgeous. She wore boots and blue jeans, and the backpack straps tugged mightily at her shoulders due to the heavy load inside. She held a red silk flower on a long stiff stem and stumbled on the deserted sidewalk on Nikolskaya Street as if she were drunk. She stopped in front of the iron gate under a stone archway leading to the rear of Popov's building. She tried to light a cigarette, but her lighter (courtesy of Kit's tinkering) wouldn't light. She could see the gate guard from the corner of her eye watching her.

Yulana threw the lighter on the ground, then pretended to notice the guard for the first time.

"Do you have a light?"

"*Da.*"

She staggered slightly as she approached the closed gate. The man's massive hand reached through the bars and flicked his lighter. Yulana grasped his hand as if to steady it as she still held the flower, then touched her cigarette to the flame. She looked into his eyes and could tell he liked what he saw.

After slowly releasing his hand, Yulana exhaled sensuously. She stared at him for several beats.

"Big night?" he finally asked.

"Small night." She took a long drag and stroked the flower blossom against her cheek. "I need six thousand rubles. Now."

"Don't we all?" joked the guard.

She slowly reached through the bars and touched his chest. "I'll do whatever it takes."

The guard cleared his throat. She then moved her hand down to his belt buckle and gave it a wiggle.

"One thousand."

"Four thousand," she said.

"Fifteen hundred."

"Take a look at my face and say you won't pay two thousand."

He looked hungrily. "Okay, two thousand." He clicked a remote control and the doors silently swung open. She eased inside and then the gate closed.

"Where do we do it?"

"I'm on duty, so do me right here." He backed up against the wall into the shadows and began to unzip his pants. Standing at arm's length, she playfully stroked the flower along his groin and then up, up to just below his chin. She smiled, moved the flower near his nose and squeezed a button on the hard stem.

A blast of vapor sprayed into his face, and she quickly spun clear and stepped away from him. He looked confused, but it only took one second for the Kolokol-1 incapacitating agent to change his confused look to one of sheer terror. He took a step, wobbled, and then collapsed. Russian Spetsnaz troops had used something almost identical against Chechen terrorists—3-methylfentanyl dissolved in halothane—during the Moscow theater hostage debacle in 2002. Yulana knew the big man would be out for several hours, unless, that is, he died from the drug, as did many hostages during the 2002 theater raid. She didn't want the man to die, but the truth was, it wouldn't break her heart, either.

She placed an earbud into one ear and turned on the radio in her pocket. She clicked the TALK button three times, and after a few seconds, she heard Kit click the TALK button on his radio three times. So far so good.

Yulana moved to the rear corner of the building and chanced a scan of the parking lot. She didn't see any guards, but half a dozen late-model sedans sat parked and she couldn't tell if anyone was inside. If so, they'd see her as soon as she stepped into the open.

She pulled the radio from her pocket and whispered into it. "Kit, the parking lot."

CHAPTER 50

Kit finished binding the two rooftop guards with duct tape. He put a final piece of tape across the thin man's mouth, then answered Yulana's radio traffic.

"What is it?"

"I think I see someone sitting in one of the cars," she said.

"Wait one minute." Kit slithered to the edge of the roof and used the binoculars. He squinted and blinked and finally made out the image of a guard sitting behind the wheel of an Audi sedan. And the man was wide awake.

With haste, Kit shouldered the futuristic-looking, suppressed P90 bullpup that he had in the rig under his jacket. The T-shaped reticle of the tritium night sight glowed red in the dim light as he tried to acquire a target picture. But even the soft red glow of the optics hurt his eyes, which were now supersensitive to light due to the migraine.

Suddenly, the guard opened the door to the Audi and got out. Something was wrong; he looked concerned and pulled a pistol from his shoulder holster.

Kit tried to sight on him, but he now had a flickering, partial alteration of his center field of vision. He rubbed his eyes, then looked into the sight again.

The guard slowly walked toward where Yulana stood pressed against the building.

Kit pressed the sight tighter against his eye. The flickering in his vision now spread out to the sides, like zigzagging black-and-white lines. It felt bizarre to be gazing into state-of-the-art optics with a migraine-related visual impairment, but then, life happens.

In a few more seconds the armed thug would reach Yulana and no longer be in Kit's field of fire, so he relaxed, exhaled, sighted the weapon as best he could, then gently squeezed the trigger, because, death happens, too.

Yulana stood frozen with fear, her body pressed hard against the old building wall. She had chanced a second look into the parking lot after contacting Kit, and she feared the guard in the Audi might have seen her.

She heard a car door open and close, she heard footsteps approaching, and she wanted to run but couldn't. She stood rooted in place, petrified with fear as she slowly reached for the pistol in her purse. She tried to will her hand to move faster, but it seemed to have a mind of its own. She could barely move; how in the world would she be able to aim and pull the trigger if the guard rounded the corner of the wall?

She bit down hard on her lip, using the pain as a stimulus to action. It worked, and she raised her pistol . . . just as she heard a different sound . . . like someone had fallen on the pavement.

She took a tentative step forward, then . . .

"Sorry, I should have checked that for you. You're clear now," said Kit, over the radio.

She exhaled with relief. As blood dripped down her chin from where she bit herself, she tugged on the backpack straps, then stumbled forward.

The commercial version of the device was called Sonic Assault and was sold as a gag item. Switch it on, and the high pressure acoustic generating device causes anyone within fifteen feet to get very sick to their stomach and begin vomiting. Unless the device was turned off, the only relief was to move away from the unit. The device Yulana placed on the window ledge of the first-floor security office was much more powerful than the commercial version.

She turned it on and quickly moved away.

Boris Krutov was bored, as usual. This kind of security duty wasn't his cup of tea, because he never got to bust any heads. He much preferred working in strip joints or nightclubs. As he ran a hand through his thick black hair, he looked into the hackers' room. They didn't even notice him; all three of them wore earphones, listening to ugly music at ridiculously high sound levels. *Overpaid spoiled brats,* thought Boris, although he'd like to get his hands on the girl hacker for some horizontal recreation.

It wasn't time to rotate posts yet, but screw it, no one really cared, and the bosses were either gone or asleep. So Boris crossed to the stairwell, opened the heavy steel fire door, and trudged up the stairs to the roof. He decided to play another trick on his friends at the rooftop post, so he opened the steel rooftop door very quietly and closed it softly. He took a few steps toward the cement tower, when he saw his friends, bound up with tape, lying on the roof.

Then Boris saw a man at the northeast corner of the roof hoisting a backpack. An intruder! Boris pulled his pistol and opened fire.

Vertigo, as part of the package of symptoms experienced by migraine sufferers like Kit, usually happened during the aura phase. For Kit, it always came at the end of that phase and just before the unbearable pain of the headache itself began. Kit always got objective vertigo, where the objects around him appeared to be in motion. As he bent down to open his backpack and remove a thermite grenade, he stumbled as his world went into a spin.

And then, gunfire! Kit felt heat rip into his back. He dove to the roof and rolled as more gunfire pierced the night. Wobbly, he stood up with his sound-suppressed pistol, an FN Five-seven that held twenty-one 5.7x28mm high-velocity cartridges that can defeat most body armor—the same rounds the P90 held.

He saw a man, one of Popov's guards, but the man seemed to be moving so fast, circling Kit, that he actually saw many images of the same man. Kit understood intellectually that the vertigo was playing tricks on him, but he also knew that he made a good target just standing there. So he started firing his weapon at the images as he turned his body counterclockwise.

Kit was completely disoriented but just kept firing at the spinning images until his gun magazine was empty and the spinning form of the man was now lying prone as it continued to spin around him.

Kit knelt down and vomited again. Pain shot through his torso from the new gunshot wound. He took deep breaths, then took them quickly, oxygenating his brain. As quickly as the vertigo had come on, it faded.

Then the real pain in his head began. It was on the right side only—a unilateral migraine—and the torturous feeling began to ratchet up in intensity.

He stood, a little tentatively. No time to worry if anyone inside the building heard the guard's shots. And no time to worry about the gunshot wound to his back; if the bullet traveled in his body and pierced a major organ or blood pathway, he'd be dead soon enough.

With a bullet in him, with a migraine seriously eroding his operating capacity, and with the chance that others heard the shots and sounded an alarm, Kit decided to use the thermite now; he'd rather confirm the placement of the servers first, but he might not live long enough to do that. So he started pulling the pins on ALSG814 thermite grenades. He held three back in reserve, but he ignited twenty others, dropping them strategically on the roof above the room where the guard said the servers were located.

Thermite can burn at 4,000 degrees. The intense heat, produced through a chemical reaction, unleashed molten iron onto the roof. Since a single thermite grenade can melt through a vehicle's engine block in seconds, twenty thermite grenades burned through the corner roof section of Popov's headquarters with a searing rain of liquefied hell that Kit was sure would destroy the computer servers in the room below.

Even brief glances at the fiery thermite hurt Kit's eyes with a stabbing trauma that traveled through to the back of his skull. And extreme throbbing pain from the migraine itself now raked the right side of his brain like a ball-peen hammer slamming steel.

He moved away from the inferno and fought to focus his thoughts. His first priority was to find Kala. But he'd also have to make sure the servers were destroyed.

Vomit covered the fronts of the two guards who stumbled out from the CCTV room. The men looked green and could barely stand. A couple of guards sitting on a couch and smoking in the common room on the ground floor looked over to their comrades.

"Damn, what did you two eat for dinner?" Clearly, the guards had not heard the gunfire from the roof. The building was buttoned up tight and soundproofed.

But the nauseous guards couldn't speak.

"Go clean up, we'll watch your post."

As the sick guards headed to the toilet, the other men crossed toward the CCTV room.

The bald hacker didn't understand what had just happened, but a meteor—it must be a meteor—had just dropped onto his monitor in front of him and split it in two. Then a molten drop landed on his keyboard, and another glob hit his wrist, instantly severing his hand and instantly cauterizing the wound. As a scream formed on his lips, a blob dropped onto his waxed, shiny head and burned all the way down his spinal cord, through the chair he sat on, and burrowed into the floor.

The heavily pierced girl with the tattoos on her neck going up onto her ear screamed maniacally. Her screams caught the attention of the long-haired blond guy, who pulled off his earphones, stood up, and looked to the ceiling right as a molten mass collapsed onto him. His body simply melted, as the hellacious ooze ate into the floor.

The tattooed girl stumbled toward the door, instantly hyperventilating from abject fear. The one second it took her to open the door cost her her life, as a small drop of thermite landed on her back and pierced her with a very different kind of piercing than she was accustomed to, and burned right through her spine.

CHAPTER 51

Yulana leaned all her weight onto the battery-powered drill with a very long drill bit. The steel bit ate through the mortar with relative ease, but the wall was thick. She felt the give when the bit cleared the interior of the wall, and she backed the bit out of the cement. With shaking hands, she unwound plastic tubing and pushed the tubing through the hole she had just drilled.

She bent down to the backpack at her feet and struggled to pull out a heavy steel canister that was two feet long and eight inches in diameter. She connected the tubing to the nozzle and then turned the valve to the ON position. The Kolokol-1 gas now pumping into the ground floor was the equalizer that might enable she and Kit to pull this off; she only prayed her daughter Kala was not being held on the ground floor.

Yulana clicked the TALK button of her radio three times and heard three clicks in return. Then she ran for cover in the parking lot.

Kit felt a burning, searing pain from the bullet wound in his back as he opened the steel fire door at the bottom of the landing and entered the third floor. As he eased on a pair of sunglasses to shield his eyes from the lights, the acrid stench of burning flesh and plastic invaded his nostrils. In addition to sensitivity to light, most migraine sufferers, including Kit, had sensitivity to smells and sounds. The smell caused him to wretch, but there was nothing left to come up.

He moved forward. Strangely, the floor was eerily quiet, until a piercing alarm sounded up and down the hallway. The sound hit him like a hot poker thrust into his brain stem and caused him to stagger and cry out. He regained his balance just as a hacker who'd been sleeping bolted out of a room wearing only boxer shorts. The man stopped just short of the barrel of Kit's P90.

Sweat now poured from Kit's face in the cool confines of Popov's headquarters. The hacker blanched when he took in Kit's visage and greenish skin color.

"That's the server room?" Kit asked in Russian as he gestured to where smoke now wafted from a doorway.

"No, the server room is on the ground floor, two floors directly below that room."

Damn it! The rooftop guard confused the hackers' workroom with the server room! thought Kit.

"Who are you!?" demanded the shirtless hacker.

Kit stuck the barrel of his weapon under the man's chin. "The data from the American fiber-optic strands . . . is it all in the servers or has it been sent elsewhere?"

The man's eyes went huge. "I-I don't know."

Kit jammed the gun barrel harder. "You know."

"I-I can't say."

"You're lying again, so I'll kill you right now." Kit made like he was going to pull the trigger.

"We have it all here!" said the hacker, hurrying to get the words out. "We haven't sold access yet because we have yet to find the high-dollar strands."

Kit slammed the butt of his weapon into the man's head, and he went down, unconscious. "Appreciate your cooperation."

Kit stumbled to the hackers' room and saw the carnage. All of the computers were destroyed, but it hadn't been his intention to kill the hackers, especially in such a horrible way. The rooftop guard had either been mistaken or had lied. Yes, the hackers were spies and thieves working hard to hurt the United States of America; maybe they were the ones who had stolen his mom's life savings. Still, they weren't targets to kill, and especially not with thermite.

As shouts and commotion began to filter out from the various rooms, Kit hurried back into the stairwell; pain shot all the way up into his shoulder, and his head felt like a church bell being struck at noon.

Viktor Popov lay in a deep, satisfied sleep in a gigantic bed next to Sasha, his sexed-up red-haired personal assistant. And while ballistic ceramic sheeting lined all the walls, floor area, and ceilings of his personal rooms, the material didn't withstand temperatures of 4,000 degrees. The ceiling began to bubble, and then a dripping white-hot chemical syrup poured down onto Sasha. Her body jerked awake as her legs were amputated on the spot.

Popov woke to the sight of glowing, molten droplets raining down. He rolled clear and jumped off the bed just as a large chunk of the hackers' room upstairs, or at least the melted remains of it, collapsed onto his beautiful lover. It was the most horrific, insane, surreal sight he'd ever seen, and Viktor Popov had personally created many a horrific sight in his life.

Popov screamed maniacally as his mind simply snapped. His knees buckled, he vomited, then, head spinning, he looked up into the flames of hell. And a devil was there. For Viktor felt certain he saw Kit Bennings's face briefly appear, grinning smugly, formed from smoke and licking flames. Yes, he was sure of it.

Bennings! In his own house, his bedroom! And Sasha horribly maimed and killed. How could it be . . . ?!

Popov shuffled along in a small circle, as if most of his brain's circuits had been blown and he didn't know which way to go. He was still functioning, but his thought processes had morphed into some kind of confused morass.

Finally, some semicoherent thoughts crystallized: the deception was finished, that much he knew without a doubt. He would play out the game, fight to the last bullet, but he'd lost. It was all gone, all for naught.

Everything ruined in the blink of an eye.

He mindlessly reached for a gun and tucked it into the waist of his silk pajama bottoms as a piercing alarm ripped the night.

Room 8 on the second floor was empty, but a cursory look around told Kit that a little girl had definitely been staying there. He could search every second-floor room right now, but it was more important to make sure Kala hadn't been taken downstairs, where she would be overcome by the sleeping gas. He wobbled slightly as he donned a respirator and headed down to the ground floor.

Kit flew through the steel fire door at the bottom of the stairs. That fire door was keeping most of the incapacitating agent to the ground floor. Bodies of guards sprawled everywhere. They weren't dead but wouldn't be happy when they awoke.

Fighting excruciating pain with every step, he searched all the rooms, but there was no sign of Kala. He found the server room in the northeast corner. The thermite had eaten all the way through the second and third floors, and most of the server towers were already destroyed. He used the remaining three thermite grenades just to make sure the job was absolutely complete.

Yulana aimed very low and pulled the trigger. Her father had instructed her on how to shoot firearms when she was a young teen. She knew she had to breathe, to not jerk when she pulled the trigger. Still, this was incredibly hard for her to do, since Viktor Popov held her terrified daughter Kala in his arms as he stumbled barefoot in pajamas across the parking lot toward a Mercedes.

His hair tousled, his eyes wild with some kind of insane incomprehension, he fired back at Yulana, holding the gun one-handed, but he didn't really aim. Perhaps he was firing at apparitions, perhaps at the ghosts of those he had already killed, who, sensing some kind of reckoning, were now appearing on the scene for a resettling of accounts.

Yulana wiped at her tears. *Kala! Sweetheart! It's Mommy!* She could see the unspeakable fear on her daughter's face, and simply ran toward her.

CHAPTER 52

Popov made it into the Mercedes and locked the door. He felt safer because the vehicle was armored: thick armored windows, armor plates in the doors, and run-flat tires, and it would take a tank to stop him. *Do you have a tank, Bennings?! And, my God, she shot at her own daughter! I was holding her daughter, and she shot at me. What kind of mother does that? She is unfit, doesn't deserve to have this child at all.*

Viktor felt confused, he felt sick, he was tired. He put the car into gear just as Bennings ran out of his burning building.

Maybe he could just run him over?

Bennings started shooting some kind of gun—why was the man wearing sunglasses at night?—but the bullets just glanced off the windshield. Where were all of his men? Where was Dennis? *Once again, I will have to finish the job myself.* So he tromped on the gas and veered toward the American. But then he slammed on the brakes and screeched to a stop.

Kala was bawling, and he hadn't secured her. So Popov reached over and buckled her seat belt as Kit tried to open the driver's door. The mafia don then looked out, through the driver's window into the eyes of his nemesis. The two men were no more than eighteen inches apart.

Popov looked at him, then looked through him and thought of other things. He needed to leave this place and call for more men and regroup. Yes, he needed to regroup. All was not lost after all; just a change of plans. *Have to move on. Have to go now.*

So as Bennings and Yulana emptied their magazines shooting at the tires and the engine compartment, Viktor calmly drove the Benz through the narrow stone archway, crashed through the iron gate, and turned east onto Nikolskaya.

Not quite believing what had just happened, Yulana watched Kit check inside the parked cars, but none of them had keys. After everything, after defeating the whole building, how could Viktor Popov just get into a car and drive away? It wasn't fair! It wasn't right!

Suddenly, a motorcycle roared to life, and Yulana ran forward as she realized Kit had fired up a beast of a bike. She gave him a look that told him she was coming, she was riding with him, so he nodded for her to get on, then he powered the bike after Popov and Kala, into the darkness before dawn.

She felt something wet and sticky. In the strobe of passing street-lights she saw red soaking a large part of his jacket. Kit had been shot. She tried yelling, asking if he was okay, but the roar was too loud and she needed to watch the road, to lean with him as he drove the old streets in pursuit of everything that meant anything to her.

"We need a hard, hot entry," said Buzz quietly.

"I could use one of those myself," said his LVPD detective gal pal, smiling.

Buzz winked, then tucked his Savinelli pipe into a front pocket of his assault vest. The female detective nodded to a SWAT officer, who nodded to another SWAT officer, who swung a Thor's Hammer breaching tool and smashed open the apartment door. Buzz and his lady friend rushed in right behind the SWAT guys, who were screaming, "Don't move! Police! Don't move!"

Two Russians sitting at the kitchen table in the fourth-floor apart-ment slowly raised their hands. The one with the mustache had a ra-dio in his hand, and Buzz took it from him. The Russians had been playing cards as they monitored the feed from a video camera set up on a tripod behind them, a camera pointed at the AT&T PIC across the street.

As the Russians were cuffed, Buzz pulled out his own radio and said into it, "Phase two, go! Phase two, go!"

SWAT trucks drove through the chain-link gates surrounding the old motel and crashed through a barricade that had blocked off the U-shaped parking lot. Twenty officers began a room-to-room search of the compound but didn't see a soul—until they came across four men smoking at a makeshift table in a gutted-out area next to a large deep hole in the ground into which all kinds of cabling had been run.

Jen, Angel, and half a dozen SWAT coppers didn't bother buzzing the buzzer at the PIC's gate, they just drove through it. At the entrance to the building, a startled employee wearing baggy, oversized gangster pants and a do-rag under a hard hat, let them in.

"Take us to the underground room where the relay switch is for the fiber-optic trunk. And hurry the hell up!" shouted Jen as more LVPD vehicles drove into the facility.

Alex Bobrik scratched his head. Moscow wasn't answering the instant-chat connection they had been using to communicate. There must be some kind of—

The steel door to the stairwell suddenly swung open. Alex and his two assistants looked up to see police officers swarm into the cool confines of his domain.

"Freeze! Police!"

Alex watched as his female assistant with dark circles under her eyes ran across the room toward the fake panel. She pushed it inward and was about to crawl through when she was met by the barrel of a gun pointing at her from police inside the tunnel. She held up her hands and started to sob.

It has ended badly after all, thought Alex. Now he wouldn't be seeing his family for a very long time. He had always feared the whole deception had been too good to be true.

CHAPTER 53

Kit felt weak. He knew he'd lost blood and should have taken the time to put a compress on the wound. He'd also been severely weakened by the migraine. At least now the symptoms had been reduced to excruciating head pain and light sensitivity. But even with the sunglasses still on, the headlights of oncoming traffic felt like staring into a thousand suns.

He focused all of his energy on driving the bike, anticipating Popov's moves and trying to think of how in the world he could stop the Mercedes. The man had looked . . . mad? Mad as in crazy, like his mind had snapped. Not only was Popov's driving erratic, but he didn't seem to be following a coherent route. If the Benz crashed, Kala would be protected by the solidity of the vehicle and the air bags, but Popov wasn't even driving all that fast.

Had Popov called for backup with the in-dash car phone? Was he just biding his time until a carload of goons or machine-gun-toting police showed up?

This needed to end quickly for a lot of reasons, number one of which was that Kit was fading. He didn't know how much longer he could hold it together as he muscled the bike onward.

Dennis wasn't answering his cell. Neither was Mikhail. Had they made a pact with Bennings? Of course! They were hijacking the deception.

This was a coup, a purge, a putsch. When had they approached him? Probably while the major had still been in Moscow. Mikhail, his nephew, the man he'd put though eight years of university studies, had probably set up a second data center and was right now stealing the billions that rightfully were his. *Svoloch'!* Bastard!

It was finished. Over. He hadn't seen it coming at all; the marks never do.

What was left? He looked over to the child, Kala. Strange: she was crying, but he didn't hear a thing. She'd been a sweet little girl and didn't deserve to have such a *sooka*, a *shluha vokzal'naja*, a train station whore, as a mother. She could have killed the child when she fired the pistol! What kind of mother does that? What else could he do but make sure the little girl stayed safe? And she was probably hungry. She liked cakes, the staff had quickly discovered. So maybe he should find her something to eat. But it wasn't yet six A.M.; what would be open?

He remembered there were many twenty-four-hour cafés in Moscow. In fact, just around the corner—some Internet café with coffee and pastries. It was just over there.

Popov parked right in front of the Internet café and left Kala alone in the idling Mercedes.

"He left her in the car!" shouted Yulana.

Kit stopped the bike ten feet from the Benz as he watched Viktor through the floor-to-ceiling shopwindows. Yulana spun off the motorcycle and ran to the Mercedes. She threw open the door and pulled Kala into her arms.

Kit waved for her to back off, to take cover, as he painfully eased himself off of the motorcycle.

"We can go!" yelled Yulana.

Kit staggered as he shook his head, his tunnel vision locked on Popov.

"I think he's had a nervous breakdown," she said.

"People recover from nervous breakdowns."

"Please, we can just leave!" she pleaded. She held her daughter in her arms. She'd been reunited with her blessed little girl, but Yulana Petkova was shocked to realize how much she now feared for the life of Kit Bennings.

"Shhhhh," he said, gesturing for her to back off.

Kit slowly entered the shop, each step an act of mind over matter. He felt like his head was going to explode. Sweat beads carved salty rivulets on his ghostly pallor and his blood-soaked and vomit-encrusted clothing caused smarter customers to quickly exit the crowded shop. Even at this hour, geeks and IT junkies with red eyes and über-white skin in goth/slacker attire sat slumped on chairs and bench seats.

Popov stood at the counter, his back to the door. Barefoot, uncombed hair, silk pajama pants, silk robe. The clerk had bagged two cakes.

"Four hundred rubles, please."

He reached for his wallet, but of course there was no wallet. "I seem to have forgotten something," he said.

But the clerk saw the big gun in his pajama pants.

"It's okay, just take them!"

Popov nodded; that sounded right. He turned around and saw a bloodied man standing in the doorway. The man looked vaguely familiar.

Yes! He had been one of them! He was one of the men who had come that night and shot dead his twin three-year-old daughters. Popov himself had tracked down and killed four of the attackers, but the fifth man had eluded him all of these years. And now here he was, standing in front of him. This time, Viktor wouldn't miss.

Bennings saw the hint of recognition in Popov's otherwise vacant eyes. The old bull of a Mafia don was moving his hand onto his gun. As Kit stepped forward, the gun came free of Popov's waist. Kit wrenched it from the Russian's hands and flung it across the room.

He held Popov with his left hand as he grabbed a tablet computer from a group of slackers and smashed it into Popov's face, breaking the glass screen. Another slacker hadn't even noticed all of the commotion, as he mindlessly played a video game on his large smartphone, which was plugged into a socket, charging.

As Popov screamed a howl of rage, Kit grabbed the teenager's phone and violently shoved it all the way into Popov's open mouth. He vised his arm around the Russian's jaw, locking his mouth closed and forcing the phone down his throat. The former KGB strongman's eyes grew so large they looked ready to burst, and his body violently convulsed as he slowly choked to death, with the phone's power cord dangling from his lips.

Popov went limp, and his eyes rolled up into his head. Kit dropped him to the tile floor as a dozen strangers watched in awe.

"TMI . . . too much information." Kit jerked the power cord from Popov's mouth and pocketed it.

Barely able to stand, Bennings tossed several thousand rubles onto the counter, dealt out thirty thousand more to the slackers, and then stumbled out.

The cool night air felt good. Kit lurched forward, feeling as physically spent as he could ever recall feeling. But it was over now. He knew an American doctor on Zubovsky Boulevard. He knew he needed medical attention right now. He blinked and looked to the ground, concentrating on placing one foot in front of the other.

Just then a yellow golf ball rolled right up to him.

CHAPTER 54

Kit looked up toward the Mercedes, where his eyes locked on a familiar visage. A face he'd last seen behind the controls of a gigantic bulldozer.

Dennis Kedrov, rosy-cheeked and smiling, ran a hand through his blond hair as he held a Makarov 9mm. Mikhail Travkin stood to the side and slightly behind Dennis. Six goons held guns on Yulana, who was holding Kala.

Kit's finger found the P90's trigger; he quickly pivoted the subgun from the oversized shoulder rig. He stood ready to shoot, although he swayed slightly, fighting mightily to stay conscious. Kit had killed Travkin's uncle, Viktor Popov, just moments ago with his bare hands. And Travkin had to have witnessed that through the huge café windows. Meaning this was now a blood feud for both sides.

Bennings felt cold, very cold, in the brisk Moscow air of an early spring morning. He knew he could kill Travkin, and maybe the blond guy before he'd be shot down dead by the goons. Fair enough.

Travkin took a small, slow step forward, with his arms out to his sides. "A lot of blood was tragically shed tonight. With Viktor Popov's untimely passing, we could easily be persuaded to wipe the slate clean. With you and your government."

"You're Mikhail Travkin, Popov's nephew."

"Correct."

Kit's eyes panned from Mikhail to Dennis. He quickly calculated the brand-new dynamic that equaled the new leaders of Popov's kingdom. Business was business, after all. "You were the number-two guy, but now you're number one." He looked at Dennis. "And you're the new number two."

"Correct again."

"Did either of you have anything to do with what happened to my mother and sister?"

"Quite the contrary. We were against involving you at all, Major Bennings. My uncle was his own worst enemy and would not listen to reason."

"Where is my sister?"

"You haven't heard?" asked Dennis surprised. "She was rescued by police detectives in Las Vegas."

Kit was unable to hide the look of hope that crossed his face. Could it be true?

"Both of her captors were killed," said Dennis.

"Friends of yours?" asked Kit pointedly.

"You know how it is. Sometimes you have to work with people you don't really like."

"May I?" asked Travkin, gesturing that he wanted to reach into his pocket.

Kit nodded his assent, and Travkin produced a smartphone. His fingers flew like hyped-up digits on the touch screen. He then slowly bent down, placed the smartphone on the ground, and kicked it over to Bennings.

Pain ripped through his torso as Kit slowly, carefully stooped down and picked up the phone. Sweat dripped from his chin as his head spun. It was all he could do, it took every last ounce of his strength and mental capacity to stand up and hold the phone at eye level so he could glance at the screen showing the *Los Angeles Times* online news story about Staci, while still keeping his sight picture on Travkin's chest.

He lowered the phone.

"Looks like the slate is already clean."

"And your government?"

"I'm sure they're anxious to close the book on this whole episode. I won't advise them otherwise."

Bennings looked at the two men for a long moment. Who would make the first move?

Travkin gestured, and the goons lowered their guns. They backed away from Yulana and Kala and moved toward a waiting limo.

Sirens sounded in the distance.

Smiling, Dennis put away his pistol. He and Travkin crossed to the limousine, got in, and drove away.

Yulana ran to Kit while she held Kala. Bennings holstered his weapon and started to collapse, when she grabbed him and held him upright.

"Can you drive, Mrs. Bennings?" he said, barely audible.

"With pleasure, my husband."

CHAPTER 55

DCI John Stout had to eat it. Not only was the loss of Herb Sinclair a gut punch to CIA's SAD operational capabilities in Russia, but his man had been a traitor. In addition to the Sinclair fiasco, the magnitude of the economic and intelligence disaster that had been avoided put a lot of juice from Wall Street and D.C. into Kit Bennings's corner, so neither the national security adviser, the secretary of the army, nor Stout and his CIA could touch Bennings and his merry band of marauders. And the president had personally ordered Stout to attend the secret ceremony now unfolding at a nondescript government office on K Street.

Kit Bennings, Yulana and Kala Petkova, Buzz Van Wyke, Angel Perez, Jen Huffman, Staci Bennings, and Detectives Bobby Chan and Ron Franklin also attended, in addition to Secretary of Defense Bartok and Secretary of State Margarite Padilla.

Bennings's uniform looked slightly bulky from all the bandages he was wearing underneath it.

Since Buzz Van Wyke was a CIA contract employee, John Stout presented him with the Intelligence Medal of Merit, one of the higher awards the agency can give. But Buzz knew that due to the politics of the affair, his days of contract employment for the CIA were over . . . at least as long as Stout was DCI.

Angel Perez and Jen Huffman, both active-duty military members of the Activity, were awarded army Distinguished Service Medals, promoted one rank, and issued 100 percent permanent disability retirements, effective immediately. Of course, there was nothing wrong with either of them; this was the government's way of nicely getting rid of them while at the same time giving them some financial largesse.

Newly promoted Lt. Col. Kitman Bennings was also awarded a handful of medals, including the Homeland Security Distinguished Service Medal. And he was also to be medically retired from the army. Tomorrow. Like with Perez and Huffman, the discharge would be honorable and there would be a substantial financial payout. They were all being "fired" under the best possible terms, but they were still being fired.

The earlier words of the president's chief of staff, Donna Ibrahim, had been utterly prescient as to how to handle the whole affair.

"They'd be pinning an inmate number on you if you hadn't come through. You know that, don't you?" asked Padilla softly as she pinned a State Department medal onto Kit's uniform.

"I think there's more honor among the thieves in the prison system than the thieves here in D.C.," said Kit with a straight face.

Padilla looked shocked for a moment, then said, "I think you're probably right." She straightened the medal, then looked him in the eye. "You were right about some other things, too. I was very angry with those things you said to me on the phone. But the more I thought about it . . . Let's just say that in life, teachers can be found in unlikely places at inconvenient times. You taught me something important, and I won't forget it."

Kit smiled. He extended his hand, but instead, Padilla embraced him in a hug and gave him the kind of pats on the back you give someone for a job well done.

Kit saluted and turned away from Padilla. He drilled his eyes into the CIA director's. Bennings understood very well that going rogue could not be tolerated by the government, but the punishment didn't have to include assassination. Or jail time for Buzz, Angel, and Jen, as Stout had requested. Kit's friends were elite special operators, and simply losing their careers was a terribly harsh punishment. Kit knew that a man like Stout would continue to secretly wield his enormous power to exact vengeance on him and the others . . . unless the DCI was put in check. Which is why Bennings crossed to the director and extended his hand.

As a politician, Stout extended his hand expecting a handshake; as a man who had killed many with his bare hands, Kit locked the DCI into a painful grasp, causing Stout to wince.

"Nineteen twenty-one Third Street, Arlington, unit three-two-two. She's only twenty-three, and those kinds of extramarital affairs don't track well with the president's female supporters."

"What are you—?"

"Don't deny it, Stout. I have evidence. And I'm not even mentioning the secret bank accounts overseas. 'The nation's top spy'? Yeah, right. You're just a party hatchet man good at covering up a lot of dirty laundry. Send any more shooters after me, and I will reduce you to a dung stain. Pull the slightest crap against me, my team, or my family . . . well, you get the idea."

Bennings gave an extra hard squeeze to Stout's hand, creating the distinct sound of bones snapping, as Stout's knees buckled and the man let out a cry of pain. He released the DCI with a shove and then crossed over to his group.

"Friend of yours?" asked Staci, who had her good arm as far around Bobby Chan's substantial waist as it would go, which wasn't very far. Her other wrist was still in a cast, and so was her injured knee.

Staci had essentially swapped fiancés. Blanchard, whose business in Tokyo had been too important for him to cut short, had been unceremoniously dumped by her when he eventually got back to Chino Hills.

Chan, on the other hand, had stayed glued to her from the moment he carried her out of the fleabag flophouse on West Tropicana. The chemistry between two people can't be analyzed in a lab; Staci and Bobby had the kind of personal love chemistry that can be so elusive in life. It was fun just watching them.

"Just had to work out a little business understanding with Mr.

Stout, there," said Kit as he slipped off the silver chain around his neck that held the key given to him by his father. He held it out for Staci.

"Time for you to take this, Sister."

Staci limped over to him and put her big brother in a bear hug. She then took the necklace and pendant and draped them back over Kit's head. "And let you shirk your responsibilities? No way."

Before Kit could protest, Bobby Chan cut in. "Kit, don't get me wrong, the ceremony was nice and all that, but this place has the charm of a quarantine ward at a tropical disease hospital. Can we go somewhere and get some chow? And maybe a beer and a shot?"

"Vodka?" asked Yulana, who was holding Kala's hand, trying to keep her from running off.

Kit eased an arm around his wife and exchanged smiles with Buzz, Angel, and Jen. "You know, Sis, I'm glad I didn't get to rescue you, and that Detective Chan got the honor instead. Because he's going to fit into the family, just fine."

And with that, they departed.

"When should I make the approach?"

"Before he leaves D.C.," said Margarite Padilla to the man in the ten-thousand-dollar Armani suit.

"What if Bennings says no?"

"Would you say no to what we, I mean, what *you* are offering him and his team?"

"Would I say no? Of course I would, because I'm not crazy. Did you see what he just did?! He broke the DCI's hand!"

"Bennings will take the offer. It's a special operator's dream come true. Our only problem is, which assignment do we give him and his team first?"